USA TODAY [barcode obscures text] **n** has books in prin[...] with Mills & Boon [...]s, HQN and other imprints. [...]ITA® finalist, she has won both a *RITA®* and Romantic Times Reviewer's Choice Award. Mother of four, Catherine lives in South Carolina where she enjoys kayaking, hiking with her dog and volunteering in animal rescue. FMI, visit: catherinemann.com

Lynne Graham lives in Northern Ireland and has been a keen romance reader since her teens. Happily married, Lynne has five children. Her eldest is her only natural child. Her other children, who are every bit as dear to her heart, are adopted. The family has a variety of pets, and Lynne loves gardening, cooking, collecting allsorts and is crazy about every aspect of Christmas.

Cathy Williams is a great believer in the power of perseverance as she had never written anything before her writing career, and from the starting point of zero has now fulfilled her ambition to pursue this most enjoyable of careers. She would encourage any would-be writer to have faith and go for it! She derives inspiration from the tropical island of Trinidad and from the peaceful countryside of middle England. Cathy lives in Warwickshire her family.

Passionate Encounters

Passionate Encounters
A Price
Worth Paying

CATHERINE MANN

LYNNE GRAHAM

CATHY WILLIAMS

MILLS & BOON

First Published in Great Britain 2022
by Mills & Boon, an imprint of HarperCollins*Publishers* Ltd,
1 London Bridge Street, London, SE1 9GF

www.harpercollins.co.uk

HarperCollins*Publishers*
1st Floor, Watermarque Building,
Ringsend Road, Dublin 4, Ireland

ISBN 978-0-263-30555-5

MIX
Paper from
responsible sources
FSC™ C007454

THE BILLIONAIRE RENEGADE

CATHERINE MANN

To Barbara Collins Rosenberg – an amazing agent and a dear friend.

One

He was back.

Felicity Hunt didn't need to see more than the buff-colored Stetson resting on his knee to know Conrad Steele hadn't heeded her request that they stop seeing each other. The man threatened the balance she'd worked so hard to create in regaining her professional life after her divorce.

But the Alaskan oil magnate had a reputation for determination. The smooth-talking kind that persisted until he won.

Well, he wouldn't win her.

Although he was sure pulling out all the stops to gain her attention today in the hospital's enclosed memory garden.

Conrad was currently leading story time, pint-size patients gathered around him in a heart-tugging cluster.

On her way back from supervising a critically ill

three-year-old who'd just entered the foster system, Felicity steeled her resolve to keep this man at arm's length. Easier said than done. As a social worker at Anchorage General Hospital, she had a soft spot for her young clients.

Children sat in wheelchairs and on floor mats, wide-eyed with rapt attention focused on the cowboy spinning a tale about a magical horse. His deep voice rumbled over the words, the book all but dwarfed by his large hands. He kept it open for his audience to see, the current page containing a watercolor image of the horse with a blanket and saddle over its back.

A little girl raised her hand with a question. "What's hanging off the saddle?"

"Those are stirrups, for the rider's feet," Conrad answered, tapping his boots on the floor. He then expanded the explanation with ease, his knowledge of all things equine shining through.

His gaze rose from the children, colliding with Felicity's as she leaned against a pillar. The air crackled between them with a connection she should have been used to by now, but the potency still caught her unaware. Just a look not more than three heartbeats long left her shaken long after he returned his attention to the book.

God, he was handsome in a rugged, movie star way with a strong jaw and cheekbones. His dark hair was trimmed neatly, hints of silver at his temples tempting her fingers to stroke. And those eyes, pale blue like the hottest of flames.

He had broad shoulders that filled out his crisp white shirt just so, his suit coat draped over the back of the rolling chair. His red silk tie drew her attention to the strong column of his neck.

This was a man others leaned on.

She forced even breaths in and out, willing her heart rate to slow. The scent of plants and flowers mingled with the antiseptic smell of the highly sterilized space.

Fidgeting with the badge on her silver lanyard, Felicity knew she should walk right out of the memory garden, and she would, before he finished the story.

Meanwhile, she couldn't stop thoughts of how she'd met Conrad, of how he'd pursued her with such flattering intensity. Her work as a county social worker had brought her to this hospital often, and his nephew had been dating a friend of Felicity's who volunteered in the NICU. Felicity had finally caved and dated Conrad briefly, against her better judgment, but she'd broken things off just before Christmas and taking on a new job.

It was a dream come true being hired on as a hospital social worker for underage patients. The recent change offered all the more reason she needed to stay focused on her career, and not on romance. Her broken marriage had left her full of crushing heartbreak. The grief had taken its toll on her at the office, crippling her concentration. She'd labored long and hard to rebuild her résumé. She refused to endure another setback in her professional—or personal—life.

After Conrad closed the last page of the book, he turned over story time to a volunteer with puppets. Felicity let go of her lanyard, her fingers numb. She'd gripped it so hard the ridges bit into her skin.

She'd waited too long, lost in thoughts of this man. If she moved quickly, she could still make an escape...

But wouldn't that delay the inevitable?

She couldn't just walk away today without confronting Conrad about his refusal to give her space. Her heart sped.

Conrad slid on his suit jacket, then scooped up his Stetson and overcoat. He wove his way through the audience, past geraniums spilling over the side of terracotta planters, massive urns with trees and a babbling stone fountain. While the puppeteer set up her portable stage, children stretched and wriggled, mats rustling and IV poles clinking. Conrad paused, leaning to answer a question from a young girl with a bandanna covering her bald head, then continued his journey across the indoor garden.

And his eyes were locked on Felicity.

Felicity exhaled hard, her heart double-timing against her will. He didn't miss a beat in his beeline to her, his long legs eating up the space between them, boots thudding on the tile floor.

"Hello," he said simply, his head dipping low enough his breath caressed her cheek. "It's good to see you."

She bit her lip and struggled to keep her gaze off his mouth and on his eyes, memories of their brief time together bombarding her. "We should step out. I wouldn't want to disrupt the performance."

Taped flute music started as the puppeteer slid into place behind the stage. The children stilled for the rest of the entertainment.

Conrad opened the door leading out of the memory garden and into the busy hallway, winter coat draped over his arm. Staff in scrubs mixed with visitors in street clothes, and the flow of human traffic streamed both ways, the opposing currents somehow weaving around each other fluidly. The wide corridor sported a wall of windows showcasing a snowplow making its way through the lot beside a towering parking garage.

Conrad clasped her elbow and guided her to a nook lined with vending machines. The simple touch set her body on fire. His equally hot gaze made her feel like a siren in spite of her businesslike pin-striped skirt and ruffled white blouse.

He planted a hand on the wall, his shoulders blocking out the corridor, making a public space suddenly intimate. "Congratulations on your new job."

So he did know, probably from her friend Tally Benson, who was dating Marshall Steele—Conrad's nephew. Felicity had the confirmation. His time here wasn't coincidental. He was looking for her.

Frustration—and an unwanted tingle of pleasure—filled her. "Tally told you?"

"Marshall did," Conrad acknowledged. "I didn't know you were looking to make a change at work."

She struggled to focus on his words, difficult to do with the spicy scent of him filling her every breath.

"I wasn't unhappy at my other position, but this is a dream job of mine." All the more reason she needed to keep her focus narrowed.

"They're lucky to have you." His hand was close enough to stroke her hair, but he didn't move.

The phantom touch, the promise, was just as potent.

Enough polite chitchat. "Why are you here? I'm not buying this sudden interest of yours for story time with sick children."

"You didn't want our date from the bachelor auction last month, so I'm fulfilling the time purchased here."

She'd been irate when he'd paid the money in her

name for his time at the charity bachelor auction. She didn't like being manipulated. Another reason she was irritated to see him here today, despite the way his nearness made her temperature spike.

Still, she couldn't deny he was doing a good thing for the patients, many of them here long term in the pediatric oncology ward. "That's very altruistic of you. What made you think of reading books instead of something like volunteering in the gift shop?"

"I like kids, even though I don't have any of my own. I've always been a proud and involved uncle. And my family's charity foundation is initiating a number of projects here at Anchorage General."

Could that be true and she just hadn't heard about it yet? Or was he making another excuse to pursue her because she'd had the nerve to say no to a Steele?

"What kinds of projects?"

"We're starting with a program donating books to patients." He answered without hesitation.

She believed him. About that much at least. "That's a wonderful thing to do, but I need to make sure you know, my interest is not for sale."

His easy smile faded. "Neither is my honor. My family has always supported this hospital out of gratitude for their top-notch care. My nieces and nephews were born here. My niece Naomi underwent cancer treatment here—and then went on to deliver her twins here. The book donation is a part of the new pilot program."

"New pilot program?" she couldn't resist asking, the professional in her intrigued. So much for playing it as cool and formidable as the Alaskan tundra.

"The Steele and Mikkelson families' new charity foundation is looking for more ways to make a difference at the hospital. One of those ways is to provide children with new books, volumes they can keep so there's no risk of germ cross-contamination with shared materials."

How could she find fault with that plan? She couldn't. "That's really thoughtful. I'm sure the children and parents will be very grateful."

Finances could become strained with long-term hospitalizations, so much so that even buying books was a luxury.

"Today's package for each child included a copy of the story they just heard." A half smile tugged on his mouth, those signature Steele eyes full of promise.

It had been a riveting tale, no question, especially when read by a larger-than-life cowboy. "You said *ways*—plural—of helping here. What else is the foundation doing?"

She was curious, yes. But she also needed to know where to avoid him so she didn't keep testing her resolve where he was concerned.

"The vote was taken yesterday, so technically, it's okay for me to share now even though the press release won't go out until tomorrow." His smile widened and her stringent resolve waned.

"Okay, I'll admit it. You've got my interest—on a professional basis only."

His brows shot up almost imperceptibly. "Of course." His smile was confident—and sexy. "We're making a donation to the oncology ward in honor of my niece. They'll be renaming it, to be made official at a dinner for the hospital board of directors and the charity foundation board."

His words sunk in. This wasn't a simple book drop-off or some quickly concocted plan to bump into her in passing. He and his family's charitable foundation had a genuine, vested interest in being a part of this hospital's financial landscape.

Realization filled her with the inescapable truth—and she couldn't deny a shiver of excitement. "You're not going anywhere, are you?"

Stetson in hand, Conrad watched Felicity walk away in a huff down the hospital corridor.

He was definitely getting under her skin, and that was a good thing. Damn straight, he wasn't going anywhere. He had wanted her since the first time he'd seen her. He'd worked to win her over since then, not an easy task as she was still stinging from her divorce. But then, he wasn't one to shy away from a battle.

Letting his gaze linger on her, he stepped away from the vending machines and back into the flow of foot traffic in the wide corridor, winter coat over his arm. Felicity's sleek brown hair was pulled back into a neat French twist, midday sunlight through the window reflecting off honey-colored streaks.

Her pin-striped skirt was both professional yet also appealing in an understated way as it hugged her curves, sweeping down to touch the top of her knee-length leather boots. The ruffles on her blouse drew his eyes to her neck and wrists. Not that it took much to bring his attention to her.

He was selective, dating professional women who weren't interested in a walk down the aisle. He'd had a brief marriage and a near miss, having been left at the altar by his fiancée. His attempts at happily-ever-after had left him gun-shy.

Then when his older brother had lost his wife and child in a plane crash, seeing his brother's unrelenting grief had cemented Conrad's resolution to stay single. He'd devoted himself to helping bring up his nieces and nephews. He loved kids. It hadn't been a hardship to lend a hand to his overburdened big brother, Jack. Conrad was fifteen years younger and had energy and time to spare. He couldn't help wondering, though, if the fact that his brother's kids were grown now attributed to some restlessness on Conrad's part.

His gaze zoned back in on Felicity as she stepped into an elevator. She certainly had his attention and he imagined she would have at any time in his life. He'd hoped things would go a little more smoothly today, but he also enjoyed a good challenge.

He started toward the elevators just as the double set of electric doors opened, a blast of cold air gusting inside. A familiar face stopped him short. Marshall. His nephew. The middle child in Jack Steele's brood, Marshall was a bit of a recluse, preferring to oversee the original homestead ranch. He'd never voiced an interest in the day-to-day operations of the family's oil business.

They'd all had to step up, though, when Jack Steele had become engaged to the widowed matriarch of their corporate rival, the Mikkelson family. Shortly after that, Jack had suffered a fall from a horse that could have killed him, but didn't. Still, it had left him with a recovery from spinal surgery that had lasted months.

Even though Jack had married Jeannie Mikkelson, the family had still been in turmoil at a critical juncture in the merger into the combined companies that became Alaska Oil Barons Inc., with stock prices fluctuating as a result. They needed to provide a unified, stable front. Hopefully the charity foundation—with both the Steeles and Mikkelsons at the helm—would help blend the families while also reassuring investors.

Marshall closed the last few feet between them, shaking snow off the brim of his hat. "What are you doing here? Is something wrong?"

"Everything's fine." They were all still a little jumpy after Jack's accident, and then Shana Mikkelson's aneurysm. A larger family meant more cause for concern as well as happiness. "I was delivering the books to the children's ward, am just finishing up reading one."

"Seriously? I suspect a different agenda here." Marshall's brown eyes narrowed, the quiet perception in the depths so like the gaze of Marshall's mother, who'd died in a plane crash. "Felicity's working here full-time now, isn't she?"

"I recall reading to you when you were a kid," Conrad dodged neatly.

"As *I* recall, you were doing it then for extra credit for your high school English class."

He waved dismissively. "Two birds with one stone. I'm a multitasker."

"Ah, like today." Marshall held up a hand. "No worries if you don't want to talk about Felicity. I'm here to pick up Tally and take her to lunch. Are you still coming by tomorrow with Nanuq and Shila?"

He'd been housing a couple of horses for Marshall since one of his two barns had burned and he needed some flex space for his animals while the rebuilding was under way. The aesthetics weren't complete, but the stalls were secure and warm. Nanuq and Shila, which meant white bear and flame, were ready for transport.

"Absolutely. See you then."

In fact, he could use a ride to work out the tension he would no doubt feel after the impending confrontation with Felicity. Before the day was out, she would learn just how closely they would be working together.

Striding down the hospital corridor toward her office, Felicity wished it was as easy to haul her thoughts away from the first-floor lobby and one big sexy distraction in a Stetson.

But then her nerves had been a mess since she'd bumped into Conrad. She needed to get herself together before the meeting with her new boss. Felicity wove by a nurse with a vitals cart and a cluster of visitors lost in their conversation.

Her new supervisor had been cryptic about the reason for the meeting other than to say it was about a way for Felicity to make a mark in her job. Her interest was piqued. She couldn't get there fast enough. Looking down to pull her notes from her portfolio bag, she nearly slammed into someone—

Tally Benson, waving at her.

"Hello there," her friend exclaimed in surprise. "I'm just finishing up volunteering. I thought I wasn't going to see you today. How's the new job?"

"I'm excited about the opportunity." The words sounded hollow in Felicity's mouth, making her wonder why she bothered faking emotions with her friends. Back in high school, she'd briefly tried out for a school production of *King Lear* because her foster mom loved Shakespeare. During the course of her tryouts, Felicity had realized masking her feelings required a lot more work than actors onstage and on-screen made it out to be.

Strangely, during her work, she'd never had to fake an emotion she didn't feel. Her deep well of empathy supplied her strength as she moved through the difficult spaces of social work.

Today, she felt like that high schooler reading lines. The words didn't match her body's articulation of apprehension, intrigue.

"Then why are you frowning?" Tally scrunched her nose.

Felicity adjusted her lanyard, unable to resist asking, "Did you know that Conrad is reading to the kids in pediatrics?"

She opted to dodge the question that had too much of a matchmaking vibe. "I've heard the family's charitable foundation has big plans for the hospital."

And that level of donation couldn't be a simple romantic ploy. Renaming a wing involved a significant amount of money. She felt small for having accused him of reading to the kids for show.

Felicity forced a smile. "The hospital is lucky to have such a generous benefactor."

"To be honest, I'm a little overwhelmed by the family. There are so many of them." And the redhead would certainly know that since not too long ago she'd been hired to help Marshall around the house while he recovered from a broken arm. Now they were a couple. "But the charity foundation has been a rewarding way to get to know them."

When the Steele patriarch had married his rival's widow, the business world had been full of reports about the merger of their two companies and there had been fluctuations in the market with concerns about who would take the helm. There still hadn't been an official announcement of who would be the CEO for the newly formed Alaska Oil Barons Inc., but she'd heard rumblings they were closing in on a choice.

"Oh," Felicity remembered, reaching into her portfolio bag, "I have your letter of recommendation ready." She had convinced Tally to apply for a scholarship to pursue a degree in social work. The woman was a natural.

Tally's smile beamed, her eyes watering. "Thank you." She took the envelope, sliding it carefully into her purse. "Your support and encouragement means the world to me. I'm afraid to get my hopes up that I'll get in, much less receive the scholarship."

Hope was a scary thing, no question. Felicity remembered too well how difficult it had been to trust in a positive future after her divorce. "I'm rooting for you. Let me know the minute you hear."

"I will," Tally promised, giving her a quick hug. "I should let you go. Let's do lunch soon and catch up. My treat."

"Sounds great. Let's keep in touch…" Felicity backed away with a smile and a wave before spinning toward her new office. She lifted her key card and swiped her way into the space—all hers with a window of her own. She could see the snowy mountains and make the most of what little daylight there was during an Alaska winter. She still had boxes stacked in the corner, but had started unpacking the most important items first. Starting with a bulletin board of thank-you notes from parents and newly adopted clients, along with a few childishly drawn pictures she'd framed. These meant more to her than any accolades, seeing how her work made life better for children who were helpless.

She understood the feeling too well.

Swallowing back a wad of emotion, she searched through the stack of files on her desk until she found the one she was looking for under a brass paperweight, a Texas buffalo. She glanced at the clock and gasped. She needed to get moving.

She locked her door, then raced down the hall toward the elevator bank, her leather boots scuffing against the tile floor in her speed. Just ahead, an elevator door began to slide close.

"Wait," she called. "Please hold that elevator."

A hand shot out and the doors bumped back open. Sighing in relief, she angled through sideways.

"Thank you," she said breathlessly. "I'm running late for a meeting."

A masculine voice chuckled from the other side of the packed elevator.

A familiar masculine voice.

She closed her eyes. "Hello, Conrad."

What were the odds?

Gathering her composure, she opened her eyes to find him standing next to a young nurse who was making no effort to hide checking him out. And he gave no acknowledgment to the flirtatious behavior, which Felicity had to admit moved her. He dated widely, but she'd never heard a negative word about him from other women.

Damn it. She didn't need these thoughts. "Fifth floor, please."

She made a point of reviewing the proposal she wanted to give her boss about a new playlist of music and movies for the children in oncology during treatment time.

The elevator slid open again and the cluster of occupants departed, leaving Felicity alone with Conrad. It must have been too much to hope for that he would leave too and make this easier on her. Another part of her whispered that his presence shouldn't bother her this much.

He stepped up alongside her. "Would you like to go out to dinner?"

She tucked her papers away. "You're persistent. I'll give you that."

"Don't you want to know more about the foundation's plans for the hospital?"

She looked up sharply, her gaze colliding with his. A shiver rippled through her as the spicy scent of his aftershave filled her breaths in the small confines of the elevator. Quite simply put, he was yummy, and also offering information she craved.

"I'm intrigued. But I have to say no thank you to dinner."

He chuckled softly.

"Laughing at me certainly isn't going to win me over."

"Trust me, I'm not laughing at you. You do amuse me, but it's your wit, which I admire and find sexy as hell." He grinned at her. "Am I doing better?"

Sighing, she searched his face, his too-damn-handsome face. "I don't understand why you're still pursuing me."

"You're just that amazing." His eyes held hers again, stirring more of those tingles up and down her spine, making her imagine what it would be like to lean into him, just a hint.

The elevator doors slid open, the movement and

people on the other side jarring her out of her daze. Securing her bag, she stepped forward. There was no denying the attraction between them. That had never been in question.

Even now, she could swear she felt the warmth of him just behind her. Because she did.

He'd followed her out of the elevator, on the very floor of her meeting with her boss about an exciting new opportunity. On the very day Conrad had mentioned his family's charity foundation beginning new endeavors at Anchorage General. With the children. Foreboding swelled through her.

Gesturing forward, Conrad smiled. "It's going to be a pleasure working together."

Two

Conrad knew better than to push his luck.

He held the door open for Felicity on their way back out of her boss's office an hour later. Follow-up meetings had been scheduled for brainstorming potential initiatives for the Steele-Mikkelson charity foundation, to best utilize their donations. They just needed to coordinate with Isabeau Mikkelson for times that worked for her as well, since she was the foundation's official PR person.

Their primary goal? To have a prospectus in place to unveil at the banquet for the board next month. The next four weeks would offer the perfect opportunities to win over Felicity.

And if she still said no after that? He didn't want to believe that would happen. But he also wasn't a jerk. It wasn't like the two of them had fallen in love at first sight.

Still, he was certain they could have one hell of an affair.

He stopped at the elevator, the set of her shoulders telling him he'd pushed his luck far enough for one day. He pulled out his phone and stepped away from the sliding doors. She shot a surprised look his way and he stifled a smile, surfing his emails by the window to check for updates before heading back to the office.

An hour later, he strode down the corridors of the Alaska Oil Barons Inc.'s corporate offices. He served on the board of directors for his brother's company, while maintaining an investment business of his own.

Windows along the length of the corridor overlooked the frozen harbor. The other wall was lined with framed artistic photographs of the Alaskan countryside. This building had been the Steele offices, and since the merger, it was the primary headquarters. The Mikkelson tower was still open and filled to capacity, and the styles of the two offices had begun to merge. The chrome decor of the Steele building now sported some metal-tipped teak pieces.

Conrad opened the conference room door. The lengthy table was already more than halfway full. At the head, his brother, Jack sat, beside his new wife, Jeannie Mikkelson-Steele, whose influence extended well beyond changes to the furniture.

Jack leaned back in his seat, waving his brother into the room. "We're just waiting for Naomi to arrive. How did things go at the hospital?"

Conrad rolled a chair away from the table and placed his briefcase on the sleek, polished wood. "The kids were grateful for the books and the story time."

Jack smiled slowly. "I was talking about the meeting with Felicity Hunt, her boss and the hospital's PR director."

Taking his seat, Conrad used the excuse of pulling out paperwork to delay answering the question. The last thing he needed was an overeager family spooking Felicity.

From his briefcase, he pulled an extra copy of the children's book he'd read at the hospital. He passed the paperback to Glenna Mikkelson-Steele—Jeannie's oldest daughter. "I brought this for Fleur."

To everyone's surprise, Glenna had married Jack's oldest son, who many had thought would assume the family helm. But Broderick had held firm to his position of splitting the CFO duties with his wife so they could focus on their growing family. Everyone in the family was stretched thin, and the acting CEO had moved to North Dakota for a less taxing position so he could spend more time with his wife and start a family.

The board was in final talks trying to lure Ward Benally from the competition. Landing him would be a coup. He worked for a rival company and was a respected—and feared—leader in the oil industry. Benally was also a tough negotiator—which made hammering out a contract a challenge, but it would be a boon if they pulled it off.

Conrad was doing his best to help his family through the transition of the merger. He slid another copy to the far end of the table where Trystan Mikkelson— black sheep of the family—sat with his very pregnant wife. The company's PR consultant, Isabeau Mikkelson, rested one hand on her very pregnant stomach and her other hand on her service dog's head. The Labrador retriever assisted in alerting to Isabeau's diabetes, especially important with a baby on the way.

Jack snagged an extra copy from his brother's briefcase, fanning through the pages. "And your meeting?"

"I'm not sure what you mean," Conrad evaded while pulling his tablet from his briefcase. "I attended. We discussed data and look forward to having Isabeau at the next meeting."

"And Felicity was okay with being the point person with you when Isabeau's unavailable?" Jack pressed.

Couldn't his brother have brought this up away from all these prying eyes? "She's professional. And this is business."

Jack grinned. "Would you have volunteered for the charity board if she wasn't involved?"

Conrad snapped his case shut. "I've always been loyal to the family." That went without saying. Although it was best to go ahead and address the elephant in the room. "I'm not denying I want to spend more time with her. It's nice how life lines up sometimes."

Saving him from further questions, Naomi Steele-Miller pushed open the door. His niece had faced death as a teen and many had thought she wouldn't survive cancer. Conrad hadn't been sure how his brother would make it through losing another child after Breanna. Thank God, that hadn't happened.

And as it turned out, he hadn't lost Breanna either.

Standing, Conrad pulled out a chair for his niece. Brea and Naomi had looked so much alike as children. How was it that they'd all missed any resemblance when Breanna, posing as Milla Jones, had taken a job as a receptionist? Of course, her hair had been bleached blond.

Could they have all been thrown off by something that simple?

Although Brea and Naomi were fraternal twins, not identical.

Naomi pulled her chair into place. "Thank you for being patient. Sorry I'm late. It took longer to settle the girls than I expected."

Conrad snagged another copy of the children's book and passed it to his niece. An attorney for Alaska Oil Barons Inc., she had only just started coming to work without her twin daughters in a double stroller. She and her husband worked from home as much as possible. Her husband, Royce, was a research scientist for the corporation.

Jack took a swallow from his water glass before starting. "No need to apologize, Naomi. Everyone else only just arrived."

Everyone?

Strangely, there were no other board members there—or rather, no one who wasn't a family member. Could this meeting have a different agenda?

Jack cupped the glass, his jaw tight. "Shana called with an update into the investigation."

Conrad straightened in his seat. Shana and Chuck Mikkelson were taking a train ride to North Dakota to house hunt for their upcoming move. Chuck was taking a job heading up offices at that end of the pipeline. For her to call, it must have been important. All eyes were trained on Jack.

"Milla Jones—Brea—has made contact through an attorney. She's willing to talk as long as there's legal representation present."

Conrad couldn't miss the toll this was taking on his

older brother. Stark lines fanned from his eyes, dark circles underneath.

Jack shook his head, scraping his hand through his hair. "She's our Brea, but she wants lawyers to be involved in the reunion? It's so surreal."

Jeannie rested a hand on her husband's arm. "She's been gone a long time. There's no telling what she's been through. Let's focus on the fact she's reached out."

Broderick snorted in disgust. "Because she got word we were closing in on her."

"That's rather cynical," Jack said.

"I'm just setting realistic expectations, Dad. No matter who she is, we can't forget she was leaking corporate secrets before she ran away without a word to any of us."

Jack pushed his water glass away. "No matter what happened when she came here as Milla Jones, she *is* our Breanna. Nothing is more important than that."

Nods made their way around the table, some more reluctant than others.

Jeannie rolled her chair back. "Let's break for a few, get our heads in the game again, then reconvene to discuss the latest round of contract negotiations with Ward Benally."

A wise suggestion to take a breather, given the tension pulsing from both the Steeles and the Mikkelsons. There'd been recent allegations made that someone in the Mikkelson family could have been involved in Brea's disappearance. It seemed inconceivable, but then so did the possibility that Brea could truly be alive.

These days, anything was possible.

Conrad tossed his tablet into his briefcase. Since he'd weighed in with his written feedback, Conrad took the opportunity to step out of this portion of the meeting.

Once back in the corridor, he turned on his cell and it immediately buzzed with missed calls and texts.

And right at the top of the list of those who'd phoned? Felicity Hunt.

Felicity tried not to stare at her phone on her kitchen counter.

Calling Conrad had been an impulsive move, which was surprising in and of itself since she wasn't the impulsive type. But when a friend from work had texted her with questions about a rumor regarding Breanna Steele… Felicity had found herself remembering a discussion with Conrad about how devastating his niece's disappearance had been for him.

Felicity punched in Conrad's number before she could think.

Property in Alaska was costly and social workers didn't bring in large paychecks. Since she lived alone and spent most of her free time at work, it made sense to rent a one-bedroom apartment. She hadn't brought anything from Texas with her anyway, preferring to leave all her furniture and the bad memories associated with it behind her.

Her living area was tight, but comfy, with a generic tan sofa alongside a space-saver rattan chair, and her one indulgence—a fat, raspberry-colored reading chair perched by the window and under a skylight. She missed her Texas sun but couldn't deny the magnificence of the views here were unrivaled.

She'd wanted a place far from memories of her painful past, and she'd found a haven here.

Turning back to her coffeepot, she tapped the "water only" feature to make tea. She pulled a mug from the

cabinet, a stoneware piece she'd bought at a local fes-
tival. Leaving her belongings behind had offered the
opportunity to explore new styles and reinvent herself.

She'd kept the most important things in her life, letters from people who cared about her. Foster siblings.
Her final foster parents. A social worker who'd made a
world of difference in her life.

Her work meant everything to her. She still couldn't
ever turn her back on the career that gave her purpose.
Her life's calling was to make the same difference for
helpless children.

A mantra she repeated to herself daily.

More than once daily lately, since Conrad Steele had
entered her world.

She blew in her tea before taking a sip. The warmth
soothed her nerves.

Her phone chimed, and she reached for the cell while
lifting her mug for another drink. The name on the
screen stilled her hand.

Conrad Steele.

Her heart leaped at the incoming call, too much. But
she wasn't going to play games by making it ring longer. She was an adult.

She thumbed the speakerphone. "Hello, Conrad."

"I see I missed a call from you."

In spite of insisting to herself this was no big deal,
she found herself tongue-tied. "I don't want to be pre-
sumptuous. I just wanted to make sure everything's
okay."

"Things are still on track for the hospital donations.
No need to be concerned."

She hated that he thought her reason for calling could
be only self-serving. "I heard there's news about your

niece. I don't want to pry and invade your family's privacy, but I thought of you—"

"You're not prying. You're being thoughtful. Thank you. I know you have ties to the family through your friendship with Tally. You care."

"I do."

His heavy exhale filled the phone. "Brea has reached out. We don't know the full story as to where she's been and why she came back the way she did, pretending to be someone else. But at least we're going to have answers."

"This has to be so difficult for you."

"My brother is tied in knots," he said tightly.

She knew him well enough to realize how deeply this would affect him, too. He was close to his family. One of the things that drew her to him. "And you're taking a backseat to your own feelings since you're an uncle."

"Are you using those counselor skills on me?"

"It's second nature, I guess." She just hadn't thought she was quite so transparent. Or maybe he was that perceptive. Either way, she needed to choose her words more carefully.

"I'll be fine. Thank you again for the concern," he said softly before continuing. "Was there another reason for your call?"

She needed to work with him, but also needed him to understand her position. "I got a text from a coworker with information I thought I should pass along."

"What kind of information?"

"The rumors are already churning about Milla Jones possibly being your missing niece. Photos of Milla— Brea—have been circulating."

"Yes, we had those released when we first started our investigation."

"Everyone in the break room has been talking about the volunteer who filed a report about the same woman delivering flowers to patients one night." She toyed with her lanyard. "The volunteer said she plans to notify your family, but I wanted to make sure you knew."

"Delivering flowers? That's strange."

"My friend said a volunteer came to her and explained she was approached by Milla and paid a large sum of money to loan her volunteer smock. Unethical on so many levels, which is why she didn't come forward sooner."

"How long ago did this happen?"

"Last fall. I'm sure the Steele family will be notified through official channels soon."

"Last fall? That's around the time when Naomi's twins were born."

A chill went through her to think of Breanna Steele stalking the halls incognito to see her twin's newborn babies. Hospital security was paramount, especially in the maternity ward. The babies all wore bracelets that would set off alarms if they were taken from the floor. But still. This was more than a little unsettling.

What had happened to Breanna that caused her to distrust her own family so deeply? A sense of foreboding rolled over Felicity, born of too many years on the job, telling her that finding the woman wasn't going to bring an easy, happy reunion.

Conrad cleared his throat. "Thank you for sharing that information. I'll pass it along."

"I hope it helps in some way."

"Every piece of this crazy puzzle is helpful." He paused for a moment. "Was there something else?"

"Actually, yes. I want us to start fresh for the good of the hospital project."

"What do you mean by starting fresh?"

"A working friendship, on neutral ground." She couldn't be any more succinct than that.

"I've made it clear I want more. Is that going to be a problem for you?"

"And it's clear we have to work together. I can be professional." She hoped. If only he wasn't so damn hot.

Except she knew it was more than that. There were plenty of attractive men in the workplace and she didn't find herself tempted by them, not in the way this man seemed to seep into her thoughts no matter how hard she tried to put him out of her mind.

"Okay, then," he continued, "do you ride?"

She couldn't hold back her laugh. "Do I know how to ride? I'm a Texan."

His chuckle sent a thrill up her spine.

"Alright, then, Felicity. I'm helping exercise my nephew's horses while his second barn is rebuilt. Bundle up and join me."

It was just horseback riding. Not like a romantic dinner out.

And still, she found herself far too excited at the prospect of spending more time with a tempting man she'd vowed never to see again.

Conrad had spent the last twenty-four hours trying to get Felicity's voice out of his head. Attraction was one thing. Total loss of focus? That was unacceptable.

He'd worn himself out in his home gym in preparation for her arrival in hopes of giving himself a much-needed edge.

Warmth from the shower still clung to his skin as he made his way across his in-home basketball court. Stretching his arms overhead, he exhaled hard as he closed the distance to the door. He combed his fingers through his damp hair, anticipation zinging through him over this outing with Felicity.

Opening the door, he left the harsh fluorescent lights of his gym behind. As his eyes adjusted to the gentler light in his wood-paneled living room, his boots thudded on the pine flooring as he picked his way around the large area rug and black-and-tan sectional. Light filtered in from the large windows, filling the oversize tray ceiling.

Yanking his heavy coat off the rack and snagging his black Stetson, he opened his door and shrugged into the wool coat, which still had the lingering scent of antiseptic and hand sanitizer from all his time at the hospital. Even a pine-scented gust of wind that caused snow to stir slightly didn't completely dissipate the hospital smell.

It wasn't altogether unpleasant, though. The smell reminded him of Felicity. The sexy social worker who'd agreed to meet him today at the small barn that loomed slightly to the north. To call it small felt like a misnomer. More like, small as far as his family's standards went. There was room for only ten horses and one tack room. But large, relatively speaking. He lived a good life.

Snow covered the tiered roof, icicles spiking from the eaves. Three horses trotted around the front paddock. Literally frolicking in the snow. Sally, the oldest mare he owned, played with an oversize ball. Careening around it like a little filly. The old chestnut mare still so full of life and wonder.

His brother had a larger barn with more rides, but then, he had children. Conrad had his horse and mounts for his nieces and nephews to ride when they came over. But he led a bachelor's existence, more scaled back than his brother's.

That wasn't to say Conrad hadn't once envisioned a life for himself with kids and a spread like his brother. But that wasn't in the cards for him. He'd seen that clearly after the breakup of two significant relationships. He'd given it his best shot, only to get his heart stomped and the betrayal stung him still.

So he'd thrown himself into helping his brother. He'd watched Jack's kids grow up, had helped with them as much as his brother would allow. Conrad led a full life.

His boots crunched in the snow as he moved toward the barn. Conrad opened the latch to the climate-controlled stable. Warmth brushed against his cheeks as he grabbed the necessary tack for today's ride. He placed the saddles one by one on the built-in saddle racks on the walls of the barn. Hung the bridles next to them. He returned to the tack room for grooming supplies. Settled into his routine.

A whinny emerged from down the barn. Jackson, his palomino stallion, poked his golden head out. Ears flicking in anticipation, matching Conrad's own pent-up energy. Setting the grooming supplies down, he moved toward his horse. Gave the stallion a scratch behind the ears as he slipped the leather halter over Jackson's head.

Leading the palomino to the first crossties, he

clipped the golden horse. Jackson adjusted his weight, popping his front right hoof on an angle, and let out a sigh that seemed almost bored. Of all the horses Conrad had ever worked with, he'd never come across one with so much personality. And a personality that matched his so well.

Giving the horse another scratch, Conrad determined which ride he would choose for Felicity. Glancing around the barn, he settled on Patches. A quiet, steady pinto gelding, well mannered.

Conrad retrieved Felicity's mount and began grooming Patches first. As he finished grooming the pinto, he heard the distinct sound of a car engine approach and then fall silent.

A few moments later, Felicity walked into the barn. He was half-surprised she'd shown. For a moment, the world seemed to tilt as he was struck by her natural beauty, the curves visible even through her snow gear.

Her brown hair was swept into a thick braid draped over one shoulder. Her deep purple parka matched her snow pants. Her scarf was loose around her neck, but long enough to cover her face if the wind picked up.

She tugged the ends of the fringed scarf tighter as she approached him. "Well, hello, Conrad. I have to confess, I didn't expect this."

Her eyes flitted to the open door behind her, gaze lingering on his one-story home, which overlooked a mountain range.

"What *did* you expect?" He finished currycombing Jackson, who stretched his neck out far, releasing a shuddering shake from ears to tailbone. Conrad bent over, hoof pick in hand, watching her out of the corner of his eyes.

"I envisioned you living in a penthouse condo. Not a…well, a home."

"Technically, this—" he motioned around the space "—is a barn."

She laughed, the wind through the open door carrying a whiff of her citrus scent, mixing with the familiar smell of leather and hay. "You're right. It is. But I was referring to your house, as well."

Interesting how she saw space when he thought of his estate as scaled back. Releasing Jackson's hoof, Conrad made his way to the door. Shut it to keep out the cold. No use freezing before they started riding.

"It's not the size of my brother's, but I don't need as much room."

"It's still very spacious, especially by Alaska standards with property being so expensive." She winced, setting her leather bag on the recessed shelving near where the saddles hung. She positioned the bag near the helmets he'd always made children wear. "That was crass of me to mention money."

"Not at all. High real estate prices here are a fact." Hefting Patches's saddle and saddle pad off the rack, he slung the bridle over his shoulder.

A glance at Felicity's wind-pinkened face filled his mind with thoughts of skimming kisses over her before claiming her mouth. The memory of her was powerful, so much so, it could tempt him to move too fast and risk the progress he'd made with her. Drawing in a steadying breath, he focused on the task of readying the horses.

As he moved toward the pinto, Patches's ears flicked as if interested in the conversation at hand as the saddle settled on his back. Conrad was a hard worker, but plenty of people worked hard and didn't have this kind of luxury. He knew luck had played in as well and he didn't lose sight of that. After adjusting the girth, he slid the bit into the horse's mouth, fiddling with the chin strap. He placed the reins on Patches's neck. The well-trained horse didn't move, but stood at attention as Conrad tacked up Jackson.

"Even in Texas, I grew up in smaller places, my parents' apartment, then foster homes. This is incredible."

He warmed at how she expressed appreciation for the life he'd built, rather than comparing it with Jack Steele's sprawling compound. Conrad passed her the reins to Patches, the wind blowing the loose strands of her hair forward. His hands itched with the urge to stroke her hair back.

Too easily, he could lose himself in looking at her. But if he made a move, she would likely bolt.

Patience.

He offered her a leg up out of courtesy but also to determine her skill. He would be able to tell if she was as good a rider as she claimed by the way she sat in the saddle. How she positioned her body and weight.

Felicity seemed to be a natural.

Now confident she could hold her own, he led his horse out by the reins. The sun was high and bright, reflecting off the snow in a nearly blinding light. Closing the barn door behind him, he led Jackson a few steps away from the steel-reinforced door. Conrad pulled himself into the saddle, hands adjusting the reins by muscle memory.

Pressing his calves into Jackson's sensitive side, he urged the horse toward an open gate. He figured this enclosed area would be safer—just in case Felicity lost her seat. Much easier to contain than potentially chasing Patches through the wilderness.

Felicity skillfully picked up the reins, bringing Patches to attention as she set her horse beside his. "Have you heard anything more about your niece?"

"We've locked down a time for Brea's arrival. We'll be meeting with her attorney present—at her request." The hair on the back of his neck bristled at all the ways things could go badly.

"This can't be easy for any of you."

He pushed his weight in the saddle, grounding down. Nothing about Brea's return had been something he could have imagined. At least not like this.

"We never dreamed we could have her back at all. We're staying focused on the fact she's alive." Truthful, but it didn't negate the hell of wondering what led her to infiltrate the company, to resent and mistrust them all to this degree.

"I hope it's not awkward if I ask, but is there a chance her mother is alive, too?" An eagle soaring overhead cast a wide-wingspan shadow along the snow ahead of Felicity.

"No, none," he said without hesitation. "Mary's body was thrown from the plane. They were able to make a positive ID. With Brea, they only located teeth in the charred wreckage."

It never got easier discussing that part of the aftermath.

She shivered. "Your family has been through so much."

"Nothing guarantees life will be easy." The glare of the sun along the icy pasture was so bright he shielded his eyes with his hand. "We're just lucky to have each other for support along the way."

"That's a healthy outlook."

Her words made him realize she was listening with a professional ear. "I recall you saying you became a social worker because of growing up in foster care. What made you decide to switch to the hospital position?"

Her posture grew surer as she answered him, guiding Patches around snow-covered bushes. "As a child, I saw what a difference a caring professional could make, in my life and in others'. There are so many components, from the caseworker, to the courts, and yes, too often, hospitals. This gave me another avenue to make a difference."

"You're certainly doing that." He respected her devotion to her job, one of the many things that had attracted him to her. He'd thought her career focus would also make them a great pair. He'd thought wrong and needed to figure out another way around to win her.

"I'm grateful to your family for what they're doing for the hospital." Wind blew flurries around her horse's hooves. "The children in oncology... I don't need to spell out their needs for you. You saw it with your niece Naomi."

"I did. What kinds of needs do you see for the children in the hospital?" he asked, to make the most of working together. And because he found he was genuinely curious in her input.

"That's such a broad question."

He tilted his head, looking forward on the trail in the pasture and checking for uneven ground that could be masked by the snow. "Say the first thing that pops into your head."

"I have a list in my office on staffing and structural needs," she said, still not answering his question.

But he understood how her professional instincts might be in play, not wanting to commit to an item when there was a more important need.

"Send me the list. I feel certain we can address those issues. What else?" he pressed. "Something you didn't even imagine could go on your wish list." He pushed Jackson into a slow trot, the palomino's stride putting slight distance between them. Glancing over his shoulder, Conrad saw a determined smile settle on Felicity's face.

Keeping her hands low on Patches's neck, she clicked her tongue, coaxing the horse into a smooth jog. Though the horse's pace increased, Felicity's seat stayed steady. Flawless execution.

"Well, the children in behavioral health could use more pet therapy teams."

Felicity's roots might be Texan, but she held her own with the horse and the cold like she'd lived here her whole life. He was surprised and impressed. "We're on it. Isabeau Mikkelson is on the committee for PR and she brought up that very subject in an earlier meeting."

"She and her husband live on a ranch outside Juneau, right?"

"Yes, she just arrived in town today. They're staying with the family during her last trimester of pregnancy. She's high risk because of her diabetes, and they want to use the same doctor Naomi had for the delivery."

"I'm glad they have the support of so many relatives. Are you sure she's up to the task of helping with this?"

Even with Isabeau being high risk, he hadn't considered something could go wrong. "She checked with her doctors first and got the okay. She's been going

stir-crazy taking off work and this was a good compromise. She's been helping pick up slack, too, that would
have been covered by Jeannie's former assistant, Sage
Hammond."

"What happened to Sage?"

"She took a sudden sabbatical to Europe. Really left
the family in a lurch, kind of surprising since she's
related to Jeannie." He shrugged. "Anyway, Isabeau
raised the idea of pet therapy since she has a service
dog for her diabetes. Even though a service dog is different from a therapy dog, Isabeau's a great resource
on the topic. She's familiar with the various roles a pet
can play in health care."

Felicity nodded. "A service dog performs a task for
one person for life, and a therapy dog provides comfort in groups or for a number of different people individually."

"Exactly. We're looking into therapy dog programs
for individual room visits as well as group settings.
Having a couple of dogs present during reading time
would be a great place to start."

"That sounds wonderful. You've clearly put a lot of
thought into this." She glanced at him. "Your family,
too. It's not just a…"

"Not just a promotional tool? No. That's not to say
we aren't happy for the good press, because our success gives us more charitable options."

"I'll do my best to be sure the money's spent wisely
so the foundation can do even more."

"I'm sure you will." Applying slight pressure with his
reins, Conrad looped his horse back toward the barn.
Created somewhat of a bad circle in the snow.

Felicity maneuvered Patches to follow him. "How are you so certain?"

"You were willing to come riding with me today in spite of pushing me away with both hands," he said with a cocky grin.

Silence fell between them. The only sounds echoing in the air were the crunch of horse hooves against fresh snow.

She shook her head, her smile half amused. "I don't dislike you."

He laughed, appreciating how she didn't dish out flattery just because he had money to donate. "Watch it, or my ego will overinflate with the lavish compliments."

"I don't mean to be rude. I just want to be sure we're clear that this is business."

He needed to make sure she understood. "I would never make a move without your consent."

"But that's not the same as continuing to pursue me," she said with a wry smile, her cheeks turning red from the wind.

"You're too perceptive for me to even try to deny that."

"As long as you're clear on where I stand."

"Yes, ma'am." He tapped the brim of his Stetson, tipping it slightly in salute. "We should get back before your Texas roots freeze out here."

They'd reached the gate again. Conrad guided Jackson through the opening. Though if he was being honest the horse knew it was time to return home. A renewed pep in his step, Jackson moved toward the barn. Patches let out a low nicker as they drew closer to the structure.

He'd made progress with Felicity and his quest. He'd

meant it when he said he wouldn't leverage the attraction between them until she gave him the green light. But he was a patient man. He could still spend time with her. Get to know her better. Persuade her that they could have something special.

In fact, he welcomed the challenge—as well as the distraction from the stress of his niece's complicated return.

Three

Breanna Steele still struggled with thinking of herself by her birth name. She'd been Milla Jones for over fifteen years. It felt like longer, in fact, since the Brea days were distant, muddied by so many factors since the plane crash.

Pushing away her in-flight meal, she pressed her fingertips against the cool glass of the airplane window. Since the plane crash all those years ago, flying sent her stomach into knots. Particularly when the private jet was so small, just like that aircraft all those years ago. But the transportation had been chartered by the Steeles. Snow-covered mountains sent her nerves into overdrive so she returned her focus to the main cabin.

Her lawyer accompanied her, a young attorney who'd taken her case pro bono, looking to make a name for himself. He was cutthroat. All the more reason to trust him with a future so scary and unsure.

Taking the flight offered by the Steeles had made her nervous, but ultimately it was the logical thing to do. She'd also been very clear in her acceptance that she'd left safeguards in place if anything happened to her. The world would know exactly where she'd been.

People thought she was acting paranoid. She didn't care.

She tore apart the roll, tossing the pieces into her bowl of uneaten salad. Stress had taken a toll on her appetite. Since the death of her "adoptive" parents last year, she'd been unable to resist searching for answers about her past. Her mind was a jumble. She'd been brought up by a couple—Steven and Karen Jones— who'd protected her from the threats of her family's crooked connections.

She'd been told her Steele siblings died as well in the crash and the accident was such a haze, she'd believed it. Steven and Karen had insisted they were keeping Brea safe from threats existing in her birth father's world.

Finding out after the Jones's deaths that her real dad and her siblings were alive had been a shock, one that started a steamroll of questions about other things. Still, loyalty to Steven and Karen, who'd saved her, was tough to break. She'd told herself they lied about her siblings to keep her safe from her father, who'd orchestrated her biological mother's death. Brea still believed that to a degree. So much so that she could only envision meeting with the Steeles with lawyers present for her safety—and so she didn't end up in jail.

There was also the whole matter of her wrangling a job at Alaska Oil Barons Inc. under her fake name and leaking business secrets. She'd wanted revenge for their abandonment. Now she was beginning to realize things might not be that simple. But she still needed to be careful.

As the plane began its descent into Anchorage, she shivered. Afraid, but resolute. The time had come to face her past, to make peace so she could move forward free of any entanglements with the Steeles.

Free of the pain of realizing they never really searched for her.

Never could she be a part of the Steeles' world of lies and a fake sense of family.

Felicity found disentangling her feelings when it came to Conrad Steele was easier said than done. Their simple ride together had left her more confused than ever.

Fidgeting with her long, silver necklace, she looked at her half-eaten turkey-and-hummus sandwich. She contemplated grabbing it off the pile of vintage travel books she'd used to decorate her office. Unlike her co-workers, Felicity didn't have many pictures of family and loved ones plastered in every square inch of her office.

Not that she wasn't sentimental. Instead, she had a few handwritten cards displayed, pinned to a corkboard. These mementos helped her through the dark days, when the important work she did weighed heavy on her mind. Felicity needed reminders of light.

Compelled by memories, Felicity reached for the letter Angie, the social worker who made all the difference in her life, penned upon Felicity's acceptance of her first social worker job. She hadn't worked here long, but already files were piling up on her desk. The workload was heavy, but each day came with opportunities to touch lives. Already, she'd added a new note to her board, a thank-you from a young patient and her parents, alongside others from the past she'd brought from her other job.

She gathered up the files and stowed them in a drawer, trying to tidy up before Conrad Steele and Isabeau Mikkelson arrived. Felicity kneed the drawer closed. Her office wasn't as grand as anything in Conrad's work world, but she was proud of her new space, with a corner window. Her framed diplomas might not be Ivy League, but she'd finished with honors, the first in her family to attend college. She'd worked two jobs to put herself through. It had taken her an extra year in undergraduate school, as well as an extra semester to complete her master's in social work. But she'd never given up on her dream.

People like Conrad didn't understand what it was like to have no family support. She didn't blame him or resent him for that. However, she couldn't help but feel they came from different planets and he could never fully understand her journey.

A tap on her door pulled her from her thoughts. She smoothed back her hair on her way across the room. Nerves fluttered in her stomach at just the prospect of seeing Conrad. She willed herself to take three slow breaths, in through her nose and out through her mouth, the way she coached patients to do.

She opened the door. There wasn't enough air in the room to calm her reaction to the man on the other side of the threshold.

Conrad's broad shoulders filled out the designer suit jacket, his overcoat and Stetson in hand. "Isabeau's running a little behind. Her OB doctor was held up."

"Come in." Felicity gestured through, willing herself not to think about how much smaller the space was with him inside.

He hung his coat and hat on the rack in the corner before turning back to face her. "Isabeau said she should be here in about ten minutes."

They were going to discuss procedures for including more therapy dogs in the pediatric ward. Felicity had seen amazing results from therapy dogs with children, but she wanted more information on channels for ensuring the dogs were the right fit. She knew enough to realize that just because a dog was affectionate didn't make it a therapy dog candidate.

Isabeau had information on programs that tested dogs and provided training to the therapy dog's owner. She'd also mentioned discussing the different levels of work, varying from simply sitting with a reading group to assisting someone in a recovery setting.

Conrad tapped along her note board and framed art from patients. "These notes and pictures are incredible."

"They've gotten me through some rough days at work."

He shot her a wide smile. "This beats my wall of fame, hands down."

"You won't find me disagreeing with that," she couldn't resist retorting, grinning back. "There's an indescribable thrill when my job works the way it should."

"I can hear that in your voice." He sat on the corner of her desk, the Alaska skyline stretched out behind him through the window. "That compassion is what makes you such a success."

She leveled a stare his way. "I'm also not won over

by idle flattery. You don't know enough about my work to judge how successful I am or am not."

"I do know, from your wall there and your boss's confidence in you to represent the hospital with the charity foundation."

His words stopped her short, stirring confusion. She'd been so certain Conrad had orchestrated their working together on the program. "Oh, uh…"

"What?" he asked. "Is something wrong?"

"I'm just…surprised." She searched his face. "I thought you pressured my boss into choosing me for the project."

"Absolutely not," he said without hesitation. "You don't know me all that well or you wouldn't say it, much less think it. When it comes to business, I'm no-nonsense. My brother has the soft heart."

"He seems gruff and you're all smiles." She studied him for a moment longer even though she could swear she knew every handsome detail of his face, every line that spoke of experience. He was all man and she was far, far from unaffected. "And that's how you two catch people off guard in negotiations. People don't expect gentleness from your brother and ruthlessness from you."

He ran a hand through his dark, gray-flecked hair, hand stopping on the back of his neck. A boyish kind of charm that she hadn't noticed he'd possessed. Conrad—a complex man of many mysteries.

"Ruthless? Ouch." He clapped a splayed hand over his heart. "How did I go from all smiles and charm to ruthless so fast?"

She wasn't sure. Just when she thought she had him

pegged, he surprised her. "I guess I'm learning to get to know you. Wasn't that your goal in pursuing me?"

"You could say that, although I was hoping for something more persuasive than *ruthless*."

"Ruthlessness can be a good thing, when channeled properly."

His blue eyes heated, the air crackling between them. "And do you think I've been channeled properly?"

She ached to lean in closer to him to see if the temperature continued to rise the nearer she came. And then she realized...she was being played.

Felicity angled back. "I ask questions for a living, you know, and it's to keep someone talking rather than having them do the asking."

"Busted." He shrugged unrepentantly.

Fine. She could go toe-to-toe with this man. "My training also makes me believe you only want me because I'm telling you no."

"Let's test your theory." He lifted her hand, the calluses on his fingertips touching her skin, arousing her. "Say yes to a date. See if my interest evaporates. It won't, by the way. But go ahead. Try."

"Now you've changed to charming again." She should pull her hand from his. Should. But didn't.

Instead, her imagination ran wild with the possibility of having his raspy touch all over her body. Her senses filled with the crisp, outdoorsy scent of him.

A cleared throat in the doorway broke the spell like a splash of chilling reality. She tugged her hand away quickly. But she was certain he didn't miss her guilty flinch.

Felicity took in a very pregnant Isabeau, whose slender hand rested gently on her baby bump. She wore a violet knit sweater dress, her shoulder-length red hair perfectly styled into loose romantic waves. Even in her eighth month, Isabeau had a chic style that she put to use in her PR profession. Felicity had been impressed with her when accompanying the Steeles to the ballet last month.

Isabeau looked at them with curiosity in her eyes. "I'm sorry to be late. Thank you for waiting."

Thank goodness Isabeau hadn't commented on, well, the obvious. Felicity adjusted the second chair so it was closer to the pregnant woman. "How was your appointment?"

Smiling her thanks, Isabeau sank into the seat with a sigh. "We're watching the baby's weight because of my diabetes." Diabetes could cause a baby to be larger. "But, thankfully, all appears to be on track. I'll finish up plans for the hospital dinner and still have two weeks to put my feet up before my son is born."

Isabeau and Trystan had shared the gender news, but were keeping the name a secret.

Conrad patted her shoulder. "That's great news from the doctor."

His concern was undeniable. And touching. He cared for his family. Felicity knew that already, but the reminder, especially right now when she was feeling vulnerable, made her edgy. She needed to distance herself. Work had been her buffer for years and she embraced that now as a way of understanding the people around her.

And she needed to maintain that sense of professionalism. She worried about appearances and letting her guard down around him.

She gestured toward Conrad's chair. "We have a lot to cover, so let's get started."

However, with her skin still burning from his touch, she knew she was only kidding herself if she thought it wouldn't happen again.

Ninety minutes later, Conrad packed his briefcase, the meeting drawing to a close. Felicity had kept the discussion businesslike, moving the agenda along at a brisk pace. Isabeau was already retreating toward the elevator, the office door still open.

Leaving Conrad alone with Felicity. Worries about Brea showing up and the unrest in the family dogged him. Being around Felicity felt like the only time he wasn't hounded by the sense that his family was on the brink of another disaster.

She thumbed through a stack of new children's books on her desk. "I'm impressed with how seriously you and the committee are taking the reading selection. It's going to be incredible having therapy dogs sit with the children during story time."

"We're certainly adding to our family library for the little ones." Try as he might, he felt his gaze drawn to the curve of her pink lips. Natural beauty shone through in her delicate eyebrows, arching as she smoothed back a strand of brown hair.

"Naomi's twins were born here."

He nodded as he packed a children's book away. "And Glenna and Broderick's daughter, too. Her adoption is almost complete."

"Adoption?" Felicity passed him a stack with the rest of the books.

As she leaned forward, he noted the way her blouse hugged her body, suggesting well-appointed curves. Felicity had the kind of beauty that few possessed. It was about more than her looks. It came from her confidence, the way she carried herself.

Damn mesmerizing.

"It's complicated." He tucked the rest of the storybooks into his briefcase, keeping his distance for now. He wasn't going to push his luck. "Baby Fleur was abandoned on my brother's doorstep with a note from the mother saying she didn't know if the father was Broderick...or Glenna's first husband."

She raised an eyebrow. "I've dealt with some complex placements. That had to be so difficult for everyone."

"Turned out that Glenna's first husband had cheated on her just before he died." He wasn't sure why Felicity hadn't booted him out of the office yet. "The baby is, in fact, his biological child. But in the time waiting to learn the paternity results, Glenna and Broderick bonded hard with Fleur."

She leaned in, clearly invested in the story. He would take any opportunity—any conversation—to build a firmer connection between them. Stolen time. A date could still be possible. He could feel her interest crackle in the space between them. "And her biological mother?"

He should have realized Felicity's professional instincts would kick into gear. "Signed over her rights to them for a private adoption." He snapped his case closed and locked. "We couldn't love Fleur any more if she was Broderick's."

"That's how it should be." She tapped one of the framed thank-you notes.

"I agree. Naomi's twins were conceived with an anonymous sperm donor. Yet, Royce is one hundred percent committed to being their father. He even delivered them in a car in a snowstorm."

One of the crazier moments of the last year. But one that his family had welcomed and embraced with open arms. His family anchored him through hard times. With the Steeles so on edge, he found himself…searching.

A bad reason to want this date with Felicity so much? Maybe. But he wasn't giving up.

She angled her head, hair tumbling in front of her eyes. He fought the urge to reach across the desk and sweep it behind her ear. "How did I not know all of this about the Steeles and Mikkelsons?"

"We're a big family. There's a lot to know." He held her gaze for a moment before turning toward the door. He'd made more progress than expected today. And he was only getting started on his plans for seduction.

Only four days had passed since her meeting with Conrad, and Felicity was starting to worry that by the end of the week, she might not have any space left to move.

Her office was overflowing with gifts—Swiss chocolates, outrageously expensive Vietnamese coffee beans and two lavish floral arrangements. The scent of roses, lilies and freesia filled her office.

She needed to walk the flowers down to the children's ward for the nurses' station to share with patients who could use a pick-me-up. She felt decadent keeping them for herself even for the short term but it had been a hectic week, each day more stressful than the one before. And today had been the worst, starting early with eleven children being admitted to the hospital for neglect.

But pampering herself with candy and flowers wasn't going to make that any easier. She needed to stop dwelling on thoughts of Conrad Steele.

She scooped up her cell phone to take with her and noticed she had somehow missed a call from Isabeau. Tapping Redial, she didn't have to wait long.

Isabeau picked up on the second ring. "Hi, thanks for getting back to me so quickly. I have a favor to ask."

"Let me pull up my file on our plans so I'll have it handy for reference." She typed in her password to bring the computer screen back to life.

"Actually, this isn't about business. It's a personal favor." Isabeau's voice was so heavy with concern it had Felicity sitting up straight with worry.

"Of course." Felicity turned away from her computer, her focus fully on the call. "What do you need?"

A pause filtered through the phone.

Felicity felt as though her heart became dislodged from her chest, climbing into her throat. Threatening to spill out on her desk amid budget requests and case files.

"Would you be willing to sit in when the family meets with Breanna?" The words fell out in a fast tumble with a nervous edge. "There will be lawyers present, as if it wasn't already going to be tense enough. I think they would benefit from having you there."

Felicity agreed that having professional help present would be wise, but she wasn't as sure she was the right person since she knew the family. Not to mention, Isabeau was a Mikkelson, not a Steele.

And there was the whole crazy draw to Conrad to

deal with. "What does the rest of the family have to say?"

A sigh signaled the weariness Isabeau felt.

"Jeannie agreed, and she's going to talk to Jack about it. He listens to her."

While she appreciated Isabeau's heart was in the right place, Felicity still wasn't sure she was the person for the task. "There are other counselors in the area. I would be glad to give you a list of recommendations."

"But we know you. You know us, and that's no small task, given our huge family tree," Isabeau said wryly. "But if you're not comfortable, I understand."

Felicity weighed her decision and chose her words carefully. Things were complicated enough, given her feelings for Conrad.

Feelings?

Felicity pushed aside the wayward thought and settled on a compromise. "If Jack and the others agree, then I'm glad to do what I can to help with any issues that may arise."

"Thank you. That's a huge relief." A shaky sigh whispered through the phone. "It's all just so…surreal. Brea coming…being alive, her being this Milla person who was out to harm the company."

"I realize this must be stressful for you. I hope you're taking care of yourself and the baby."

"Of course I am," Isabeau said quickly in a way that Felicity interpreted as the end of the conversation about Breanna. "My husband is waiting on me hand and foot, as is the rest of the family. All I have is this project to think about until my son is born."

Felicity laughed along with her, even through an ache that lodged in her chest over the woman's words as they finished the call. Her grip tightened on the silent cell until her fingers numbed.

There'd been a time when Felicity had dreams of being pregnant, with a doting husband as excited as she was. Yes, her ex had wanted children, but she'd sensed trouble in the marriage and wanted a steady home first. Something that never happened because her ex was a drug addict, hooked on prescription meds. She still couldn't believe how long it had taken her to discover his addiction. She was a counselor, for heaven's sake.

But he was that good of a liar, twisting her inside out over time.

In a last-ditch effort, she'd begged him to go to counseling together in addition to checking into a rehab center. He'd delayed and delayed until she realized he was never going to change. He didn't want to. Two weeks after she booted him out, he moved in with another woman.

Felicity knew she'd dodged a bullet. The heartache would have only been worse the longer they'd stayed together. Still, sometimes, when she heard about other happy couples living the dream, it made her remember all that pain. The betrayal. And yes, it even made her question herself, although she knew in her gut she'd done everything she could.

Well, everything except having chosen someone different from the start. She could forgive herself for one mistake. But if she repeated the past? She would have no one to blame but herself.

The scent of roses drew her attention back to the arrangements from Conrad. She really did need to get them out of her office. And the staff would appreciate the chocolates. If only it was that easy to get the man out of her mind. But this was a start.

Juggling the two arrangements with the box of chocolates tucked under her arm, she made fast tracks down the corridor. She stepped out of the elevator on the floor for pediatric oncology…and stopped short as she caught sight of children seated in a circle in the play area. Story time? It appeared so. She'd forgotten the discussion about having readings here for patients too ill to go to the memory garden.

Or maybe her subconscious had nudged her this way.

Sighing at herself, she secured her grip on the flowers and chocolates. If Conrad saw her giving away his gifts, then so be it. Maybe it was for the best.

As she walked closer, she realized it wasn't a male voice, but rather a woman's voice reading, a familiar voice. Her friend Tally, who was engaged to Marshall Steele, held up the kids' favorite book about the magical horse.

Felicity passed the flowers and candy to a nurse with a smile, her attention drawn to the children as Tally told them to go to the window for a surprise.

Curious, Felicity stepped closer, helping a little boy struggling with his wheelchair. Gasps and squeals of delight filled the air. She parked the wheelchair at the window that overlooked the parking lot.

And found a sight that tugged her heart far more than any roses or chocolate.

Below the window, Conrad Steele sat astride his horse just like the hero in the storybook, confident, strong…

And tipping his Stetson in greeting.

Four

Even from across the parking lot, on his palomino, Conrad could see Felicity was fired up. She charged through the sliding doors out into the elements. The wind tore at her cape as she picked her way past a pile of sludge a snowplow had pushed to the side.

From the scowl on her face, she wasn't happy.

Sexy as hell. But definitely not happy.

He guided his horse closer, anticipation sizzling through him with each step of Jackson's hooves. He hadn't planned on seeing her, but he was damn glad for the opportunity to square off with her, all the same.

Drawing up alongside her, Conrad gave a gentle tug to the reins. "Hello, beautiful. How's your day going?"

"What are you doing?" Her words were soft, but steely.

"Hopefully, I'm charming a bunch of sick children."

He lifted his Stetson and waved it at the windows where the children were lined up watching. His horse shifted his weight from front hoof to front hoof as if gearing up for a dance and show. Sometimes, he swore the palomino could read his thoughts as they formed.

Sighing, she tugged the hood of her cape over her ears. "And this has nothing to do with your quest to wear me down."

"You're assuming I planned on you seeing me, which I didn't since I expected you to be in your office." And that was the truth. It stung him that she still thought only the worst of him. Although if she already thought that of him, he might as well make the most of the moment. "But hey, if it dazzles you as well, then that's just a win-win. Let's give them a show."

She eyed him warily. "What do you mean?"

He extended a gloved hand. "Join me."

Picturing the scene now, he imagined the oohs and aahs of the children as he rode off with Felicity. A classic cowboy hero move. A movie brought to life on their doorstep. Some bit of light he could offer them.

And offer for himself, if he was being honest.

For a moment she didn't move. Just stood assessing him as he contemplated how to advance if this impromptu idea backfired.

Backing up a step, she hugged her cape tighter around her. "You're kidding."

Only one step back, though. She still seemed to be assessing, contemplating. Seizing the indecision, he pressed forward.

"Not at all. Ride with me." He might not have planned this, but suddenly he wanted her to join him as much as he wanted his next breath. "The horse trailer is just around the corner, but the children don't know that. You'll make their day without risking frostbite."

She chewed her bottom lip for so long he was sure she would say no and bolt back into the hospital. Then her chin jutted and she extended her gloved hand. He clasped it and as soon as she placed her foot in the stirrup, he gave a firm tug, maneuvering her in front of him in a smooth sweep. No question, she was at home on a horse. He hadn't expected to find this common ground with her. A pleasant surprise. And one he intended to make the most of.

As she straddled the horse, her bottom nestled against him in a sweet pressure that made his teeth ache. His arms slid forward to clasp the reins. Damn, she felt good, right here where she belonged.

He guided the horse forward with a quick *click, click*. His thighs pressed against Felicity's legs. The closeness sent their chemistry into overload. His libido sure had a way of betraying him around this woman.

He knew this would be short-lived and she would raise those barriers in place soon enough. But for now, he let himself enjoy the sensations of being close to her, the rocking of the horse's gait generating a tantalizing friction of her body against his.

She glanced back at him, a wry smile on her face. "The children really did enjoy seeing you out here. Thank you for making the arrangement with Tally."

"I have to admit it was Marshall's idea when he heard Tally planned to read today. He said he would have done it, but he had an appointment." And now Conrad wondered if somehow his nephew had engineered this. Even if Felicity hadn't seen him out here on the horse, she would have heard about it. And while he was enjoying having her in his arms, he preferred to keep his family out of his relationships as much as possible.

Which posed a problem since Felicity was good friends with Marshall's fiancée. Hell, this was complicated.

He stopped Jackson to let a car ease past, the child in the backseat watching them with wide eyes. No doubt, the children in the hospital weren't the only ones noticing this impromptu jaunt.

"Well, thank you all the same for taking time off from the office to do this for the children."

Was it Conrad's imagination, or did she lean back into him more?

"I can work from home this evening." An image filled his mind of the two of them side by side on his sofa, laptops open. The thought caught him up short. That kind of shared time ventured into the relationship realm, something more than recreation or sex.

Jackson stopped at the end of the horse trailer, waiting. Conrad cleared his mind and focused on the present. He swung out of the saddle and held up a hand for Felicity, even though she could clearly handle a dismount on her own. He wanted to touch her again, to feel her fingers clasp his.

Then they were standing face-to-face, their breaths filling the air between them with puffy clouds that mingled, linked. He wanted to kiss her, but needed her to make the move. They were in her workplace and he knew better than to risk alienating her with a public spectacle.

He'd already pushed his luck with the shared horseback ride.

So he stepped back and took to heart the flash of disappointment in her eyes.

He removed the saddle and saddle pad from Jackson. To his horse's credit, he didn't need to slip the bridle off and tie him to the trailer. His palomino had no interest in bolting. He grabbed a hard brush, running it down the horse's strong frame. Jackson shook from ears to tail, seeming to enjoy the post-riding care. Grabbing the horse's halter, he unhooked the bridle, slid it down his arm. Conrad led Jackson into the trailer, aware of her gaze on him. She hadn't left, and that boded well. He didn't intend to let the opportunity pass.

"Can I convince you to warm up in the truck cab with me? I have a thermos of hot coffee." Latching the trailer door shut, he shot her a grin.

"Coffee…my weakness," she said with a rueful smile.

"I remember." He made a point of remembering everything about her.

And he intended to use whatever leverage he could in his quest to get her into his bed. Hopefully, sooner rather than later.

Climbing into Conrad's truck, Felicity wondered if *she* needed her head examined. As if things weren't complicated enough between them, now she had the meeting with Breanna to consider, too. Did Conrad know she would be sitting in? Still, she couldn't bring herself to ask him. She was enjoying this.

It was just a simple cup of coffee, she reminded herself. Except nothing about this man or her feelings for him were simple.

She was making just one reckless decision after another when it came to him. First, climbing on the horse—her body still tingled from the proximity. Then, agreeing to sit here in the close confines of the king cab, heater blasting and carrying the spicy scent of him.

But reason had left her right about the time she'd sat in front of him in the saddle, her body coming alive in a way that made her question her decision for distance. His effect on her was potent. Intoxicating. And damn near irresistible.

The truck wasn't the luxury SUV he usually drove. No, this was a working vehicle. While it appeared to be only a couple of years old, the truck had been used often and hard. The leather seats wore the look of many cleanings. Snow and ranch life had taken a toll.

His gaze landed on her toying with her lanyard. "That's a really pretty piece."

"Thank you. Lanyards are my weakness." She tried not to be aware of his eyes on her hand, which happened to be right at breast level. His look wasn't of the ogling sort or disrespectful, but it was…aware. "I have a collection of them."

He passed her a travel mug of coffee.

She let go of her necklace and took the drink, inhaling the java scent. "Heavenly. Thank you. I really needed this."

"Long day?"

She nodded, touched by his insight. "I was called in before breakfast for an emergency."

There had been an influx of eleven children admitted for signs of neglect after child services pulled them from a commune. The children would be placed in foster care. The intake had been emotional for all the staff, who had worked to reduce the stress for the already traumatized youths. Every time she thought she'd seen it all, she learned otherwise.

Conrad reached behind him to the backseat. "I have some power bars in my emergency kit."

"I snagged some fruit from the cafeteria. Thanks, though."

He dropped the bag back to the floorboards. "You're a tough lady to pamper."

"Or incredibly easy to pamper. Keep bringing me coffee like this." This wasn't hospital coffee. This was the good stuff.

And now she realized why she'd joined him. She needed this time away from the office and the strain of a rough day. Maybe it was unwise to indulge, but she wanted this momentary escape.

She searched for a way to extend their time together awhile longer. "Tell me what it was like growing up here."

Draping an arm along the back of the seat, he angled to face her. "Our dad and mom were busy building the business, so Jack and I didn't have a lot of supervision. Jack was expected to look out for me. Which he did. He took me horseback riding, fishing, hiking, kayaking. Wherever he went, he let me tag along."

"You two are close," she said, more to keep the conversation going than anything. She already knew how much his brother meant to him. His sense of family was one of the things that made him all the more tempting.

"We are. Although once he and Mary got married, because my parents were getting older, I was left to my own devices more."

"How so?" she asked, curious about Conrad as a little boy. She recalled there being about fifteen years between the brothers, so Conrad would have still been quite young then.

"Unlimited computer time. That's when I started playing the stock market."

"As a kid?" she asked in surprise.

A wry smile crossed his lips that she noticed more than she should.

"I used my father's profile."

"He didn't notice?" She wondered just how much he'd been left on his own. No wonder he'd reached out to his brother's family.

"Oh, Dad noticed…eventually. He saw the profit margins increase at a much higher rate." He shrugged. "So he set me up an account of my own and began loading it up with allowance money to invest—as long as I would give him tips."

"And that was the start of your company."

"Yes, ma'am."

He truly was a self-made man. She was impressed. *Surprised.*

"I seem to recall reading that you got a master's degree in engineering. But how did this young entrepreneurial side of you never make it into the press?" She swirled the hot coffee in the mug, tendrils of steam carrying a light scent of cinnamon and nutmeg.

"I prefer to keep a lower profile than my brother." He tapped her forehead. "What are you thinking?"

Her stomach fluttered at his touch, reminding her to proceed with caution despite the electricity he ignited in her skin. "I'm trying to decide if you're being honest or just trying to tell me what I want to hear."

His smile faded. "I'm always truthful. Always."

She realized she'd insulted him. He took his honor seriously. That…tempted her.

While she might have wanted to escape from the

stress of work, this conversation was bringing a whole new host of problems. She was playing with fire.

Felicity drained her coffee and passed him the cup. "I should get back to work."

He took the mug, his fingers sliding around her wrist, holding her. "Felicity?"

The connection between them grew stronger, making her ache for more. Just a taste of him. Unable to resist, she swayed toward him, just a hint. But it was enough.

His head dipped and his mouth met hers, fully, firmly. He tasted of coffee and winter, of passion and confidence. And he set her senses on fire with a simple stroke of his tongue. As much as she tried to tell herself it was just a kiss…that her reaction was because of abstinence…this kiss, this man, moved her in a way she'd never felt before.

She gripped his coat and pulled him closer, the heat of him reaching even through his clothes, her gloves, into her veins. The world outside faded away, the truck cab a warm haven of isolation and temptation. Much longer and she would be begging him to take her home, and more.

Then a gust of warm air whispered between them and she realized he'd pulled away. She opened her eyes to find him studying her from the driver's seat. Unmistakable desire flamed in his gaze, but he was pulling away.

Giving her the space he'd promised?

That made her want him all the more.

He stepped out of the truck, walked around the hood to her side and opened her door. "I'll see you tomorrow."

His words were a promise.

One she couldn't bring herself to deny.

* * *

Walking away from kissing Felicity had been tough as hell.

But Conrad knew it was the right move. Aside from being in a public parking lot, he could sense she still wasn't ready to take things to the next level. He'd made too much progress to risk a setback by pushing too fast.

He was a patient man.

Patient, and frustrated.

Thank goodness he had the distraction of a family card game at his house. He'd rather play pool on his vintage table. There was something calming about the angles. Like riding, sizing up shots calmed him to his core. But today, he and his brother, Jack, opted to gather the Mikkelson and Steele men for cards. Chuck and his wife had moved to North Dakota, but they made use of the family's private jet for trips back to Alaska.

Playing games together was a carryover from Conrad's childhood when his brother taught him to play.

Jack Steele stood in front of the wet bar, whiskey glass in hand, talking on the cell phone to Jeannie.

Conrad moved to the high counter that separated Jack from him. The housekeeping staff had left an array of snack food on the tan-and-brown-flecked granite countertop. Grabbing a plate, Conrad shoveled some fresh Parmesan fries onto his plate, along with two Reuben sliders. He swiped a bottle of beer and made his way back to the table. He scooped fries into his mouth and chewed, trying to push the memory of Felicity's lips from his mind.

An unsuccessful venture.

Chuck filled his plate, pouring nuts and fries sky

high. Opting for the sparkling seltzer water, he returned to the table.

Conrad sat in silence for a moment, listening to the cadence of his brother's laugh. It was good to hear that sound given the events of the last year and the strange reemergence of Brea. Conrad was grateful Felicity had agreed to sit in when Brea met with the family. He couldn't even begin to imagine what time apart from her birth family could do to a child who'd disappeared at her age.

A creak from the door to the game room cut through his thoughts. He cranked his head to the side to see a man in the door frame. Conrad did a double take as Royce entered.

Naomi's husband, a renowned, brilliant scientist who worked for the company, Royce was…eccentric and reclusive. He had proved a great father to the twins, but he tended to spend his downtime on solo activities rather than hanging out with the extended family.

His near-midnight-colored hair was slightly disheveled. Looked like he had come from hours of working out a formula. Knowing Royce's dedication to his work, Conrad's assessment was probably correct.

Conrad swiped the surprise from his face over the scientist's unexpected attendance. "You're joining us?"

Royce shrugged, dressed in a plain black sweater, opting for understatement always. "It's too cold for fishing." He looked at the spread, then moved for the fries and popped one into his mouth. "Hope you don't mind that I let myself in."

With Royce's showing up, all the men in the extended family were present. It would make for an interesting poker game. And a welcome distraction. "We rank better than freezing your ass off. Nice to know."

"I came for the beer." Royce nodded to Jack as he tucked away his cell phone and stepped behind the bar. "How's Aiden doing?"

"Haven't heard from him," Jack said tightly, pulling the tap handle down and filling the frosted glass.

Aiden had dropped out of college. The teen said he wanted to learn the family business from the ground up. His father had suggested working summers, then. Aiden had declined.

Conrad could see both sides.

Their dad had booted him and Jack out when they'd each turned eighteen. It had been tougher for Jack since he'd already been in love with Mary, ready to tie the knot. They'd started a family right away. Jack's education had taken long, hard hours.

Things had been easier for Conrad since he'd been on his own, using every free minute to study for higher scores, grateful his investment savvy could pay the bills. And he hadn't been providing for a family or reading bedtime stories to kids then.

Jack shot a glance Conrad's way. "Don't send him money."

Conrad held up his hands. "I have no intention of doing any such thing." He took a swig of his beer, savoring the hoppy notes from the seasonal brew. "I may take him out to dinner next time I'm on-site, but my wallet will stay otherwise closed."

As much as he'd filled his wish for kids with Jack's children, Conrad was 100 percent clear on who their father was.

At the poker table, Chuck began shuffling decks.

Conrad tipped his beer to Chuck. "How did the house hunting go?"

"We're going to build. We found the land we want, and now we're having an architect draw up plans. If all goes well, it should be done by the time our name comes up on the adoption list."

"That's great." Jack placed a plate of sliders and nuts on the table, his piercing eyes fixed on Chuck as he sat. "I hope you have a suite there for Jeannie, because once there's a grandchild, there'll be no prying her away."

Chuck smiled. "We're counting on it." He turned to his brother, Trystan, offering him the deck to cut. "How's Isabeau?"

"The doctor says she's doing well, but I gotta confess, her diabetes scares me." His hand shook as he stacked the cards again for Chuck to deal.

Conrad toyed with his chips in front of him as the cards were dealt. "If you need anything, just ask."

Trystan scrubbed a hand over his jaw. "Keep an eye on her during the meetings. Make sure she isn't over-doing."

"Consider me on it," Conrad said without hesitation.

Trystan smiled his thanks. "If there's anything I can do in return, let me know."

"I believe Marshall already beat you to the punch." Sliding his cards from the table, Conrad leaned back in his chair.

"What do you mean?" Trystan fanned the hand he'd been dealt.

"Sending me to the hospital to ride a horse during story time." Conrad slid a card to the center, while the others at the table looked on with undisguised interest.

Marshall tossed chips into the middle of the table. "I

figured Felicity would either see or hear about it, which would bode well for you. Did it work?"

"She was impressed," Conrad admitted, memories of that kiss filling his mind.

Grinning, Marshall sipped the seltzer water. "I've always thought you two would make a nice couple."

Broderick leveled a shocked look at his brother. "Tally has certainly made a change in you."

Marshall swapped out two of his cards. "Uncle Conrad has always been there for us. He deserves a family of his own."

"Hey," Conrad interjected. "We're talking about me dating Felicity. Neither of us is marriage material. We're married to our jobs, which makes us a good match for a relationship."

Marshall cocked an eyebrow. "Funny, but I always thought you were more self-aware than that."

Conrad scratched along the logo on the beer bottle. "I invited you all here for cards, not a gossip circle."

And in fast order, he won the hand. If only wiping the knowing looks off their faces could be that simple. Unlikely, since if he had his way, they would all be seeing a lot more of him with Felicity on his arm.

Five

Felicity fidgeted with her phone as she sat in the waiting area outside the Alaska Oil Barons Inc. conference room, the meeting with Breanna Steele still a half hour away. This confrontation had the potential for healing—but she feared that it was more likely to tear open old wounds. She'd arrived early to gather her thoughts, and be on hand to get a read off everyone as they arrived.

Nerves fluttered in her stomach over seeing Conrad, but she was determined not to let them distract her from helping this family. She still hoped to steer them to another counselor, but they'd reached out to her. The sound of footsteps drew her attention from her phone, unable to quell the leap of excitement over seeing Conrad today... Except it wasn't him.

Disappointment stung, too much. She'd definitely

made the right choice in limiting her help to today's meeting. Objectivity was difficult around Conrad.

She forced a smile of welcome for Isabeau Mikkelson... and her friend Tally, who also happened to be Marshall Steele's fiancée.

The redheads could have been sisters. Certainly they'd formed a bond as future in-laws in the sprawling family. Did the Steeles and Mikkelsons know how lucky were to have so much support not just from each other, but from their extended family? Hopefully Breanna would see that, too.

The weight of today's meeting returned to the forefront of Felicity's mind. While she had been trained to navigate difficult spaces such as this, her stomach knotted as she tried to imagine Breanna's position. Tried to unpack all the ways warring emotions probably tore at her.

All would be revealed soon enough.

Tally smiled with relief as she drew closer to Felicity. "Thank you for coming. It's reassuring to have you here."

Standing, Felicity tucked away her phone. "I'm glad to help however I can. There's no way anyone could be prepared for a situation like this."

Isabeau glanced over her shoulder as staff passed in the hallway. Pregnancy elevated her beauty, giving her the glow of a Madonna painting by one of the old masters. She sighed in her flowing maternity dress, her ruffled cap sleeves dipping down as her shoulders relaxed. She looked from Tally to Felicity, and said in a low voice, "The family is all so stalwart it worries me. They even scheduled a business meeting right after this to continue negotiations with the final candidate for the CEO position."

"It's not unusual for people to cling to the familiar when they feel other things are out of their control." Although Felicity had to question the wisdom of holding such an important business negotiation after what would undoubtedly be an emotionally draining meeting with Breanna Steele.

Isabeau eased down to sit in an overstuffed leather chair, one gentle hand atop her baby bump. Leaning into the plush leather with her other elbow, she rubbed her temple as she stretched her shapely legs. "We'll all feel better once the new CEO is in place. If our families can lock in a deal with Ward Benally, he's just the sort of take-charge guy who's needed right now. No one will need to 'babysit' him through the transition."

"I think he's got Marshall's vote, too. Although, speaking of take-charge guys…" Tally's mouth pulled up into a wily smile as she turned toward Felicity. Tally rested a hip against the reception table, her sleeve brushing against the arrangement of wildflowers. "What's up with you and Conrad? You can tell me to mind my own business and I won't be offended."

Felicity weighed her words and opted for simple and succinct, hoping to quell any matchmaking. "He wants a relationship. I need to focus on my career. There's nothing up."

Tally scrunched her nose and tapped Felicity's arm. "You know what they say about all work and no play…"

Isabeau laughed softly, her eyes twinkling. "And the chemistry between you two lights up a room."

Bracing her shoulders, Felicity needed to nip this kind of talk in the bud. She knew how to wield silence as well as words. After giving herself a moment to gather her thoughts, she continued, "Did you bring me here to help or to match-make?"

Isabeau's smile faded and she touched Felicity's wrist. "I would have asked you to come today regardless."

"Okay, then," Felicity said, Isabeau's words bringing the importance of this meeting back into focus. "Let's concentrate on that."

Voices from the corridor had them all sitting upright fast, heads swiveling toward the new arrivals. Felicity's skin tingled as she heard Conrad's deep timbre stroke her senses as he spoke to his brother.

The two men paused in the archway, immersed in discussion. Felicity's gaze was drawn to Conrad's profile. His handsome face was tense, lips drawn taut in a line as his features attempted neutrality. But she'd been trained to read people. She could feel the tension radiating from him over the confrontation to come. But he stood shoulder to shoulder with his brother, head dipped, listening to Jack.

That show of support touched her. Deeply. The ability to put aside personal pain to help another wasn't as common as it should be.

As if he could feel her watching him, Conrad looked up, his gaze colliding with Felicity's. The emotion in his eyes was so raw, beyond what she'd even suspected. She ached to reach out and comfort him. It was all she could do to keep her feet planted.

Tally cleared her throat. "Nothing up between the two of you, huh?"

Felicity glanced at her friend, realizing she wasn't fooling anyone, least of all herself. How ironic that only moments after she'd insisted her devotion to work precluded any relationship, she was so tempted by Conrad.

She hadn't been good about articulating issues to her ex-husband, so she'd been careful to face her problems—at work and in her personal life—head-on since then. But with Conrad, she'd been so certain that he was the problem and kept throwing herself in his path to deal with him. Only to realize Conrad wasn't the issue so much as her—she was damned attracted to him and there was no escaping that fact.

She needed to make it clear to the family that, based on how things went today, she would make a recommendation for another counselor to see them through this tense time with Breanna.

Because in order to get Conrad out of her head, Felicity was going to have to confront the attraction head-on, sooner rather than later.

Brea was sick to her stomach.

Even knowing this meeting was exactly what she wanted, what she'd planned for, bracing herself to enter that conference room full of Steeles and Mikkelsons rattled her. Having her lawyer at her side didn't ease the knot of panic in her chest.

The last time she'd been here, she'd hidden her true identity. She hadn't relied on her family not recognizing her as an adult. She'd bleached her hair and wore colored contact lens. That disguise had offered a buffer between her emotions and her return, a protective shield. Now, with her real name revealed and her hair dark again, she felt exposed walking into a meeting as…herself.

Whatever that meant.

She'd once considered herself a Steele, first and foremost, part of a big, loving family. Then her world had been rocked by the accident. Doctors told her the concussion she'd suffered was severe, a part of what made processing all that happened immediately afterward so difficult.

But she couldn't deny the truth that someone connected to her family had killed her mother, and almost killed Brea in the process. She didn't know whom to trust. She only knew now that her adoptive parents were dead, and she was questioning everything.

And she couldn't rest until she had answers, safety and, most of all, resolution. She needed to move forward with her life and she couldn't do that until she made peace with her past.

She also needed to make sure the company didn't prosecute her for leaking corporate secrets. She hadn't planned on doing that when she'd wrangled her way into the organization undercover. She still wasn't sure how her better judgment had gotten away from her. She'd been so caught up in a need for revenge and wanting to strike back. That time was still a fog of frustration, betrayal…and heartbreak.

Somehow, she'd let her emotions get the better of her. Anxiety had her shaking in her ankle boots. Was she sweating? Her whole body felt on fire. But she didn't dare show her apprehension by dabbing her brow to check.

Throat running dry, her lips parched, she attempted to find something here and now to anchor her. Finding something here and now in this place though? That was part of the problem.

Hooking her thumbs into the sleeves of her black

turtleneck sweater, she did her best to channel her alter ego, the one who had provided a degree of armor last time she was here. With her family.

With determination she did not feel, she gripped the stainless steel door handle leading to the Steele conference room. Her lawyer kept even stride next to her. Brea tried to imagine herself like some warrior princess striding into the battlefield with her loyal second in command.

She worked to keep her eyes off the faces of the people gathered at the long, dark conference table. People she'd once called family. She'd accomplished putting them out of her mind for the years she'd been away. She'd slowly stopped thinking of them in the interim. Her adoptive parents had helped her with that, reminding her that letting go of those connections was important for healing.

These people were all her enemies, after all. One of them was most likely responsible for the accident that had thrown her life into disarray and killed her mother. It was best not to linger on any good memories. She definitely couldn't afford to let emotions get the better of her now.

She continued her measured walk to the table. Chin high. Resolved. She fought down the rise of nerves that threatened to undo her calculated mask of neutrality and power.

Which became harder with the weight of their gazes on her. Unable to resist, finally, she looked into the eyes of her family.

She lingered first on her uncle Conrad. The strangeness of the supposedly familial connection chilling her blood. Images of someone else's life flashed in her mind. Her uncle helping her onto a paint horse, teaching her where to place her weight in the saddle. Her twin sister's peal of laughter and whispered secrets. Brea knew better than to let her eyes linger on Naomi, the toughest one of all to forget.

An avalanche of half-formed memories threatened to bury her alive. Right here. In the thick tan carpet of the Steele boardroom. Her eyes flicked away from her family members at the table, searching the visible Alaskan wilderness beyond the glass planes.

Part of her wanted to spin away and make a run for it. Cast aside all identities, all knowledge. Make her life in a small cabin in the woods. Become a recluse, take up knitting or writing. Avoid people and all the pain they caused.

But Brea bit down on the impulse to flee, made herself look at each person. But then her gaze landed on her father. His sharp blue eyes full of pain—and tenderness. The tightness in her chest intensified. She would do better to keep her eyes off those from her past.

She'd seen them all before during her time here working as Milla Jones. But this was the first time they'd *really* seen her, knowing who she was.

Would she have ever had the nerve to come back if they hadn't run the DNA test and found out her true identity?

She honestly wasn't sure.

Stanley Hawkins, her attorney, pulled out a chair for her. With an outward control she was far from feeling inside, Brea sank into the chair. The young lawyer took his seat next to her, and the rest of the group followed suit.

Her attorney, who'd taken the case pro bono, gave her

an almost imperceptible nod of encouragement before he placed a manila folder in front of him, his green eyes as wild as a jungle. Formidable for someone his age, Stanley did not back down. He cleared his throat after what seemed like years of suffocating silence.

"I have a statement prepared by my client." He passed pages around the table. "It details her life after the airplane crash."

A flash of pain chased across Jack's face. Real? Or affected for the others at the table? "Is this really necessary? I had hoped we could talk through what happened, rather than read about it."

Her attorney shook his head, as she'd been clear with him about what she wished. "My client is present and cooperating, in spite of her concerns about her personal safety."

She tried not to notice how many of those seated winced at his words. Could they really not know that fear for her life motivated her? She'd been so busy protecting herself, she hadn't really considered that her siblings could have been snowed by their father, as well.

Jack bristled, his chest puffing out as he held the paper in a white-knuckled grip. He clung to it the way someone would hold on to the edge of a cliff. One miscalculation would mean a tumble to certain death.

"I don't know what happened to you in the years we were apart, but I hope with time you'll remember how very much you were—are—loved by your family. None of us would do anything to hurt you."

In the space of half of breath, Stanley leaned forward in his chair, putting his hand on top of the folder. "And yet someone did. Hearing that a Mikkelson could be involved in that long-ago plane crash does little to put my client's fears to rest. Perhaps it's time to end this for today."

"Everyone, let's breathe." A woman in the back corner of the room spoke up. She'd been sitting in the shadows, and Brea had missed noticing her when entering the room.

Brea leaned to whisper in her lawyer's ear. "Who is that?"

Before the attorney could ask, the woman scooted her chair closer. "Brea, I'm Felicity Hunt, a family friend. I'm also a counselor."

Brea's shoulders braced defensively. "If you're here to force me to change my plan for this meeting, you're not going to succeed."

Felicity held up a hand. "Actually, I think you're right to handle this in the manner that you're most comfortable. This statement is a good place to start."

Brea eased back into her chair, without relaxing her guard. "All of you went to a lot of trouble to track down Milla Jones." If only they'd put forth that effort into investigating the crash. "You've found her—me. I'm here to cooperate." For her siblings' benefit, in the event that some could be trusted, she added, "I don't want to give the impression that I'm less than understanding of how stressful this is for each of you."

Jack held the paper in a tight grip. "Are there questions you would like to ask us?"

Plenty. But she was shaking so hard on the inside, she feared she would fly apart if she spoke. It was tougher than she realized, seeing them all with the truth out there between them. So many of her childhood memories were a jumble. She loved her adoptive parents...but she'd once thought she loved the people at this table, too.

Now? She didn't know what she felt except afraid.

And determined not to let that fear show.

Brea did her best to school her features, keeping her tightly linked hands under the table. Anything to mask the whir of emotions and half memories threatening to steal air from her lungs.

Her eyes slid to Naomi. To her twin. To the bond that felt as real as the grain of the wooden table beneath her palm. As steadying, too. Somehow, despite everything.

Naomi's face softened slightly, her jaw loosening as an audible breath escaped her lips. She nodded, her ponytail bobbing.

Swallowing, Brea readied herself. "I have a question about a memory. Or what I think is a memory, anyway. Naomi, maybe you could shed some light here?" Brea's voice felt strange in this too-still room. All around the table, her family leaned in.

"Of course. I'll do my best," Naomi vowed.

Pursing her lips together, Brea attempted to articulate the memory as best she could. "When our mother would tuck us in at night, did she sing us a song about bear cubs that chased the northern lights?"

Naomi blinked, surprised at the question. There were harder questions floating around Brea's brain, but for now? Brea needed to find something real to hold on to. While Naomi's loyalty to the people at this table would be stronger than anything for a long-lost sister…the connection between them was still undeniable. It had drawn Breanna to the hospital the night Naomi's twins were born, even though going there had been a risk.

"She did. Then she would turn on a night-light that simulated the colors of the northern lights on the ceiling. We would fall asleep staring at it, talking about all our dreams." Naomi's voice was gentle, mournful.

Brea didn't trust herself to speak. She couldn't afford to show vulnerability. She tapped her attorney's foot with hers in their prearranged cue for when she was ready—or needed—to end the meeting.

Her lawyer touched the back of her chair, standing. "I want to thank you all for this initial meeting. My client has had enough for the day."

Brea kept her eyes forward, letting the room become a blessed blur as she pushed the chair back from the table. Turned toward the door. Stanley again in perfect stride.

"We'll be in touch soon," Stanley called over his shoulder to the murmuring Steeles, who were poring over the written statement.

Writing that document had been hellish. But it was easier than speaking the details. She'd kept it as factual as possible, telling of the couple who'd saved her from the wreckage, protected her and brought her up as their own in their off-the-grid community.

Taking a shaky breath, she willed her legs to move faster. Needing to be away from the claustrophobic space of that conference room. From the questions that gnawed at her.

As they turned the corner near the elevator, Brea's heart dropped from chest to stomach. She'd caught the figure only in her peripheral vision, but she'd known him from before. From when she pretended to be Milla Jones. A towering, charismatic man who drew her attention by the sheer force of his eyes. A dangerous attraction, given he was a driven power broker. Just the sort of man—like her family—whom she would do well to steer clear of.

Ward Benally—rumored to be the new CEO of the company—strode past. Brea pressed the button impatiently. Needing fresh air and open sky more than before.

Apparently, it was business as usual around here, in spite of a meeting that had her struggling not to sink to her knees. She should have known better than to give her so-called family the benefit of the doubt.

Conrad braced his hands against the wet bar in the conference room, not sure how he was going to get through the business meeting with Ward Benally. But it was the only time the CEO candidate had been able to meet. Conrad reached for the crystal pitcher and poured himself a glass of water.

He was drained. Completely.

His neck was tight, his whole damn body tense, from the post-Brea conversation. From the pain evident in his brother and his brother's kids.

Seeing Brea today knocked the wind out of everyone. Even Conrad, who prided himself as the man who could swoop in with a sincere, well-timed gesture to sidestep tragedy.

Not today. Not even close.

It should be so simple. His niece was alive despite all the evidence suggesting otherwise. The family was reunited. But somehow, something so joyous had taken a dark turn. Reopened old wounds for his family and dealt new ones.

Brea's decision to end the meeting so quickly had left everyone rocked. Naomi had voiced fears that her answer had triggered the reaction, blaming herself for the way the meeting unfolded. Jack had been deathly silent, reminding Conrad how close they'd come to losing him in a riding accident a year ago. How much more strain could his brother's body take?

A hand on Conrad's shoulder pulled him back to the present. He turned to find Felicity watching him through concerned eyes. He'd wanted her here for his family, but found himself grateful there was someone here who saw this was hell for him, too.

He set aside his water glass. "Thank you for being here today."

Her hazel eyes softened. "I don't know how much help I was."

"After Brea left, you said all the right things to help the family manage their expectations." The meeting had been frustratingly short, with little from Breanna. He was most grateful for how Felicity had handled things afterward, quietly talking them through the aftermath.

She took a step closer, her silky brown hair sliding forward along her face. He resisted the urge to test the texture of a lock and tuck it behind her ear.

Her citrus scent filled his breaths, the flowing bells of the sleeves of her dress brushing the air as she moved past. She was all he saw, despite a room full of family filling chairs on the other side of the room.

"Conrad, you're so worried about them, but this has to be difficult for you, too."

Her words alone were a comfort, but he needed to keep his focus on his family. "Today was a big step." He drew in a deep breath. "I need to get to work. Thanks again. I don't know how to repay you."

"You can take me out to dinner tonight."

Her offer stunned him silent. He looked at her, trying to read her expression and find a reason for her about-face. Was she simply offering to help him talk through today's stressful reunion? Or did she want to talk about the hospital dinner party?

Regardless, it wasn't an opportunity he would let pass. His day from hell was finally looking up. "Consider it a date."

He intended to make this next meeting the shortest ever. In his mind, he was already out the door early, more than ready to spend an evening with the most captivating woman he'd ever met.

Six

Jack Steele had suffered the worst blows from life nearly twenty years ago when the plane had gone down with his wife and daughter on it. Today should have been the best day of his life with the return of his daughter from the dead. Instead, it was his second worst.

The weight of that strained meeting, of Breanna's accusatory expression, chilled him to his soul. His eyes closed tight against the pain, his head fell to rest in his hand. He'd been in a fog afterward, lasting through the entire hour afterward when Ward Benally had come in.

Jack was struggling still.

It had taken everything inside him to convince Jeannie she should still accompany Isabeau and Trystan to the ultrasound. But he'd known how important it was to her. Family was everything.

Sinking lower, he pushed back in his rolling ergonomic leather chair, stopping inches away from the floor-to-ceiling recessed bookshelves that formed the wall behind him. Pivoting in the chair, he looked at a family photograph beneath one of the spotlights.

From before. When his family—and heart—were whole. In the photograph, Brea slung an arm around Broderick. An innocent, toothy grin on her face.

The picture seemed like pure fiction at this point. Jack's normally steady resolve balked. Spinning the chair forward and around, he saw ghosts of Brea everywhere. Saw her as a baby crawling across the plush rug, Mary making sure she didn't travel to the tile floor. Saw her at eight with her sleek silver book bag excitedly chattering about her science class.

An avalanche of memories that seemed irreconcilable with his present life.

What had happened to his daughter to make her turn her back on her family so soundly? She clearly remembered them all. How could all those years in a happy family mean nothing to her? The fear and rage radiating from her had been soul crushing.

He couldn't believe—or understand—how the child he and Mary had loved so deeply could have turned against him. The rest of the family had seemed to take comfort from the counselor present, but Jack had been too numb, too stunned to process anything that was said.

A tap on his door sent him sitting up straight again, scrubbing a hand through his hair to shake off his mood. His younger brother, Conrad, appeared, a force to be reckoned with in his well-tailored black suit and slightly loosened red tie.

Ever since Conrad was a kid, Jack had thought his brother moved like a jungle cat. Slow, determined strides. Predatory instinct in the boardroom. A silence that commanded respect. It was part of the reason they made a good team.

Conrad tucked into the room with that familiar swagger. "I thought you were cutting back on office hours to spend more time with that beautiful new wife of yours."

Jack hadn't expected to find love again after Mary died, and he certainly hadn't expected to fall for the matriarch of a rival family. But Jeannie had stolen his heart. Completely. And he knew she was as torn up about the rumors surrounding her family's involvement in the crash as he was. "I'm heading out soon."

"I would ask if you're okay, but there's no way anyone could be alright after what shook down today."

True enough. "Having Felicity present was a good idea." Even if he hadn't been in the right frame of mind to listen. "I'm just sorry that Breanna didn't give us an opening to talk at all."

"Give it time. She's here. That's a start," his brother said wisely.

Jack pinched the bridge of his nose, his eyes stinging with tears. "I know. I have my baby girl back. That's what matters most. Knowing she's alive…"

Jack appreciated that Conrad gave him the space to regain control. His brother had always been intuitive that way, seeming to understand that an overt sign of comfort would only make things worse. This silent support, his brother's way of being there and helping, had carried Jack through some of the most hellish times imaginable.

"Thank you, brother. There's no way I can repay you for all you've done for me over the years."

"You'd do the same for me," Conrad said with a half smile.

Jack liked to think so, but had he missed opportunities, being so wrapped up in his own life? "You look like you're on your way out. I don't want to keep you."

"I can stay awhile longer," Conrad said, but didn't sit.

"I'm good. Really." He eyed his brother. "Big plans?"

Conrad looked to the windows on the west wall for a moment as if considering the question. He cocked his head back to Jack. "Dinner out with Felicity."

Surprise lit through him. "I thought she gave you the boot. Glad things have turned around."

Conrad shook his head dismissively. "Thanks, but I'm not here to talk about me. How are you doing? That was one helluva rough meeting earlier."

His brother had always been a good listener, but talking wouldn't fix this. "I'm fine. Really. And you're right that I should go home to my wife."

Conrad lingered, his bright blue eyes sharp and searching. "If you're sure."

Jack closed his laptop for emphasis. "Absolutely. And thank you."

"Anytime," Conrad said, backing toward the door, closing it behind him on the way out.

Jack sagged back in his chair again, not ready to go home, in spite of what he'd said to his brother. Jeannie was the epitome of support, but he couldn't miss the tension in her over rumors that her brother, Lyle, had somehow been involved in the crash. Jack loved her and trusted her implicitly. However, he couldn't expect her to remain totally objective when it came to her siblings. It was best not to burden her.

He would have to deal with this on his own. He just prayed he would get his daughter back without further damage to his family.

Her heart racing, Felicity swept on mascara.

She still couldn't believe she'd asked Conrad out after all her vows of swearing off relationships. But that tragic family reunion had tugged at her every last heartstring until she'd found herself reaching out to him now rather than later as she'd originally planned.

Committed, she was going to look her best. She dug through the modest array of makeup in her teal bag. Lately, she'd simplified her daily routine to moisturizer and mascara for work. She couldn't remember the last time she'd reached for fancier products or performed a more elaborate routine. Not since her divorce.

That thought almost made her drop her makeup bag in the trash.

Felicity picked up the simple pearl drop earrings. They were her favorite pair. She'd splurged when she'd graduated from her master's program. They were among her most valued possessions, and she broke them out only for special occasions. Like nondate dates with a handsome man.

Stomach fluttering, she pulled out the shimmery metallic powder and swept it onto her lids. She blinked, satisfied with the light glow. She added a brush of color along her cheekbones, then gave her lips a pop after applying the neutral color, surprised to find she was smiling.

Surprised, and guilt-ridden as she reflected on the emotional turmoil of the day. She hoped the Steeles would accept her recommendation for a counselor. They were going to need all the help they could get to navigate this reunion to a peaceful resolution.

But that was out of her control now. She should be focused on her dinner date. Although now that she thought about it, she wondered if it had been selfish to ask for tonight. His family might need him. She reached for her phone to call him and reschedule, or maybe she should cancel—

The doorbell echoed through her apartment.

Her stomach flipped like she was a teenager rather than a mature woman. Backing from the bathroom mirror, she snagged a long silver necklace and draped it over her head, the tassel falling to rest against her black sweater.

She was halfway across the room before she realized she'd been almost running. So much so that she practically stumbled into the tall bookcase on the wall in the living room. Rocked the books on social inequity within the child care system that stood as stalwart companions in her tiny one-room apartment. Smoothing her sweater, she did her best to regain composure, her heels clacking on the wood floors as she moved away from the kitchen-living room toward the door.

She wasn't sure going on this date was wise. But ignoring the attraction hadn't worked. She needed to face it, face *him*, head-on.

Willing her breath to even out, she pulled open the door.

Conrad stood in the hallway, a box of candy in hand. His gaze skimmed her up and down, lingering on her red leather boots before sliding back up to meet her eyes. "Has anyone told you lately how gorgeous you are?"

His words shouldn't have the power to send her heart into overdrive, but they did. The more time she spent with him, the more she desired him. Could the reality possibly live up to the expectation building inside her?

Now there was a strange thought—hoping for bad sex so she could get over thinking about him.

She'd given Conrad an opening by asking for this date, and she couldn't deny she wanted to spend more time with him—wanted *him*—but she still needed to be careful. "Thank you for the compliment. Let me get my coat and we can be on our way."

He followed her inside. "You aren't smiling at the compliment."

"I'm flattered, truly." She pulled her overcoat from the hall closet.

"But…"

She needed to make sure he didn't read too much into this evening out. Hugging her coat, she turned back to face him. "I want to be fair to you."

"How about you let me worry about myself. I'm a big boy."

"Yes, you are." And just that fast, she realized she'd revealed how drawn she was to him in spite of everything she'd said. She couldn't pretend tonight had been a simple dinner invitation. In fact, nothing had been simple since the first time she'd seen him two months ago when she'd given Tally a ride home from volunteering at the hospital.

She couldn't pull her gaze away from the allure of his clear blue eyes. He passed her the black foil box of candy, gold bow glinting in the bright hall light. Their fingers brushed, and the air crackled with awareness.

She skimmed a finger along the intricate bow without taking the box. "I'm not sure what to make of this."

"Romance," he said, his voice husky.

"I thought you were romancing me with donations to the hospital." Was that breathy tone hers?

"At the celebrity auction? Yes, I was. Now, my part in the hospital program has taken on an official and professional angle. I can't let my feelings for you interfere with the financial decisions I make."

"Oh." Her eyes went wide.

"That wasn't what you were expecting to hear."

"Not at all," she had to admit. "But it's a good answer. An honorable one."

Inclining his head, he gestured to the box of candy. That wit shining in his blue eyes. Crackling and collapsing her senses until her focus was solely on him, the way his lips moved as they formed words.

"Then you'll accept the chocolates."

She laughed, clutching the box to her chest. "Try to pry them out of my hands."

He grinned back at her. "Tally told me you had a weakness for chocolate."

Felicity placed the candy on the half-moon table next to a succulent plant. "It's no fair how you keep getting all the inside scoop. What's your weakness?"

His eyes flamed. "You."

Her breath hitched in her chest as his head dipped. His mouth slanted over hers, warm, firm. Tingles spread through her at the first touch. She clenched her fingers in his jacket, anchoring herself in the wash of sensation, the fine fabric of his lapels and the sweep of his tongue over hers. The deeper she sank into the kiss, the more he brought her body alive again, the more she realized she was right in thinking this connection couldn't be ignored.

He brushed his mouth along hers a final time, lingering for another toe-curling moment before he backed away. "We should go before we're late for our reservation."

Conrad hadn't expected dinner with Felicity to flow so effortlessly, from appetizers to desserts. The conversation had been easy, entertaining, distracting him from thoughts of his niece and fractured family for long stretches at a time. No doubt, Felicity was a brilliant and engaging woman.

And she entranced the hell out of him.

Conrad held out her coat for her while they waited for the valet to bring his SUV around. He draped the satin-lined dark wool over her shoulders, his fingers brushing along her neck. The light scent of flowers tempted him to indulge in touching her longer.

As she swept her hair free from the collar, she looked over her shoulder at him, smiling. "Thank you for a lovely evening."

Was that a promise of more in her eyes? He was learning this woman was beyond predicting. He pushed the restaurant door open and followed her outside into the bitter cold under the awning. "Then let's do it again."

"Why don't we wait to see how this night together finishes?" The curve of her smile had his full undivided attention as their footfalls crunched into the snow-flecked sidewalk.

Now he was certain that was a promise of more and that prospect stopped him in his tracks on the salted walkway.

At his abrupt stop, she grabbed his arm fast. Her feet slipped on a slick patch of ice. He caught her, his arms clamping around her, hauling her against his chest. His heart hammered at how close she'd come to falling. Her hair teased his nose and he could have stood this way all night.

If it weren't for the fact they would freeze to death.

He scanned for his SUV and found it in line behind three other idling vehicles, waiting. Without another thought, he scooped her into his arms and began walking to his red SUV.

"You're going to slip on the ice," she gasped.

"You already did that." Conrad secured his hold, enjoying the sweet press of her hands gripping the lapels of his overcoat.

"Yes, I did slip. And it hurt. Please put me down before the same happens to you," she pleaded as they strode by a stretch limo. The passengers climbing inside whistled and called out to him and Felicity.

"Are you okay?" he asked, alarmed and mad at himself for not checking her over right away.

"Just twisted my ankle a little." Her breath was warm against his neck. "I can walk, though."

"You'll only risk more damage to your ankle. And I'm not going to fall."

"You sound confident."

"At least you didn't call me arrogant," he said with a half smile. "Although, you wouldn't be wrong."

"Do all the Steele males act this way?" she asked as they stopped beside his vehicle.

The valet stepped from behind the wheel, engine still running, and opened the passenger door.

Conrad turned to the side and angled her into the

leather bucket seat. "By 'act this way,' do you mean helping a wounded individual make her way back to the car safely?"

Her laughter floated on the brisk breeze. "I can't believe you managed to say that with a straight face."

He closed her door and settled behind the wheel, heater blasting. "I told you. I'm arrogant."

"And yes, I acknowledge that you're charming, too." Her eyes glistened with a lightheartedness that still knocked him on his ass.

"Glad to hear my hard work's paying off." He wanted to stroke snow from her hair, to kiss her. But he needed to know. "How does your ankle feel? Do we need to go to the emergency room?"

She unzipped her boot and flexed her foot a couple of times. "Only a little sore. It's going to be fine."

He hauled his gaze off the slim line of her leg and onto the road as, finally, the cars began moving forward. "Glad to hear. I imagine you didn't get much practice walking on ice in Texas."

"That would be an accurate guess. I thought I'd gotten better, though, having lived here for seven winters." She looked at him sidelong.

He steered the SUV onto the road, headlights streaming ahead, windshield wipers sweeping snow off the windshield. "How is it our paths have never crossed before you brought Tally home from the hospital when her car broke down last month?"

Her fingertips tapped the glass lightly.

"You and I don't exactly run in the same social circles." Her voice was dry.

And hinted at more of those reservations on her part he'd hoped to have already overcome tonight.

"That's been entirely my loss," he said, and meant it.

She shifted in the seat, angling toward him. "You just don't ever let up, do you?"

"I'm only being honest." He could feel himself losing precious ground with her.

"Let's just say I'm not an overly trusting person by nature."

A challenge? He accepted. "Then I'll have to work on earning your trust."

She toyed with a lock of her hair, and he sensed an opportunity opening up between them again, especially with the way she leaned toward him.

Her head tipped to the side. "How do you intend to do that?"

"Let's start now. Ask me anything," he invited her. "And rely on those counselor skills of yours to determine if I'm being honest."

"Do you ever wish you'd left Alaska?"

He wondered at her reason for asking. But he'd promised her the truth and he would deliver. "My family's here. My business is here. I'm able to travel as much as I wish."

"You didn't answer my question." She warmed her hands in front of the heater vent.

"Ah, you're good at this." He respected her intelligence, her devotion to her job, her quick wit…hell, so many things, other than the fact she had been so determined to push him away. Hopefully, that was changing. "The answer is no, I don't wish I'd left. I'm happy here. It's my home."

"What are your favorite childhood memories growing up here?"

Why did she want to know? He searched for a reason, so he could figure out the best answer to roll out that would win her over. While he wasn't certain of her motivation for that question, he did know she regretted not having a family. "Jack would take me sledding. He was well past sledding days himself. Yet, he was patient with me."

The memory scrolled through his mind. His much older brother trekking them out to the best hill on Steele land. He always made it an adventure. Named the animal sounds they heard. Would stay out in the cold for hours.

"Where were your parents?"

"Working long hours. Taking long business trips." He gripped the steering wheel. "Our parents weren't neglectful, if that's what you're implying."

"That's how you and your brother grew so close?"

Yeah. His brother had damn near brought him up. Even picked him up and dropped him off from school most days. They were a tight family unit. Family, their father always said, was the cornerstone of everything. "He looked out for me."

"And you felt like you owed him," she prodded. Gently, but he felt the pressure of the statement.

"It's not a matter of owing anyone anything. It's just what we do for each other." He shot a glance her way. "What? You don't believe me?"

"I completely believe you." Her beautiful face was earnest, basking in the glow of the dash light. "It's just... well... I read about this kind of bond and I see it with siblings sometimes. I just didn't expect to hear this from you. You're lucky to have each other."

"Yes, we are." He knew she'd been in foster care, but

he hadn't given thought to her biological family. "Do you have siblings?"

"I do. Half siblings. We were split up before we even finished elementary school." She scratched a fingernail along the armrest, repeatedly, the only sign that relayed how the discussion upset her. She always kept her emotions close to the vest. "We tried to keep in touch for a while, but other than the occasional message online, we've gone our separate ways. Actually, I have more contact with my last foster family."

How she'd built a life for herself in spite of everything that had been thrown her way was admirable. Rare. "You're so damn incredible, you steal my breath."

Her mouth spread into a wide smile. "Well, that's a good thing. Because as much as I've tried to ignore the attraction between us, I'm not having any luck."

He struggled to follow her shift from discussion of family and admirable character to…attraction. "Felicity—"

She pressed her fingertips to his lips. "Time to stop talking and take me to bed."

Seven

Felicity had known from the second she issued the dinner invitation to Conrad that they would very likely end up in bed together. And now that they were stumbling through her front door in a tangle of arms and legs and passion, she couldn't bring herself to regret the decision.

Her fingers dug into his shoulders as he pressed her against the hall wall. She stroked her booted foot along the back of his calf, looking forward to no barriers between them. The press of his body to hers with the solid wall of muscles and thick ridge of desire stirred the need inside her higher, hotter. She breathed in the lingering scent of his soap—sandalwood, patchouli and *man*.

Sliding her hands under his custom-fit jacket, she explored the breadth of his back, her nails scoring along the fine silk of his shirt. In her restless roving, her elbow bumped the hall table. The box of candy he'd brought earlier slid to the floor.

At the thud, he looked to the side. A smile creased his handsome face. Easing back a step, he leaned down to scoop up the wrapped box. "It's my pleasure to indulge your weakness. I'd like to learn what else you have a weakness for."

The promise in his words and in his blue eyes set her on fire, leaving her eager to learn the same about him. His mouth pressed to hers again as they made their way deeper into her apartment. The warm glide of his tongue brought hints of their after-dinner coffee and how easy the conversation had been between them. He was a bold, brilliant man and that attracted her every bit as much as his well-honed body.

She steered him, her body against his, kissing and walking and wanting. She wrestled his coat off, and her cape slid to the floor as they moved. Shedding the layer didn't begin to cool her off, however. As she stumbled past her tufted leather sofa, foot catching on the rug, her desire for this man went from a blaze to a wildfire.

Why had she ever thought this was a bad idea?

The connection between them was combustible and undeniable. She would indulge. Her heart was on lockdown. She deserved this much for herself.

Felicity saw her living room only in glimpses as she charted a course for her bedroom, moving quickly past the bookcases full of professional reading and a collection of her favorite romance novels. She bumped open her bedroom door, her haven.

Her place wasn't a high-end mansion like those his family owned. But it was hers. A space for decompressing after the stress and weight of social work. The downy blush comforter in her room accompanied three rows of pillows—just like a posh upscale hotel room. Her bedside table sported a half-read book, open and facedown to save her place. And yes, in spite of her personal life where happily-ever-after had ceased to be an option, she still gravitated to romance novels, books where life turned out for the best in spite of obstacles. She needed that uplifting message after the stress of her work life.

Right now, she was far from wanting to chill out, and her little decadences in the room would serve a new purpose. From the high-thread-count sheets to the essential oils diffuser steaming sweet lemongrass.

He tossed the candy on the bed, the box landing with a thump an instant before the backs of her knees hit the mattress. She fell into the soft give of the comforter, the toes of her leather boots just grazing the carpeted floor.

Kneeling, he tugged the zipper down one of her red boots, inching off her sock and kissing his way along her calf. Peeling away her restraint along with the leather. She flung her arms back, her eyes sliding closed as she savored the sensation of his mouth on her skin.

Imagined his lips all over her.

Anticipation notched higher.

He took his time slipping her out of her dress, kissing her shoulders and murmuring sweet words in her ear as he unveiled new places to his touch. She told herself to savor the moment, to relish every touch, but her fingers grew impatient. Her hands twisted in his shirttails when she tugged them free. Her lips lingered on the hard planes of his chest when she slid aside the garment.

With a hiss of breath between his teeth, he threw aside the rest of his clothes in a haphazard array on the floor. She elbowed up to take in the naked magnificence of him, from his broad shoulders to his lean hips. To his thick arousal against his six-pack stomach.

A smile of sensual intent lit his face an instant before he dropped to his knees again. Between her legs.

Her breath caught in anticipation. He nudged her wider, dipping his head to nuzzle, then give her the most intimate of kisses.

A breathy sigh carried a soft moan between her lips as her eyes slid closed. Her elbows gave way and she sagged back on the bed, surrendering to the magic of his touch and tongue. His hands skimmed upward to caress her breasts, his thumbs teasing and plucking her nipples into tight, tingling buds. She twisted her fists in the sheets, tension building. All too soon, she soared toward release, her body arching into each ripple of sensation pulsing through her.

Air teased over her bare flesh, every nerve ending alive and in the moment. She struggled to gather her thoughts enough to give him the pleasure he'd brought her. She elbowed up just as he angled over her to kiss her neck.

"Hold that thought," he said just before he popped a truffle into her mouth.

When had he opened the box? She must have languished longer than she'd thought after the incredible orgasm he'd given her. She let the truffle melt on her tongue, the creamy chocolate and raspberry filling saturating her taste buds.

Conrad angled away and she clasped his arm. "Where are you going?"

"Not far." He reached for his suit jacket. "I'm just getting protection."

"I have some in the bedside table." She reached for the drawer, her elbow bumping a jar of sunflowers and daisies. They breathed life into this space, pulling together the pale metallic lamps with beaded lampshades that cast a dusky, beckoning glow on the bed.

"So you planned for this," he said with a smile, a condom packet between his fingers.

"I had a strong sense this was a definite possibility." She picked up the open candy box and placed it beside the lamp. She couldn't resist scooping out two more truffles.

"Just so we're clear… I need to make sure you want this."

Angling up to sit beside him, her hip against his, she popped a truffle into his mouth to silence him. "If you recall, I asked you on the date. I want this. And I know my own mind."

"You're one hundred percent right about that."

She put the other truffle between her teeth, drawing him toward her to share. The candy and kiss blended, their legs tangling as he rolled on top of her.

The hard planes of his chest called to her fingers, the heat of his skin searing through her palms. He stayed in shape, but she'd already known that from their outing riding horses and the way he'd carried her to his SUV. Still, feeling the cut and ripple of those muscles without any barriers between them outdid her expectations.

She nipped his bottom lip. "How do you know just what to do to have me melting faster than those chocolates on my tongue?"

"I'm just listening to you, to your body."

A man who listened. She could get turned on by

that alone. And yet he brought that and so much more to the bedroom.

She slid her hand between them, stroking the length of him, learning the hard, velvet feel of him. His low growl of appreciation spurred her on until he angled away, panting. He tore open the condom packet and sheathed himself.

The intensity of his gaze, the urgency in his taut jaw, echoed the feelings swirling through her. She stroked her feet up his calves on her way to hook her legs around his waist. Open. Eager. For him. He thrust inside her, filling her not just with his body, but with a fresh wash of sensation. Her nerve endings sizzled to life in a way she'd been so long without.

In fact, right now, she couldn't recall ever experiencing this incredible kind of a connection. He was everything and yet also had her wanting more. More of him. More of this.

Her hips rolled against his, her breasts teased by the hair bristling his chest. Conrad's husky moans matched hers, their whispers of pleasure and encouragement creating a sensual symphony between them.

Conrad threaded his fingers through the tangled locks of her hair, kissing her. Or was she kissing him?

Both perhaps, because this was a meeting of equals between them.

And already she felt another wave of release ready to crash over her. She did her best to hold back, to hold on to this moment awhile longer, because truth be told, trusting in the future was hard as hell for her. But the building passion couldn't be denied. The orgasm slammed into her without warning, stronger than the one before, wrenching a cry of bliss from her throat.

Her nails sunk into Conrad's shoulders, biting in with half-moons.

His breathing heavy, sweat dotting his brow, he followed her with his own completion, the muscles along his back tensing under her touch. His pleasure launched another ripple of aftershocks through her already sated body. Her arms slid from him in an exhausted glide to rest on the bed.

The scent of them lingered in the air, filling her every ragged gasp.

Before the perspiration cooled on her body, she wondered what the hell she'd done. Because no way was this a one-time deal. And that realization rocked her. So much so, she needed space to deal with it.

She pressed a kiss to his temple before easing out from under him. Already, she had to resist the urge to climb right back into his arms. "I'll make us some coffee before you go."

He sat up, sheet wrapped around his waist, his chest sporting the light scratches she'd left on his skin in the heat of the moment. "You're booting me out of your bed."

"I thought you would be relieved."

"Hell no." He sat on the edge of the bed, studying her through narrowed eyes. "I think we could have an incredible affair."

"I agree, but I've been clear there can't be feelings involved between us." She searched for the words to explain why she was sending him away. "Sleeping over takes this to a level that, well, I'm not comfortable with."

"Understood." He clasped her hand, tugging her closer until she stood between his knees. "I can't see us being able to ignore that while we're working together on the hospital dinner."

She could see his point. "What exactly are you suggesting we do about it?"

"Let's call these next few weeks a no-pressure window of time to see each other, to be together." His thumb caressed the sensitive inside of her wrist over her racing pulse.

"And when the event is over, we go our separate ways? Just like that?"

"If that's what you want, then yes."

Could she trust him?

She wanted to. And she also wanted to have more nights like tonight with him—while keeping her heart safe. "What if I agree to that, but we still take things one day at a time?"

"For another chance to be with you? I say, hell yes." He tugged her onto his knee, his other hand sliding up to cup her breast. "What do you say we make use of your stash of condoms before we have that coffee?"

Even knowing she might regret it later, she sank back into the covers with Conrad, already losing herself in another chocolate-flavored kiss.

The next day, Conrad pulled up outside his brother's waterside mansion. Nestled up against an iced-over lake, the impressive structure seemed to double in size, its dynamic log-cabin-inspired reflection flickering on the glass-like surface of the water. Wind tore through the lone pine tree near the water's edge. A shiver in the tree's spine as it bowed forward.

Over coffee at four in the morning, Conrad had asked Felicity to join him for this family gathering and he was surprised she'd agreed. Especially since she'd held firm to her decision that he couldn't spend the night.

He'd gone home to shower, returning to pick her up just before lunch. He couldn't deny he was pleased to have her by his side today, at this luncheon around the indoor pool. No question, his brother needed to have the support of his family. In reality, all of them needed this, a positive get-together, after the stressful meeting with Brea.

Conrad shifted his SUV into Park as Felicity gathered her pool bag. "Thanks for coming along."

"I enjoy your family." She angled across the center console to kiss him quickly. "Just no PDAs when we're inside, please."

"Understood."

Sex with Felicity had been even more incredible than he'd expected—and his expectations had been mighty damn high. He'd half thought she would boot him out, and granted, she'd tried. But he'd been given this window of time with her and he intended to make the most of it.

He exited the SUV, boots punching through the snow as he made his way over to her door. Conrad's eyes locked with hers, that electric recognition passing between them. Offering his hand, he helped Felicity out of the car. Regretted that they had to make their way to the house's side entrance, which would lead to a glassed room, heated indoor pool and people. Even in the subdued touch her leather gloves provided, Conrad hungered for more time alone with her.

She stepped through the threshold, Conrad following her into the din of noise. His family milled around the indoor pool area. His youngest niece, Delaney, sat on the gray stones that flanked the pool, feet casually moving in the water. Her infectious peals of laughter echoed in the glass and wood hall.

A large table filled with hummus, pita, kalamata olives, pineapple and strawberry spears, juicy moose burgers and garlic lime chicken wings drew the attention of the majority of his family. His older brother, Jack, handed a red plate to Jeannie as she smiled at some private joke. Across the pool, near the floor-to-ceiling glass wall sporting a breathtaking view of snowcapped mountains and feathering pine trees, Isabeau lay out on a lounger, fanning herself. She rested a hand on her pregnant stomach, a calm smile on her face as Trystan kept her well stocked with water and food. Her service dog was tucked under the lounger, head on her paws, ears and face alert.

"You made it!" Jeannie exclaimed across the pool, her eyes bright and welcoming. Marshall clapped Conrad's back in greeting on the way to the array of food. Royce and Naomi laughed with the twins in the pool, doting over them with care. Broderick and Glenna nudged little Fleur in her baby float, their daughter squealing in delight, kicking her chubby legs underwater.

Felicity waved to all as she dashed for the changing room. Conrad opened a beer, taking a swig before he ducked into the other changing area. He stepped back out just as Felicity rounded the corner to return. Conrad's heart threatened to jump out of his chest and skip across the room.

Sexy as hell, Felicity walked toward him in a sleek emerald green one-piece with a plunging neckline. Her curves perfectly highlighted threw him back into memories of their night together. The taste of her on his lips. The suit and her beauty reminded him of a mermaid, a siren, luring him in.

Picking up flatware, Felicity joined him in line. She scooped hummus and pita onto her plate before adding skewers of pineapple and strawberry. Conrad placed a burger onto his own dish, feeling Felicity studying him through narrowed eyes.

He glanced at her. "Is there something wrong?"

Smiling, she gently brushed shoulders with him. "I'm just curious. This doesn't seem like your kind of party."

"Maybe I'm doing research for the next kids' story to read to sway you with my Machiavellian plan."

"Is that true?"

His levity fled. "This is my family. They're here. I'm here." He couldn't help wondering. "Why are you?"

"My friend invited me."

She'd called him a friend. That was progress of sorts, given they were also lovers. "Well, what a smart friend I am for wrangling the opportunity to spend the day with you in a swimsuit."

"I could say the same." She snapped the waistband of his swim trunks playfully, then blushed, looking around quickly to see if anyone had noticed.

His fingers ached to touch her, pull her in for a kiss. Given the scenario, his throat hummed with a rumble of appreciation, eyes locking hard with hers.

Conrad leaned in to steal a quick kiss from Felicity, but the erratic barking of Isabeau's dog interrupted him. Tearing his eyes from Felicity to the lounger across the pool, he watched Trystan's expression fill with concern as he launched to his feet, leaning over Isabeau. Jeannie was already across the pool. Shouting mixed in with the dog's increasingly urgent barks, launching panic.

Isabeau was going into premature labor.

A half hour after the family departed for the hospital in a fast caravan of vehicles, Brea still sat in her car, where she'd hunkered down and watched with binoculars from a hidden vantage point as they'd partied. She hadn't lived in that home long, her father having built it as they grew older and needed more space. But she'd still had time to make memories there.

She should take the rental car out of Park and leave, but she was so caught in the past, she hadn't been able to make that move. Hours had passed since she pulled her little sedan into this hidden spot near the gates. Like a hawk, she'd watched the Steele mansion with a macabre interest. Unable to tear herself away.

Waves of memories presented themselves to her. As each receded, she felt more hollow and raw. Once upon a time, she had dared Broderick to hang from the rafters of the boathouse like a bat. He'd done it, stalwart and brave in the middle of the night.

Once upon a time, she'd wanted to be a mermaid with her sisters in the indoor pool. Brea made them stay in the water practicing synchronized mermaid dives until their hands turned pruney.

Once upon a time, she had been happy there as a Steele. In that house that loomed so far from her. A pain lodged in her chest that felt much like a knife piercing her ribs.

How could they all be so happy, so unaffected, when her world had been blown all apart?

She couldn't help but think her reappearance hadn't

rocked them all that much. Sure, they wanted her around, but she wasn't one of them anymore. They'd moved on. The bond had been broken. Any joy in seeing her was…out of nostalgia.

That confirmation of her suspicions should have reassured her, but it just hurt. More than it should. She couldn't allow the Steeles to have this kind of power over her.

A three-knuckle tap on her passenger window disrupted her thoughts. She cranked her neck to the left. Ward Benally's fox-like gaze met hers.

As if her emotions weren't raw enough.

She spotted his sleek SUV parked a few feet ahead. She didn't know a lot about him, but if he was now a part of the Steele and Mikkelson corporate empire, then she'd best keep her guard up around him.

Tipping her chin, she rolled down the window, the cold air washing over her. Centering her as she met his deep blue eyes, which she cursed herself for noticing so acutely. "Yes?"

"Mind if I climb in with you before we talk? I'm freezing my ass off out here." He glanced pointedly at the empty passenger seat.

She studied him for a moment, resisting the urge to tell him to go back to his own vehicle. The more she learned about him, the safer she would be. He wore a well-tailored coat that showed off his finely toned body. His brown hair covered mostly by the black stocking hat making him somehow even more attractive.

Since he'd already seen her lurking around, there was no need to bolt. The damage had been done. She might as well make the most of the inside scoop he could offer her on her family's world.

She tapped the locks and gestured to the passenger seat of her rental car. After he climbed in, she turned off the low-playing radio and turned up the heat. "So you're the CEO who's going to take over my father's company."

He folded into the bucket seat, his large frame a tight fit in the compact vehicle. "The business belongs to the shareholders, from both the Steele and Mikkelson corporations."

"I stand corrected." She conceded that point, but nothing more. He was an outsider and the Jack Steele she'd known growing up would never have turned his business over to a stranger. Another mystery. "You owe both my father and stepmother for your advancement."

"It's my understanding that none of your siblings or your stepsiblings could be convinced to take on the job." He nodded, his angled jaw flexing.

She sat up straighter. "Are you implying there's a reason no one will step up?"

"A lot of reasons, I imagine." He fell silent, his eyes on her.

"What?" she asked, fidgeting uncomfortably.

That fox stare of his pinned her again. "I'm trying to figure you out."

"Why?" she fired back. "Are you interested?"

Whoa. Where had that come from?

"Only interested in the chaos you're causing." He tapped the dash decisively. "My first priority, if I decide to accept the job, will be getting this company on stable footing again. What is your priority?"

Brea let her smile turn as icy as her Alaskan birthright. "What do you think?"

He removed the stocking cap, his textured brown

hair standing on edge. Disheveled in a way that made Brea want to run her fingers through it.

His hands squeezed around the knit hat as he casually said in a gruff voice, "I'm guessing some kind of self-interest."

That surprised her. And intrigued her. "I appreciate how you don't tiptoe around me like my family does."

"That's because I don't care. And they do. Sadly. Because it doesn't seem like you give a damn about them."

"You don't know the first thing about me."

The heat in the air crackled between them as they stared at each other. His pointedness magnetized and enraged her.

"I know you've been avoiding the Steele family." He gestured to the mansion with his hat. "So I think it's strange that you're out here spying on them."

Spying? She didn't like that word at all. Or the sense that's how he saw her, as someone who lurked and stalked. "What you think isn't of significance to me. Is there something I can help you with?"

"Actually, yes. I need to find out where everyone is. I need to drop off some paperwork and no one's answering at the gate."

A tart laugh burst from her lips. She angled toward him, lowering her voice conspiratorially. "That's because they all just hauled out of here in a caravan of cars."

"And you're still hanging out because?" He didn't miss a stride, leaning in with a dramatic whisper of his own.

She blinked. She wasn't giving him any more information than necessary.

He lifted his hands innocently. "Okay, none of my

business. Except for the fact that—as you said—I'm a lock to be the new CEO of Alaska Oil Barons Inc. And as the head of that company I think it's in my best interest to make sure you don't intend to do something that harms the business."

"Is that a threat?"

His head snapped back. "No. Not at all. I had no intention of giving off that impression."

"You can understand I'm not too trusting of the people around here."

He cocked an eyebrow. "And I'm sure you can understand why people around here aren't too trusting of you right now."

"Point made. Get out of my car."

"Can do. I need to figure out where that caravan of Steele vehicles was heading anyway." He tugged a lock of her hair. "Nice chatting with you, Breanna Steele."

The door slam vibrated the car and she wished she could have attributed the tingle she felt to the gust of wind that had blasted through. But she knew full well it was from that infuriating man.

A man she couldn't allow to distract her. Not now. Not when her future, her life, her sanity, was at stake.

Balancing a tray of coffees and a bag of pastries, Felicity channeled her college waitressing days as she moved into the waiting room. Carefully maneuvering around the green chairs that had seen better days, she distributed the sweets and coffee to Conrad's family. Appreciative nods and murmured thanks lifted up from all around.

Food and coffee would not mitigate the risk Isabeau was in as she labored a month early. The baby was coming, and the road to the safe delivery of the child would be hard fought.

Still, sitting idly by had never been Felicity's style. So she did the best she could to offer temporary distractions.

Felicity's heart was in her throat for this family as they worried about Isabeau. Trystan had been beating himself up for not insisting she never set foot out of bed, even though the doctor had assured them all had looked well at the last appointment.

They would feel better when that baby was in the world and Isabeau was healthy.

Marshall scooped up the last apple pastry, and Felicity slumped in one of the green chairs by Conrad. She'd sat here a year ago with the sister of one of her clients. A flashback to that day involuntarily played in her mind's eye, along with memories of her own marriage. About the time she'd wanted to start a family, her relationship had begun crumbling. She hadn't understood why then. But later realized that was when her husband's drug use had started.

She'd beaten herself up for a long time, not understanding how she—counseling professional—could have missed the signs. Only later, with some distance and proof, had she realized he was just that adept of a liar.

Tears stung her eyes as she stared at the board of baby photos from ward deliveries, all those healthy babies and happy families, all the joy around them now with other relatives getting news that everything went alright. She prayed for similar news today for this family as she watched nurses in scrubs scurry down the hallway.

Conrad blew into his cup of java. "Thank you for this. I appreciate your sticking around to help here."

Her hands moved on their own volition to stroke behind his ear. He leaned into the touch, settling into the chair more. Somehow, despite all the signs for why she didn't need this complication, she found herself unable to leave.

No. That wasn't quite right.

She didn't want to turn her back on this man. This kind, complicated man.

Felicity gently massaged his temple, hand tracing circles in his dark hair. "I figured you would want to sit with your family for updates, and if I hadn't come, you would have been the one making runs for coffee and pastries."

"Probably so." He let out a chuff of air, nodding.

A chime of bells dinged—an indication a baby had been delivered. The whole family turned toward the double doors. Waiting. But no doctors came. The room's collective hush faded. Whispers of conversations started again in their private nook where they couldn't be overheard.

"I enjoyed myself earlier." Felicity scooped her legs underneath her. She leaned against him. Their shoulders touching. "You're so good with the kids. I know you say you've wanted to be there for your brother, but…"

"Why am I not married?" He supplied the obvious question.

"I don't mean to be rude or pushy…"

"You're certainly not the first to ask. It's a reasonable question and given the shift in things between us, you have every right to ask. I almost made it to the altar. We had the reception hall reserved…and she got cold feet."

She'd heard he'd had a very serious relationship in the past, but hadn't realized things had gone so far. She felt selfish thinking she'd had the corner on the market for painful pasts. "I'm sorry to hear that. What happened?"

"Why does it matter?" He bristled.

"I guess my career makes me ask questions without even thinking." She dunked a piece of the pastry in her coffee.

"Or as a means of keeping people from asking about your life. Maybe if I had asked more questions before, I would have understood you better."

She chewed the bite of pastry, grateful for the pause it gave her before answering. Conrad may not have her training, but he was sharp. Attentive. And perhaps all too close to the mark.

She cleared her throat with a sip of coffee, knowing she owed him the same kind of answers she sought from him. "I believe I was clear when I broke things off last Christmas. I had a rotten first marriage. I'm focused on my career, now more than ever, with the new position at the hospital."

He stretched his legs out in front of him, crossing his feet at the ankles. "Surely you can't think one bad man represents the entire male population. Your career must tell you otherwise."

"If that's true, what if I just don't like you? It's not like we went out for very long."

He laughed, locking eyes with her. "I believe we're past that now."

A blush heated her face. "Point taken."

He patted over his heart. "I think that may well be the nicest thing you've said to me."

"Considering I've pushed you away more often than not, I don't think that's saying much." A hint of regret stung as she thought of how forceful she'd been. She'd been pushing him away because of her own shadows.

"Then make it up to me by letting me take you home when we finish here."

As she weighed her answer, the bell chimed. A new baby. The doors opened and a nurse walked through, calling for them. "The doctor wanted me to let you know Isabeau is fine. And the baby boy is doing well for a preemie."

An eruption of cheers rivaling any college touchdown echoed in the waiting room. Felicity was swept into the movement of this family, exchanging hugs with not just Conrad, but the rest of the clan. A beautiful, happy family moment, and she cherished it. Felicity was caught right up in the middle of the celebration. If she wasn't careful, she would get caught up in this family the same way she'd gotten caught up in the man.

Eight

Three hours later, as she stepped into Conrad's home, Felicity wasn't any closer to stemming the excitement singing through her. There was just too much beauty in the day for the moment to be denied. The happiness made her realize how long it'd been since she felt this way—not bracing herself for the next storm life had to offer her.

After buffering herself from life for so long, this new ease and happiness had been unexpected. Strange, even. But she wasn't ready to let it go yet. She decided to savor it just awhile longer. Tomorrow would come all too quickly.

Right now, she wanted to ride the joy of knowing the baby was okay. And yes, it had been a wonderful afternoon with Conrad.

Shrugging out of her red wool coat, Felicity stepped farther into the entryway. Drank in the small details she now recognized as Conrad's signature, understated style.

A wall of windows on the far side of the living room boasted a stunning vista of snowcapped mountains, eliminating any need for art. The room was dominated by nature, with sleek silver cliff sides jutting through and tall trees that fluttered in the wind. Even now, the view still took her breath away.

"This is…quite a place." Her whole apartment would fit in the living room with space to spare.

He tossed his Stetson on a coatrack hook. "Are we going to discuss my overprivileged life again?"

"No, I understand you made your own fortune." She passed her coat to him and placed her bag on the leather sofa.

"And I understand that my home life was stable, giving me advantages you didn't have," he said, his eyes cautious.

She couldn't help but think that despite all of Conrad's charm, he moved as warily through relationships as she did.

She did appreciate that he was trying to show her he'd heard her concerns, but she didn't want to hash through that now. She wanted to live in the moment. "How about we just deal with the present?"

"Sounds good to me." His hands fell to rest on her shoulders, massaging lightly.

She swayed nearer, drawn to the heat of his touch. "We'll be working together on the hospital event even more closely now that Isabeau's had her baby. Let's keep our focus on that, rather than the past."

His thumbs stroked along her collarbone in sensuous, slow swipes. "I'm not going to pretend last night didn't happen."

"Me either." She couldn't. What they'd experienced together was rare, and absolutely unforgettable. Still, she needed to be clear with him before she could feel comfortable indulging that attraction again. "But please understand, I'm not walking back on what I said about not being in the market for a long-term relationship."

"I heard you." His hands glided up to cup her face, fingers spearing in her hair. "And I also remember you suggested that since we can't avoid each other for the next three weeks, we might as well make the most of that time."

She couldn't agree more. Stepping into his embrace was so easy. So natural. Felicity arched up onto her toes just as his head lowered, their mouths meeting with ease and familiarity now, a perfect fit that stirred anticipation. Their bodies were in sync, the attraction so tangible neither of them seemed able to resist.

She wasn't sure how long it would take to see this through, but she was determined to take all she could until then.

He tasted of the berry cobbler they'd had for dessert, topped with the best vanilla ice cream she'd ever had. Everything about this family brought the best of the best to even the simple pleasures of life. They weren't pretentious, but they were privileged. Quickly, she pushed away the thought that threatened to chill her and wriggled closer.

His hand slid down her arm in a delicious glide until he linked fingers with her, stepping back. "Follow me."

"What do you have in mind?"

"Trust me," he said, blue eyes full of irresistible intent.

* * *

Conrad tightened his grip on Felicity's hand. Leading her through his home, his mind set on exactly where he wanted to take her. During the entire party at his brother's place, Conrad had fantasized about getting Felicity into his own pool. Preferably, naked.

Images of her curved body, dark hair slick on her breasts, set his heart racing. Feeling her quickening pulse in their laced hands, he maneuvered through the living room, winding around the sectional and leather recliners. Her footfalls were soft against the thick rug on the hardwood floor as they passed the large dining table, which saw use only when he'd hosted holidays for his brother the year after he lost his wife and daughter.

Conrad pushed the thought aside, as he smoothly opened glass sliding doors to his own heated, enclosed pool area.

The space was private, even with glass walls. The tint was one-way, with an incredible view overlooking a cliff and snowcapped mountains in the distance. No one could approach from that side.

Felicity turned in a slow circle to take it all in, her red leather boots clicking on the mosaic tile flooring. "This space is breathtaking."

Her smile pleased him.

He couldn't take his gaze off her. "*You* are breathtaking."

A fire lit in her eyes as she stepped back to peel off her sweater dress. Inch by inch, she bunched the knit fabric up, revealing creamy skin one breath at a time. She whipped the dress the rest of the way over her head, tossing it onto a pool lounger and shaking her silky hair back into place. Static lifted strands in a shimmery electric halo around her slim face.

She was bold and beautiful as she stood in a black lace bra and panty set, still wearing her red leather boots.

His pulse hammered in his ears, all the blood rushing south. Fast. Leaving him hard with desire, his feet rooted to the spot as he watched her.

She reached behind her, unhooking her bra. The straps slid forward along her arms, the cups holding on to her breasts for a moment before the scrap of lace fell to the tiled floor. She shimmied her panties down her legs and stepped out of them.

His breath hitched in his chest. Her beauty, confidence and sensuality lit up the room. Moving forward, he lifted both hands to sketch a finger along her collarbones, down to her breasts, the tightening buds encouraging him to continue. He traced farther, farther still until he dipped to stroke between her legs. Already, she was damp and ready for him. Her knees buckled and she grabbed his shoulders, her eyes sliding closed with a sigh.

He reclined her onto a padded poolside lounger to remove her boots as he'd done the first time they were together.

"I don't think I could ever grow tired of this." Her eyes blinked open, the hazel depths full of shadows that reminded him of the time limit she'd put on their affair. The last thing he wanted was for her thoughts to already be jetting toward leaving.

He touched her lips, silencing her, before he stepped back to toss away his own clothes in a speedy pile. He snagged a condom from his suit pocket before lowering himself over her. She beckoned him with open arms, her knees parting. He didn't need any further invitation. Stretching over her, he pressed between her legs, inside her welcoming body.

Her sighs, the roll of her hips, the caress of her skin against his—all of it teased his senses. The water feature tapped an erratic symphony that matched his speeding heart—her answering heartbeat against his chest.

He lost himself in sensation, in her floral scent and the mist of salt water from his pool. The glide of their bodies against each other as perspiration dotted their skin. He waited what felt like an eternity to get her into his bed since the first time he'd laid eyes on her. In reality, it had barely been two months. But time had shifted in that moment when he'd seen her, his every waking and sleeping thought leading him to pursue her.

And he didn't intend to let up. This woman was one in a million, a class act with sex appeal that seared him clear through. He thrust deeper, her legs hitching up and around his waist, drawing him closer still as her hips encouraged him on.

A flush spread over her skin, her head pressing back into the cushions from side to side. Seeing the oncoming tide of her completion sent a fresh surge of pleasure through him. Her moan grew louder, becoming a cry of bliss. The warm clasp of her pulsed around him, bringing him to a throbbing finish that rocked him to the core. His arms collapsed and he fell to rest, blanketing her. His orgasm shook him once more, a shudder racking through him. Her hands on his back, his butt, teasing every last bit of sensation from his tingling nerve endings.

Once their labored breaths slowed, he hefted himself off Felicity and lifted her in his arms. She smiled up at him and looped her arms around his neck without a single protest, seeming to trust wherever he intended to take her.

He strode toward the pool, the tile cool against his bare feet. Carrying her down the steps, he plunged them both into the heated waters, the stone fountain feature spewing a shower into the deeper end. A saltwater pool, there was no chlorine to sting the air or skin. Just the glide of soft, warmed waves over them.

Neither of them spoke afterward. He smoothed her hair back, his forehead resting against hers, their breaths mingling. It had been an intense couple of days, with Brea's return, making love to this woman, the emergency C-section of Isabeau's baby boy.

And he couldn't deny having Felicity by his side had made all of it easier. She'd supported him. It was also an unusual dynamic since he was more often on the giving end. He wasn't quite sure what to make of that. And he wasn't in any state of mind to untangle those thoughts.

Felicity had a hold over him that exceeded anything he'd felt for any other woman. And that scared the hell out of him.

Felicity stared at her lover as he slept, his head denting the pillow beside her. After they had sex by the pool, they'd swam playfully, then showered together. Her body was mellow and sated, her still-damp hair gathered in a loose knot on her head.

She hadn't meant to stay through the night, but time had slipped away as they'd made love again and talked into the early hours. The long dark nights of an Alaskan winter had made it all too easy to lose sight of the approaching morning.

In the gentle rays of moonlight streaming through the window across his room, Conrad looked peaceful. Sexy and chiseled, but the light revealed a softer side of him. The kind of light that sent her mind wandering, probing possibilities. A seductive space to imagine.

Combing her fingers through his coarse hair, she could swear that he leaned into her touch. She took in the strength of his body as she sank into the down feather pillows. For the span of a breath, she allowed herself to picture an impossible future. One where she moved through this space—Conrad's space—dressed in this room of cool grays and breathtaking views. Shared a bed and a life with this bewitching man. What it might be like. What that life would taste like, fresh berries, his lips, mountain air singed with pine scent... Incredible sex, a shared interest in supporting and bettering others.

She'd prided herself on dating people with less traditional good looks. But there was no denying that Conrad had a movie star face, with his strong cheekbones and jawline.

Even the hints of gray in his hair grew in with perfection, just the right amount sprinkling at the temples.

He was a handsome man, completely comfortable in his own skin.

Given he was the younger brother of an immensely successful businessman, Felicity marveled all the more. She would have expected a younger brother to struggle at least a bit to find his place in the world.

Not Conrad. He'd built his own business, while still supporting his brother's business and personal ventures.

Maybe that was why Conrad had never tried marriage again after the failed engagement.

Who the hell would have time for more? His life was packed.

Or maybe she was just giving herself a convenient out for keeping barriers between them.

Sliding out of the bright white, high-thread-count sheets, she landed gently on the tan carpet. Toes luxuriated in the softness as she gathered her clothes from the nearby chair.

Before they slipped into bed last night, Conrad offered her a tour of his place. She'd never been in a home quite this large or extravagant. No question, the home was amazing, from the pool to the media room. He even had a workout area and indoor basketball court, perfect for enjoying during long Alaska winters.

She knew her worth. Understood that she was a smart woman with a great career. A catch in her own right.

Still, there were times she wondered what drew Conrad to pursue her so intensely. He could have anyone he wanted. Certainly, even someone much younger. She'd half expected that after their first time together, the thrill of the chase would fade for him and he would walk away.

But he hadn't.

The previous morning had brought the invitation to join him at his family's get-together. And then here, as well. He'd been attentive, while giving her space, a difficult balance to achieve.

Slipping into her black lace panties, she cast a casual glance back at Conrad. His chest steadily rising and falling.

She wasn't sure what to make of him.

And until she figured that out, she needed to maintain some distance between them. Sitting to hook her bra behind her back, she willed her mind and body to sync.

She needed to hold strong to her decision to keep this simple. She would not—could not—linger for a romantic breakfast.

She tugged on her sweater dress, then resecured her damp top knot. Hair she'd defiantly grown out after her messy divorce. Her ex had preferred her with a shoulder-length bob. When the divorce process started, she'd resolved to do something small and symbolic for herself. So she let her hair grow long and wild. A reminder to herself she'd never be compromised or caged like that again.

A rustle of the sheets gave her only a moment's warning before he spoke.

"How about coffee before you leave? I wouldn't want you falling asleep behind the wheel." He swung his legs from the bed. "Or better yet, I'll call for a driver."

His hair was mussed from her fingers, his jaw peppered with a five o'clock shadow. He was every bit as appealing as when he was decked out in a custom-fit suit. She needed to get moving or she would be tempted to crawl back into that bed for the rest of the night… maybe longer.

"There's no need for that." She pulled on her fluffy socks and tall boots, ready to find that distance she'd been thinking about. "I didn't mean to wake you."

"More like you were sneaking off. No need to do that. I heard you loud and clear about your 'no sleepovers' rule."

"Well, technically I did sleep over, even if I didn't fall

asleep." She dropped a quick kiss on his mouth. "But I also meant what I said about making the most of this time while we're planning the hospital event. Avoiding the attraction would make those meetings miserable."

"I'm glad we're in agreement on that."

She pointed to his phone. "Could you check for any message about Isabeau and the baby?"

"Of course." He scooped his cell off the dresser and thumbed through. "All's going well. He's still on oxygen, but is eating well and alert. Would you like to see some photos?"

"Yes, please." She rushed to his side and leaned in to look at the screen. The pinkish newborn had oxygen tubes around his tiny face in the stark white warmer. A fighter already. At five and a half pounds, so tiny, but bigger than they'd feared. A sting of regret pinched her as she thought of the children she'd once dreamed of having.

"They've named him Everett, which means strong."

She touched the screen lightly. "He's beautiful. Congratulations, Uncle Conrad."

"Great-uncle. Good God, that makes me sound old," he said, although he showed not the least bit of vanity. Just a wry laugh.

"You're a good bit younger than your brother. You could still have children of your own." How had she let that loaded statement slip from her lips? Especially when she'd vowed to keep things simple between them. This was not a simple question, by a long shot. Yet she couldn't help but wonder how he felt about not ever being a father.

"What about you?" he dodged her question, his face inscrutable.

She weighed her answer, trying to decide whether to speak or run far and fast. She opted for the truth. "I've considered adopting an older child. The timing just hasn't been right."

He stroked a strand of her hair back, cupping the side of her face. "You would be a phenomenal mother."

The tender sincerity in his words touched her in a way that stirred her heart, too much.

"Thank you." She passed back his phone. "But this conversation has gotten entirely too serious for our ground rules about this affair."

He cupped her hips and drew her close. "Then by all means, let's not lose focus."

She laughed, appreciating that he didn't push the point. "I'll take that coffee, thank you."

"Lucky for you, I know exactly how you like it."

That wasn't the only preference he'd taken note of, and it didn't escape her attention. Was he that thoughtful? Or was she being played?

She hated being suspicious, but her instincts in the romance department had led her so horribly astray, she couldn't bring herself to let her guard down.

Living in the moment was far safer. She kissed him once more. "I'll take that coffee to go, please."

Jack rubbed the back of his neck, exhausted.

The day spent at the hospital visiting baby Everett, helping Trystan and Isabeau, had proved to Jack more than ever that it was time to hand over the reins of the business. He wanted—needed—to focus on his family. The sooner he could wrap up this call with Ward Benally, the better.

Leaning against one of the windowpanes on the

wall of windows, Jack searched the lake while listening to Benally on speakerphone. Fading sunlight filtered through the blinds in Jack's private library, casting the room in a weary twilight glow. It matched his mood. His fingers rested on the blinds, opening up the view ever so slightly. As if there'd be a magic answer out there about winning back Brea if he could just see better.

If only it were so simple. If only anything made sense to him anymore.

Benally said his goodbyes on the other end of the phone.

"Thank you," Jack said. "Yes. We'll talk soon."

He placed the cell phone on the vintage desk. It had belonged to Jack's great-grandfather. A man Jack remembered in flashes. Images mostly, if he were being honest. But his grandfather had built and carved the wooden desk. Embedded scenes of the Alaskan tundra into the wood—elk, bears and cresting mountains. The well-worn wood gave Jack a sense of solidity.

The library served as a refuge for Jack and Jeannie as their ever-expanding family filtered in and out of the common areas of the house. He didn't mind retreating here. The walls were warmed by shelves of books and a plush, red Oriental rug. A crystal chandelier descended from a recessed point in the ceiling. Years ago, he'd painted that ceiling sky blue. A reminder of hope in the days after his family suffered unimaginable tragedy.

Jack was a detail man.

"Jack?" Jeannie called from the sofa, where she sat with boxes of papers at her feet. "Who was that on the phone? Was it something to do with Isabeau and the baby? I should get back to the hospital."

Jeannie gathered her blond hair—streaked with glistening gray—into a ponytail. A move Jack had learned to associate with action, unrest and intervention. Jeannie's bright blue eyes turned cloudy as worry set in her jaw.

He made fast tracks across the room to rest a hand on her shoulder, to reassure her. "Relax. That wasn't Trystan."

She pressed a hand to her chest in relief. "Thank heavens."

The NICU allowed only a limited number of visitors and Trystan and Isabeau had made it clear they wanted the nighttime alone to bond with their baby. Odds were in the infant's favor, but a tiny preemie was still a frightening proposition for all.

A call to come to the hospital would likely only mean the worst.

The fire crackled, adding warmth to the cool, fading light from the overcast sky. Snow fell harder, in bigger chunks outside as night approached. While he would drop everything to be at Trystan and Isabeau's side, a small pang of guilt and relief passed through him. Relief, because no call from the hospital meant the baby's stability. Guilt because he'd merely exchanged one crisis for another.

Their joint families could not seem to catch a break or a breather. His heart was heavy. The contents of Brea's written statement had only made things worse as she detailed the off-the-grid family who had rescued her at the crash site, then brought her up as their own.

The people who'd saved her had stolen her, and that was eating him up inside.

Jack dropped to sit beside Jeannie on the sofa. He would rather talk about anything except that damn statement. "That was Ward Benally. He had some questions for the board. He's a tough negotiator. We'll be lucky to get him."

Jeannie smiled warmly, her pink lips pressing together. She turned her head, running gentle fingers through his still-thick hair. "And you're truly alright with giving over control of the company to an outsider?"

She stroked from his head down to the nape of his neck. With an expert touch, she massaged him softly.

"Are you?" He brought her manicured hand over his lap, massaging her palms as he knew she enjoyed.

She leaned her head against his shoulder. "Well, none of our children seem interested in the position."

"They're forging their own paths. That's admirable." He tapped the boxes at her feet with his boot. "What's all of this?"

"I'm sorting through old letters from my brother and sister." She glanced at Jack with pain-filled eyes. "I don't want to believe that Lyle and Willa could have anything to do with what happened to your family. But I can't bury my head in the sand."

Her fear cut through him. While he wanted—needed—answers about the crash that had torn apart his family, he couldn't ignore how explosive those discoveries might be.

He leaned toward the box, sifting through the contents, aged paper brittle to the touch. As fragile as the future. "What are you expecting to find in these?"

"I don't know exactly. Maybe something that places them in the wrong place at the wrong time. Or even some hint that one of them had a connection to the airplane mechanic involved."

It had been quite a blow to realize Marshall's fiancée's father had been the mechanic who'd worked on the plane that fated flight. Tally's dad had killed himself out of guilt, so now they couldn't ask him if his role had been deliberate or accidental.

And if it had been deliberate, why? At whose instigation?

"Have you found anything?"

"Nothing concrete, I'm afraid. But there's a lot here to sort through." The words practically leaped out of Jeannie's mouth.

"Can I help?"

"You could, but I'm not sure it's the best idea. You don't know them the way I do. You might miss a subtext, or a reference to something in our past that seems innocuous."

Suspicion lit. Was she trying to keep him away from those letters for another reason?

There was no denying that Jeannie's siblings had sketchy pasts. Her brother had been mixed up in shady deals more than once. And Willa had man problems and drug problems that had led her to give up her son, Trystan, for Jeannie to raise, and Jeannie had embraced the boy into the fold unreservedly. Most didn't even know he wasn't her biological son.

One thing Jack was certain of. If Jeannie's family had been in any way involved in that crash, Jeannie had no knowledge of it. He trusted her.

If only he could say the same about her siblings. Hell, even about her first husband.

And although Jack trusted her, how would any negative news about her family affect his children? Affect how they felt about Jeannie?

He'd thought the worst of their families' feud had passed once he and Jeannie had married. There was no way he could have foreseen anything like this.

A knot formed in Jack's throat. He'd been given this second chance at happiness, one he'd never expected to find. And he'd been so damned grateful. But how could he have guessed that the Mikkelson-Steele divide might have far darker depths than old mistrust or even corporate espionage?

Because he'd also never imagined that the return of his long-lost daughter could threaten to tear his marriage apart.

Nine

Conrad intended to make the most of the time he had left with Felicity planning the hospital charity dinner. Sleeping together had in no way eased the sensual tension during those working sessions. In fact, it only increased since now he knew just how good they were together.

Sitting beside her at the table in the Alaska Oil Barons Inc. boardroom, he reviewed the financial spreadsheet while she finalized the seating chart now that the RSVPs were locked down. Felicity left work early once a week for them to hammer out details for the event. The rest was accomplished between them by text and emails. This would be their final, in-person meeting since the hospital dinner was scheduled for the end of the week.

The gust from the heater vent carried the floral scent of her shampoo, tempting his every breath. The same scent that clung to his pillow after they were together.

For the past two weeks, he'd done his best to romance her out of bed, as well. Time was running out.

He'd taken her on a dinner cruise, with stunning glacier views. Another night, they'd gone to a dinner theater. He could still hear the melodic sound of her laughter echoing in his head, reverberations calling to mind her soft skin, her supple lips.

He stole a sidelong glance at her. She swiped along her tablet, rearranging the seating chart graphic with one hand. With the other, she popped chocolate-covered pretzels into her mouth. A gift he'd sent her. It made him smile to see he'd chosen well.

"I'm glad to see you stopped giving away my gifts to the nurses' station." He stole a chocolate pretzel from the dish.

She grimaced, hair falling in front of her slender face, calling attention to her angled jaw. "I didn't mean for you to know that."

"It was the nicest way I've ever been rejected," he said with a grin. "I'm glad we've moved past that, though."

For how long?

"You're spoiling me so much, I've had to double my time on the treadmill." She pulled the dish closer. "Not that I'm giving these up."

Her playfulness reignited the barely banked fire in him. He was enjoying the hell out of getting to know the different sides of her. "I'll have to look into chocolate coffees."

"You're going to melt me." She stroked her foot along his calf under the table, out of sight of anyone who might walk by the conference room.

He slid a hand down to caress her leg, the linen of her suit warmed from her body. "That's my intention."

Footsteps and conversation from the hall broke them apart quickly.

Part of the rules—no one could see them. No PDA. Felicity had held hard and fast to this.

Withdrawing his hand to the top of the long table in the Steele building, he already missed the feeling of her. She leaned forward in her office chair. Imperceptible to outside eyes. But a secretive flick of her eyes told a different story. Ever so slightly closer to him without arousing any kind of suspicion.

Fire burned in his blood.

He glanced at the seating chart. With the board of directors for the hospital and the Alaska Oil Barons Inc., with their plus-ones and special guests, the dinner party included just over one hundred. It would also mark the first official function for Ward Benally as the new CEO.

"What do you think of Ward Benally?"

"What I think doesn't matter." She swept her finger along the screen, shifting the table placements, swapping around the location for the musicians' stage. "The decision's already been made to move forward with the hire."

"So you don't like him?" he pressed.

"I've barely met the man," she answered. Evasively? Or diplomatically?

He'd learned that her years of social work made Felicity's face sometimes hard to read. She knew how to bury emotions and feelings. To center her features in an expression of neutrality. Conrad had learned to treat her unguarded emotions as a treasure.

"I'm curious about your impressions of him. You have good instincts." He meant what he said. The more time he spent with her, the more he enjoyed her beyond just sexual attraction. "Maybe it's from your training. Or maybe it's innate in you and that's what drew you to the profession. Regardless, I'm curious what you think."

Pushing her tablet away, she rolled back her chair, turning it toward him. "You want tips on how to handle him as the head of the company."

"Partly," he admitted, but couldn't deny it was more than that. "I also want to protect my brother. I'm not sure he's at the top of his game right now."

Her bright eyes met his. He felt her intelligence sparking as she nodded.

"That would be understandable for your brother, given the shock of finding out his daughter's alive—and that by her own admission in her written statement, she chose not to contact him."

Conrad had trouble wrapping his brain around Brea's recounting of having lived with a family off the grid who had claimed her as their own. It was…too much. He needed to focus on what he could handle, control and change.

The present.

"I need to be sure Benally is the right person to take over this company my family has poured their hearts into."

Felicity splayed her hands on the table, her voice soft yet empathetic. "As I understand it, the recommendation may have come from your brother, but you told me the board had to vote. The process of checks and balances is there for a reason."

True enough. It was still difficult to see his brother step down and pass over the company to someone out of the family. Although it felt hypocritical to complain when Conrad wasn't willing to take the helm either.

"Then what do you think of Benally?"

"Cutthroat businessman. He'll do well for your company," she said without hesitation.

"That simple?"

"He's the type who lives, eats and breathes the job. That's my impression."

Relief swept through him. "Okay, then. I can rest easy that the company will thrive."

"You trust my opinion that much?" Her mouth curved into a surprised smile.

He did. Her brain was every bit as sexy as the rest of her. "That's why I asked."

He lifted her hand and pressed a kiss to the inside of her wrist, giving her fingers a quick squeeze before letting go.

Her pupils widened in response. A surge of desire pumped through him, along with a vow to kiss every inch of her later when they were alone.

She cleared her throat and rolled her chair back to the conference table. "What are we going to do about entertainment since the string quartet bowed out?"

The cellist had come down with influenza, which had progressed into pneumonia. The others in the group were showing symptoms of the flu. Even if they recovered in time, the risk that one of them might be contagious was too great. The last place they needed to be performing was in a hospital full of vulnerable patients.

Conrad spun his smartphone on the conference table. "I called Ada Joy Powers and she tentatively committed as long as her agent confirms the scheduling works. Ada Joy was a big hit at the steampunk gala last November."

"Are you sure we can afford her and stay within budget? She's such a big name and the steampunk gala was a huge affair." Felicity studied the budget sheet before looking back up at him.

He hesitated before answering, but then she would find out eventually anyway. "I'm going to cover the cost. That will give us more money to apply to the menu."

"That's very generous of you."

"Something needed to happen fast. I took care of it. The expense is minor."

She laughed. "To you maybe." She tipped her head to the side, her silky hair fanning forward. "So you have Ada Joy Powers's personal number…"

Was she jealous? "Is that a question?"

"I know I've said I'm not interested in a long-term relationship, but I don't take sleeping together lightly." She clasped her hands together so tightly her knuckles went white. "I expect exclusivity for the time we're together."

Of all the things he could have predicted she would say, this wasn't on the list. But he was damn glad to hear it. "Good. Because so do I."

Her gaze locked with his, and he'd been with her long enough now to read her expression with total clarity.

She wanted him. Now. As much as he wanted her.

To hell with work.

He slid back his chair at the exact same moment she did the same. And he knew just where he intended to take her.

Felicity hadn't even known there was a penthouse apartment in the Alaska Oil Barons Inc. headquarters. Conrad told her it was for the occasions when one of the family had to work late.

He'd also said it was the nearest, fastest place he could bring her, this luxury condo with towering ceilings and an incredible view of the icy bay. Even this emergency stopover for the Steele and Mikkelson families could easily fit three of her apartments. Her heeled boots reverberated on the hardwood floor that connected the living room to a recessed kitchen and dining area. Intricate stonework on the walls framed the window overlooking the bay. And that was as much attention as she wanted to give the place.

The man in front of her was far more enticing.

She stroked the back of his neck as he tapped in a code locking the door. He continued to type along the panel, the fireplace glowing to life. The makings of an idyllic evening. The flames crackled, an echo she felt in the way Conrad's blue eyes fell on her. Even through his button-up shirt, Felicity could make out the suggestion of the hard planes of his chest. Over the past two weeks, his body had become seared in her memory. She craved him. On so many levels.

Enticed, she drew his head down to hers, his kiss intoxicating. His briefcase thudded to the hardwood floor along with her purse. They walked deeper into the living room, their legs tangling as they tugged at each other's clothes. His fingers made fast work of the buttons on her blouse. She swept aside his suit coat and tugged his crisp shirt free of the waistband, sighing with pleasure as she reached bare skin, stroking up his broad back.

Nibbling his way to her ear, he whispered, "I take it to mean you approve of the place."

She loosened his tie, then tugged it off. Slowly. One seductive inch at a time.

"Have you brought anyone else up here before?" She

hated the words the moment they left her mouth, much like when she'd asked about Ada Joy. A spiral of doubt and pain opened beneath her, threatening the here and now. Years of hurt from her failed marriage screamed in her ears.

Felicity shut down the thoughts before they threatened to steal this moment from her. Time was running out until the dinner, her deadline for this relationship. She shouldn't care about his answer. What they had was casual.

She pressed her fingers to Conrad's lips. "Don't answer. Just kiss me."

She was a stronger woman than that. She didn't need affirmations.

He pulled her hand from his mouth. "I have not brought anyone here. Anytime I stayed in this place, I stayed alone."

His answer mattered. Too much. And the affirmation filled a hollow place inside her.

She forced herself to breathe. "Well, I'm happy you thought of it now."

"You're an inspiration."

"Get ready to be majorly inspired."

Her mind filled with possibilities, a list she intended to put to good use. She lost herself in the power of his kiss, his touch, pausing only to snag a condom from his wallet. The urgency pumping through her veins surprised her, given how often they'd been together over the past weeks. But rather than dulling the edge, sating the need, her desire for him ramped up. She couldn't get the rest of his clothes off fast enough. His discarded garments mixed with hers in a trail over the thick Persian rug until they were both bare, skin to skin.

This man undid her in so many ways. Keeping her boundaries in place around him was a constant battle, to the point she sometimes wondered why she bothered. He was so good at sliding right past them when she least expected it. Like when he'd asked her what she thought of the new CEO hire. As if he deeply valued her opinion.

Damn it. Enjoy the here and now.

She let go of the thoughts and just held on to him. She tapped him on the chest, nudging him toward the large-striped club chair.

Grasping the armrests, he sat, his gaze a blue flame heating over her. Setting her on fire. She stepped between his knees and took her time rolling the condom into place, savoring the feel and heat of him.

She straddled his lap, her hands flat against his chest. Her eyes locked on his, she eased herself down, taking him inside her. His chest rose and fell faster under her palms, his pulse quickening against her fingertips.

He gripped her hips, guiding her as she met him thrust for thrust. Deeper. Faster. Their speeding breaths synced, sweat glistening and slicking their flesh. Desire built inside her, crackling through her veins as hotly as the flames in the hearth. Her breasts grazed his chest, his bristly hair teasing her overly sensitive nipples to taut peaks.

This man moved her in a way none had before. Not even her ex-husband.

Again, she pushed away thoughts of the past and focused on the present, on taking the most from this moment. Savoring every blissful sensation. The future could be faced later.

She deserved this, wanted this, craved more. Everything.

And he delivered, intuitively knowing just where to touch and stroke her to the edge of completion, easing up, then bringing her to the brink all over again until she was frenzied with need. Unable to restrain herself any longer.

Her head fell back, her cries of pleasure riding each panting breath as her orgasm built, crested, crashed over her in a shimmer of sensation. He thrust once, twice more, his hoarse groan mixing with her sighs, his finish shuddering through him.

Sated, she sagged against his chest. His hands stroked along her back, quiet settling between them with an ease that should have been a good thing. Instead, it made her uneasy.

She rested her head on his shoulder, the scent of him so familiar now. They were sinking into a relationship, a real one, in spite of all her attempts otherwise. He was getting through to her. And as much as she wanted to trust him—to trust herself—that was easier said than done. Her heart had been broken beyond repair.

Felicity tried to enjoy the steady rise and fall of his chest. Tried to let the happiness of this moment touch her. Conrad ran a gentle hand up and down her spine, wrapping closer to her.

But she couldn't shake the fear of what came next. Of the way the boundaries needed to be drawn before irreparable damage touched her soul again.

She couldn't risk losing herself in this man. Not after how hard she had fought for her peace, her quiet but meaningful life.

She needed to get through to him—and herself— that this couldn't last.

* * *

An hour later, Conrad drew Felicity to his side, their legs tangled in the sheets. He'd been honest with her about never having brought anyone here before. He'd never been one to mix business and pleasure.

Something about Felicity had him throwing out his personal rule book from the first time he'd seen her.

The sex between them had been as amazing as ever, but he sensed something was bothering her. And with their timing running out, Conrad knew he needed to attend to the issue now.

She shivered against him and he pulled the downy comforter over them.

"Is that better?" he asked. A second fireplace sputtered dulled orange flames, bathing them in subdued light. The night sky glowed with winking stars and remnants of northern lights. He couldn't have asked for a better, more romantic setting on the spur of the moment.

"Perfect," she said, tipping her head back to smile at him. "I'm glad you brought me here."

Her words reassured him. Maybe he was just imagining that she was pulling away, just a flashback to his ex, which wasn't fair to Felicity. "And just in time. The place will be going to Ward Benally once he starts with the company. He made it a condition of accepting the job. Apparently, he's that much of a workaholic."

She laughed softly. "And you're not?"

His hand slid to cup the sweet curve of her bottom. "Work is the last thing on my mind right now."

"Luckily, we're on the same page." She teased her fingers along his chest.

"Hold that thought," he said, dropping a quick kiss

on her lips before easing away. He slid from under the comforter, leaving the bed to get his briefcase from the living room. He returned, enjoying the way her eyes followed his every move.

"Is it something with work?" She sat up, hugging the sheet to her breasts.

Her loose hair in the firelight made her look like a statue of the goddess of the hunt. But this goddess was all flesh and fire.

He shook his head, dropping the briefcase on the foot of the bed. He typed in the password, then pulled it open. Anticipation pumped through him as he pulled out a long jewelry box with a ribbon.

"Another gift?" Her eyes lit with curiosity as she tentatively stroked the ribbon. "You already gave me the chocolate pretzels today."

"And I helped you eat most of them." He laughed a bit sheepishly as he sat on the bed.

She squinted at him, the blanket falling from her slender shoulders. Shadows danced across her bare body. His gaze skimmed from the soft curve of her breasts to the smile on her face. Damn. *Mesmerizing* didn't even begin to explain the effect Felicity had on him.

"We shared." She took the package from him tentatively. "Thank you. You're going to spoil me."

"I'm certainly trying." In countless ways, this woman astounded him.

She helped so many people; he enjoyed pampering her. He waited while she tugged the ribbon slowly, taking her time like a kid drawing out the excitement. She creaked open the box to reveal the gift.

A pearl lanyard for her hospital badge.

Her eyes lit with surprise—and appreciation. "Oh my goodness, this is so gorgeous. And truly thoughtful."

She drew the lengthy strand out of the box and slid it over her neck. The necklace settled between her breasts, the pearls luminescent against her creamy skin.

Conrad joined her in the bed again, knowing he would carry this vision of her in his mind every time he saw her wear it. "I'm glad you like it. I saw it when I picked up a gift for Everett." He grinned, thinking of the newest member of his ever-growing family.

"What did you choose for him?" She linked her fingers with Conrad's.

"A silver bank shaped like a bear." The baby had improved beyond even the doctors' best expectations and was going to be released from the hospital by the end of the week.

"That sounds precious." She draped a leg over his, leaning against the leather-padded headboard with him. "I know you've been a huge part of your nieces' and nephews' lives. But do you ever wish you had children of your own? You didn't answer when I asked earlier."

An image of a very different time clouded his mind. When he'd lain in bed with his fiancée, kissing her as they dreamed about having a full house, at least four kids, she'd laughed as she kissed his ear. How full his heart had been in that moment.

Despite the pain, Conrad considered Felicity's question. After a moment, he answered in a quiet voice. "My fiancée and I had planned on a large family, but when she walked away…" He shrugged. He hadn't been interested in revisiting an emotional shredder.

"It's not too late for you. Men have less of a biological clock than women."

He couldn't help but wonder… "Are you asking me to father a child with you?"

"No!" she said quickly, almost insultingly so, "no. I was just making conversation." A flush creeping over her face, she pulled back, swinging her legs off the bed. "I'm going to get something to drink. Can I bring something for you?"

He recognized her move for what it was—avoidance. He clasped her elbow. "Wait. Let's keep talking about this. You mentioned wanting to adopt an older child. Did your ex-husband object to that?"

She hesitated so long he thought she would leave anyway.

Then she sat on the bed again, hugging a pillow to her stomach. "He was on board with as many children as I wanted."

"But…?"

Pain flashed through her hazel eyes, so intense it weighted the air and had him reaching for her.

She shook her head, her hold on the pillow tightening. "He was a drug addict."

Her grip on the pillow intensified. Even in the dull light, Conrad could make out the whites of her knuckles as her fingers dug in.

Shock stilled him. He'd known their marriage was troubled, but he never would have guessed this. He stayed silent, sensing she was on the edge of bolting if he said the wrong thing.

She chewed her bottom lip, then continued, "I didn't know for a long time because he was also an incredible liar. We'd been going to counseling for years and he even managed to fool the professionals…for a while. I know too well how a person can be manipulated into believing falsehoods. The lies are so insidious over time, the liar hones their skills, you start to doubt yourself and your perception of reality. It's frightening. And it's real."

The strength of her conviction—the old anger—leaped from her words, a hint of what she'd been through. He touched her arm, feeling inept to deal with the depth of her pain. Wishing he had more to offer. He barely stemmed the need to find her ex and make the bastard pay for hurting her.

"Felicity, I'm so sorry."

"That's not my point. I'm sharing it now to help you understand Brea as well—"

"We're not talking about Brea. This is about you."

"That's my past." She blinked fast, her face molding into the neutral expression that he'd seen her adopt for work.

In the past? Clearly it wasn't given how insistent she was on keeping him at arm's length.

"Are you so sure about that?"

She raised an eyebrow. "You're not in a position to preach about letting go of the past." She held up a hand. "Never mind. Forget I said that. I need to go home."

The pillow carelessly discarded, Felicity moved past him. A coldness descended in the room. A draft that rivaled the Alaskan weather outside. She walked back to the living room, and he followed to find her gathering her clothes.

He considered calling her on her avoidance, but outright confrontation didn't seem in his best interest, given the set of her shoulders. "It's late to be on the road."

"I'm an adult," she said, stepping into her panties and pulling on her bra. "I know how to drive in snow."

He could see the determination in her eyes, but no

way was he letting her get behind the wheel when she was this upset. "And I'm a gentleman. I'll drive you."

She exhaled hard, deflating the pain as she gave a small nod.

Even as he saw the acceptance in her expression, he knew without question, when he took her home, she wouldn't be inviting him inside. He recognized the distancing look in her eyes all too well. He'd seen it before.

In the eyes of his ex, just before she'd walked out of his life.

Ten

Intellectually, Jack understood that he and Jeannie had so much to celebrate with the grandbaby's recovery and the company soon to settle in with a new CEO, which would give them all more time to enjoy their growing family.

Unfortunately, the intellectual understanding didn't reassure him the way it should.

As he sat in the hospital cafeteria with Jeannie for lunch, waiting for the doctor to finish checking Everett, Jack struggled to will away the impending sense of doom dogging him since he'd come across Jeannie sorting through that box of old letters. With each day that passed and no word from Brea or her lawyer, the frustration grew.

He needed to do something to fix things with his family. He just wanted peace and normalcy for all of them.

Cradling his coffee cup, Jack focused his attention

on his wife. "Would you like me to get you something else to eat?"

Stress lined Jeannie's face, dark circles under her eyes as she picked at her salad. "This is fine, thank you. I'm just not that hungry."

"We can try somewhere more appetizing after we visit Everett."

She nodded noncommittally, dodging his gaze. Then her eyes widened as she looked past him and waved.

"Felicity?" Jeannie called, appearing grateful for the distraction. "Come join us."

The hospital social worker paused at the elevator, then strode toward them, carrying a small blue basket. She stopped at their table, lifting the gift. "I was going to drop off some things for Trystan and Isabeau, snacks and a little present to welcome Everett."

"That's thoughtful of you," Jeannie said. "We're going to plan a baby shower after Everett's released and settled in. I hope you'll be able to attend."

"I would like that, thank you." Felicity smiled warmly, but there was something…off…in her eyes that Jack couldn't quite pinpoint.

Something to do with Conrad?

A buzzing incoming text distracted Jack from their conversation and he glanced at his cell. A message from Brea's lawyer. Jack's heart hammered with wariness.

He read through the message, then read it again in surprise.

Hope tugged at him like a magnet. Unease and mistrust jerked him back. The warring emotions cinched his shoulders tight, jaw tensing.

Jeannie touched his wrist. "Is everything alright?"

"It's a text from Brea's attorney." He tucked his

phone back into his pocket, his body on autopilot. "She wants to attend the hospital charity dinner."

Jeannie gasped, pressing a hand to her chest. "I don't know what to say, what to think." She turned to Felicity. "What's your opinion?"

Felicity cradled the basket in her lap, her eyes concerned. "Are you asking me as a friend?"

Jack leaned forward with a heavy sigh, wanting to believe this was a positive sign but remembering too well the unrelenting anger in Brea's eyes. "I would welcome your feedback based on experience."

Felicity looked from one to the other, waiting as a couple walked past. Once their conversation was private again, she said, "Just so we're clear, I'm offering an opinion as a counselor, but not as your counselor."

Jeannie pushed away her salad. "What do you mean by not being our counselor?"

"I'm too close to you all to step into that role," she said apologetically. "I thought I made it clear when I attended the first meeting that it was with the understanding the family would look into long-term counseling with someone else."

"And we will," Jack reassured her. "Once we're all a family again, we realize we will have a lot to work through."

Felicity leveled a steady, no-nonsense stare at them. "Sooner rather than later would be best for everyone. Every time you see her is going to be fraught with stress for all of you and you're going to regret it if you feel you haven't done everything possible to get through this."

Jack heard her, but still wrestled with why this needed to happen now. Brea was back and reaching out. "We understand she's not thinking clearly...but given time, now that she's heard the truth..."

"Jack," Felicity said, her voice taking on a professional calm. "She has been gone from you longer than she was with you. She was so young when she lost you all. Keep in mind it's highly doubtful her adoptive parents didn't hear about your family's tragedy. It's my impression the crash was big news in that area."

"Yes..." He remembered the days after the crash in flashes. Headlines. Newspaper clippings. Sound bites on local news sources. A horrifying reel of images from the wreckage.

"But do you understand she was in essence a kidnap victim?" Her blunt words sliced through the antiseptic air. "Just because we have no reason to believe she was physically abused by them, that doesn't take away from the psychological trauma. Have you heard of Stockholm syndrome?"

Jeannie gasped. "Brainwashing by a captor?"

"Basically, yes." Felicity nodded, leaning closer. Careful to keep her voice low so it wouldn't echo in the room. "How you behave now is more important than I think you realize, not just for getting her back, but for facilitating her healing."

Her words resonated, deeply, offering Jack the first real hope he could actually do something. Strange how he hadn't thought of how counseling for himself and his family could help Brea. He'd been more focused on her needing to seek a professional.

Felicity pushed back from the table. "You have an incredible family. I know you're facing some unthinkable challenges, but together? My money's on you all."

Smiling her reassurance, Felicity stood, grasping the gift basket to leave.

As she walked away, Jack turned his attention back to Jeannie. "I think it's time to take Felicity up on the offer to speak with someone about how to reach out more effectively." He squeezed Jeannie's hand. "My heart is being torn in two thinking about how scared my little girl must have been, how those people took advantage of that and stole…"

His throat closed with anger and pain just talking about it, affirming all the more that he needed help seeing this through.

"Jack, I'm here for you," Jeannie said, holding tight. "Whatever you need, however I can help. We'll face this together."

"Thank you," he said, so grateful not to be alone any longer thanks to his beautiful wife, always at his side. How had he gotten so damn lucky? "Jeannie, have I told you lately how grateful I am you took a chance on me?"

He stroked a thumb along her wrist, their wedding bands glinting.

Smiling, she stroked his cheek. "I seem to recall you saying it a time or two."

"I just want to make sure you know that no matter what happens with Brea, I love you." He couldn't imagine a future without her.

Tears filled her blue eyes. "Even if—God forbid—it turns out my brother and sister had something to do with that awful tragedy?"

The words clawed at his soul. It would hurt if that was the case. And he could see it already hurt her. He couldn't bear to see her in this kind of pain. Felicity was right that he hadn't fully grasped the toll this was taking on all of them. He needed to rectify that. Jeannie—and what they shared—was too precious to risk.

"No matter how much our family means to us, we can't control their actions. I do know that if they are guilty of something, you had no knowledge of it. That's all that matters. Whatever shakes down, we'll deal with it. Together."

He lifted her hands to his mouth, pressing a kiss over her ring with a promise of forever he looked forward to fulfilling.

With Jeannie at his side, he could face whatever the future held.

Felicity sank down into her chair behind her desk, her emotions raw from visiting baby Everett. Seeing Trystan and Isabeau's happiness had blindsided her in a way she hadn't expected. She didn't begrudge them their joy, but it made her think of those dreams she'd had during her marriage. Reminded her of the depth of her ex-husband's betrayal.

Of course, seeing the baby was only half the reason for the resurgence of those emotions. The bigger part of the equation was her exchange with Conrad about having children. He was getting under her skin, burrowing his way toward her heart, making her feel things she couldn't afford to feel.

She gripped the edge of her desk, willing her nerves to ease. She'd taken a couple of days away from Conrad in hopes of regaining some distance, some objectivity. Because he was becoming too important to her, too fast.

A tap on the open door drew her eyes upward. Conrad stood in the void as if conjured from her thoughts.

The man before her was no trick of the imagination or hallucination. His solidity—his existence and presence here—ignited some spark deep in her soul.

When she felt the flames within her, she knew the time for the affair had expired.

She was interested in him on so many levels beyond just the sexual and that made her vulnerable. She could get hurt. By indulging in these dates over the past few weeks, she'd opened herself up for pain.

He leaned a shoulder on the door frame, his hands surprisingly empty of any gift. Not that she needed presents. But she couldn't help but wonder. Was he easing off the romance?

"Hello," she said, staying behind her desk, moving two files around as if she was busy and not just sitting around daydreaming about him.

"You've been avoiding my calls." His expression was inscrutable. But his words were crystal clear.

"Could you close the door? I don't want to broadcast my personal life at work." She waited until he stepped into her office and sealed them alone together inside. She held up the two folders. "I've been swamped. But everything's in place for the event."

"That's not what I meant, and you know it." He rounded her desk, but didn't touch her, just leaned against the window.

Guilt pinched. She wasn't being fair to him. She stood, flattening her hands to his chest and giving him a welcoming kiss.

A kiss that seared her to her toes and threatened to weaken her resolve to give herself time to sort through her feelings. She smoothed his lapels. "Things have been intense between us."

A half smile twitched at his mouth, but didn't quite reach his eyes. "I'm glad to hear you admit that."

Drawing in a shaky breath, she searched for the words to make him understand how this was tearing her up inside. "I just needed some space to get my thoughts together."

"And did you intend to at least tell me that rather than just ignoring my calls?" The first hints of anger clenched his jaw.

She braced her shoulders, anxiety tightening her chest. "I've never lied to you about where I stand. You knew from the start that I'm not ready for a serious relationship."

"You're too busy lying to yourself," he shot back.

Anxiety turned to anger. How dare he patronize her and her concerns.

Her hands fell from his chest. "That's not fair."

He lifted an eyebrow. "But it's true."

"No, no… You don't get to talk to me that way." She held up a hand, putting arm's length distance between them. Away from him and temptation. "But if we're going there, then what about you? You play at being a father to your nieces and nephews because it saves you having to commit to something that might actually be a risk to your heart."

He crossed his arms over his chest, his blue eyes snapping. "Sounds like you have me all figured out. Why are you so afraid of an affair with me if you're certain I'm never going to commit? Or was that part of the draw? No risk to your heart? And as a bonus, I come with this great big family you always wanted growing up."

She gasped, pain slicing through her. "How dare

you use what I shared about my ex and my childhood against me."

Her past rose like a monster from the bay. A nightmare where ghosts wandered. She could taste years of loneliness on her tongue. Feel the weariness settle in her bones and joints.

She recalled the time when everything she owned collapsed into a small pink backpack. The time in fourth grade when the most popular boy in junior high laughed at her because she didn't have parents to talk at career day. And yes, her upbringing had made her all too vulnerable to her ex-husband's false charms and empty promises of family.

Pain threatened to steal her resolve to stand up for herself as she did her best to shove down the memory of shuffling from foster home to foster home.

"I'm only calling it as I see it." The anger eased from his face, and he shook his head, sighing with frustration. "You spout off about getting help and moving on and yet you won't take your own advice."

Tears burned behind her eyes, but she would be damned if she would break down and cry in front of him. "If I'm so broken, then you're better off without me." She strode to the door and opened it, gesturing out into the hall. "Just go. Get out of my office."

She stood stone still. Unflinching, with an apparent resolve she didn't come close to feeling.

He searched her expression silently for so long, she thought he might not leave. Just when she was about to weaken and say something, he nodded tightly. He strode across the office and out the door, angling through, careful not to so much as brush her.

The silence after he left was deafening, the weight

of what had just happened sweeping over her in the aftermath. Numb, she let the door close behind him, unwilling to let anyone see her like this. Her legs folded and she sank into a chair, stunned at the depth of her anger. Her grief. Her pain over having pushed Conrad out of her life.

She wanted to trust what they had together. She wanted to believe that a real relationship was possible for her, but she didn't know how to reconcile her own past. He'd been uncannily correct in that regard. She felt like a hypocrite, touting the benefits of therapy to deal with such a monumental issue when she couldn't get past her own ghosts.

Unable to fight back the tears, she let them flow. How had things gotten out of control so quickly? Sure, she'd given herself a couple of days apart to get her emotions under control. She'd thought she was making progress, until today when she kept running into Steeles and Mikkelsons at every turn.

And it wasn't likely to get much better with their active role in charitable endeavors at the hospital. If she hadn't just changed jobs, she would have seriously considered a move. Even now she found herself considering it. There was a time she'd thought her job was everything. Yet…it didn't feel like nearly enough.

And now she had nothing else left.

Conrad couldn't believe how badly he'd mismanaged the confrontation with Felicity. Everything he'd planned to say had flown out of his head. So much for being the rational businessman. But nothing about his feelings for Felicity was rational.

Their fight had gutted him, leaving him shaken and

clueless on how to fix things. He wanted to believe the break wasn't permanent, but Felicity had been wary from the start. And she'd been pulling away for days.

His drive to cool down landed him on the road to his brother's house. A sign that Felicity was right about his using Jack's family as a substitute for having one of his own? There may have been some truth to that.

As he turned the corner to Jack's driveway, he lowered the radio. A classic rock song's guitar riff faded in favor of the distinctive crunch of tires on hardened snow and gravel.

If he was honest with himself, he'd been on edge after taking the gift to Everett. All the talk with Felicity about having children came flooding back. He'd genuinely thought he was okay with his decision not to become a parent. Now? If he couldn't have a family with her...

The thought threatened to swamp him. He pushed it aside, trying his damnedest not to think about the woman who meant everything to him.

Hopefully hanging out with his brother and the horses would provide the distraction he needed so desperately right now.

Pulling through the security gate, he spotted his brother outside the barn and shifted his SUV into four-wheel drive. Alongside the pasture fence, he put his vehicle into Park.

Jack's barn mirrored the rustic mansion, reminiscent of a log cabin. The facade of the interlocking wood panels seemed to reflect the red hues of the setting Alaskan sun.

Stepping out into the compacted snow, Conrad yanked his gloves from the passenger seat. The sun grew heavy in the horizon, beginning to sink behind the trees and mountain line across the lake. Shrugging his coat on, he walked through the snow, moving toward his brother, who was wearing a puffy winter coat, focused on the horses playing in the pasture.

Conrad pulled on the gloves, fingers thankful for the reprieve from the quickly dropping temperature.

When Conrad was about ten feet out, Jack turned around. A vague surprise danced in his brother's half smile.

Jack nodded, his black Stetson obscuring his brother's normally inquisitive eyes. "What brings you out this way?"

Two feed buckets jutted from the snow, dinner for the horses that currently cantered in the white pasture. Abacus, a bay quarter horse, circled wildly around a lone pine tree at the center of the turnout. He let out a bellowing whinny that reverberated across the property.

Conrad stuffed his gloved hands into the pockets of his jacket as a gust of wind rolled off the bay. "Just at loose ends and thought I'd swing by."

"Uh-huh," Jack said even though his face was clear that he wasn't buying it. Still, he stayed silent, waiting.

He offered his brother one of the pails of feed. Conrad grabbed the red bucket, following Jack to the feeding troughs. They plowed through the snow. Silent except for the sudden attention of Abacus and his paint counterpart, Willow.

The horses circled, galloping for the feeding area. The strong muscles of the horses working overtime as they raced each other. Almost like brothers, siblings engaged in play.

Conrad's mind filled with images from decades ago,

of Jack teaching him to ride when their parents had been too busy. He was lucky to have those memories and so many more. Yet he'd deliberately hurt Felicity by throwing it in her face that she didn't have any such memories of her own.

He felt like a selfish ass—for what he'd said to Felicity and for bothering his brother when Jack had heavy burdens.

"How are you doing with all the Breanna mess?" Conrad inspected the feed in his bucket, knowing his brother didn't buy that he was telling the whole story or that he'd come to talk about Breanna.

Jack glanced over at Conrad, pouring the feed in Abacus's feeding trough. "I'm fine. Jeannie and I have contacted a counselor to help us through. I've been leaning on you too much and that's not fair to you."

Conrad nodded, dumping the contents of his bucket into Willow's trough. Going through the motions of feeding the horses only proved to him how empty his life was. "I want to be here for you. I'm your brother."

The two horses broke their gallop, relaxing into an enthusiastic trot. Ears perked forward, excited for their evening meal.

"And I want to be here for you. So let me." Jack stroked the paint's neck. Willow snorted into his food, chomping loudly. "Now tell me. What really brought you here?"

Conrad hadn't intended to burden his brother, but Jack's face showed he wouldn't back down.

And Conrad was confused as hell, to say the least, and he could use his brother's feedback. The man had somehow managed to have two good marriages when Conrad hadn't been able to manage one. "I've screwed up."

"What happened?"

The fight with Felicity flooded his mind again, her every word and his own unguarded responses. "Felicity gave me my walking papers."

On instinct, Conrad reached out to touch Abacus's neck. The bay looked up from his food, stretched his long neck, leaning over the fence so Conrad could scratch him. The horse's tongue hung out to the side as Conrad tried to find comfort in the silken coat. His usual ritual wasn't cutting it today. The ache over losing Felicity still consumed him.

"I'm sorry to hear that. You two seemed like a great couple. Any hope this will blow over?"

Abacus chuffed, returning to his food. "She was pretty clear." And he'd bungled the whole conversation. He rubbed the kink in the back of his neck. "Her ex-husband really did a number on her."

Guilt flashed through him because he'd just done a number of his own, throwing her past in her face.

"Like your ex did a number on you," Jack said.

"Worse." And he felt guilty as hell for using what she'd shared against her. He prided himself on being a better man than that. He'd lost his mind in the exchange. Lashed out at her in the most unproductive way.

Jack grabbed the discarded feed buckets, stacking them together. "Must have been bad, then, since what happened to you kept you from committing for so long."

His head snapped back. But he couldn't deny the truth of what his brother had said. Conrad had allowed that one rejection to taint all his future relationships. How much worse it must be for Felicity with all she'd been through.

She'd been honest with him about her wary heart. And he'd pushed anyway. "You don't pull any punches."

"We're brothers. You've always been there for me, and I'm trying to be better about being there for you." Jack clapped a hand on Conrad's shoulder, squeezing. "Jeannie and I took Felicity's advice and contacted the counselor she recommended. So you don't need to worry about me. I'm grateful for all you've done. Now, it's time for you to have your own life."

Felicity had spoken with Jack and Jeannie? She was doing more for his family than he was, and she hadn't said a word. More guilt stung him.

Having devoured their meal, the horses waited at the gate. Abacus pawed the snow-covered earth, digging a trench with his front right hoof.

Jack tossed one of the halters and lead lines at Conrad. He caught it, the action as natural and familiar as breathing. How many times had they done this routine over the years?

Conrad thought about Felicity's words again about using Jack's family as a substitute for his own. As a way to protect his heart.

And it was past time he accepted there was truth in that.

For the first time in two decades, he allowed himself to want that future. With Felicity.

"What if I can't win her back?"

"What happens if you don't try?"

Fair statement. But that didn't help Conrad with the *how*. "What do you suggest I do? I've romanced the hell out of her."

"I'm sure you have," Jack said.

Conrad followed his brother, securing Abacus in a

halter. They moved back toward the barn, the horses eager to be out of the cold.

"Just like you did with all the other women you've had affairs with over the years."

"She's different," Conrad said without hesitation, the truth of that resonating deep in his soul. He led Abacus into the stall, unhooked the halter and gave the horse a pat between the ears.

His brother, who had finished putting Willow into the neighboring stall, appeared at the gate. "Then why are you treating her the same? Tell the woman that you love her."

The obvious truth of his brother's simple advice broadsided Conrad.

His time with Felicity had been about more than romance and sex. He was mesmerized by her intelligence and compassion. The confident way she faced life, whether it was at work or riding a horse. Everything about her called to him at a soul-deep level.

Somehow, Felicity had slipped under his radar and stolen his heart.

He was completely in love with her.

Now he had to convince her he was worthy of her trust.

Eleven

Felicity wished she could blame her exhaustion on prepping for the party. However, even though she had worked herself into the ground getting this hospital dinner under way, her lack of sleep came from a broken heart.

And in this ethereal, romantic landscape with the memory garden full of flowers and twinkling lights in the trees?

It made her heart cinch, balking under the pressure of hopes and whims she had done her best to smother to keep herself safe. Futile efforts, though, she realized, as she gazed up at the elaborate centerpiece. Cherry blossoms with pink tea roses weighed heavily from the center of the table, making the glass-enclosed space seem like a fairy garden, filled with possibilities.

Except Felicity felt only a pang of regret as she smoothed the white shimmery tablecloth in front of her.

Two days had passed since her argument with Conrad, and her sadness only intensified, especially when she'd seen him this afternoon as she'd finalized the last of the setup. Thankfully there had been enough traffic with the caterers and florists to help her keep her distance.

The event was going off without a hitch, and she should be celebrating. She swirled a glass of sparkling wine, taking in the flickering lights strung from the ceiling, which gave the appearance of nested constellations.

Slow, sensual piano chords melted under the roaring conversation among guests.

As she leaned back in her chair, her eyes wandered to the boughs of pink and white flowers blanketing the stage where Ada Joy Powers would offer her soulful crooning after the keynote speech that should be starting soon.

Dinner had passed over her lips. The blackened salmon, rich mashed potatoes and vegetable medley as nondescript as water even though the caterer was without peer and her dining companions raved. Food simply lost its appeal as her heart sank further, her emotions taking up all the space in her mind. Replacing her hunger with nausea and dizziness.

Felicity did her best to smile at her tablemates, offer polite conversation. Words left the aftertaste of ash, and the longer she stayed at this event, the more the lump in her throat swelled, her chest tightened. Maintaining a smile of neutrality took all her effort.

It seemed like she had to actively remind herself not to cry every few minutes. She paid such attention to her own internal mantra she barely noticed her waiters dressed in crisp white uniforms clearing her plate, bringing her dessert.

The event moved forward.

Felicity felt stuck in the moment of her fight with Conrad. Forced to replay the scene in her mind again. And again.

Now, the event was in full swing, the keynote speaker behind the microphone and dessert under way. Grateful she didn't have to make small talk with the strangers at her table any longer, she felt able to breathe for the first time since Conrad had left her office.

Her sorbet sat untouched in front of her, berries beginning to float in the melting treat. She'd made a last-minute change to the seating arrangements, ensuring she didn't sit with any of the Steele or Mikkelson family. She just couldn't make small talk with them, not even with her friend Tally. The last thing they needed was more tension, given how stressed they all had to be about Brea Steele's surprise request to be present tonight.

Felicity's gaze trekked to Brea's table, where the woman sat with Conrad and her lawyer. The rest of the table was filled with Steele and Mikkelson siblings since Jack and Jeannie had to sit at the table of honor with the new CEO, Ward Benally.

All had their attention focused on the podium.

The voice of the keynote speaker floated through the room. Thomas Branch, the lead actor from the hit wildlife show *Alaska Uncharted*, leaned on the podium. His voice as rich and gravelly as the outdoor landscapes he showcased to scores of viewers. The rugged, dark-haired actor had first made his name in action movies, but he'd left the big screen for television after the death of his wife, to be more available for their new-born son. Conrad had secured the speaker, just as he had the vocalist.

Unable to resist, Felicity stole a look at Conrad since no one would notice with their attention focused on the dynamic speaker. Conrad took her breath away. He appeared every bit as comfortable in the tuxedo as he did in jeans and a Stetson. He was a brilliant, magnetic—and compassionate—man.

When she'd taken her new job, she'd thought her world was on track. How could Conrad have worked his way into her life so completely in such a short time until her days felt empty without him?

She thought back to what he'd said about her only wanting him for his large family. And she couldn't deny how much she'd enjoyed getting to know them. But she knew in her soul there had been more to her relationship with Conrad than that. It had been real and powerful, despite her efforts to keep her emotions in check.

Blinking away tears, she forced herself to focus on the speaker as a distraction before she embarrassed herself by losing it altogether.

"I'm honored to be here tonight for the renaming of the children's oncology ward, a testimony of hope for the future. This project is a beautiful tribute to the Steele family and their strength. Like Jack and Jeannie, I lost my spouse. She died too young, and I know how hard it is to get over that. Yet, Jack and Jeannie have found a way to honor that love while embracing the future with a new happiness…"

Felicity pressed a shaky hand to her mouth. She'd chosen the wrong time to pay attention to the speaker. Her heart was in her throat. She couldn't keep her gaze off Conrad any more than she could hide from the truth of why she'd pushed him away. She'd been terrified. Not of loving him, because she had already fallen for him, deeply, irrevocably so.

She'd been afraid of what would happen if he loved her back.

If that happened, there would be no hiding from taking a chance on a future with him.

The speaker's words rolled around in her mind, chastising her for not having the courage to risk her heart a second time.

Her gaze lingered on Jack and Jeannie, seeing the love between them against all odds. More than anything, Felicity wanted to be the kind of person who continued to grow and love, instead of the kind of person who let a bad experience keep her in a shell of self-doubt forever.

Brea sat in the darkened corner of the greenhouse party, preferring to watch unobserved, with her back to the wall. So far her identity had been kept a secret from everyone except the family—and Ward Benally, since he was taking over the company and they all thought she was some kind of corporate spy.

Three bold piano notes resounded in the enclosure, and an eruption of applause animated the air with palpable energy. Ada Joy Powers slunk onstage in a swanky, vintage floor-length violet gown. Her hair cascading over one shoulder, pink lips outlined in a sensual Cupid's bow. Looking like a princess from another world as the spotlight accented her curves.

Ada Joy smiled brightly, thanking the audience. "Count me in, will ya?" she called to the piano man.

He flashed a toothy grin of his own, responding with a "three, two, one" before loosening his fingers on the keys. His hands played a lively tune across the ivories. Soon, a violin joined the fold.

"Give me…" Ada Joy belted. "Give me the moon and shadows. I'll keep you…"

Brea twisted her napkin in her lap to occupy her twitchy hands under the cover of the table, resisting the urge to bolt. She was through running.

No. She would stay. Learn to stay, at any rate.

So much of her life felt punctuated by movement. Shifts that still left her reeling.

What might happen if she stayed put for a change? If she let herself unwind in this space, near the people she'd once called family? She could simply trace the contours of her old life. See how it felt.

Except the problem was Brea had no idea what might happen. But her heart urged her to find out. To favor stillness.

She'd come to this event against the advice of her attorney. And she still wasn't certain what had compelled her to ask to be present. Part of her had been sure her request would be denied since they wouldn't be able to control her here. She could definitely make a scene and ruin their event if she chose. However, if that had been her goal, she could have accomplished it long ago.

Returning to Alaska last year and then coming back now had been about something else altogether. A search for more than safety.

Because safety would have been best achieved by staying away.

She was in search of peace.

The sense of being watched made her jump with nerves. She turned quickly to find... Ward Benally.

She searched for her attorney, but he was nowhere in sight, and the rest of her table's occupants had taken to the dance floor. How could she have been so preoccupied? So careless? And if her family had been keeping their distance because of her lawyer, then why hadn't they come over once he left? The fact that they were giving her space instead of pushing like they had after the first meeting surprised her. She wondered what had caused the change.

Ward dropped into an empty chair beside her. "Thank God your lawyer finally had to use the restroom. I was starting to think I would never find you alone."

Well, that explained where the lawyer went. "Unless there's a line at the men's room, which there never is, he'll be back soon. You should go."

Brea kept her eyes fixed forward on Ada Joy, whose arms raised as she delivered an elongated high note.

Ward didn't budge. "I'm curious why you're still around. I thought for sure you would disappear into another country, this time one without extradition."

"You're rude," she snapped, turning away from the stage to look at him hard.

He seemed so relaxed in his custom-fit tuxedo. He flexed his jaw. Arrogantly. "Just curious why you're sticking around if you intend to hold everyone at arm's length."

That was actually a good question, not that she intended to give this arrogant man a compliment. "We all need answers and this seems the best place to get them."

Her gaze drifted to the table where Naomi, her twin,

sat with her head turned toward the stage. Naomi's hand reached for Royce. An embrace of love, one Brea could recognize from across the room.

So many years had separated her from her twin. And yet...

She felt a pull toward her sister. A tether that connected them beyond typical familial lines. A deeper connection, a deeper version of love.

Yes. That is what she felt when she looked at Naomi. The kind of love that only existed between sisters, intensified by their twinship.

That alone made Brea's presence here worth it. She'd known returning was the only option the day she snuck into Naomi's room to see her nieces.

"Why now?" Ward leaned forward, his voice a whisper against Ada Joy's powerful vocals.

None of his business. If she wasn't telling her family, she sure wouldn't tell him. "I understand that you're looking out for the company, but don't you think this is between my father and me?"

Ward crossed his arms over his chest, leaning back in his chair, his gaze too perceptive. "That's the first time I've heard you refer to him as your dad."

His observation stole the wind from her lungs. Except she couldn't deny he was right.

She sipped her champagne. Swallowed, bubbles tickling her nose. Took a second to gain her composure.

"Facts are facts. He *is* my father," she said with more nonchalance than she felt. "And the facts are going to show I have done nothing to harm the company."

"You didn't leak secrets to cause chaos during the consolidation of the Mikkelson and Steele companies?"

She gave herself a moment with another strategic

sip of her champagne. "I may have spoken to the press and stirred the pot. And I may have shared more than I should, but I didn't do anything near what I've been accused of."

"Okay." His dark eyes focused on her lips. A faint blush threatened to stain her cheeks.

"You believe me?" She nearly buckled under this moment of unexpected softness.

His sarcastic laughter cut through her.

So much for that. Brea felt heat and anger rise in her throat.

"I believe you're not going to tell me anything more." He scraped back his chair. "I see your watchdog is back, so I'll go now."

His fingers lingered on the back of her chair as he moved past, just grazing her bare shoulders. The scent of musk and spice hung in the air, staying with her in ways that simultaneously intrigued and infuriated her.

What had he hoped to accomplish with this chat other than to get under her skin? If so, he had succeeded.

She'd said far more than she'd intended, and he'd gotten her to question her own motives with only a few words. She could understand why he'd been chosen to head the company.

But she wouldn't make the mistake of letting her guard down around him again. Important to know, since she'd made a decision tonight.

She wasn't going anywhere anytime soon.

Conrad wondered how much longer this dinner party could continue.

He'd been waiting for the right moment to approach

Felicity. He wanted to stack all the odds in his favor. But even if his plan to win her back was a bust, he wasn't giving up. He intended to prove he could be trusted with her heart.

As if drawn by a magnet, Conrad's eyes found Felicity in the buzzing crowd. Her black, floor-length dress stopped his breath. Flowing material gathered in a suggestive arch on her left shoulder, plummeting into a deep V that accented her breasts. Her other shoulder was bare, the asymmetrical cut further deepened by a deep slit in the hem that revealed her well-toned legs.

Try as he might, he couldn't take his eyes off her. His mouth dried, heart pumping overtime. A helluva woman.

Her gaze met his across the room, holding, the air between them crackling with awareness. She didn't look away. Instead she took a step forward. All the encouragement he needed. He strode toward her, shouldering through the crowd until he reached her. Or rather, she met him halfway in the middle of the dance floor.

He hadn't planned that part, but then he hadn't expected to see the relief and wary joy in her eyes either. He held out his arms in an invitation to dance.

Again, she surprised him by stepping into his arms without hesitation. He gathered her against his chest, the feel of her familiar and so very welcome. He rested his head against the top of her head, breathing in the scent of her shampoo and losing himself in the slow music with her.

His hand roved up and down her back in time with the jazz tune. "The party's almost over, but I don't want what we've shared to end."

There.

He'd begun to lay his thoughts bare. Knew he needed to fight for this intelligent, sexy woman.

"I don't want to keep having an affair," she said, her breath warm against his chest.

But her words chilled him. "You're still breaking things off with me?"

His heart sunk. Was he too late? He knew his words the other day had found their mark. Dealt her pain. Conrad wanted to take them back. Spend his days proving that moment wrong.

"No, not at all." She looked up at him, her heart in her eyes. "I'm saying I want more than an affair. I want us to have a future."

Her admission filled him with so much relief, he refused to let the opportunity pass. He would do his best to reassure her. "I'm happy to hear that, because…" He drew in a bracing breath, about to utter the most important admission of his life. "I've fallen in love with you. And I want the opportunity to prove you can trust my love will last."

Her arms slid up around his neck and she stepped closer into his embrace, swaying. "That's so wonderful to hear, because I've fallen in love with you, too."

Of everything he'd imagined she would say back to him, this hadn't been on the list. But he didn't intend to complain.

"You're making this too easy for me. I owe you an apology for the way I spoke to you. I was speaking to you from my own fears, and that wasn't fair to you."

"I said some hurtful things to you, as well."

"Wait. I need to say this. You were right about so many things." He swallowed hard but refused to give her anything less than his best. "It rattled me seeing

Trystan and Isabeau, and realizing that without a doubt I'd buried my own wish for kids in my relationship with my nieces and nephews. But I don't want to hide from my own future anymore."

Her eyes showed no condemnation, no *I told you so*. Just quiet acceptance and love. Best of all, love.

He held her closer, her body a perfect fit to his. "I deserve a happy future, and more importantly—to me—so do you. Starting now."

"Right now? I'm intrigued." She smiled up at him, her hazel eyes warm as a Texas summer. She whispered in his ear, her breathy words sending shivers down his spine. "You can still romance me. I won't complain."

He knew she appreciated his gifts, but this time together meant more to her. As he mulled that over, it made sense. She'd received precious little attention from the people in her life, instead always giving hers to them.

He intended to make up for that, spoiling her in every way possible.

"Just what I wanted to hear." His heart fuller than he'd even dared hope, he guided her off the dance floor, exchanging a look with his brother. Jack had agreed to take care of the party wrap-up if Conrad persuaded Felicity to leave early. Which he had. "Come this way, my love."

He snagged their coats on the way out, their path down the corridor lined with potted trees covered in small white lights. He couldn't wait to get her alone. The sliding doors opened to the outside.

Where his horse—Jackson—waited in the parking lot.

Felicity gasped in pleased surprise. Damn straight,

he still intended to romance her. Conrad took the reins from the groom and swung into the creaking saddle. The smile in her eyes rivaled the glistening stars.

He reached a gloved hand down for Felicity, and she clasped it without hesitation. He drew her up in front of him, then took a blanket from the groom and draped it over her legs. He set the horse into motion, the clop, clop of the hooves echoing his heart hammering against his rib cage at having her close again.

Tucking her head under his chin, she hugged the blanket tighter. "You weren't kidding when you said you planned to keep romancing me."

"I've been thinking we should pick out your next gift together. Something along the lines of a ring with a diamond so big it rivals the northern lights."

She stilled against him, tipping her face up to look at him. "Are you…?"

"Proposing?" While he hadn't planned that part, it felt right. "Yes, yes, I am. I want you to marry me, to be the mother of those incredible older kids we're going to adopt. To be my wife, my partner for life."

"Of course I will." She sealed her answer with a kiss, before whispering against his lips, "You are the love of my life. You are my future. And I look forward to making our dreams come true together."

A sigh of relief and happiness racked through him. He'd hoped this would be her answer, but had intended to be patient if she'd said no. Now, knowing that she was his and he was hers…his dreams had already come true, thanks to her.

She slid her arms around his waist. "I've been thinking."

The gesture felt right. Natural.

"About what?" Conrad squeezed his calves slightly. Jackson perked up, his ears attentive as they maneuvered toward the deserted side road. The clop of Jackson's hooves softened, cushioned by the fresh powder of snow.

They moved farther down the road. Snow clung to the pine branches that flanked the road. A giant moose moved through the shadows of the trees. Illuminated only by the silver moonlight.

She leaned closer. Settled into him, deepened her seat in the saddle. A whisper leaped from her lips. "Let's elope."

Had he misheard? "As in get married now?"

She laughed softly, her breath puffing into the cold night air. "That's generally what *elope* means."

The more he thought about it, the more her proposal felt right. "You're sure?"

"I'm sure that I love you," she said, staring up into his eyes with all that love shining through, "and that I don't want to wait to spend the rest of my life with you."

He also realized she was offering this to alleviate any fears he might have of a repeat of a broken engagement. He needed to be certain this was right for her, though. "And you trust me?"

"I trust *us*."

Smiling, he lowered his mouth to hers, kissing the woman who would soon be his wife, who would forever be in his heart.

* * * * *

THE BILLIONAIRE'S
BRIDAL BARGAIN

LYNNE GRAHAM

CHAPTER ONE

CESARE SABATINO FLIPPED open the file sent by special delivery and groaned out loud, his darkly handsome features betraying his disbelief.

There were two photos included in the file, one of a nubile blonde teenager called Cristina and the other of her older sister Elisabetta. Was this familial insanity to visit yet another generation? Cesare raked long brown fingers through his luxuriant black hair, frustration pumping through every long lean line of his powerful body. He really didn't have time for such nonsense in the middle of his working day. What was his father, Goffredo, playing at?

'What's up?' Jonathan, his friend and a director of the Sabatino pharmaceutical empire, asked.

In answer, Cesare tossed the file to the other man. 'Look at it and weep at the madness that can afflict even one's seemingly sane relatives,' he urged.

Frowning, Jonathan glanced through the sparse file and studied the photos. 'The blonde's not bad but a bit on the young side. The other one with the woolly hat on looks like a scarecrow. What on earth is the connection between you and some Yorkshire farming family?'

'It's a long story,' Cesare warned him.

Jonathan hitched his well-cut trousers and took a seat. 'Interesting?'

Cesare grimaced. 'Only moderately. In the nineteen thirties my family owned a small island called Lionos in the Aegean Sea. Most of my ancestors on my father's side are buried there. My grandmother, Athene, was born and raised there. But when her father went bust, Lionos was sold to an Italian called Geraldo Luccini.'

Jonathan shrugged. 'Fortunes rise and fall.'

'Matters, however, took a turn for the worse when Athene's brother decided to get the island back into family hands by marrying Luccini's daughter and then chose to jilt her at the altar.'

The other man raised his brows. 'Nice...'

'Her father was so enraged by the slight to his daughter and his family that Lionos was eternally tied up in Geraldo's exceedingly complex will.'

'In what way?'

'The island cannot be sold and the two young women in that file are the current owners of Lionos by inheritance through their mother. The island can only be regained by my family through marriage between a Zirondi and a Luccini descendant and the birth of a child.'

'You're not serious?' Jonathan was amazed.

'A generation back, my father was serious enough to propose marriage to the mother of those two girls, Francesca, although I would point out that he genuinely fell in love with her. Luckily for us all, however, when he proposed she turned him down and married her farmer instead.'

'Why luckily?' Jonathan queried.

'Francesca didn't settle for long with the farmer or with any of the men that followed him. Goffredo had a narrow escape,' Cesare opined, lean, strong face grim, well aware that his laid-back and rather naive father could never have coped with so fickle a wife.

'So, why has your father sent you that file?'

'He's trying to get me interested in the ongoing, "Lionos reclamation project",' Cesare said very drily, the slant of his wide, sensual mouth expressing sardonic amusement as he sketched mocking quotations marks in the air.

'He actually thinks he has a chance of persuading *you* to consider marriage with one of those two women?' Jonathan slowly shook his head for neither female appeared to be a show-stopper and Cesare enjoyed the reputation of being a connoisseur of the female sex. 'Is he crazy?'

'Always an optimist.' Cesare sighed. 'In the same way he never listens when I tell him I haven't the smallest desire to ever get married.'

'As a happily married man and father, I have to tell you that you're missing out.'

Cesare resisted a rude urge to roll his eyes in mockery. He knew that, in spite of the odds, good marriages *did* exist. His father had one, after all, and evidently Jonathan did too. But Cesare had no faith in true love and happy-ever-after stories, particularly not when his own first love had ditched him to waltz down the aisle with an extremely wealthy man, who referred to himself as being seventy-five years young. Serafina had dutifully proclaimed her love of older men all the way to the graveyard gates and was now a very rich widow, who had been chasing Cesare in the hope of a rematch ever since.

Cesare's recollections were tinged with supreme scorn. He would never make a mistake like Serafina again. It had been a boy's mistake, he reminded himself wryly. He was now far less ignorant about the nature of the female sex. He had never yet lavished his wealth on a woman who wasn't more excited by his money than by anything else he offered. A satisfied smile softened the hard line of his wide, expressive mouth when he thought of his current lover, a gorgeous French fashion model who went to great lengths to please him in bed and out of it. And all without the fatal suffocating commitment of rings or nagging or noisy kids attached. What was not to like? It was true that he was an extremely generous lover but what was money for but enjoyment when you had as much as Cesare now had?

Cesare was less amused and indeed he tensed when he strolled into his city penthouse that evening to receive the news from his manservant, Primo, that his father had arrived for an unexpected visit.

Goffredo was out on the roof terrace admiring the panoramic view of London when Cesare joined him.

'To what do I owe the honour?' he mocked.

His father, always an extrovert in the affection stakes, clasped his son in a hug as if he hadn't seen the younger man in months rather than mere weeks. 'I need to talk to you about your grandmother...'

Cesare's smile immediately faded. 'What's wrong?'

Goffredo grimaced. 'Athene needs a coronary by-pass. Hopefully it will relieve her angina.'

Cesare had stilled, a frown line etched between his level ebony brows. 'She's seventy-five.'

'The prognosis for her recovery is excellent,' his father told him reassuringly. 'Unfortunately the real problem is my mother's outlook on life. She thinks she's too old for surgery. She thinks she's had her three score years and ten and should be grateful for it.'

'That's ridiculous. If necessary, I'll go and talk some sense into her,' Cesare said impatiently.

'She needs something to look forward to…some motivation to make her believe that the pain and stress of surgery will be worthwhile.'

Cesare released his breath in a slow hiss. 'I hope you're not talking about Lionos. That's nothing but a pipe dream.'

Goffredo studied his only son with compressed lips. 'Since when have you been defeatist about any challenge?'

'I'm too clever to tilt at windmills,' Cesare said drily.

'But surely you have some imagination? Some… what is it you chaps call it now? The ability to think outside the box?' the older man persisted. 'Times have changed, Cesare. The world has moved on and when it comes to the island you have a power that I was never blessed with.'

Cesare heaved a sigh and wished he had worked late at the office where pure calm and self-discipline ruled, the very building blocks of his lifestyle. 'And what power would that be?' he asked reluctantly.

'You are incredibly wealthy and the current owners of the island are dirt-poor.'

'But the will is watertight.'

'Money could be a great persuader,' his father reasoned. 'You don't want a wife and probably neither of Francesca's daughters wants a real husband at such a young age. Why can't you come to some sort of business arrangement with one of them?'

Cesare shook his arrogant dark head. 'You're asking me to try and get round the will?'

'The will has already been minutely appraised by a top inheritance lawyer in Rome. If you can marry one of those girls, you will have the right to visit the island and, what is more important, you will have the right to take your grandmother there,' Goffredo outlined, clearly expecting his son to be impressed by that revelation.

Instead, Cesare suppressed a groan of impatience. 'And what's that worth at the end of the day? It's *not* ownership, it's *not* getting the island back into the family.'

'Even a visit after all the years that have passed would be a source of great joy to your grandmother,' Goffredo pointed out in a tone of reproach.

'I always understood that visiting the island was against the terms of the will.'

'Not if a marriage has first taken place. That is a distinction that it took a lawyer to point out. Certainly, if any of us were to visit without that security, Francesca's daughters would forfeit their inheritance and the island would go to the government by default.'

'Which would please no one but the government,' Cesare conceded wryly. 'Do you really think that a measly visit to the island would mean that much to Nonna?' he pressed.

'The right to pay her respects again at her parents'

graves? To see the house where she was born and where she married and first lived with my father? She has many happy memories of Lionos.'

'But would one short visit satisfy her? It's my belief that she has always dreamt of living out her life there and that's out of the question because a child has to be born to fulfil the full terms of the will and grant us the right to put down roots on the island again.'

'There is a very good chance that clause could be set aside in court as unreasonable. Human rights law has already altered many matters once set in stone,' Goffredo reasoned with enthusiasm.

'It's doubtful,' Cesare argued. 'It would take many years and a great deal of money to take it to court and the government would naturally fight any change we sought. The court option won't work in my lifetime. And what woman is going to marry and have a child with me, to allow me to inherit an uninhabited, un-developed island? Even if I did offer to buy the island from her once we were married.'

It was his father's turn to groan. 'You must know how much of a catch you are, Cesare. *Madre di Dio*, you've been beating the women off with a stick since you were a teenager!'

Cesare dealt him an amused look. 'And you don't think it would be a little immoral to conceive a child for such a purpose?'

'As I've already stated,' Goffredo proclaimed with dignity, 'I am not suggesting you go *that* far.'

'But I couldn't reclaim the island for the family *without* going that far,' Cesare fielded very drily. 'And if I can't buy it or gain anything beyond guaranteeing Nonna the right to visit the wretched place one more time, what is the point of approaching some stranger and trying to bribe her?'

'Is that your last word on the subject?' his father asked stiffly when the silence dragged.

'I'm a practical man,' Cesare murmured wryly. 'If we could regain the island I could see some point of pursuing this.'

The older man halted on his passage towards the door and turned back to face his son with compressed lips. 'You could at least approach Francesca's daughters and see if something could be worked out. You could at least *try...*'

When his father departed in high dudgeon, Cesare swore long and low in frustration. Goffredo was so temperamental and so easily carried away. He was good at getting bright ideas but not so smooth with the follow-up or the fallout. His son, on the other hand, never let emotion or sentiment cloud his judgement and rarely got excited about anything.

Even so, Cesare did break into a sweat when he thought about his grandmother's need for surgery and her lack of interest in having it. In his opinion, Athene was probably bored and convinced that life had no further interesting challenges to offer. She was also probably a little frightened of the surgical procedure as well. His grandmother was such a strong and courageous woman that people frequently failed to recognise that she had her fears and weaknesses just like everyone else.

Cesare's own mother had died on the day he was born and Goffredo's Greek mother, Athene, had come to her widowed son's rescue. While Goffredo had grieved and struggled to build up his first business and establish some security, Athene had taken charge of raising Cesare. Even before he'd started school he had been playing chess, reading and doing advanced maths for enjoyment. His grandmother had been quick to recognise her grandson's prodigious intellectual gifts. Unlike his father, she had not been intimidated by his genius IQ and against a background of loving support Athene had given Cesare every opportunity to flourish and develop at his own pace. He owed his *nonna* a great deal and she was still the only woman in the world whom Cesare had ever truly cared about. But then he had never been an emotional man, had never been able to understand or feel truly comfortable around more demonstrative personalities. He was astute, level-headed and controlled in every field of his life yet he had a soft spot in his heart for his grandmother that he would not have admitted to a living soul.

A business arrangement, Cesare ruminated broodingly, flicking open the file again. There was no prospect of him approaching the teenager but the plain young woman in the woolly hat and old coat? Could he even contemplate such a gross and unsavoury lowering of his high standards? He was conservative in his tastes and not an easy man to please but if the prize was great enough, he was clever enough to compromise and adapt, wasn't he? Aware that very few people were cleverer than he was, Cesare contemplated the startling idea of getting married and grimaced with distaste at the threat of being forced to live in such close contact with another human being.

'You should've sent Hero off to the knackers when I told you to!' Brian Whitaker bit out in disgust. 'Instead you've kept him eating his head off in that stable. How can we afford that with the cost of feed what it is?'

'Chrissie's very fond of Hero. She's coming home from uni next week and I wanted her to have the chance to say goodbye.' Lizzie kept her voice low rather than risk stoking her father's already irascible temper. The older man was standing by the kitchen table, his trembling hands—the most visible symptom of the Parkinson's disease that had ravaged his once strong body—braced on the chair back as he glowered at his daughter, his gaunt, weathered face grim with censure.

'And if you do that, she'll weep and she'll wail and she'll try to talk you out of it again. What's the point of that? You tried to sell him and there were no takers,' he reminded her with biting impatience. 'You're a bloody *useless* farmer, Lizzie!'

'That horse charity across the valley may have a space coming up this week,' Lizzie told him, barely even flinching from her father's scorn because his dissatisfaction was so familiar to her. 'I was hoping for the best.'

'Since when has hoping for the best paid the bills?' Brian demanded with withering contempt. 'Chrissie should be home here helping you, not wasting her time studying!'

Lizzie compressed her lips, wincing at the idea that her kid sister should also sacrifice her education to their daily struggle for survival against an ever-increasing tide of debt. The farm was failing but it had been failing for a long time. Unfortunately her father had never approved of Chrissie's desire to go to university. His world stopped at the borders of the farm and he had very little interest in anything beyond it. Lizzie understood his reasoning because her world had shrunk to the same boundaries once she had left school at sixteen.

At the same time, though, she adored the kid sister she had struggled to protect throughout their dysfunctional childhood and was willing to take a lot of grief from her father if it meant that the younger woman could enjoy the youthful freedom and opportunities that she herself had been denied. In fact Lizzie had been as proud as any mother when Chrissie had won a place to study Literature at Oxford. Although she missed Chrissie, she would not have wished her own life of back-breaking toil and isolation on anyone she loved.

As Lizzie dug her feet back into her muddy boots a small low-slung shaggy dog, whose oddly proportioned body reflected his very mixed ancestry, greeted her at the back door with his feeding bowl in his mouth.

'Oh, I'm so sorry, Archie…I forgot about you,' Lizzie groaned, climbing out of the boots again to trudge back across the kitchen floor and fill the dog bowl. While she mentally listed all the many, many tasks she had yet to accomplish she heard the reassuring roar of a football game playing on the television in the room next door and some of the tension eased from her slight shoulders. Watching some sport and forgetting his aches and pains for a little while would put her father in a better mood.

Her father was a difficult man, but then his life had always been challenging. In his case hard work and commitment to the farm had failed to pay off.

He had taken on the farm tenancy at a young age and had always had to work alone. Her late mother, Francesca, had only lasted a few years as a farmer's wife before running off with a man she deemed to have more favourable prospects. Soured by the divorce that followed, Brian Whitaker had not remarried. When Lizzie was twelve, Francesca had died suddenly and her father had been landed with the responsibility of two daughters who were practically strangers to him. The older man had done his best even though he could never resist an opportunity to remind Lizzie that she would never be the strong capable son he had wanted and needed to help him on the farm. He had barely passed fifty when ill health had handicapped him and prevented him from doing physical work.

Lizzie knew she was a disappointment to the older man but then she was used to falling short of other people's expectations. Her mother had longed for a more outgoing, fun-loving child than shy, socially awkward Lizzie had proved to be. Her father had wanted a son, not a daughter. Even her fiancé had left her for a woman who seemed to be a far more successful farmer's wife than Lizzie could ever have hoped to be. Sadly, Lizzie had become accustomed to not measuring up and had learned to simply get on with the job at hand rather than dwell on her own deficiencies.

She started her day off with the easy task of feeding the hens and gathering the eggs. Then she fed Hero, whose feed she was buying solely from her earnings from working Saturday nights behind the bar of the village pub. She didn't earn a wage at home for her labour. How could she take a wage out of the kitty every week when the rising overdraft at the bank was a constant worry? Household bills, feed and fuel costs were necessities that had to come out of that overdraft and she was dreading the arrival of yet another warning letter from the bank.

She loaded the slurry tank to spray the meadow field before her father could complain about how far behind she was with the spring schedule. Archie leapt into the tractor cab with her and sat panting by her side. He still wore the old leather collar punched with his name that he had arrived with. When she had found him wandering the fields, hungry and bedraggled, Lizzie had reckoned he had been dumped at the side of the road and, sadly, nobody had ever come looking for him. She suspected that his formerly expensive collar revealed that he had once been a much-loved pet, possibly abandoned because his elderly owner had passed away.

When he'd first arrived, he had hung out with their aging sheepdog, Shep, and had demonstrated a surprising talent for picking up Shep's skills so that when Shep had died even Brian Whitaker had acknowledged that Archie could make himself useful round the farm. Lizzie, on the other hand, utterly adored Archie. He curled up at her feet in bed at night and allowed himself to be cuddled whenever she was low.

She was driving back to the yard to refill the slurry tank when she saw a long, sleek, glossy black car filtering off the main road into the farm lane. Her brow furrowed at the sight. She couldn't picture anyone coming in a car that big and expensive to buy the free-range eggs she sold. Parking the tractor by the fence, she climbed out with Archie below one arm, stooping to let her pet down.

That was Cesare's first glimpse of Lizzie. She glanced up as she unbent and the limo slowed to ease past the tractor. He saw that though she might dress like a bag lady she had skin as translucent as the finest porcelain and eyes the colour of prized jade. He breathed in deep and slow.

His driver got out of the car only to come under immediate attack by what was clearly a vicious dog but which more closely resembled a scruffy fur muff on short legs. As the woman captured the dog to restrain it and before his driver could open the door for him Cesare sprang out and instantly the offensive stench of the farm yard assaulted his fastidious nostrils. His intense concentration trained on his quarry, he simply held his breath while lazily wondering if she smelt as well. When his father had said the Whitaker family was dirt-poor he had clearly not been joking. The farmhouse bore no resemblance to a picturesque country cottage with roses round the door. The rain guttering sagged, the windows needed replacing and the paint was peeling off the front door.

'Are you looking for directions?' Lizzie asked as the tall black-haired male emerged in a fluid shift of long limbs from the rear seat.

Cesare straightened and straight away focused on her pouty pink mouth. That was three unexpected pluses in a row, he acknowledged in surprise. Lizzie Whitaker had great skin, beautiful eyes and a mouth that made a man think of sinning, and Cesare had few inhibitions when it came to the sins of sexual pleasure. Indeed, his hot-blooded nature and need for regular sex were the two traits he deemed potential weaknesses, he acknowledged wryly.

'Directions?' he queried, disconcerted by the disruptive drift of his own thoughts, anathema to his self-discipline. In spite of his exasperation, his mind continued to pick up on the fact that Lizzie Whitaker was small, possibly only a few inches over five feet tall, and seemingly slender below the wholly dreadful worn and stained green jacket and baggy workman's overalls she wore beneath. The woolly hat pulled low on her brow made her eyes look enormous as she stared up at him much as if he'd stepped out of a spaceship in front of her.

One glance at the stranger had reduced Lizzie to gaping in an almost spellbound moment out of time. He was simply...*stunning* from his luxuriant black hair to his dark-as-bitter-chocolate deep-set eyes and strong, uncompromisingly masculine jawline. In truth she had never ever seen a more dazzling man and that disconcertingly intimate thought froze her in place like a tongue-tied schoolgirl.

'I assumed you were lost,' Lizzie explained weakly, finding it a challenge to fill her lungs with oxygen while he looked directly at her with eyes that, even lit by the weak spring sunshine, shifted to a glorious shade of bronzed gold. For a split second, she felt as if she were drowning and she shook her head slightly, struggling to think straight and act normally, her colour rising steadily as she fought the unfamiliar lassitude engulfing her.

'No, I'm not lost... This *is* the Whitaker farm?'

'Yes, I'm Lizzie Whitaker...'

Only the British could take a pretty name like Elisabetta and shorten it to something so commonplace, Cesare decided irritably. 'I'm Cesare Sabatino.'

Her jade eyes widened. His foreign-sounding name was meaningless to her ears because she barely recognised a syllable of it. 'Sorry, I didn't catch that…'

His beautifully sensual mouth quirked. 'You don't speak Italian?'

'The odd word, not much. Are you Italian?' Lizzie asked, feeling awkward as soon as she realised that he somehow knew that her mother had been of Italian extraction. Francesca had actually planned to raise her daughters to be bilingual but Brian Whitaker had objected vehemently to the practice as soon as his children began using words he couldn't understand and from that point on English had become the only language in their home.

'*Sì*, I'm Italian,' Cesare confirmed, sliding a lean brown hand into his jacket to withdraw a business card and present it to her. The extraordinary grace of his every physical gesture also ensnared her attention and she had to force her gaze down to the card.

Unfortunately, his name was no more comprehensible to Lizzie when she saw it printed. 'Your name's Caesar,' she pronounced with some satisfaction.

A muscle tugged at the corner of his unsmiling mouth. 'Not Caesar. We're not in ancient Rome. It's Chay-zar-ray,' he sounded out with perfect diction, his exotic accent underlining every syllable with a honeyed mellifluence that spiralled sinuously round her to create the strangest sense of dislocation.

'Chay-zar-ray,' she repeated politely while thinking that it was a heck of a fussy mouthful for a first name and that Caesar would have been much more straightforward. 'And you're here *because*…?'

Cesare stiffened, innate aggression powering him

at that facetious tone. He was not accustomed to being prompted to get to the point faster and as if the dog had a sensor tracking his mood it began growling soft and low. 'May we go indoors to discuss that?'

Bemused by the effect he was having on her and fiercely irritated by his take-charge manner, Lizzie lifted her chin. 'Couldn't we just talk here? This is the middle of my working day,' she told him truthfully.

Cesare gritted his perfect white teeth and shifted almost imperceptibly closer. The dog loosed a warning snarl and clamped his teeth to the corner of his cashmere overcoat, pulling at it. Cesare sent a winging glance down at the offending animal.

'Archie, *no*!' Lizzie intervened. 'I'm afraid he's very protective of me.'

Archie tugged and tugged at the corner of the overcoat and failed to shift Cesare an inch further away from his quarry. To the best of his ability Cesare ignored the entire canine assault.

'Oh, for goodness' sake, Archie!' Lizzie finally exclaimed, crouching down to physically detach the dog's jaw from the expensive cloth, noting in dismay that a small tear had been inflicted and cherishing little hope that the damage would not be noted.

Whoever he was, Cesare Sabatino wore clothing that looked incredibly expensive and fitted too well to be anything other than individually designed for its wearer. He wore a faultlessly tailored black suit below the coat and his highly polished shoes were marred only by the skiff of mud that continually covered the yard at damp times of the year. He looked like a high-powered businessman, tycoon or some such thing. Why on earth was such a man coming to visit the farm?

'Are you from our bank?' Lizzie asked abruptly.

'No. I am a businessman,' Cesare admitted calmly.

'You're here to see my father for some reason?' Lizzie prompted apprehensively.

'No…I'm here to see you,' Cesare framed succinctly as she scrambled upright clutching the still-growling dog to her chest.

'Me?' Lizzie exclaimed in astonishment, her gaze colliding with glittering eyes that gleamed like highly polished gold, enhanced by the thick black velvet fringe of his long lashes. Below her clothes, her nipples pinched almost painfully tight and a flare of sudden heat darted down into her pelvis, making her feel extremely uncomfortable. 'Why on earth would you want to see me? Oh, come indoors, if you must,' she completed wearily. 'But I warn you, it's a mess.'

Trudging to the side of the house, Lizzie kicked off her boots and thrust the door open on the untidy kitchen.

Cesare's nostrils flared as he scanned the cluttered room, taking in the pile of dishes heaped in the sink and the remains of someone's meal still lying on the pine table. Well, he certainly wouldn't be marrying her for her housekeeping skills, he reflected grimly as the dog slunk below the table to continue growling unabated and his reluctant hostess removed her coat and yanked off her woolly hat before hurriedly clearing the table and yanking out a chair for him.

'Coffee…or tea?' Lizzie enquired.

Cesare's entire attention was still locked to the wealth of silver-coloured silky hair that, freed from the woolly hat, now tumbled round her shoulders. It was gorgeous in spite of the odd murky brown tips of colour that damaged the effect. Dip-dying, he thought dimly, vaguely recalling the phrase being used by one of his team who had showed up at the office one day with ludicrously colourful half-blonde, half-pink locks. He blinked, black lashes long as fly swats momentarily concealing his bemused gaze.

'Coffee,' he replied, feeling that he was being very brave and polite in the face of the messy kitchen and standards of hygiene that he suspected might be much lower than he was used to receiving.

In a graceful movement, he doffed his coat and draped it across the back of a chair. Lizzie filled the kettle at the sink and put it on the hotplate on the ancient coal-fired cooking range while taking in the full effect of her visitor's snazzy appearance. He looked like a city slicker who belonged on a glossy magazine cover, the sort of publication that showed how fashion-conscious men should dress. To a woman used to men wearing dirty, often unkempt clothing suitable for outdoor work, he had all the appeal of a fantasy. He really was physically beautiful in every possible way and so unfamiliar was she with that level of male magnetism that she was challenged to drag her eyes from his lean, powerful figure.

Dredging her thoughts from the weird sticking point they had reached, she went to the door of the lounge. A businessman, she reminded herself doggedly. Successful businessmen—and he looked *very* successful—were cold-blooded, calculating individuals, ready to do anything for profit and divorced from sentiment. He certainly emanated that arrogant vibe with his polished image that was so totally inappropriate for a male visiting a working farm. 'Dad? We have a visitor. Do you want tea?'

'A visitor?' Brian Whitaker rose with a frown from his chair and came with shuffling, poorly balanced steps into the kitchen.

Lizzie removed mugs from the cupboard while the two men introduced themselves.

'I'm here about the island that Lizzie and her sister inherited from your late wife,' Cesare explained calmly.

The silence of astonishment engulfed his companions. Lizzie studied him wide-eyed while her father turned his head towards him in a frowning attitude of incredulity.

'It's a rubbish inheritance…nothing but a bad joke!' Lizzie's father contended in a burst of unrestrained bitterness. 'It stands to reason that an inheritance you can't use or sell is worthless… What use is that to anyone? So, that's why you're here? Another fool chasing the pot of gold at the end of the rainbow?'

'Dad!' Lizzie exclaimed in consternation at the older man's blatant scorn.

She wished she had guessed why the Italian had come to visit and scolded herself for not immediately making the association between his nationality and the legacy left to her and Chrissie by their mother. Over the years the island that couldn't be sold had been a source of much bitterness in her family, particularly when money was in such short supply. She lifted the kettle off the range and hastily made the drinks while she wondered what on earth Cesare hoped to achieve by visiting them.

'I'll put your tea in the lounge, Dad,' she said, keen to remove her father from the dialogue, afraid of what he might say in his blunt and challenging way.

Brian Whitaker stole a glance at the Italian's shuttered dark face, not displeased by the effect of having had his say. 'I'll leave you to it, then. After all, the only reason *he* could be here is that he's coming a-courting!' he completed with a derisive laugh that sent a hot tide of colour flaring below Lizzie's pale skin. 'Good luck to you! Lizzie was ditched by the neighbour a couple of years ago and she hasn't been out on a date since then!'

CHAPTER TWO

LIZZIE WANTED THE tiled floor to open up and swallow her where she stood. Being humiliated in front of a stranger felt even more painful than the snide comments and pitying appraisals from the village locals that had followed the ending of her engagement to Andrew Brook two years earlier. A month later, Andrew had married Esther, who had already been pregnant with their son. She stiffened her facial muscles, made the tea and the coffee and even contrived to politely ask if the visitor took sugar.

Wide, sensual mouth set in a grim line, Cesare surveyed Lizzie's rigid back view, noting the narrow cut of her waist and the slender, delicate curves merely hinted at by the overalls. Her father had been cruel taking her down like that in front of an audience. Not a date since, though? He was astonished because, unflattering as her clothing was, Cesare had immediately recognised that she was a beauty. Not perhaps a conventional beauty, he was willing to admit, not the kind of beauty that set the world on fire but certainly the type that should make the average male look more than once. What was wrong with the local men?

'Sorry about Dad,' Lizzie apologised in a brittle

voice, setting the coffee down carefully on the table in front of him, catching the evocative scent of some citrusy cologne as she briefly leant closer and stiffening as a result of the sudden warmth pooling in her pelvis. Never had anyone made her feel more uncomfortable in her own home.

'You don't need to apologise, *cara*,' Cesare parried.

'But I should explain. My parents resented the will—personally, I never think about it. Unfortunately, the island was a sore point in our lives when I was a child because money was tight.'

'Have you ever visited Lionos?'

'No, I've never had the opportunity. Mum went once with one of her boyfriends and stayed for a week. She wasn't too impressed,' Lizzie revealed ruefully while she scanned his lean, strong face, taking in the high cheekbones, straight nose and hard, masculine mouth before involuntarily sliding her gaze upward again to take another sweep of those absolutely devastating dark golden eyes of his. 'I think Mum was expecting luxury but I believe the accommodation was more basic.'

'The will endowed the island with a trust and I understand a caretaker and his family live nearby to maintain the property.'

Lizzie cocked her head to one side, her shattered nerves slowly stabilising at his lack of comment about her father's outburst. Pale, silky hair slid across her cheekbone and Cesare looked up into those wide hazel-green eyes framed with soft honey-brown lashes, and suddenly he was aware of the heavy pulse of heat at his groin and the muscles in his broad shoulders pulled taut as ropes as he resisted that sirens' call of lust with all his might.

'Yes. But the trust only covers maintenance costs, not improvements, and I understand that the house is still firmly stuck in the thirties. Mum also assumed that the caretaker would cook and clean for them but instead the man and his wife told her that they weren't servants and she had to look after herself,' Lizzie volunteered wryly. 'All in all she found it a very expensive jaunt by the time they'd paid someone to take them out to the island and deliver food while they were there.'

'Naturally you want to know what I'm doing here,' Cesare murmured smoothly.

'Well, I don't think you've come a-courting,' Lizzie fielded with a shrug that dismissed her father's gibe but completely failed to hide her discomfiture at that crack.

'Not in the conventional sense,' Cesare agreed, lean fingers flexing round the mug of coffee. It was barely drinkable but he doubted if she expended much concern when it came to the domestic front, which was hardly surprising when it was obvious that she was struggling to keep the farm afloat single-handedly. She was leaning back against the cooking range with defensively folded arms, trying to appear relaxed but visibly as tense as a bow string. 'But I do think we might be able to come to a business arrangement.'

Lizzie frowned, dragging her wandering gaze from his lean, extravagantly handsome features with a slight rise of colour, scolding herself for her lack of concentration, questioning what it was about him that kept her looking back at him again and again, long after curiosity should have been satisfied. 'A business arrangement?'

'I don't think your sister enters this as she's still a teenager. Obviously as co-owner of the island, you would have to confer with her, but I'm willing to offer you a substantial amount of money to go through a marriage ceremony with me.'

Her lashes fluttered in shock because he had knocked her for six. Inexplicably, his cool sophistication and smooth delivery made the fantastic proposition he had just made seem almost workaday and acceptable. 'Seriously? *Just* a marriage ceremony? But what would you get out of that?'

Cesare told her about his grandmother's deep attachment to the island and her approaching surgery. As she listened, Lizzie nodded slowly, strangely touched by the softer tone he couldn't help employing when talking about the old lady. His screened gaze and the faint hint of flush along his spectacular cheekbones encouraged her scrutiny to linger with helpless curiosity. He was not quite as cold and tough as he seemed on the surface, she acknowledged in surprise. But she could see that he was very uncomfortable with showing emotion.

'Isn't circumventing the will against the law?' she prompted in a small voice.

'I wasn't planning to publicise the fact. For the sake of appearances we would have to pretend that the marriage was the real deal for a few months at least.'

'And the "having a child" bit? Where does that come in?' Lizzie could not resist asking.

'Whether it comes into our arrangement or not is up to you. I will pay generously for the right to take my grandmother to the island for a visit and if we were to contrive to meet the *full* terms of the will, you and your sister would stand to collect a couple of million pounds, at the very least, from selling Lionos to me,' he spelt out quietly. 'I am an extremely wealthy man and I will pay a high price to bring the island back into my family.'

Millions? Lizzie's mouth ran dry and she lost colour, eyes dropping to focus on the long, lean brown fingers gracefully coiled round the mug of coffee. For a split second she saw her every hope and dream fulfilled by ill-gotten gains. Her father could give up the farm tenancy, and she and Chrissie could buy him a house in the village where he would be able to go to the pub quizzes he loved and meet up with his cronies. Chrissie would be able to chuck in her two part-time jobs, concentrate on her studies and pay off her student loans. Being freed from the burden of the farm would enable Lizzie to go and train for a job she would enjoy. Archie could get some professional grooming and a new collar and live on the very best pet food…

It became an increasingly stupid dream and she reddened with mortification, hands clenching by her side as she suppressed her wild imaginings in shame at how susceptible she had been when tempted by the equivalent of a lottery win.

'I couldn't have a child with a stranger…or bring a child into the world for such a purpose,' she confided. 'But if it's any consolation, just for a minute there I wished I was the sort of woman who could.'

'Think it over,' Cesare suggested, having registered without surprise that the suggestion of oodles of cash had finally fully engaged her in their discussion. He rose fluidly upright and tapped the business card he had left on the table top. 'My cell number.'

He was very big, possibly a foot taller than she was, with broad shoulders, narrow hips and long, powerful legs.

'Yes, well, there's a lot to think over,' she muttered uneasily.

He reached for his coat and turned back to her, dark eyes bright and shimmering as topaz in sunshine. 'There are two options and either will bring in a profit for you.'

'You definitely talk like a businessman,' she remarked, unimpressed by the statement, ashamed of her temporary dive into a fantasy land where every sheep had a proverbial golden fleece. Could it really be that easy to go from being a decent person to a mercenary one? she was asking herself worriedly.

'I am trying to negotiate a business arrangement,' he pointed out drily.

'Was it *your* father who once asked my mother to marry him?' Lizzie could not stop herself from enquiring. 'Or was that someone from another branch of your family?'

Cesare came to a halt. 'No, that was my father and it wasn't a business proposal. He fell hard for your mother and they were engaged when she came over here on holiday. Having met your father, however, she preferred him,' he advanced without any expression at all.

But Lizzie recognised the unspoken disapproval in the hard bones of his lean, strong face and she flushed because her mother had been decidedly changeable in her affections and there was no denying the fact. Predictably, Francesca had never admitted that she had actually got engaged to their father's predecessor. But then every man that came along had been the love of Francesca's life until either he revealed his true character or someone else seized her interest. Her mother had always moved on without a backward glance, never once pausing to try and work on a relationship or considering the cost of such continual upheaval in the lives of her two young children.

'I'm afraid I'm not a sentimental man,' Cesare imparted. 'I'm innately practical in every way. Why shouldn't you make what you can of your inheritance for your family's benefit?'

'Because it just doesn't seem right,' Lizzie confided uncertainly. 'It's not what my great-grandfather intended either when he drew up that will.'

'No, he wanted revenge because my grandmother's brother jilted his daughter at the altar. My great-uncle was in the wrong but plunging the island into legal limbo simply to keep it out of my family's hands was no more justifiable,' Cesare countered with complete assurance. 'It's been that way for nearly eighty years but I believe that we have the power to change that.'

'The ethics involved aren't something I've ever thought about,' Lizzie admitted, resisting the urge to confess that the island still seemed no more real to her than that fabled pot of gold at the end of the rainbow that her father had mentioned.

Cesare smiled with sudden brilliance, amused by her honesty and her lack of pretence.

His smile almost blinded her, illuminating his lean, darkly handsome face, and she wanted so badly to touch him for a disconcerting moment that she clenched her hands into fists to restrain herself. She was deeply disturbed by the effect he had on her. Indeed, she feared it because she recognised her reaction for the fierce physical attraction that it was. And nobody knew better than Francesca Whitaker's daughter how dangerous giving rein to such mindless responses could be for it had propelled her mother into one disastrous relationship after another.

In the smouldering silence, beautiful, dark golden eyes fringed with velvet black held hers and she trembled, fighting reactions she had never experienced so powerfully before.

'My offer's on the table and I'm willing to negotiate with you. Discuss it with your sister and your father but urge them to keep the matter confidential,' Cesare advised smoothly, staring down into her upturned face, attention lingering on the lush contours of her lips as he wondered what she would *taste* like. 'We could go the full distance on this… I find you appealing.'

And with that deeply unsettling comment, Cesare Sabatino swung on his heel and strode back out to the limousine sitting ready to depart. The driver leapt out to throw open the door for his passenger and Cesare lowered his proud dark head and climbed in.

Appealing? Lizzie pushed her hair back off her brow and caught her surprised reflection in the small age-spotted mirror on the wall. He was really saying that he could go to bed with her and conceive a child with her if she was willing: that was what he meant by the word *appealing*. Her face flamed. She was *not* willing. She also knew the difference between right and wrong. She knew that more money didn't necessarily mean more happiness and that a child was usually better off with a mother *and* a father.

Yet the image of the tiny boy she had glimpsed cradled in her former fiancé's arms after the child's christening in the church had pierced Lizzie with a pain greater than that inflicted by Andrew's infidelity. Lizzie had always wanted a baby and ached at the sight of infants. When Andrew had left her for Esther, she had envied Esther for her son, *not* her husband. What did that say about her? That she was as cold at heart and frigid as Andrew had once accused her of being? Even remembering that hurtful indictment, Lizzie winced and felt less than other women, knowing that she had been tried and found wanting by a young man who had only wanted a warm and loving wife. Lizzie knew that, in choosing Esther, Andrew had made the right decision for them both. Yet Lizzie had loved Andrew too in her way.

Her eyes stung with moisture, her fingers toying with the ends of the brown-tinted hair that Andrew had persuaded her to dye. The dye was growing out, a reminder of how foolish a woman could be when she tried to change herself to please a man…

But where on earth had her strong maternal instinct come from? Certainly not from her volatile mother, who in the grip of her wild infatuations had always focused her energies on the man in her life. Lizzie had not been surprised to learn of the impetuous way Francesca had evidently ditched Cesare's father to marry Lizzie's father instead. Hard Yorkshire winters and life on a shoestring, however, had dimmed Brian Whitaker's appeal for her mother and within weeks of Chrissie's birth Francesca had run off with a man who had turned out to be a drunk. His successor had been more interested in spending Francesca's recent legacy following the death of her Italian parents than in Francesca herself. Her third lover had been repeatedly unfaithful. And the fourth, who married her, had been violent.

Lizzie had always found it very hard to trust men after living through her mother's grim roll call of destructive relationships. She had struggled to protect the sister five years her junior from the constant fallout of moving home and changing schools, striving to ensure that her sibling could still enjoy her childhood and wasn't forced to grow up as quickly as Lizzie had. Almost all the happy moments in Lizzie's life had occurred when Chrissie was young and Lizzie had the comfort of knowing that her love and care was both wanted and needed by her sibling. When her sister left home to go to university it had opened a vast hole in Lizzie's life. Archie had partially filled that hole, a reality that made her grin and shrug off her deep and troubled thoughts with the acknowledgement that it was time to get back to work and concentrate on what really mattered.

'Marry him and stop making such a production out of it!' Brian Whitaker snapped at his daughter angrily. 'We don't have any other choice. The rent is going up and the bank's on the brink of calling in our loan!'

'It's not that simple, Dad,' Lizzie began to argue again.

But the older man wasn't listening. He hadn't listened to a word his daughter had said since the letter from the bank had delivered its lethal warning. 'Simple would have been you marrying Andrew. He would have taken on the tenancy. I could still have lived here. Everyone would have been happy but could you pull it off?' he derided. '*No*, you had to play fast and loose with him, wanting to *wait* to get married!'

'I wanted to get to know him properly, not rush in. I wanted our marriage to last,' Lizzie protested.

'You might as well have parcelled him up for Esther and handed him over. Andrew was our one chance to keep this place afloat and you threw him away,' he condemned bitterly. 'Now you're mouthing off about all the reasons why you can't marry a man and have a child just to improve *all* our lives!'

'A lot of women wouldn't want to do it!' It was Lizzie's parting shot, tossed over her shoulder as she stomped back into the yard with Archie dancing at her heels. A week had passed since Cesare Sabatino's visit and her father had reasoned and condemned and outright ranted at her every day for her reluctance to accept Cesare's proposal.

Hopefully, Chrissie would not be singing the same tune, Lizzie reflected ruefully as she drove her father's ancient, battered Land Rover Defender down the lane to collect her sister off the train. She had told Chrissie all about Cesare's visit on the phone and her sibling had urged her to follow her conscience and refuse to pay heed to her father's grievances.

That was, however, proving a much more major challenge than she had expected, Lizzie acknowledged heavily. Almost insurmountable problems were forming ahead of her like a string of dangerous obstacles. They could not afford to pay a higher rent when the tenancy came up for renewal and that reality would render them homeless. They could not even afford to live if the bank demanded that the loan be repaid as they were threatening to do. And *where* would they live, if the worst came to the worst? Her father had no savings. Yes, it was all very well following her conscience, Lizzie conceded wretchedly, but right now it was no good at all as a blueprint for economic survival.

Sadly, the stress of the constant arguments and anxiety was taking the edge off Lizzie's usual happy anticipation at the prospect of having her sister home for a couple of days. Chrissie, pale silver hair caught up in a sensible ponytail, blue eyes sparkling with affection, was waiting outside the station, two big cases by her side and a bulging rucksack on her slender shoulders.

'My goodness, you've brought back a lot of luggage… but it's not the end of term,' Lizzie remarked in bewilderment, thinking out loud while Chrissie concentrated on giving her a fierce hug of welcome.

'I've missed you so much,' her sibling confessed. 'And I'm going to ask you all over again—why have you still not had your hair dyed back to normal?'

'I haven't had the time…or the cash,' Lizzie muttered, hoisting a heavy case and propelling it across to the Land Rover.

'No, you're still punishing yourself for not marrying Andrew.'

'They're teaching you psychology now on your English course?' Lizzie teased.

Luggage stowed, Lizzie drove back home. 'I should warn you…Dad's on the warpath.'

'He wants you to marry the Italian and make our fortunes, right?' Chrissie groaned in despair. 'Dear old Dad, what a dinosaur he is. He tried to pressure you into marrying Andrew for the sake of the farm and now he's trying to serve you up on the altar of that stupid island! Well, you don't need to worry, you're not going to come under any pressure from me on that score. We've lived all our lives without the excitement of being rich and what you don't have, you don't miss!'

In spite of her stress level, Lizzie managed to smile. After an unrelieved overdose of her father's reproaches, Chrissie, with her positive outlook, was like a little ray of sunshine. 'You're right,' she agreed even though she knew that her kid sister was not very grounded. Chrissie had always been a dreamer, the creative one with the fluffy romantic and idealistic ideas.

In fact, while she watched Chrissie hurtle across the yard to pet her elderly pony, Hero, and feed him an apple from her pocket, her heart sank from so bald a reminder of her sister's tendency to always look on the bright side even if there wasn't one. Didn't Chrissie appreciate that if they lost their home, Hero would be one of the first sacrifices?

'I've got a surprise for you…' Chrissie told her, almost skipping back to Lizzie's side to help her unload her luggage. 'I'm home for good!'

Lizzie turned incredulous eyes on the younger woman. 'What are you talking about?'

'I'm dropping out of uni…I'm coming home,' Chrissie proffered, her soft mouth set in an unusually firm and purposeful line. 'Even with the two jobs and the student loan, I can hardly afford to eat and my overdraft is *massive*, Lizzie. I'm fed up with it, especially when I know you're slogging away here every hour God gives and still barely scratching a living. I'm going to get a job and help you whenever I can. I'm all grown up now—it's past time I pulled my weight on the home front.'

Shock was reverberating through Lizzie, closely followed by dismay. Much as she missed her sister, the very last thing she wanted was to see Chrissie throw away her education to come home and vegetate. In any case, it was a moot point that they would even have a home to offer her sibling in a few weeks' time. 'I didn't realise that you were having such a struggle.'

'I didn't want you worrying,' Chrissie confided. 'But I've learned a lot. I'd no idea it cost so much just to live. I can't possibly work any more hours, though. I've already had a warning from my tutor about my standard of work slipping... I'm so tired I'm falling asleep in lectures.'

And that was the moment when Lizzie reached her decision. What security her family had was vanishing fast but it was within her power to change everything for the better. How could she stand by and simply do nothing for her family while their lives fell apart? At the very least she should go through with the wedding to enable Cesare to take his grandmother back to the island for a visit. Whatever he paid her for that service would surely settle their outstanding bills and enable her to find a rental property in the village. But how could she go further than that? How could she have a child with him so that he could legally buy Lionos and resolve all her family's financial problems?

The answer came to Lizzie in a blinding flash of

light and she could barely credit that she had not seen the solution sooner. Cesare had said he was very practical and the answer she came up with would not only make the threat of intimacy with a stranger unnecessary but would also be a supremely sensible approach. Suddenly the sensation of weighty responsibility and dread on her shoulders and spine evaporated and she straightened, even cracking a brief smile at the heady prospect of finally being in full control of her life again.

'You're going back to university on Sunday, young lady,' Lizzie told her kid sister firmly. 'You will quit your part-time jobs and concentrate on your studies. I will ensure that you manage.'

'You can't marry the guy, Lizzie!' Chrissie gasped in horror. 'You simply *can't*!'

Lizzie thought fast and breathed in deep before she sat down at the kitchen table. 'Let me be honest with you. I've spent eight years working round the clock on this farm. I've had no time for friends and I've had very little social life. I have no decent clothes or jewellery and I don't even know how to put on make-up properly.'

'But that doesn't mean you have to give way to Dad and make a sacrifice of yourself.'

'Has it occurred to you that maybe I *want* to marry Cesare and have a child? He's a very handsome man and you know how much I've always wanted a baby. I also would like to have enough money not to worry myself sick every time a bill comes through the letter box!' Lizzie declared, her heart-shaped face taut with vehement composure as she watched Chrissie frown and suddenly look unsure of her ground.

'I'm deadly serious,' Lizzie continued with dogged determination. 'I *want* to marry Cesare. It's the best thing for all of us and, believe me, I'm not the sacrificial type.'

'I never thought…I never dreamt…' Bemused and uncertain of such an explanation from the big sister she had always loved and admired, Chrissie shook her head, frowning at her sibling. 'Are you sure, Lizzie? Have you really thought this through?'

No, Lizzie hadn't thought it all through and was determined not to run the risk of doing so before she had tied the official knot. Whatever happened she was going to marry Cesare Sabatino and miraculously sort out her own and her father's *and* Chrissie's problems. No other action now made sense. So, it would be scary and would entail deception—well, she would get braver and she would learn some new skills. My goodness, hadn't she just told a barefaced lie to the sister she loved?

She walked into her bedroom and lifted the business card Cesare had left behind. Before she could take fright, she tapped out the number on her mobile phone and then studied the blank message space.

Will agree to marry you. Talk about the rest when we next meet.

Cesare blinked down at the text and then glanced across the dinner table at Celine, whose sleek blonde perfection had entranced him for longer than most women managed. In his mind's eye, however, he was no longer seeing the French fashion model, he was seeing a slender platinum blonde with luminous green eyes surrounded by soft brown lashes. Surprise was cutting through his satisfaction, perhaps because he had had the weirdest conviction that Lizzie Whitaker would say no to the temptation of the cash he had offered. He wondered why he had thought that, why he had assumed she would be different from any other woman.

Women liked money and he liked women: it was a fair exchange in which neither of them need feel used or abused. Hadn't he learned that a long time ago? Athene would be able to return to her childhood home for a visit at the very least. Was Lizzie Whitaker planning to meet the *full* terms of the will? Raw anticipation of an entirely different kind infiltrated Cesare and he frowned, bewildered by the flood of undisciplined hormones smashing his self-control to pieces. He was thinking about Lizzie Whitaker, *only* thinking about her and he was as aroused as a teenager contemplating sex for the first time.

'You seem distracted,' Celine remarked tentatively.

Cesare studied her without an iota of his usual lust, exasperated by the games his body was playing with his usually very well-disciplined brain. 'A business deal,' he proffered truthfully.

Goffredo would be overjoyed at the news of the upcoming wedding while Cesare was simply stunned at the prospect of getting married, whether it was a business arrangement or not. *Married!* The delicious food on his plate ebbed in appeal. Dense black lashes screened his gaze. It was rare for him to take a night off and somehow Lizzie Whitaker had contrived to kill any notion he had had of relaxing with Celine. What was it about her that unsettled him? After all she was a pretty standard gold-digger, willing to do virtually anything to enrich herself, and how could he criticise her for that reality when he had baited the hook?

CHAPTER THREE

'I DON'T KNOW what the arrangements are likely to be,' Lizzie told her father while she paced the kitchen, a slim figure clad in jeans and a sweater and workman-like boots. 'Look, I've got a few things to check outside. I might as well keep busy until Cesare arrives.'

'What sort of a name is that he has?' Brian Whitaker scoffed.

Lizzie dealt the older man an impatient glance as she put on her jacket because he had no excuse to be needling her or disparaging Cesare. But everything, she told herself in an urgent little pep talk, was *good* in her world. Chrissie had returned to university and soon she and her father would no longer need to worry about rent rises and bank debts they couldn't cover. 'It's an Italian name, just like mine and Chrissie's and Mum's and it's completely normal. Let's not forget that Cesare is about to wave a magic wand over our lives.'

'Even the Garden of Eden had the serpent,' her father countered with a curl of his lip and his usual determination to have the last word.

Lizzie drank in the fresh air with relief and walked to the stone wall bounding the yard to check the sheep in the field. Lambing hadn't started yet but it wouldn't be long before it did. If she had to leave home before then, Andrew would probably take the ewes, she was reasoning in the detached state of mind she had forged to keep herself calm since she had sent that text to Cesare. There were no successes without losses, no gains without costs and consequences. In the middle of that sobering reflection while she watched the lane for a car arriving, she heard a noise in the sky and she flung her head back in the fading light to look up.

A helicopter was coming in over the valley. As she watched it circled the top of the hill and swooped down low to come closer and then noisily hover. For a split second, Lizzie was frozen to the spot, unable to believe that the helicopter was actually planning to land in a field with stock in it. The craft's powerful lights splayed over the flock of fast-scattering sheep, which ran in a total panic down the hill. Lizzie ran for the gate, Archie at her heels, and flew over it like a high jumper while shouting instructions to her dog to retrieve the flock.

Heart pounding, she ran down the hill at breakneck speed but was still not fast enough to prevent the sheep from scrambling in a frantic escape over the wall at the foot and streaming across the next field towards the river. Sick with apprehension, she clambered over the wall and ran even faster while watching as Archie herded the frightened ewes away from the water's edge. The noise from the helicopter unluckily intensified at that point because the pilot was taking off again and the sheep herded close together and then took off terrified again in all directions.

Someone shouted her name and she was relieved to see Andrew Brook racing down the hill to join her. Struggling desperately to catch her breath, while wondering anxiously where Archie had disappeared to, she hurried on towards the riverbank to see if any of the animals had gone into the water. Andrew got there first and she saw him stooping down in the mud over something, whistling for his sheepdog. One of the sheep had got hurt in the commotion, she assumed, hurrying down to join him.

'I'm so sorry, Lizzie. He's hurt. He was too little to handle them in a panic like that,' Andrew told her.

Lizzie looked down in horror at the small prone body lying in the mud: it was Archie and he was whimpering. She knelt in the mud. *'Oh, no...'*

'I think it's only his leg that's broken but there could be internal injuries. He was trodden on,' Andrew, a stocky dark-haired man in his late twenties, reminded her.

'That *crazy* helicopter pilot! Are people insane?' Lizzie gasped, stricken, while Andrew, always resourceful, broke a small branch off a nearby tree, cut it to size with the knife in his pocket and splinted it to Archie's leg, wrapping it in place with twine.

'Nobody should land in a field with animals in it,' Andrew agreed. As Lizzie comforted her pet with a trembling hand he unfurled his mobile phone. 'We'd better get him to the vet. I'll ring ahead to warn Danny.'

Andrew's dog had retrieved the sheep and on the walk back uphill they were returned to the field from which they had fled. Lizzie was in shock and wildly dishevelled by the breakneck pace of her downhill marathon, sweat breaking on her brow, tears trickling down her cheeks as she held Archie's small, shivering body as gently as she could to her chest. Back in the yard, Lizzie went straight to the Land Rover and settled Archie on the front passenger seat.

'I'll come with you,' Andrew announced. 'I know how you feel about that daft dog.'

'Thanks but I can manage,' Lizzie assured him with a warm smile that acknowledged how comfortable she could still feel with her former boyfriend.

'That's the ex-fiancé—Andrew Brook, our neighbour,' Brian Whitaker informed Cesare, who was stationed beside him outside the back door of the cottage. 'They grew up together. I always thought they'd make a match of it but then he met Esther and married her instead.'

Cesare told himself that he had no desire for that information. He was already irritated that Lizzie hadn't been waiting to greet him—didn't she appreciate what a busy man he was? Now watching her smile beguilingly up at her ex-boyfriend, who was an attractive, stalwart six-footer, he was even less impressed. When she looked at the other man like that and squeezed his arm with easy intimacy it made him wonder why they had broken up and that dart of inappropriate curiosity set his even white teeth on edge, sending another wave of annoyance crashing through him.

'Lizzie!' her father called as Andrew strode back home across the couple of fields that separated their properties.

Lizzie turned her head and focused in bewilderment on the tall, darkly handsome male poised by her father's side. Her heartbeat suddenly thudded like a crack of doom in her ears and her throat tightened. Sheathed in an immaculate grey pinstripe business suit worn with a white shirt and scarlet tie, Cesare looked very much at odds with his surroundings but he still contrived to take her breath away and leave her mind briefly as blank as white paper. 'Good grief, when did you arrive? I didn't see a car.'

'I came in a helicopter...'

Lizzie, the Land Rover keys clenched tightly in one hand, froze. She blinked in fleeting bewilderment and then headed towards Cesare in a sudden movement, rage boiling up through the cracks of anxiety and concern for her dog and her flock. '*You're* the bloody idiot who let a helicopter land in a field full of stock?' she raked at him incredulously.

In all his life, nobody had ever addressed Cesare with such insolence. A faint frown line etched between his ebony brows, he stared at her as if he couldn't quite believe his ears. Indeed he was much more concerned with the reality that, in spite of her awareness of his visit, his bride-to-be still looked as though she had strayed in from a hostel for the homeless. A streak of dirt marred one cheekbone and her clothes were caked in mud and displaying damp patches. But when he glanced higher and saw the luminous colour in her cheeks that accentuated her hazel-green eyes and the contrast of that tumbling mane of admittedly messy white-blonde hair, he registered in some astonishment that even had she been wearing a bin liner it would not have dampened her physical appeal on his terms. His usual high standards, it seemed, were slipping.

'What's the problem?' Cesare enquired with perfect cool, reasoning that some sort of cultural misunderstanding could have provoked her sudden aggressive outburst.

'The problem is...'

'Don't shout at me,' Cesare sliced in softly. 'I am not hard of hearing.'

'Your pilot landed that helicopter in a field full of sheep...and he should be shot for it!' Lizzie framed rawly. 'They were so terrified they fled. All of them are pregnant, only days off lambing. If any of them miscarry after that crazed stampede, I'll be holding *you* responsible!'

For a fraction of a second, Cesare recalled the pilot striving to persuade him to land a couple of fields away but the prospect of a time-wasting muddy trek to the cottage had exasperated him and he had insisted on being set down as close as possible to his destination. 'The mistake was mine, not the pilot's. I chose the landing spot,' Cesare admitted, startling her with that confession. 'I know nothing about farming or the care of animals. Naturally I will compensate you and your father for any loss of income that results.'

'Well, the man can't say fairer than that,' Brian Whitaker cut in, sending his furious daughter a warning glance. 'Let that be the end of it.'

'Archie was *hurt*!' Lizzie protested fierily, shooting Cesare a seething look that warned him that even admitting his mistake was insufficient to soothe her. 'The flock trampled him at the river. I'm taking him to the vet now for emergency treatment and I haven't got the time...or the patience...to deal with you!'

Cesare watched in disbelief as his future bride unlocked the rusty vehicle several feet away and began to climb in.

'You've done it now. She treats that stupid dog like her firstborn!' Brian Whitaker muttered impatiently and retreated back indoors, bowing out of the situation.

With the split-second timing that matched Cesare's lightning-fast intellect, he strode forward and opened the passenger door of the Land Rover to take the only step left open to him. 'I'll accompany you to the vet's,' he informed her flatly.

Very much disconcerted by that announcement, Lizzie flicked him a frowning appraisal. 'You'll have to hold Archie.'

Cesare, so far out of his comfort zone that he already felt as if he were trapped in something of a nightmare, finally noticed that it was a two-seat vehicle and that the scruffy dog lay comatose on the only seat available for his own use.

Lizzie leapt back out of the car. 'I'll move him and *then* you can get in,' she told him, racing round the back of the vehicle to scoop up Archie in trembling hands and usher him in.

'I could drive,' Cesare pointed out drily.

'You don't know where you're going and I know where the potholes are,' Lizzie told him incomprehensibly as she very gently rested Archie down on Cesare's lap. 'Please make sure he doesn't fall.'

Tears were choking Lizzie's throat. Archie was so quiet and he had never been a quiet dog. Right at that very minute, he could be *dying*, his brave little life and loving spirit ebbing away, and that was why she wasn't going to waste time arguing with Cesare Sabatino about anything.

'Is he still breathing?' Lizzie demanded, turning out onto the road.

'I can feel his heart beating,' Cesare proffered quietly, blocking out his uneasy awareness that the vehicle stank of animals and was far from clean. He stroked the still body for want of anything else to do and was startled when the dog twisted his head to lick at his hand.

'He trusts you,' Lizzie informed him.

'He doesn't have much choice in the matter,' Cesare fielded, reckoning that he had been sent to Yorkshire solely to suffer. In his opinion she drove like a maniac. He had spent the day travelling and his day had started at six in the morning in Geneva. Now it was eight in the evening and, not only had he not eaten for hours, but he was also convinced that many more hours would pass before he could even hope for the opportunity. He knew she had no idea that he had planned to take her out to dinner and, since he didn't have a woolly fleece and cloven hooves, it would never occur to Lizzie to feed him.

Unaware of her unwelcome passenger's thoughts, Lizzie rammed the Land Rover to an abrupt jolting halt in a small car park. Carefully carrying Archie, Lizzie stalked into the surgery, leaving Cesare, a male who was unaccustomed to being ignored, to follow her. An older man greeted them and carried the dog off to be X-rayed, leaving Lizzie and Cesare in the small, dull waiting room.

In consternation, Cesare watched Lizzie fighting off tears again. Driven by a desperate masculine urge to shift her thoughts to what he viewed as more positive issues, he murmured, 'So, we're getting married?'

Lizzie marvelled at his lack of compassion and understanding. Did he really think she was in any frame of mind to discuss that while she was waiting to hear whether Archie would live or die? 'Yes, but it won't really be a marriage,' she parried, striving not to look at him because he really had the most stunning dark golden eyes and every time she looked she ended up staring and she didn't want him to notice her behaving like a silly schoolgirl.

'We're not going for gold, then,' Cesare assumed, referring to the requirement for a child in the will while surveying her down-bent head with a sense of deep dissatisfaction that took him aback. Why was he feeling that way? Common sense suggested that he should settle for taking Athene for a visit to Lionos and think himself lucky to have gained that much from the exchange.

A tangle of silvery hair brushed the delicate cheekbones of Lizzie's heart-shaped face and she glanced up through the silken veil of her lashes, green eyes clear and direct. 'Well, yes, we are. I've thought of a way round that.'

'There's no way round it,' Cesare informed her impatiently, marvelling at the luminous quality of those tear-drenched eyes.

'AI,' she declared quietly.

His straight ebony brows lifted. 'AI?'

'Artificial insemination. We use it with the stock and we can do it that way too,' Lizzie muttered in an undertone, trying not to succumb to discomfiture because he was *really* staring at her now as if he had never heard of such a process. 'I mean, that way there's no need at all for us to get up close and personal. We can both conserve our dignity.'

Cesare was staggered by the suggestion. 'Dignity?'

he queried thinly, his first reaction being one of male offence until his clever brain examined the suggestion. For him, it would be a win-win situation, he acknowledged grudgingly. He would not have to sacrifice his freedom in any field because the marriage would be a detached charade from start to finish. That *was* the civilised sensible approach because there would always be the risk that sexual involvement could muddy the waters of their arrangement. But while his intellect reinforced that rational outlook, he discovered that he was curiously reluctant to embrace the concept of a child fathered in a lab rather than in the normal way and equally reluctant to accept that Lizzie Whitaker would never share his bed.

'Well, obviously neither one of us would want to be put in the position where we would have to have sex with a stranger.'

Without warning, unholy amusement burnished Cesare's lean, darkly handsome features. 'I don't think you know much about the average male.'

Colour flared like a banner in Lizzie's cheeks. 'And if that's the sort of man you are, I don't think you should be boasting about it!' she snapped pointedly.

Cesare breathed in slow and deep and resisted the urge to ask her if she ever lightened up. It was something of a shock for him to discover that there was a woman alive utterly impervious to his looks and charisma. He didn't believe in false modesty and had been well aware since the teen years that he could attract women in droves, a success rating that had only been enhanced by his gradual rise to billionaire status. Lizzie, however, put out no encouraging vibes and was not remotely flirtatious.

Watching the cool forbidding expression spread across his lean bronzed face, Lizzie took fright and said, 'I'm sorry...I'm too worried about Archie to mind what I say. I didn't intend to be rude but you must understand that two people with as little in common as we have really do need a get-out clause when it comes to having a baby,' she framed with a shy upward glance. 'And if I agree to that, there would be additional safeguards I would require.'

'Such as?'

Lizzie breathed in deep. 'You would have to agree to take on the role of acting as a father to the child until it grew up. Obviously we'll marry and then divorce... whenever.' Lizzie shifted an uncertain hand. 'But a child has specific needs from a parent and those needs must be met with love and security from *both* of us. That would be quite a responsibility for you to take on for the next twenty years and I need to be sure that you're willing to accept that.'

A very faint darkening of colour across Cesare's spectacular cheekbones highlighted his discomfiture. He had assumed that Lizzie was planning to discuss the financial rewards for her willingness to fulfil the terms of the will and her true, infinitely more responsible and caring angle of interest had pierced him with a rare sense of guilt. 'Why are you so willing to take on that responsibility?' he prompted.

'I've always wanted a child of my own,' Lizzie responded, quite comfortable and secure in making that admission. 'But I don't really want a man to go *with* the child, so the arrangement you suggested would probably suit me best of all. At the same time I don't want to raise a fatherless child, so an occasional father such as you would be is even more acceptable.'

Cesare was quietly stunned by those statements. The women he socialised with were never so frank about a desire to conceive either now or in the future. He wondered if she was still in love with her ex or simply some sort of man-hater because it was unusual for so young a woman to decide that she wanted to live her life alone. And then in dawning dismay he heard himself say, 'Are you gay?'

Lizzie turned bright pink but recognised why he had interpreted her words in that light. 'No, that's not the problem,' she responded stiffly, determined to keep her reasons for her solitary choice of lifestyle strictly private. There was no requirement whatsoever for her to explain herself to him and she was grateful for the fact.

'If we had a child together, I would hope to meet all your expectations of a father,' Cesare informed her with quiet conviction. 'As it happens, I have a very good father of my own and appreciate the importance of the role he plays.'

Lizzie nodded. 'That was my only real concern… Oh.' She hesitated but there was no way of avoiding the most pressing requirement. 'If we're to proceed with this I'm afraid I'll need some money from you upfront. I have to be honest—we are all stony broke. My sister needs some cash to stay on at university and I'll have to rent a property in the village for my dad because when I leave, he'll be relinquishing the tenancy of the farm.'

Absorbing the fluctuating expressions of embarrassment and apprehension skimming her heart-shaped face, Cesare sent her a soothing smile. 'Naturally it's not a problem. I expected something of the sort.'

'You knew how we were fixed...*before* you visited?' Lizzie queried in surprise.

'I never enter a situation blind,' Cesare countered unapologetically.

Danny the vet appeared in the doorway. 'Archie will be out in a minute. My nurse is just finishing up with him. His leg's broken and he's had a blow to the skull, which means he's a little woozy, but other than that he seems fine.'

After the vet had explained his treatment and proffered medication for the coming days, Archie emerged in the nurse's arms, a cast attached to one small leg and a balloon collar round his neck to prevent him from nibbling at it. Lizzie gathered him close, tears tripping from her eyes again as she huskily thanked the older man while Cesare insisted on taking care of the bill.

'I'm very attached to Archie,' Lizzie explained, dashing tears of relief from her eyes with her elbow. 'You can drive back if you want. The keys are in my pocket.'

Cesare fished out the keys and unlocked the car. 'I was hoping you would fly back to London with me tonight.'

'*Tonight?*' Lizzie exclaimed in disbelief. 'That's impossible!'

'We have a tight time schedule. I have everything arranged. Is it really impossible?' Cesare prompted drily. 'You appear to have no presentable clothes and can't need to pack much.'

'But I have to sort out somewhere for Dad to live and move him out of the cottage.'

'I have staff who will hire professionals to deal with those tasks for you,' Cesare told her with complete cool. 'You've had your say. I have agreed to your terms and now I need you to come to London.'

It was bite-the-bullet time, Lizzie registered, angrily colliding with brilliant dark eyes as hard as jet. He was being unreasonable. Surely there was no excuse for such haste? But what choice did she have? The arrangement having been agreed, he was now in charge of events. 'I'll have to call in with my neighbour to ask him to look after the flock.'

'Andrew Brook?'

Lizzie stiffened. 'Yes.'

'Why did you break up?'

'That's private,' Lizzie told him waspishly.

Cesare gritted his teeth. 'We'll go and see him now, so that you can make your preparations.'

Lizzie left Archie asleep in the Land Rover. Esther opened the door and her look of dismay mortified Lizzie, although she had always been aware that Andrew's last-minute exchange of would-be wives had caused Esther almost as much heartache and humiliation as it had caused Lizzie. People had condemned Esther for sleeping with a man who was engaged to another woman. They had judged her even harder for falling pregnant and thereby forcing the affair into the open and some locals had ignored Esther ever since.

Andrew sprang up from the kitchen table while Lizzie carried out introductions whereupon Cesare startled her by taking charge. 'Lizzie and I are leaving for London tonight—we're getting married,' he explained. 'Lizzie wants to know if you'll take her sheep.'

Lizzie saw the surprise and relief darting across Esther's face and looked away again, her own colour high. Esther would be glad to see her leave the neighbourhood and she didn't feel she could really blame the other woman for that, not after the way people had treated her.

'This is a surprise and it calls for a celebration,' Andrew pronounced with genuine pleasure. 'I didn't even know you were seeing anyone, Lizzie.'

Home-made peach wine was produced. Cesare found it sickly sweet but he appreciated the sentiment while he watched and read his companions and made certain interesting deductions. Andrew Brook appeared fond of Lizzie but no more than that. Indeed his every look of warmth was for his wife, who was a rather plain, plump young woman who couldn't hold a candle to Lizzie in the looks department. Lizzie, on the other hand, Cesare could not read at all. She chatted but was clearly eager to leave as soon as was polite.

'Are you planning to enlighten me yet?' Cesare drawled when they returned to the Land Rover, his Italian accent licking round the edges of every syllable in the sexiest way imaginable.

Lizzie was bitterly amused by that stray thought when she didn't do sex or even know what sexy was. That had lain at the heart of her disastrous relationship with Andrew when she had learned that she was simply one of those women who did not like to be touched. She had assumed—*wrongly*—when she agreed to marry him that her own response would naturally change as time went on and they became closer. But that hadn't happened and her feelings hadn't changed.

'Andrew had an affair with Esther while we were engaged and she got pregnant. We broke up six weeks before our wedding day and he married her the following month. They're very happy together,' Lizzie explained flatly. 'That means I've got an unused wedding gown in my wardrobe, so I'll bring that down to London.'

'No!' Cesare sliced in with innate distaste. 'I will buy you another dress.'

'But that's silly and wasteful when there's no need for it!' Lizzie reasoned in bafflement.

'If we are trying to persuade my family that this is a genuine marriage, you will need a designer gown with all the usual trimmings.'

'But how could anyone possibly believe it was genuine? We're chalk and cheese and we only just met.'

'You'll be enjoying a full makeover in London and only my father knows when we first met. By the time I'm finished with you, they *will* believe, *cara*,' Cesare insisted.

'And what if I don't want a makeover?'

'If you want to be convincing in the role you're being paid to take, you don't have a choice,' Cesare told her softly. Of course she wanted a makeover, he thought grimly, unconvinced by her show of reluctance. She was willing to do just about anything for money. Hadn't she already demonstrated the fact? She was prepared to become a mother simply to sell the island to him. But then to be fair, he acknowledged, he was willing to become a father to buy Lionos although, in his case, he had additional and far more presentable motives.

What was the use of working so hard when he had

no heir to follow him? What easier way could he acquire a child to inherit his empire? He had seen too many marriages explode into the bitterness and division of divorce, heard too many stories about children traumatised by their parents splitting up. The will had given him a chance to avoid that kind of fallout *and* the imprisonment of taking 'for ever after' vows with one woman. A marriage that was a marriage only on paper and a child born prior to a low-key civilised divorce would suit Cesare's needs very nicely indeed.

Out of Cesare's response, only one phrase assailed Lizzie: *you're being paid*. It was an unwelcome but timely reminder and she chewed at her full lower lip, restraining a tart response. Hopefully within a couple of months he would have no further use for her and she would get her life back and, even more hopefully, a life that would stretch to include the sheer joy of becoming a mother for the first time. When that time came, maybe she would be able to find some sort of work training course and accommodation near Chrissie. Or maybe that was a bad idea, she reflected uneasily, suspecting that her sibling had the right to her independence without a big sister hovering protectively somewhere nearby.

'A moment before we go inside…' Cesare breathed, striding round the bonnet of the rusty farm vehicle.

A frown drew Lizzie's brows together as she hovered by the back door. When he reached out and tugged her close, Lizzie was so taken aback that she simply froze. His hands came up to frame her cheekbones and she gazed up into glittering golden eyes that reflected the lights shining out from the farmhouse windows, her nostrils flaring on the faint fresh scent of his cologne and the underlying hint of clean, fresh man.

At that point while she was mulling over why he smelled so good to her, Cesare lowered his proud dark head and kissed her. Lizzie stopped breathing in shock, electrified by the sensation and taste of his firm sensual mouth on hers with her heart hammering and her pulse racing as if she were riding a Big Dipper at an amusement park. He nibbled her lower lip and thunder crashed in her ears, the earth literally moving when he swiped his tongue along her full lower lip in an erotic flick that made her quiver like a jelly.

Forbidden warmth burst into being inside her, swelling her breasts, tightening her nipples, spearing down between her legs in a twin assault on her senses. A hard urgency now laced the passionate pressure of his mouth on hers and her head fell back, lips parting by instinct to welcome the deeply sensual dart of his tongue. He pulled her closer, welding her to every powerful line of his lean, powerfully masculine body with a big hand splayed across her hips to hold her in place and in spite of their clothing she felt his arousal, the hard, unmistakeable ridge between them. With almost superhuman force of will because she was on the edge of panic, Lizzie pressed her hand against his shoulder to push him back from her and, to be fair to him, he freed her immediately.

'That's enough,' she framed unevenly, her breath rasping in her tight throat as an ache of what she knew could only be dissatisfaction spread at the heart of her. 'Why the heck did you do that?'

'If we intend to fool people into crediting that we are a genuine couple, we have to be able to behave like a couple…at least, occasionally,' Cesare delivered with an audibly ragged hitch in his breathing.

'I don't like being touched,' Lizzie told him in a small flat voice.

You could've fooled me, Cesare thought in disbelief, still tasting the sweetness of her soft, lush lips and struggling to suppress the rush of hungry excitement that had lit him up like a burning torch.

She was out of bounds, he reminded himself stubbornly. He was not planning to bed her. She didn't want it and *he* didn't want it either. Regrettably his body was out of step with his brain, though, and somehow she exuded all the allure of a juicy hamburger to a very reluctant vegetarian. But, Cesare reminded himself stubbornly, he could get sex anywhere. He had Celine for uncommitted sexual satisfaction. He wasn't about to risk screwing up his marital arrangement with Lizzie by flirting with that kind of intimacy. It would blur the boundaries and she might start behaving like a real wife and even start thinking that she could attach strings to him.

'So, it was just a sort of test?' Lizzie gathered in relief, assuming that it was an approach that was unlikely to be repeated very often.

'You won the gold medal for excellence, *bella mia,*' Cesare quipped, striving to will his libido back down to a manageable level but that was a challenge while all he could think about, all he could see in his head, was Lizzie spread across a bed, stark naked and not only willing but also wild. The imagery didn't help, nor did it help that he knew he, who prided himself on his detachment in business situations, was indulging in a deeply improbable but very male fantasy.

Two hours later, Lizzie was seated in a limousine with Cesare in silence. Her case was stowed, Archie was asleep on her knee and Cesare was working on his laptop. She was still thinking about that kiss, wondering what magic spark Cesare had that Andrew had so conspicuously lacked. Was it truly just a case of physical chemistry?

Frustration filled Lizzie to overflowing. There had been very few men in her life, very few kisses and she was still a virgin. Andrew had repulsed her, yet he was a young, attractive man and she had loved him. Naturally, she had assumed that she simply wasn't a very sexual woman. But within seconds of Cesare kissing her, fireworks had gone off inside her in a rush of excitement unlike anything she had ever felt. And now, for the very first time in her life, she was studying a powerful masculine thigh and the distinctive bulge at the crotch and wondering what a man looked like naked. Colour washed in a veil to her hairline and she studied Archie instead, fondling a shaggy ear as the dog slept.

It was sexual curiosity, that was all. Silly, immature, she labelled with growing embarrassment, but nothing to really worry about. After all, nothing was going to happen with Cesare. And as for that moment of panic in his arms? One kiss and she imagined she was about to tumble into an adolescent infatuation as easily as her mother had once done? No, she was much too sensible for that, she told herself soothingly. Cesare was gorgeous and well-off and arrogant and he probably slept around as such men reputedly did. He was not her type at all...

Absolutely *not* his type, Cesare was reflecting with

satisfaction. One dynamite kiss didn't alter the fact that she dressed like a bag lady, had poor manners and barely a feminine bone in her body. Or that she treated him rather like a lost umbrella someone had left behind on a train seat…

CHAPTER FOUR

THE MAKEOVER, ALONG with the shopping and the ultra-grooming at a very fancy beauty salon, shook Lizzie to her very depths.

She was transformed and she knew it and was surprised by how very much better it made her feel to see herself polished to glossiness, with that awful brown dye gone from the last few inches of her pale silvery hair. Every time she had seen that dye in the mirror it had reminded her of Andrew and the bad times, so it was a relief to be finally rid of it and stop wondering if he ironically had tried to change *her* into Esther, who had mud-brown hair of no great distinction. She regarded her long, glittery nails with positive girlish delight because she had never known such beauty tweaking could transform her work-roughened hands. The calluses were gone as well, her entire skin surface buffed and moisturised to perfection. There was no doubt about it: it made her feel like a new woman, a woman of greater assurance than she had been when she first slunk through the doors of the salon, feeling like a crime against femininity in her untouched, un-polished state.

How would Cesare view her now?

Her cheeks flushed at the thought. Why should that matter to her? What was his opinion worth? Presumably without the polishing he wouldn't have wanted to be seen out with her in public and that was a lowering reflection, she acknowledged ruefully. She had been transformed and she appreciated it, best not to think too deeply beyond that, she decided wryly. And now all dressed up to the nines she felt more armoured to cope with the hen party ahead even if it was without the support of her sister.

Sadly, Chrissie had an exam the next day and there was absolutely no way she could join Lizzie and Cesare's sisters. Lizzie was disappointed. She liked Cesare's friendly siblings very much but they were still strangers and somewhat more uncomfortably, strangers she had to keep a front up with. They thought it was a normal wedding with a bride and groom in love and happy. Unfortunately, living up to that false expectation was a strain even on a shopping and beauty trip.

'You mean, you really *aren't* pregnant?' Sofia, Cesare's youngest half-sister, gasped as she watched Lizzie down a vodka cocktail with every sign of enjoyment. 'Cesare told us you weren't but we didn't believe him.'

'This conversation is not happening,' Paola groaned in apology, the eldest of the trio of sisters, a teacher and married woman and rather more circumspect than her single, fun-loving sisters in what she chose to say. 'I'm so sorry, Lizzie.'

Lizzie smiled, masking her loneliness and chagrin. 'It's all right. I'm not offended. I know you're surprised that your brother's getting married in such a hurry—'

'When we never thought he'd get married at all,' his third half-sister Maurizia slotted in frankly.

'Obviously he's nuts about you!' Sofia giggled. 'That's the only explanation that makes sense. When I sent him that photo of you all dressed up to go out tonight, he wasted no time telling me that he wanted you to stay at home and that he saw no reason for you to have a hen night.'

Of course Cesare didn't see any reason, Lizzie reflected ruefully, glugging her drink because she didn't know what to say to his very accepting and loveable sisters or indeed to his pleasant stepmother, Ottavia, none of whom had a clue that the wedding wasn't the real thing. She had guessed, however, that his father, Goffredo, was simply playing along with their pretence but she found that same pretence stressful and knew it was why she was drinking so much and living on her nerves. Luckily Cesare had not been required to put on much of an act, she conceded resentfully, as he had taken refuge in his city apartment, after marooning her in his unbelievably luxurious town house with his family, before flying off to New York on urgent business.

Apparently it was the norm for Cesare to move out of his flashy and huge town house into his exclusive city apartment when his family arrived for a visit. Lizzie had found that strange but his family did not, joking that Cesare had always liked his own space and avoided anything that might take his main focus off business, which evidently involved socialising with his family as well. Lizzie thought that was sad but had kept her opinion tactfully to herself.

He was *so* rich: in spite of the limo and the driver and the helicopter, she had had no idea *how* rich her future fake husband was. Lizzie was still in shock from travelling in a private jet and walking into a house the size of a palace with over ten en-suite bedrooms and innumerable staff. She had then done what she should have done a week earlier and had checked him out on the Internet, learning that he was the head of a business mega-empire and more in the billionaire than the multimillionaire category.

Indeed the house, followed by the experience of being literally engulfed by his gregarious family, had only been the first of the culture shocks rattling Lizzie's security on its axis. Two solid days of clothes shopping followed by a physical head-to-toe makeover had left its mark. For that reason it was hardly surprising that she should be at last enjoying the chance to relax and have a few drinks in good company for the first time in more years than she cared to count.

Seated on his jet, furiously checking his watch to calculate the landing time, Cesare enlarged the photograph on his tablet and scrutinised it with lingering disbelief.

Don't you dare take Lizzie out dressed like that to a club! he had texted his half-sister Maurizia, with a confusing mix of anger, frustration and concern assailing him in a dark flood of reactions that made him uncomfortable to the extreme.

He still couldn't take his eyes off the photograph: Lizzie smiling as he had never seen her and sheathed in an emerald-green, 'barely there', strappy short dress with perilous high heels on her shapely legs. It was an amazing transformation. A magic wand had been waved over the bag lady. She looked fantastic and would outshine every woman around her now that her natural beauty had been polished up and brought to the fore. Her glorious mane of hair had been restored as he'd instructed, *not* cut. It gleamed in a silken tumble of silver strands round her delicately pointed face, green eyes huge, pouty mouth lush and pink. Cesare swore under his breath, outraged by his sisters' interference and the hen-party nonsense. Lizzie was no more fit to be let loose in a London nightclub than a toddler and now he would have to go and retrieve her!

'You're not supposed to be here... This is *her* night!' one of his sisters carolled accusingly as soon as he arrived at the women's table.

'Where is she?' Cesare ground out, unamused, while he scanned the dance floor.

Looking daggers at her big brother, Sofia shifted a reluctant hand to show him. 'Don't spoil her night. She's having a whale of a time!'

Cesare centred his incredulous dark gaze on the sight of his bride-to-be, a pink hen-night sash diagonally dissecting her slender, shapely body as she danced, arms raised, silvery hair flying, feet moving in time to the fast beat. What infuriated him was the sight of the two men trying to attract her attention because she appeared to be dancing in a world of her own. Suddenly Lizzie teetered to a stop, clearly dizzy as she swayed on her very high heels. With a suppressed snarl of annoyance, Cesare, ignoring his siblings' wide-eyed disbelief at his behaviour, stalked across the floor to hastily settle steadying hands on Lizzie's slim shoulders.

'Cesare…' Lizzie proclaimed with a wide, sunny smile because it only took one lingering glance to remind her how tall, dark and sleekly gorgeous he was. He towered over her, lean bronzed face shadowed and hollowed by the flickering lights that enhanced his spectacular bone structure, stunning dark golden eyes intent on her. She was really, *really* pleased to see him, a familiar reassuring image in a new world that was unnervingly different and unsettling. In fact for a split second she almost succumbed to a deeply embarrassing urge to hug him. Then, luckily remembering that hugging wasn't part of their deal, she restrained herself.

'You're drunk,' his perfectly shaped mouth framed, destroying the effect of his reassuring presence.

'Of course I'm not drunk!' Lizzie slurred, throwing up her hands in emphasis only to brace them on his broad chest while she wondered why her legs wanted to splay like a newborn calf's trying to walk for the first time.

'You are,' Cesare repeated flatly.

'I'm *not*,' Lizzie insisted, holding onto his forearms to stay upright, her shoe soles still displaying a worrying urge to slide across the floor of their own volition.

'I'm taking you home,' Cesare mouthed as the deafening music crashed all around them.

'I'm not ready to go home yet!' she shouted at him.

Lizzie couldn't work out what Cesare said in answer to that declaration. His deep-set eyes glittered like banked-down fires in his lean, strong face and he had bent down and lifted her up into his arms before she could even begin to guess his intention.

'Think we're going home,' Lizzie informed his sisters forlornly from the vantage point of his arms as he paused by their table.

'You *didn't* look after her!' Cesare growled at one of his sisters, in answer to whatever comment had been made.

'What am I? A dog or a child?' Lizzie demanded, staring up at him, noticing that he needed a shave because a heavy five o'clock shadow outlined his lower jawline, making it seem even harder and more aggressive than usual. It framed his wide, sensual mouth though, drawing attention to the perfectly sculpted line of his lips. He kissed like a dream, she recalled abstractedly, wondering when he'd do it again.

'Think we should kiss so that your sisters believe we're a *real* couple?' Lizzie asked him winningly.

'If we were real, I'd strangle you, *cara*,' Cesare countered without hesitation. 'I leave you alone for three days and I come back and you're going crazy on the dance floor and getting blind drunk.'

'*Not* drunk,' Lizzie proclaimed stubbornly.

Cesare rolled his eyes and with scant ceremony stuffed her in the back of the waiting limousine. 'Lie down before you fall over.'

'You're so smug,' Lizzie condemned and closed her eyes because the interior of the limousine was telescoping around her in the most peculiar way.

Cesare consoled himself with the hope that such behaviour was not a warning sign of things to come. How could he blame her for wanting some fun? He had a very good idea of what life must have been like for her on that farm with her misery of a father, always there at her elbow, keen to remind her of every mistake and failure. For the very first time in his life he realised just how lucky he had been with Goffredo, who saw everything through rose-tinted, forgiving spectacles. In comparison, Brian Whitaker's view of life was seriously depressing.

Lizzie opened her eyes. 'Do you want to kiss me?' she enquired.

Cesare skimmed his disconcerted gaze to her animated features, taking in the playful grin she wore. 'Do you *want* me to kiss you?'

Lizzie flushed and shifted on the seat. 'You're not supposed to ask that.'

'You expect me to act like a caveman?'

Lizzie thought about that. She had rather enjoyed being carried out of the club. Was that weird? She scolded herself for that enjoyment while mustering up a dim memory of her mother giggling and tossing her hair, eyes sparkling at the latest man in her life. Inwardly she cringed a little from the comparison she saw.

'Only when you're sober and you know what you're doing,' Cesare extended infuriatingly.

'You believe I could only want to kiss you when I'm drunk?'

Cesare suppressed a groan and studied her. If truth be told, it would take very little encouragement for him to flatten her along the back seat and take inexcusable advantage of her delightfully feminine body. 'We have a business arrangement,' he reminded her doggedly, cursing the hot swell of the erection disturb-

ing his poise because just the thought of doing anything to her turned him on hard and fast.

Her honey-brown lashes flickered. 'I'm open to
negotiation.'

'*No*, you're not,' Cesare informed her grimly, lean
bronzed face set in forbidding lines, mobile mouth
compressed. 'There will be absolutely no negotiation
on that score tonight.'

Was it so wrong, Lizzie asked herself, that she
should want to experience just once what other women
commonly experienced? She had always wanted to be
normal, to *feel* normal. Was that wrong? Indecent?
Her cheeks burned. Naturally she had picked him.
That kiss... Somehow he had become her forbidden
object of desire. How had that happened? Treacherous heat curling in her pelvis, Lizzie breathed in
slow and deep.

Cesare watched her feathery lashes dip and the
sound of her breathing slow as she slid into a doze.
Well, he wouldn't be letting her loose around alcohol
again. Sex, drink and business arrangements did not
make for a rational or successful combination. And he
was a *very* rational guy, wasn't he? Here he was being
a saint and protecting her from doing something she
would regret. Or would she? he wondered with inbred
cynicism. She was a gold-digger, after all, and sure to
be on a high after the orgy of spending that had centred on her in recent days.

He was acting against his own nature, he acknowledged grudgingly. In reality, he wanted to fall on her
like a sex-starved sailor on shore leave and keep her
awake all night. Instead he was likely to spend half the
night in a cold shower. He should have made more of

an effort to see Celine. Clearly, it was the lack of regular sex that was playing merry hell with his hormones.

Lizzie awakened as Cesare half walked, half carried her into the town house only to stop dead as Goffredo and his stepmother, Ottavia, appeared in the doorway of the drawing room.

'Your daughters are still partying,' Cesare announced. 'Lizzie was falling asleep, so I brought her home early.'

'Cesare is a party pooper,' Lizzie framed with difficulty.

Goffredo grinned and Ottavia chuckled and the older couple vanished back into the drawing room.

At the foot of the stairs, Cesare abandoned the pretence that Lizzie could walk unaided and swept her up into his arms.

'I like it when you do this,' Lizzie told him. 'It's so…so…masculine.'

'We are lucky you don't weigh more,' Cesare quipped, barely out of breath as they reached the top of the stairs.

A sudden lurch in the stomach region made Lizzie tense and she crammed a stricken hand to her mouth, mumbling, 'Cesare…'

To give him his due, Cesare was not slow on the uptake and he strode through the nearest door at speed and deposited her in a bathroom.

Lizzie was ingloriously ill. He pushed her hair out of the way, gave her a cloth, extended a toothbrush, which he unwrapped, and politely ignored her repetitive apologies for her behaviour. When she couldn't stand up again, he removed her shoes for her and supported her over to the sink.

'I don't make a habit of this,' she declared, rinsing her mouth several times over while hanging onto the vanity unit.

'I should hope not, *bellezza mia*.'

'What does that mean? The Italian bit?'

And he told her that it meant 'my beauty'.

'But that's a downright lie,' she protested, studying her bleary-eyed reflection in dismay. The make-up girl's artistry and the hairdresser's skill were no longer apparent in the flushed face, smudged eyeliner and tousled hair she now saw in the mirror.

'You need to lie down,' Cesare asserted, lifting her again so that the bathroom spun and then the bedroom that followed.

Lizzie lay flat and dead still on the bed, afraid to move lest her surroundings began revolving again. 'Where's Archie? I want Archie.'

'Archie stays downstairs.' Cesare reminded her of the household rule, announced by Primo, his imperturbable manservant, on the day she moved in.

'But that's just mean… He always sleeps with me,' she mumbled.

Cesare almost groaned out loud. She lay splayed across his bed, clearly trusting him when he didn't trust himself because she was displaying a wanton amount of bare slender thigh.

'If I can't have Archie for company, I'll have you,' Lizzie muttered. 'Lie down.'

Cesare snatched up the phone and issued a terse instruction. Within the space of a minute, Primo arrived at the door with Archie. Cesare clasped Archie and carried him over to the bed, whereupon the dog curled up obediently at Lizzie's feet with his head resting across her ankles.

'You should get into bed…you can't sleep in your clothes,' Cesare told her.

'Why not?'

Cesare released his breath in an exasperated hiss and came down on the bed beside her to run her zip down.

'What are you doing?' she whispered curiously as he smoothed the straps of the dress down off her slim shoulders.

'Making you more comfortable.' Business arrangement, *business* arrangement, bloody business arrangement, Cesare was dutifully repeating inside his head as he eased her out of the dress to expose a filmy and provocative bra and panties set in turquoise lace. He wasn't looking, he wasn't reacting, he told himself doggedly while his dark golden gaze clung of its own volition to the surprisingly full, plump curves swelling the lace cups, revealing pale pink nipples that made his mouth water and the shadowy vee at her crotch. He yanked the sheet over Lizzie's prone length so fast that she rolled and, having been disturbed and crammed in below the sheet without warning, Archie also loosed a whimper of complaint.

Lizzie stretched out a searching hand, her eyes closed. The room was going round and round and round behind her lowered eyelids and she felt lost and nauseous. 'Where you going?'

Weary after a day spent travelling and his last-minute sprint to deal with Lizzie, Cesare surrendered to the obvious. If he left her alone, might she wander off? Sleep on the floor? Have an accident? Stumble into the wrong bedroom? And what if she was sick again? 'I'm not going anywhere.' He stripped down to his boxers and lay down on the other side of the bed. A small, callused hand closed over the thumb of his right hand and held on tight. He wasn't used to sharing a bed and he liked his own space.

Lizzie settled up against a warm solid shape while Archie tunnelled below the sheet to settle down by a less restive set of feet.

Lizzie wakened with a desperate thirst at some timeless hour of the night while it was still dark. She slid her feet off the side of the bed, her soles finding the floor, and slowly straightened. A wave of dizziness immediately engulfed her and she compressed her lips hard, sober enough now to be furious with herself. Despite having hardly eaten all day she had foolishly downed all that alcohol and got carried away by the party atmosphere. Suppressing a groan of frustration, she fumbled for the switch on the bedside light and then stared in bewilderment round the unfamiliar room before focusing on the male sharing the wide bed with her.

Cesare was half naked and lying on top of the sheet she had been lying beneath. He was beautifully built with a broad bronzed torso and corded abdomen that rippled with lean muscle. One long, powerful, hairroughened thigh was partially raised, the other flat. Unshaven, he exuded a rough, edgy masculinity that made her breath hitch in her throat as she peered down at him in the lamplight. His lashes were like black silk fans and almost long enough to touch his amazing cheekbones.

She remembered asking him if he wanted to kiss

her, absolutely angling for his attention, and she almost screamed out loud at that demeaning memory. She headed for the bathroom with hot cheeks and a frustrated sense of self-loathing and shame that she could have been so silly. Had she asked him to stay with her as well? For goodness' sake, it was obviously his bedroom and he had only brought her there the night before because it was the nearest option when she felt sick. Now he had seen her in her underwear and she was mortified, although not as mortified as she would have been had he removed that as well. Her head throbbing, she drank about a gallon of cold water and freshened up as best she could without her own toiletries. She crept out of the bathroom in search of something to wear so that she could return to her own room.

Tiptoeing like a cat burglar, she opened the door into a massive wardrobe and eased back a sliding door to yank a man's white shirt off a hanger. The bra was digging into her midriff and she released the catch and removed it and the panties, wondering if she dared go for a shower. Donning the shirt, she rolled up the sleeves and buttoned it.

Being around Cesare made her feel out of control but was that so surprising? She hadn't dated since Andrew, hadn't seen the point, and before him there had only been a handful of unremarkable men. In recent times, she had had no social outlets and had only occasionally left the farm. It cost money to socialise and there had been none to spare. Being with Cesare's light-hearted sisters had been so much fun that she had forgotten to monitor how much she was drinking. One glimpse of Cesare when she was in that weakened condition had had the same effect on her as a hit man shooting her directly between the eyes. He was a very good-looking male, that was all. Noticing the fact simply meant she was female and alive and not that she wanted to pursue anything with him.

Hovering by the bed, Lizzie tried to work out how to get Archie out from below the sheet without either hurting him or waking Cesare.

'What are you doing?' Cesare husked as she yanked at the sheet to try and reach her dog. Blinking up at her with frowning dark eyes, he lifted a muscular arm to check the gold watch he still wore. '*Inferno!* It's three in the morning.'

'I should go back to my own room.'

'Don't wake up the whole household. Stay and go back to sleep,' Cesare advised her drily, flipping onto his side in a display of indifference that made her grit her teeth.

Would she wake anyone up? Stifling a sound of frustration, Lizzie doused the light and snaked back below the sheet.

Early morning was sending pale light through the blinds when she next surfaced, feeling considerably healthier than she had earlier but decidedly overheated. An arm was draped round her ribcage and she was locked intimately close to a very male body, a very *aroused* male body. A surge of heat that had nothing to do with his higher temperature pooled in Lizzie's pelvis. She eased over onto her back and looked up unwarily into heavily fringed eyes the colour of melted bronze. Her throat ran dry, her breathing ruptured.

'You're a very restless sleeper, *cara mia*,' Cesare

censured softly, his breath fanning her cheek. 'I had to clamp you in one place to get peace.'

'Oh...' Lizzie framed dry-mouthed, entranced by her view of his lean, darkly handsome features in the golden dawn light, even her hearing beguiled by his melodic accent.

'Archie, on the other hand, sleeps like the dead and doesn't move at all,' Cesare quipped. 'I've never had a dog in my bed before.'

'There's a first time for everything.'

'First and *last*,' he stressed. 'Unfortunately you wouldn't settle without him last night.'

'I'm sorry I drank too much.' Colour slowly rose to drench her porcelain skin as he stared down at her. 'Was I really awful?'

Long fingers stroked her taut ribcage, making her violently aware of the breasts swelling mere inches above. 'No, you were bright and breezy until the alcohol took its toll.'

Her breathing pattern fractured as she felt her nipples pinch tight while a hot, achy sensation hollowed between her legs. 'I'm not used to drinking like that,' she muttered jaggedly.

His golden eyes smouldered down at her and a wicked grin slanted his shapely lips, ensuring that the rate of her heartbeat accelerated. 'Don't make a habit of it.'

'Of course, I won't,' she began with a frown, tightening every muscle in an urgent, almost panic-stricken attempt to smother the sexual responses trickling through her and awakening every skin cell.

Cesare, who planned everything in Machiavellian detail, had not planned to kiss Lizzie. Having decided

not to touch her, he fully expected to abide by that pro-
hibition because he virtually never gave way to im-
pulses. Unhappily for him, the burning desire to pin
Lizzie to the bed and have wild, sweaty sex with her
had no rational base: it was driven by pure instinct.
And when she shifted her hips below the shirt that had
most definitely ridden up to ensure that bare skin met
bare skin, Cesare was lost.

One minute, Lizzie was drowning in dark golden
eyes framed by lashes longer than her own and downright jealous of the fact, and the next Cesare brought
his mouth crashing down on hers with the kind of raw,
driving passion that she was defenceless against. It
was glorious and the taste of his tongue delving deep
into the moist interior of her mouth was unsurpass-
able and an intoxication in its own right.

He traced the pointed bud of a straining nipple
and her spine undulated of its own accord, sensation
piercing straight to her pelvis. Her breasts had suddenly become achingly sensitive to the palms cupping
them and the fingers tugging gently on the promi-
nent tips. That felt amazingly good. A stifled gasp
was wrenched from low in her throat and her spine
arched, her body rising up to cradle his in an involuntary move of welcome as old as time. He skated
his fingers along a slender thigh to discover the hot
wet core of her, sliding between the delicate folds to
moisturise the tiny bud of thrumming nerve endings
above with a skilled fingertip.

Lizzie tore her lips from his to cry out, hungry beyond bearing for that sensual touch and plunging her
fingers into his tousled black hair to hold him to her.
She was no more capable of thinking about what she

was doing than she was of stopping breathing on command. Her heart was thumping, her ragged gasping breaths audible, her entire body was tingling madly with seething heat and need. With his free hand, he ripped at the buttons of the shirt. The shirt fell partially open, exposing the rounded fullness of a breast crowned by a pale pink nipple. He closed his mouth there, teasing the distended bud with the flick of his tongue and the graze of his teeth while his fingers stoked an erotic blaze at her feminine core. She shuddered, talon claws of fierce need biting into her, shock assailing her that anything physical could feel so intense that she could neither fight it nor control it.

'I love the way you respond to me, *mi piace*,' Cesare growled with satisfaction while switching his attention between her pouting breasts and sending fantastic ripples of ravishing sensation right down to her unbearably hot core.

Lizzie couldn't find her voice, her breath or a single functioning brain cell. Her entire being was welded to his every caress, wanting, needing more. And kissing an erotic path down over her flat, quivering stomach, Cesare gave her much more and she didn't have the strength of will to deny him.

With ruthless cool he zeroed in on the tender heart of her with every weapon in his erotic mastery, stroking delicate flesh with his tongue and his mouth and his expert fingers. Lizzie careened into shock at the intimacy and then moaned below the onslaught of wicked, delirious excitement. Intense pleasure followed, sweeping her up into a wild, yearning climb towards a peak that she felt she would never reach. But that climb was unstoppable. Suddenly her body wasn't her own any more and she was flying like a comet into the sun in a climax so powerful it brought shaken tears of reaction to her eyes.

Still ragingly aroused, Cesare sprang out of bed, his fists angrily clenched. What the hell had he been thinking of? No matter how great the temptation, he should *never* have touched her. They had a business agreement and a planned marriage of convenience ahead of them. They were not lovers, not friends with benefits. He did not want to muddy the waters with the kind of physical intimacy that women often assumed meant more than it did. If he wasn't careful, he might find himself more married than he had ever wanted to be, he acknowledged grimly.

Paralysed by a crazy sense of peace in the aftermath of orgasm, Lizzie closed her eyes, her body still trembling from the sweet aftermath of agonising pleasure. The mattress gave but she didn't open her eyes again until a phone rang, shattering her dream state. The phone fell silent in answer to a man's voice speaking Italian. Her lashes lifted then and she stared at Cesare while he paced the floor, mobile phone clamped to his ear. He still wore his boxers and his state of arousal was blindingly obvious. An almost painful tide of colour burned her face.

He tossed the phone down by the bed. 'Do you want the shower first?'

That prosaic question made Lizzie frantically pull the edges of the shirt she wore closed and she sat up in an agony of discomfiture. 'I'll go back to my own room.'

As she scrambled out of bed and reached for Archie, Cesare murmured without any expression at all, 'We made a mistake and we won't repeat it.'

Clutching Archie in an awkward hold, Lizzie attempted to pick up her discarded clothing one-handed. 'Is that all you've got to say?' she prompted shakily.

'It was just sex…nothing worth fussing over,' Cesare opined in a tone that was as cold as a winter shower on her overheated skin. 'Look, I'll see you downstairs in an hour. I have some papers you have to sign before I leave.'

'You're going away again?' she asked in surprise, fighting the roar of temper rising from a secret place deep down inside her.

'We have forty-eight hours to go before the wedding and I intend to use it,' he advanced calmly, deepset dark eyes hooded, wide, sensual mouth clenched hard.

Just sex…nothing worth fussing over? Lizzie mulled that putdown over while she showered. She wasn't hurt by his dismissal, of course she wasn't. *A mistake that would not be repeated.* Didn't she feel the same way as he did? What had happened shouldn't have happened. It was much more sensible if they stayed uninvolved and detached. So, if he had left her feeling a little crushed and foolish, it was her own fault for acting like an idiot and inviting such a denouement. If she couldn't quite shake off the sense of intimacy he had imbued her with, it was only because she had been more intimate with him than she had ever been with anyone else but that was a secret not for sharing…

CHAPTER FIVE

LIZZIE FASTENED THE cropped trousers and straightened the lilac cashmere sweater she wore with it. Her feet shod in flat ballerina pumps, her face lightly made up, she bore not the smallest resemblance to the woman she had been a mere week earlier.

Of course she was now in possession of a vast wardrobe and owned a choice of outfits for every conceivable occasion. Most probably many of the garments would never be worn because she could not imagine Cesare taking her sailing or out to dinner or indeed to the kind of dressy venue where she would require a full-length gown. The wardrobe was totally wasteful in its size and probable expense but she had already learned that once Cesare had instructed his underlings that she was to be dressed from head to toe in designer fashion, his orders were carried out without question.

A pity she was a little more rebellious in that line, Lizzie acknowledged wryly. A lifetime of counting the pennies meant that extravagance made her feel guilty. Breakfast in bed made her feel even guiltier although, to be honest, any excuse to escape the ghastly prospect of having to breakfast alone with Cesare had been extremely welcome.

After all, she had made a huge fool of herself the night before, hadn't she?

Lizzie inwardly cringed, colour marking her cheeks afresh. It would be a very long time, if ever, before she contrived to forget how she had writhed in ecstasy in Cesare's bed. But mercifully, they hadn't actually got as far as having full sex, she reminded herself bracingly, and she assumed that that reality would make it a little easier for her to reinstate normal boundaries between them. She was no natural wanton, never had been, had simply let alcohol, curiosity and temptation steer her briefly in the wrong direction. She wasn't like her mother either because she was not prone to sudden blinding infatuations. For years, there had been no other man for her but Andrew, a reality that had made the slow death of their relationship all the more painful to endure because it had started out with such high hopes.

It offended her sense of decency, however, that the intimacy she had shrunk from exploring with Andrew, whom she had loved, could be so very tempting when offered by a male like Cesare Sabatino, who had no respect for her at all. Cesare didn't give two hoots what happened to her or how she felt about any issue. Cesare merely wanted to *use* her to regain the island of Lionos and he thought that paying her richly for the privilege should take care of any doubts she might have.

'Mr Sabatino is in the office at the end of the corridor,' Primo informed her as she reached the foot of the grand staircase.

Almost sick with self-consciousness, Lizzie found the door ajar and walked in without knocking. Cesare's arrogant dark head flew up from his laptop, subdued fire flaring in his dark, glittering eyes at the interruption until he realised who his visitor was. A well-bred smile lightened his darkly handsome features and curved his hard mouth as he leapt upright, his attention automatically pinning to the lissom curves revealed by the casually elegant outfit she wore. In startling comparison a pink and white X-rated image of Lizzie splayed across his bed erupted at the back of Cesare's mind and he ground his teeth together as his body leapt in response to the provocation. Not for the first time he regretted the interruption that had left him burning with sexual frustration.

When he had last called Celine, he had grasped that he had a problem he had not foreseen. Aware that he was getting married, his French lover no longer wished to be seen in his company. Celine guarded her reputation because the clients who paid her a small fortune to advertise their exclusive perfume were conservative and Cesare had perfectly understood her determination to put her career first. It was, nonetheless, a challenge for him to work out how he was to cope for the next few months being married and *not* married at the same time.

He had not gone without sex for more than a couple of weeks since he was a teenager. Was he now supposed to sneak around seeking a discreet outlet? Without a doubt, he would have to avoid being seen consorting with any woman other than his wife or their marriage would appear dubious and, after going to such lengths to bring about the marriage, that was not a risk he was prepared to take. Whether he liked it or not and whether anything came of it or not, Lizzie was his only option for the foreseeable future, he acknowledged grudgingly.

'You look terrific, *cara*,' Cesare told Lizzie truthfully, politely tugging out a chair for her to use. The jasmine scent of her perfume flared his nostrils and before he could suppress the memory he recalled the wild, hot sweetness of her response. No man could easily forget that kind of passion, he reasoned, exasperated by his stubborn libido and the effect those turbulent hormones had on his usually cool intellect.

'Thanks but it's all fancy packaging, not really me,' Lizzie parried uncomfortably, because he was towering over her and close enough that she could smell the citrusy cologne that overlaid the erotic undertones of clean, warm male. Her colour fluctuating, she sat very straight-backed in her seat.

'Learn how to accept a compliment gracefully,' Cesare advised softly. 'You have a great figure, gorgeous hair and a beautiful face. Clothes merely provide an effective frame for the looks that nature gave you.'

Lizzie dealt him a pained half-smile. Unlike her, he was a master of the ready word and the right thing to say and had probably never been stuck for a quote in his entire gilded life. She evaded his shrewd gaze because she felt vulnerable, almost naked in his presence, stripped as she was of her usual working clothing and countryside assurance because his privileged world was so foreign to hers. She loved the way good clothes that fitted perfectly made her feel, but she wondered if he would still want her without that superficial gloss, a thought that made her feel inadequate and a little pathetic. In short, the spectacular luxury of his home, the costly garments and the preponderance of staff made Lizzie feel out of her depth and drowning. All she had required to crown her discomfiture was that ill-judged sexual episode that morning. 'I want you to sign these documents.' Evidently impervious to the unease afflicting Lizzie, Cesare extended a slim sheaf of papers. 'I need your permission to make alterations to the villa on Lionos.'

Her brow furrowed in surprise. 'Alterations? But you haven't even *seen* the house yet.'

'Because we won't be married until Friday,' Cesare pointed out drily. 'While we're on our honeymoon in Italy, my grandmother will be having her surgery and recuperating. As soon as she is strong enough we will fly out to Lionos and stay in the villa with her.'

'I didn't realise we were having a honeymoon.'

'It will only be a honeymoon in the eyes of the outside world,' Cesare qualified wryly.

'And your grandmother falls into that category too?' Lizzie checked.

'I've already explained that,' Cesare reminded her. 'For all that Athene's strong, she's an old lady. I don't want her to guess that our marriage is a fake. If she knew the truth she'd feel responsible and unhappy.'

'I can understand that.' Lizzie studied him uneasily. He emanated sleek, expensive elegance in a black business suit that outlined his broad shoulders, narrow hips and long, powerful legs to perfection but, unfortunately for Lizzie, she was still seeing him in his form-fitting boxers, an energising image of him half-naked and rampant with masculine potency. She chewed hard at the soft underside of her lower lip, fighting her awareness and her disobedient and thoroughly embarrassing thoughts.

'Before we can stay at the villa, however, some improvements must be made to the accommodation and for that I require your permission as the property belongs to you and your sister.'

'What sort of improvements?' Lizzie prompted with a frown.

'I want to send Primo out to the island immediately with a team of kitchen and bathroom specialists. The house needs to be brought up to date before we can live there and I want to ensure that Athene enjoys her stay.'

'But won't she be sentimental about changes being made to the house where she grew up?' Lizzie asked in surprise.

'That's a fair point but times have changed since she was a girl and I believe she'll recognise that. She's a practical woman and she likes her comforts.'

'From what my mother said, most of the soft furnishings will need to be replaced as well,' Lizzie told him in wry warning. 'Drapes, beds, sofas. I don't think it's possible to achieve so much within such a short time frame and if you don't watch out…once you start removing fitments, the villa will quickly become uninhabitable.'

His supreme assurance untouched, Cesare dealt her an amused smile. 'Believe me, if I'm prepared to throw enough money at the problem, someone will accept the challenge, *cara*.'

Lizzie shrugged because it was immaterial to her what he chose to have done to a house that she had never seen and would only briefly visit. But it was a painful reminder that Cesare only wanted her because she owned the island and could sell it to him if he married her and nobody, but nobody, could make a relationship out of that, she told herself wretchedly. None of her anxious feelings showing on her face, she dutifully scribbled her signature in the indicated places and provided her sister's address for the documents to be couriered to her.

A wholehearted smile softened her taut mouth when Archie poked his head round the door and trotted across the polished wooden floor to greet his mistress.

Cesare watched the dog receive a warm welcome and decided it was educational. Archie looked pathetic with only three working legs and the fourth in a cast and the dog played his advantage for all he was worth, rolling his tummy up in the air to be petted and then struggling pitifully to get up off the floor again. Cesare bent down to lift the terrier and help him upright again. In reaction to his sudden proximity, Lizzie rammed her chair back out of the way, her nervous response setting Cesare's teeth on edge as he straightened again.

Lizzie collided with stunning dark golden eyes fringed with black velvet lashes and forgot how to breathe, feverish tension snaking through her every muscle as she rose hurriedly from her chair again and moved towards the door, keen to be gone.

'Your father and your sister will be attending the wedding?' Cesare sought confirmation.

'Yes…' Lizzie coughed to clear her convulsed throat. 'And I'll ring Chrissie now to explain about the papers she has to sign.'

'I doubt if I'll see you again before we meet at the church on Friday,' Cesare imparted softly. 'Somehow try to practise not leaping away when I come close. It's a dead giveaway that our relationship is a sham.'

Lizzie flushed with mortification. 'Then practise keeping your distance,' she advised.

Well, that was telling him, Cesare conceded grimly. She was angry with him. He had been less than diplomatic after that phone call that interrupted them earlier that day. He ground his even white teeth together. He had only told the truth. Did women always punish men for telling the truth? If their arrangement was to work, however, he would need to make more of an effort to sustain their relationship, he acknowledged grudgingly. Women were emotional creatures. Her anxious, uneasy attitude towards him had just underlined that unwelcome reality.

Furthermore, Lizzie might be a gold-digger who had chosen money over ethics when given the choice, but how could he blame her for that when she had lived in poverty for so many years? It was not a crime for her to seek to better herself. And how could he fault her avaricious streak when, without it, she would have sent him and his proposition packing? It was unjust of him to view her in the same unforgiving light as the many mercenary women who had shared his bed, he conceded wryly. Serafina, after all, had made a straight-up choice to ditch Cesare and marry a man who had been much wealthier, even though he was also much older. He had to be less judgemental and more generous to Lizzie. In any case, as his wife and potentially the future mother of his child, Lizzie was also the equivalent of a long-term project. Somehow he would have to make her happy and *keep* her happy, because if he didn't all his plans could still come to nothing.

* * *

'You look totally amazing!' Chrissie exclaimed as Lizzie spun to show off her wedding gown, slender shoulders and arms sheathed in the finest see-through lace, her tiny waist accentuated by the fullness of her skirt.

'My brother's a closet romantic. He's going to love that dress,' Maurizia forecast as a knock sounded on the door and she and Sofia went to answer it.

'I'm having so much fun. I wish I hadn't put that exam ahead of attending your hen do,' Chrissie lamented, a slight willowy figure in the topaz-coloured bridesmaid dress that she and Cesare's sisters all wore.

Lizzie gazed fondly at her sister, thinking that she was the real beauty in the family with her perfect features and superior height.

'A pressie for you from Cesare,' Sofia announced, placing a jewel case in Lizzie's hands.

A gloriously delicate diamond necklace and drop earrings met Lizzie's stunned appraisal and a chorus of admiration rose from her companions. Of course, Cesare was playing to the gallery, assuming the role of besotted bridegroom for his siblings' benefit, Lizzie guessed. She put on the necklace and the earrings and realised that she was rather pathetically wishing that her wedding were the genuine article. She loved Cesare's family and would have given just about anything for them to be her family as well. Instead she had to live with the unlovely truth that she was deceiving them and would soon be deceiving Cesare's grandmother as well.

'You're really sure about doing this?' Chrissie whispered in the church porch as she made an unnecessary adjustment to Lizzie's gown while their father hovered, looking irritable. 'Because it's not too late to change your mind. All I have to do is call a taxi and we're out of here.'

'Are you trying to cause trouble? Of course, she's not going to change her mind!' Brian Whitaker declared in exasperation. 'That Sabatino fellow has to be the best thing that ever happened to her! At least he has an ounce of sense between his ears.'

'*We* certainly think so,' Paola piped up without hesitation. 'But sometimes the bride does get cold feet.'

'Not this one,' Lizzie countered steadily, smoothing over the awkwardness that had settled over the bridal party with her father's tactless words.

Cesare turned to look at Lizzie only when she reached the altar. Eyes the colour of melted bronze assailed her and she stopped breathing, gripped by the ferocious force of will in that appraisal. He had no doubts, she interpreted. He knew exactly what he was doing, had come to terms with the drawbacks and was concentrating on the end game. She had to do the same, she told herself urgently. She had to stop trying to personalise their relationship and stop wondering whether or not he would kiss her after they had been pronounced man and wife. Such treacherous thoughts were far removed from businesslike behaviour and utterly inappropriate, she scolded herself in exasperation.

'You look fantastic,' Cesare murmured softly while he threaded the wedding band onto her finger and she followed suit, copying his manoeuvre with less cool and more nerves.

Indeed, Cesare was taken aback by just how fabulous she looked. The effect she had on him was ever so slightly unnerving. It was his libido, he told himself impatiently. As long as he stuck to his rules of never getting tangled in anything that smacked of an emotional connection, he would be fine and perfectly happy.

And then the deed was done and they were married and there was no kiss, nor indeed any instruction to kiss the bride. Her hand trembling on Cesare's arm, she walked down the aisle, seeing a sea of smiling faces on every side of her. It was not her idea of a small wedding because the big church was crammed with guests. Out on the steps, Cesare escorted a tiny woman with vibrant brown eyes set in a round wrinkled face to meet her.

'Athene…meet Elisabetta, known as Lizzie,' he murmured quietly. 'Lizzie, this is my grandmother.'

The two women stood chatting about nothing in particular for several minutes beneath Cesare's watchful eye. Athene grinned at Lizzie. There was an astonishing amount of mischief in that unexpected grin and she squeezed Lizzie's hand. 'We'll talk later,' she promised cheerfully.

Later became much later once the bridal merry-go-round took over. The bride and groom greeted their guests at the country house hotel chosen to stage the reception, dined in splendour while being entertained by a famous singer, listened to the speeches and danced the first dance with Lizzie stumbling over her own feet. In the circle of Cesare's powerful arms and surrounded by so many well-wishers, Lizzie had to struggle to remember that their wedding was a fake.

In fact when Cesare lowered his darkly handsome

head and kissed her, Lizzie was so unprepared for the move and so taken back by it she fell into it like a child falling down a bottomless well. His mouth moved on hers and his tongue darted across the roof of her mouth and excitement leapt so high inside her she felt dizzy and intoxicated, her head tilting back, her hands tightening round his neck, fingertips flirting with the silky strands of his black hair. It was heavenly and devastating; heavenly to glory in her womanhood and appreciate that she had now discovered her sensual side and devastating to register that the wrong man was punching her buttons, simply to impress their audience.

In passionate rejection of that belittling image, Lizzie jerked her head back and pressed him back from her. 'Enough…' she muttered unsteadily.

'*Dio mio*, not half enough for me, *bellezza mia*,' Cesare rasped in a driven undertone. 'I want you.'

Lizzie had become as stiff as a board. 'We talked about that and decided that it wasn't sensible.'

'To hell with being sensible!' Cesare shot back at her with smouldering dark golden eyes framed by black velvet lashes, so breathtakingly handsome in that moment that he took her breath away. 'Passion isn't sensible…don't you know that yet?'

No, but he was teaching her what she had never wanted to know. Experimentation was acceptable to Lizzie as long as she remained in control. She didn't want to be out of control, didn't want to risk getting hurt or making a fool of herself again. Suddenly all her worst fears were coalescing in the shape of Cesare Sabatino and she had only gone and married the guy!

Sofia approached her. 'Athene wants you to come

and sit with her for a while. I expect she wants to get to know you... Cesare is by far her favourite grandchild.'

Lizzie rolled her eyes in sympathy. 'He's the only boy.'

'She practically raised him—that's why they're so close,' Sofia explained. 'Cesare was only four when our mother married his father and although he was supposed to come and live with our parents straight away, he and Athene kept on putting it off and Papa didn't like to interfere too much. Cesare's never been easy—he and Papa are so different.'

'Goffredo is a pet,' Lizzie said warmly. 'You're so lucky.'

'Cesare's too clever for his own good,' his sister opined. 'Papa was in awe of his brain and he was such an argumentative little boy.'

A smile of amusement tilted Lizzie's mouth. 'I can imagine. He likes everything his own way.'

Athene patted the comfortable armchair beside her own. 'Tell me about yourself. I'm a typical nosy old lady,' she confided. 'You talk and I ask the questions.'

Naturally there were questions about Lizzie's mother, whom Athene had met while Goffredo was dating her.

'My son could not have made her happy.' Cesare's grandmother sighed with regret. 'Francesca was always dissatisfied and she was disappointed that Goffredo already had a son. I wasn't that surprised when she broke off the engagement.'

'She wasn't happy with anyone for very long,' Lizzie admitted quietly.

'That must have been very difficult for you and your sister when you were growing up. The things that happen when you're young leave scars,' Athene remarked wryly. 'I believe that's why it's taken so long for Cesare to put Serafina behind him where she belongs…'

'Serafina?' Lizzie queried tentatively, wondering worriedly if this was some family story that she should have been acquainted with and if her ignorance would strike the older woman as suspicious.

'I didn't think he would've mentioned her to you,' Athene told her with a wry smile. 'Cesare hides his vulnerabilities very effectively.'

Lizzie resisted the temptation to admit that she hadn't believed he had any.

'Cesare fell in love with Serafina when he was a student. He wanted to marry her but she said she was too young,' Athene related, her wise old eyes resting on Lizzie's absorbed expression. 'In her first job, she met a very rich man in his seventies and within weeks they were wed.'

Lizzie froze in consternation. 'That must've been devastating for him,' she muttered ruefully, thinking that she had unkindly misjudged Cesare when she had assumed he simply had no heart and no room in his life for anything but business and profit.

'But today I know that he has finally put Serafina back where she belongs in the past,' his grandmother proclaimed with satisfaction and patted Lizzie's hand. 'Today I am joyful that Cesare has married you and changed the whole course of his life for the better.'

Lizzie suppressed a groan of disagreement. She was discovering where Goffredo's optimistic outlook came from—he had inherited it from his mother. It was a source of wonder to her that Cesare had grown up surrounded by people with such sunny natures and yet contrived to retain his cold, unemotional attitude to life. Yet he was also careful to maintain a certain distance from his loving family, she conceded reflectively, wondering if he secretly feared that his family loving softness might dull his own ruthless cutting edge.

A couple of hours after that, Lizzie boarded Cesare's private jet. Her feet, shod in spindly high heels, were killing her. Even the short walk through the airport had been too much and she collapsed into her leather upholstered seat and kicked off her shoes with intense relief.

'You did very well today,' Cesare pronounced, disconcerting her as he took his own seat opposite. 'I don't think anyone suspected the truth.'

'Your father knows,' she reminded him uncomfortably.

'He'll believe the truth for all of ten minutes. Give him a few weeks and he'll persuade himself that we fell madly in love within hours of getting married,' Cesare forecast with sardonic bite. 'That's the way Goffredo functions.'

'You have a lovely family,' Lizzie countered, colour springing into her cheeks. 'Don't be so critical. They love you very much and they aren't afraid to show it.'

Cesare stiffened until he recalled his father-in-law's behaviour throughout the day. Brian Whitaker had turned down the opportunity to make a speech, had kept to his own company in the midst of the crowd and had steadfastly managed not to smile even for the photographs. 'Your father's...different,' he conceded quietly. 'Not the demonstrative type.'

'When my mother left him, it soured him on life,' she muttered ruefully. 'And life has been tough for him ever since. He'll be more content living in the house he's hoping to rent in the village. I think it will be a relief for him not to be looking out of windows at the farm and fretting about the jobs I'm not getting done.'

'Isn't it a relief for you as well?' Cesare prompted, thinking of the long and gruelling hours of work she must have endured while she endeavoured to keep the farm going without help.

Lizzie compressed her lips and frowned reflectively. 'From dawn to dusk I worried about everything and anything and I'm not sorry to be free of that stress. The bank threatening to withdraw the loan was our biggest fear but then the rent was raised…and, that was a body blow, totally the last straw,' she confided honestly. 'That was followed by Chrissie announcing that she was going to drop out of uni and come home because we were having such a struggle. I couldn't let that happen. She *needed* to get her education.'

Cesare was listening intently. 'So that's why you suddenly changed your mind and agreed to marry me?' he breathed in a tone of disconcertion. 'I had no idea that you were under that much financial and emotional pressure.'

'But you said you *knew* our situation,' she reminded him in surprise. 'I assumed you'd used a private investigator to check us out before you came to visit.'

Level dark eyes gazed back at her, a frown line pleating his ebony brows. 'No, I didn't. I didn't know about the bank loan, the rent rise or your sister's plans to drop out. I only knew about your father's ill health and that you were trying to keep the farm afloat on your own.'

'Well, you know the whole story now,' Lizzie commented mildly. 'I was ready to sell my soul for thirty pieces of silver.'

'No,' Cesare contradicted, his sibilant Italian accent vibrating in the silence to send a current of awareness travelling down her slender spine. 'You were desperate to protect your family, regardless of what it might cost you personally. That's loyalty and I admire that trait.'

As the silence stretched, Cesare went back to work at his laptop. Driven by something stronger than he was, he found himself glancing up to watch Lizzie leaf through a glossy fashion magazine, pulling faces whenever she came on a picture of any garment she considered too extreme while absently fondling Archie's ear beneath his balloon collar. She was so very natural. What you saw was what you got from Lizzie Whitaker and he had totally misunderstood her. It was a sobering discovery for a male who prided himself on his ability to read others. He had made all too many assumptions about Lizzie, not least that she was a gold-digger, and now that he had discovered that she had been driven more by desperation than greed his innate curiosity about her was finally set free.

'Why did you dye your hair brown?' he asked her abruptly.

Lizzie twined a shining silver strand round a self-conscious finger and winced in evident embarrassment. 'Andrew didn't like my hair. He thought it attracted too much attention and that it looked white and made people think I was an old lady at first glance,' she told him uncomfortably. 'I could see his point.'

'Did you really want to please him that much?' Cesare pressed. 'Your hair's beautiful, unusual but undeniably beautiful, *cara*.'

Lizzie shrugged but her face glowed at the compliment. His lean, darkly handsome features held her intent gaze and she switched her attention back to the magazine, a pool of liquid heat gathering in her pelvis that made her squirm with chagrin. He was so very, *very* good-looking, it was natural for her to stare a little, she told herself ruefully, but she had to keep her feet on the ground and learn to distinguish between what was real and what was more probably fake.

The limousine that collected them from the airport in Italy wended its way along winding roads and through some spectacular scenery. It was late spring and the fields were green with fava beans and wheat dotted with yellow broom. Medieval villages in picturesque hilltop locations were ringed by vineyards and olive groves while the rolling hills were covered with groves of cypresses and umbrella pines. Lizzie was enchanted and plied Cesare with questions.

'You still haven't told me where we're going,' she complained.

'We're almost there.'

Lizzie stared out at the rustic stone farmhouse on the ridge of the hill and blinked because it was not what she expected. Cesare was so sophisticated that she had been convinced that they were heading for some exclusive spa. 'It just doesn't look like your style,' she breathed helplessly.

'I love old buildings. When I first saw it I was a

student out hiking with friends. The roof had fallen in, the first floor had gone and the end wall had collapsed. We took shelter in the barn during a thunderstorm,' Cesare explained as the driver turned down a dirt track that steadily climbed the hill. 'I watched the sun go down over the valley and swore I'd buy it with my first million.'

'Your first...*million*?' she exclaimed.

'It was a money pit,' Cesare told her cheerfully, his dark eyes gleaming with rueful amusement. 'I learnt that the hard way.'

The car drew up in a paved courtyard ornamented with urns full of tumbling flowers. As they climbed out, a rotund little woman in an apron hurried out to greet them. Her name was Maria and she was the housekeeper and, seemingly, Cesare's biggest fan. Ushered into a great vaulted hall, Lizzie looked around herself with keen interest, glancing through to a gracious drawing room rejoicing in a vast pale stone fireplace and an array of vibrant turquoise sofas. The outside might be antique and rustic but the inside was all contemporary elegance.

Maria led her upstairs and into a glorious light-filled bedroom with a window overlooking the valley below. Lizzie fingered the fine white linen bedding and admired the beautifully draped bed while wondering where Cesare was planning to sleep. The driver brought their cases up, closely followed by Cesare, lean and lithe in khaki chinos and an open-necked shirt that screamed Italian designer style.

'Where's your room?' Lizzie asked quietly.

'We *share*,' Cesare told her without skipping a beat.

'I'm not sharing a bed with you!' Lizzie gasped in consternation.

'We're supposed to be married. Let's stay in role,' Cesare fielded. 'Having gone this far, it would be stupid to take risks by using separate bedrooms.'

Lizzie kicked off her shoes and mulled over that argument. 'Maria's not going to talk.'

'She's not the only member of staff with access to the upper floor,' he shot back drily.

'OK…' Lizzie stood at the foot of the bed, prepared to admit that it was huge, but she was still doubtful that she could lose him in it. 'But you have to stay on *your* side of the bed.'

'Are we five years old now?' Cesare quipped, studying her with incredulity. 'You're making a fuss about nothing.'

Lizzie settled glinting witch-green eyes on him. 'I'm not used to sharing a bed. It's not nothing to me.'

'We'll discuss it over dinner,' Cesare decreed.

Lizzie threw her arms wide in emphasis, her temper mounting. 'I don't want to discuss it…I just don't want to do it!'

'Only forty-eight hours ago, you *did*,' Cesare countered, lean, strong face hard, dark golden eyes smouldering with recollection and unforgotten hunger.

Lizzie reddened. 'I was wondering how long it would take you to throw that back in my face. I was drunk, for goodness' sake,' she protested.

'At least you know what you want when you're drunk,' he riposted.

Lizzie slammed shut the door lest they be overheard arguing. 'That's a horrible thing to say!'

'Whether you like it or not, it's the truth. You want

me every bit as much as I want you. You just won't admit it.'

Lizzie was so enraged by that arrogant statement that she walked into the bathroom and closed the door behind her to escape him. The fixtures took her breath away. An antique tub took up prime position by the window while rustic stone walls and a pale marble floor provided an effective frame.

'And hiding in the bathroom isn't going to persuade me otherwise!' Cesare completed loudly outside the door.

Lizzie threw open the door again and marched out with compressed lips to drag one of the cases across the beautiful oak floor. 'I was *not* hiding.'

Cesare snatched up the case and planted it on the bed, helpfully springing the locks for her.

Lizzie hovered, her colour high, her eyes veiled.

Cesare stalked closer like a predator about to spring and she tensed from head to toe. 'Look at me, *bellezza mia*,' he urged.

Almost involuntarily, Lizzie lifted her head, platinum hair flying back from her heart-shaped face. 'Why?' she said flatly.

Lean brown hands lifted to frame her cheekbones and turn her face up. A muscle pulled taut at the corner of his wide, sensual mouth. 'I want to make a baby with you the normal way. I don't want to use artificial insemination. If we're going to become parents, let's try the natural approach first.'

He had taken her entirely by surprise. Her entire face flamed and even worse the heat darted downward to engulf her whole body. 'But that's not what we agreed.'

'We didn't agree anything. You made a suggestion. I didn't like it but I wasn't prepared to argue about it at that point and turn you off the whole idea of marrying me,' Cesare admitted without hesitation.

His sheer honesty bemused her and then touched her deep. *I want to make a baby with you.* The very words made Lizzie melt and she tried to squash her reaction and deny it. It would not be safe or sensible to have actual sex with Cesare Sabatino because it would smash the barriers she had carefully erected. But the prospect of undergoing some cold scientific procedure in a fertility clinic was, she suddenly appreciated, even less attractive to her.

'I'll think about it,' Lizzie mumbled half under her breath. 'Now, if you don't mind, I'd like to get changed into something more comfortable.'

'I'll go for a shower,' Cesare told her, peeling off his shirt without an ounce of inhibition.

Her heart hammering, Lizzie averted her gaze but the enthralling image of his bronzed, muscular torso was still seared across her vision. She pulled an outfit out of the case, nothing fancy for she had had her fill of fancy outfits that day. She caught an accidental glimpse of Cesare striding naked as the day he was born into the en suite and she almost groaned out loud. They were so different, so ill matched. He had seen it all, done it all, while she had only dreamt of the seeing and the doing. If she slept with him, she would develop feelings for him and she would get hurt because he wouldn't respond. Or maybe she would discover that she was the kind of woman who could have sex without getting more deeply involved, she reasoned abstractedly. She might not get attached to him at all, might be grateful to wave goodbye to him after a few months. How could she know how she would react?

When the shower was free, she made use of it and removed most of the heavy make-up she had worn for her big day. Applying only a dash of lipstick and blusher, she pulled on a stretchy maxi skirt and a sleeveless silk top, thrusting her feet into flat sandals. When she reappeared, a maid was in the bedroom hanging their clothes in the built-in closet and Lizzie went straight downstairs.

Cesare strode out to the marble-floored hall. 'Let me show you around before dinner,' he suggested.

'Where's Archie?' she asked.

Cesare held a finger to his handsome mouth in silencing mode and pointed into the drawing room. Archie was stretched out on a shaggy rug, his contented snores audible.

As dusk was folding in fast, Cesare showed her the outside of the house first. Lizzie stood on the covered stone terrace where Maria was fussing over a table covered in a snowy white cloth and admired the stunning view of the valley, which was overlooked by a superlative infinity pool. 'The views are out of this world. I'm not surprised you fell for this place,' she admitted, the tension of the day slowly seeping out of her.

Without warning, Cesare reached for her hand. 'This marriage can be as real as we want it to be, *bellezza mia*,' he pointed out quietly.

Her fingers flexed within the firm hold of his and her colour heightened. Real didn't mean for ever, did it? But then how many marriages truly lasted for ever? They were together now and would stay together until a child was born. The child she longed for, she reminded herself ruefully. Surely the closer she and Cesare became, the easier it would be to share their child both now and in the future?

Her lips parted almost without her volition, green eyes wide and anxious as if she was stunned by her own daring. 'I'll give it a go,' she told him softly. 'But I can't make any promises.'

Cesare smiled. It was a brilliant smile that illuminated his darkly beautiful features and enhanced his stubborn, passionate mouth. 'I'll try to make sure you don't regret it, *cara*.'

CHAPTER SIX

'MARIA IS WHIPPING out her entire repertoire for this one meal,' Cesare commented in amusement as the lazy meal wound through course after necessarily dainty course of appetising dishes.

Already unable to credit that she had agreed to try being married for *real*, Lizzie was too stressed to eat much of anything. A bite here and there was the best she could do and she proffered fervent apologies to the plump little cook when she came out to the terrace bearing her *pièce de résistance*, a fabulous layered chocolate cake.

They were about to embark on their marriage as if they were a normal married couple. And this was their *wedding night*. All of a sudden something Lizzie hadn't even had to consider in the run-up to the wedding was looming like a concealed tripwire in front of her. If she admitted that she was still a virgin he was sure to think she was a freak. After all, he knew she had been engaged. It would be better to keep quiet, she decided, and hope he didn't notice that there was anything different about her.

'You've barely touched alcohol today,' Cesare commented, wondering why she had fallen so quiet.

Not that she was ever a chatterbox, he acknowledged wryly. In fact there was always a stillness about her, a sense of tranquillity at the heart of her that was disconcertingly attractive.

'In the light of our…er…plans,' Lizzie muttered awkwardly, 'I thought it was better to abstain.'

'You're referring to the alcohol and pregnancy safety debate?'

Kill me now, Lizzie thought melodramatically. 'Yes. The argument about what might be a safe level goes back and forth, so it seems wiser just to avoid it altogether.'

'Is that why you made the most of your hen night?' Cesare asked, strong jawline tensing as he remembered her on the dance floor, full of vital energy and playfulness as she cast off her usual restraint.

'No. That wasn't planned. I missed Chrissie,' she admitted, colouring, 'and it had just been a very long time since I had been out like that and I overindulged.'

'Don't beat yourself up about it,' Cesare urged, stunning dark golden eyes shimmering in the candlelight against his bronzed skin.

He was so…hot, he was literally on fire, Lizzie reflected dizzily. And she was married to him, about to share a bed with him…and she was fretting, shrinking, *sighing* over the fact? What was wrong with her? That chemistry he had mentioned was in overdrive, lighting her up from the inside out with a prickling, tingling energy that her body could no longer contain. In an abrupt movement, she rose from the table and walked to the edge of the terrace to study the lights of the fortified village on the other side of the valley.

Her heart was as locked up tight as that village, hidden behind high defensive walls, she reminded herself bracingly. Having sex with Cesare didn't mean she was about to get silly ideas about him and start pining when he was no longer available. She had watched her mother careen blindly from one man to the next, hooked on love, her drug of choice. Lizzie had loved once and learned her lesson. If she couldn't even make it work with Andrew, there was little chance of it working with anyone else. She would have a baby to love though, she told herself in consolation.

'You're very tense, *cara*.' Cesare sighed, stilling behind her and gently resting his hands on her taut shoulders. Her delicate frame was dwarfed by his. 'You don't have to do anything you don't want to do…'

That he could read her nervous tension that accurately mortified Lizzie. In truth the problem was that she wanted him too much and feared the strength of that yearning. He turned her slowly round into the circle of his arms and she looked up at him and her knees went weak and her heart leapt in helpless response.

'I know that,' she asserted valiantly, wondering why he found the sudden change in their relationship so much easier. Were men just built that way? Was he more adaptable than she was? Or more relaxed at the concept of a marriage in which the only glue keeping them together would be sex and the hope of parenthood? *Just sex, nothing worth fussing over*, he had said after he got out of a bed where he had literally rocked her world. It was true that the only pleasure had been hers but his cold-blooded, practical take on what had happened between them had still knocked her for six. Yet she still couldn't drag her gaze from his beautifully shaped, passionate mouth.

Cesare studied her with veiled eyes, black lashes rimming the glint of smouldering gold. Desire was lancing through him with lightning-force potency, sending tiny ripples of tension through his big, powerful frame. He couldn't take his eyes off her lush mouth and the pouting crowns of her small breasts, which stirred softly below the fine silk of her top every time she shifted position.

It was years since Cesare had been so aware of a woman and he loathed the edgy bite of frustrated hunger that made him tense. He wanted to have sex with her and persuade his libido and his brain that, after all, she was just like any other woman he had bedded. He hadn't been with anyone since the day he had first met her and that bothered him. He hadn't wanted Celine when he'd had the opportunity and no other woman had since attracted his attention. Of course the problem was doubtless that his affair with Celine had run its natural course and left him bored. Lizzie was new and different, which had obvious appeal. There was even something strangely, weirdly sexy about the idea of getting her pregnant. He wasn't sure what it was but he knew that just the thought of it made him hard and ready. Given even the smallest encouragement, he would've ditched Maria's wedding banquet of a meal and headed straight for the bedroom.

Shaking off that foolish thought, Cesare gazed down at his bride with the sudden piquant recognition that she was his wife. *His* legal wife, *his* to have and to hold, *his* to protect. Without further ado, he pulled her close and kissed her, a husky growl sounding in the back of his throat when her firm little breasts brushed against his chest. She liked being carried; he remembered that and smiled. He hoisted her up into his arms and Archie scrambled up from his position of repose by the sun-warmed wall and barked in consternation at the sight of them.

'Keep quiet, Archie,' Cesare groaned. 'You can't come between a man and his wife…and I warn you, Lizzie, he's not sleeping with us tonight or any other night.'

Lizzie was challenged enough to think of sleeping with Cesare and her mouth was still tingling from the hungry pressure of his mouth. As he carried her upstairs she decided that she was turning into a shameless hussy. A gasp escaped her lips when she saw the bedroom, which had been transformed into a bower of candlelight and flowers while they had been dining. Candles flickered light from metal lanterns set round the room and lush vases of pristine white flowers completed the magical effect.

'Did you organise this?' Lizzie asked in wonderment when he settled her down at the foot of the bed.

Cesare laughed. 'No. Maria has waited a long time for me to find a wife and I think she's celebrating.'

Sudden shyness reclaimed Lizzie as he gazed down at her, the lights picking out the hollows below his high cheekbones, lending him an enigmatic quality. In that lambent light, he was truly beautiful, sleek and dark, exotic and compellingly male. With sure hands he pushed her hair back from her face, letting the long, silky strands flow down her back. He tipped up her face and claimed another kiss, feeding from the sweetness of her mouth with hungry fervour, crushing her soft full lips below his while her fingers clung to his shoulders.

'I've been thinking about this from the first moment I saw you,' Cesare growled against her reddened mouth, his dark deep voice vibrating down her spinal cord, the very essence of masculinity.

'You do talk nonsense sometimes and please don't tell me that's a compliment that I should gratefully receive. The first time you saw me I was in my dungarees and looked a complete mess!' Lizzie protested on the back of a rueful laugh.

'There's no accounting for taste or the male libido,' Cesare quipped, impervious to her disagreement. 'I saw your face, your skin, your eyes…it was enough, *delizia mia.*'

'I like it when you talk Italian,' Lizzie confided breathlessly. 'You could be reciting the multiplication tables but it wouldn't matter. It's your accent, your voice, the pitch you use.'

Surprised by that unexpected burst of loquaciousness, Cesare grinned, a slanting wicked grin that utterly transformed his lean, darkly handsome face, wiping away the cool vigilance and control that was usually etched there. 'What I like most about you is that you surprise me all the time.'

'Right now I'm surprising me,' Lizzie told him truthfully, uncertainty darkening her hazel eyes as it crossed her mind that she was behaving impulsively, not something she made a habit of after growing up with an impetuous mother. But then she was *not* her mother, she reminded herself squarely, and at the age of twenty-four was surely old enough to make her own decisions.

He took her mouth in a long, intoxicating kiss and sober thought became too much of a challenge. A ten-

sion of a very different kind began to lace her body.
She became ridiculously conscious of the silk rubbing against her swollen nipples and the dampness at
her feminine core. Her body was responding to the
chemistry between her and Cesare with a life of its
own, blossoming like a flower suddenly brought into
bloom by the sunshine. Only chemistry, *just* sex, she
reflected in an abbreviated fashion as she warded off
her insecurities. There was nothing to fear, nothing
to be ashamed of, nothing she need avoid to protect
herself. Dimly she was registering at some level of her
brain that her mother's disastrous affairs had made her
far too reluctant to take a risk on a man.

Her silk top fell in a colourful splash of silk to the
wooden floor and, with a ragged sigh of appreciation,
Cesare closed his hands to the pert swell of her breasts,
his thumbs expertly capturing and massaging the pro-
truding pink peaks until they were taut and throbbing
and the very breath was catching in her tightening
throat. Her hips dug into the mattress beneath her,
seeking to sate the hollow ache tugging at her pelvis.

One-handed, he wrenched at his shirt. 'You see
how I forget what I'm doing when I'm with you, *delizia mia*?' he rasped.

Lizzie only needed that invitation and she tugged
at his shirt, delicate fingers stroking over his taut,
muscular shoulders, adoring the heat and strength of
him. He put his mouth to her neck and skimmed the
tip of his tongue along her delicate collarbone and
then, gently lowering her flat on the bed, he roamed
down over her ribcage, sending delicious little jolts of
desire through her each time he captured the tender
peaks of her breasts.

Passion had claimed Lizzie. Her temperature was rocketing higher and higher, a sheen of perspiration on her brow, and her heart was hammering so fast it felt as if it were at the foot of her throat. Her hand delving into his luxuriant black hair, she pulled him up to her and kissed him with all the urgent hunger racing through her. He pushed her skirt up above her knees and trailed his fingers slowly up her inner thighs. Every inch of her felt stretched taut with the extreme wanting that had taken her over and she gritted her teeth as he anchored his fingers to her knickers and trailed them off. She wanted his touch so bad it hurt and she squirmed in a fever of need.

'I'm trying to go slow,' Cesare bit out raggedly, 'but I feel like an express train.'

'Talking too much,' she told him, her teeth chattering together at the unwelcome pause.

With an almighty effort, Cesare stepped back from the source of temptation. Haste wasn't cool, especially not the first time. He didn't think a woman had ever responded with that much passion to him and it was setting him on fire with overriding need. He told her that in Italian and she gave him a blissful smile, evidently glorying in the sound of his language or his voice or whatever it was that she liked. He stripped off the shirt, unzipped his chinos, pushed off everything in one urgent forceful assault on his clothing. Naked, he came back to her, revelling in the way her eyes locked to him and the sudden blush that warmed her porcelain complexion. He couldn't recall when he had last been with a woman who blushed. And in the bedroom? Never.

Lizzie was transfixed. There he was in all his

glory, her every piece of curiosity answered in one fell swoop. He scooped her up in his arms, pulled off the skirt that was her only remaining garment and settled her down, equally naked, in the centre of the turned-back bed.

Lizzie froze. 'I think we need to put out the candles!' she exclaimed, her entire body burning with embarrassment as she grasped in desperation for the sheet, which was out of reach.

In the very act of surveying her pale slender curves with rapt attention Cesare raised stunning golden eyes to study her in growing wonderment. 'I've already seen you naked,' he reminded her gently.

'That's different...I was too hung-over to be shy!' Lizzie pointed out loudly.

Cesare grinned and with a stretch of a long brown arm flipped up the sheet. 'This is not likely to hold me back,' he warned her.

As the cool cotton settled over her quivering length Lizzie lost some of her tension. Resting on one arm, she found Cesare gazing down at her with slumberous dark golden eyes. He rubbed a slightly stubbled jaw against her cheek in a sensual gesture on his path to her ready mouth.

One kiss melted into the next but as his hands roved skilfully over her, lingering on pulse points and teasing erogenous zones, lying still beneath his ministrations became tougher and tougher. Her nipples throbbed from his attentions, sending arrows of fire down to the tender, pulsing heart of her.

He stroked her and her spine arched. 'You're so wet, so ready for me,' Cesare husked.

A tiny shiver racked her slight frame, all the heat

coalescing in the swollen, delicate tissue between her thighs. She squeezed her eyes tight shut, striving to stay in control and not betray how new it all was to her. But with every ravishing caress, he seduced her away from control. Soft gasps parted her lips, her neck extending, tendons clenching as the stimulation became almost too much to bear.

'You know this will be a first for me, *cara*,' Cesare confided, running the tip of his tongue across a turgid rose-pink nipple.

Lizzie could hardly find her voice. 'What will?'

'Sex without a condom…I've never done that before and it excites me,' he admitted huskily, shifting against her thigh, letting her feel the smooth, hard length of his erection.

Lizzie was trying not to think about the size of him in that department. She was a modern woman, well acquainted with averages and gossip and popular report. Being a virgin didn't mean she was entirely ignorant, she told herself in consolation, striving not to stress as her excitement built and built. Hands biting into his strong shoulders, she lifted her hips upward, succumbing to an almost uncontrollable urge to get closer to him. He toyed with her lush, damp opening, honeyed quivers of sensations rippling through her womb, and circled the tiny bud of her arousal until almost without warning a wild, seething force of irresistible sensation engulfed her like a flood. Her eyes flew wide and she bucked and jerked and sobbed in the grip of rush after rush of intense and enthralling pleasure.

He tipped her up, hooking her legs over his shoulders in a move that unnerved her. He plunged into her tight channel and for a moment she was preoccupied with the sense of fullness, the certain knowledge that this was exactly what her body had craved throughout his teasing foreplay. In fact everything was wonderful until the hot glide of his flesh within hers sank deeper and a sudden sharp, tearing pain made her stiffen and cry out in dismay.

Cesare froze as though a fire alarm had gone off and stared down at her, dark golden eyes like hungry golden flames in his lean bronzed face. 'You *can't* be...'

Enraged by her own bodily weakness and chagrin, Lizzie dealt him a look that would have dropped a grizzly bear at ten paces. 'Well, don't stop now.'

'You're a *virgin*?' Cesare emphasised, his incredulity unconcealed as he held himself at an angle above her, muscles straining in his bulging forearms.

'How's that your business?' Lizzie slung back argumentatively.

Cesare swore long and low in his own language and cursed her stubbornness. He burned for her but he was fighting his hunger with all his might. It struck him as unjust that the hot, tight hold of her body on his gave him pure pleasure while she had only experienced pure pain.

'It's my business,' he told her grimly. 'I think this is my cue to back off.'

'No... No!' Lizzie exclaimed in consternation. 'You don't get to go that far and then *stop*... I want to know what it's like...'

In receipt of that plaintive plea, Cesare groaned out loud, belatedly recognising that marriage was proving a much bigger challenge than he had expected.

She was experimenting with him, he thought in all-male horror.

'Please...' Lizzie added, tugging him down to her, pale fingers framing his cheekbones as she reached without success for his beautiful, passionate mouth.

In the mood to be easily encouraged, Cesare shifted his hips, his entire attention nailed to her flushed and expressive face so that he could register the smallest wince she might make. Instead Lizzie smiled up at him with a look of wonderment that was uniquely soothing to his momentarily threatened male ego.

Lizzie closed her eyes again, mortified at the fuss she had made, the lengths she had had to go to to persuade him to continue. She had always believed that a man found it hard to stop in the middle of sex, so the fact that he had offered to withdraw altogether did not strike her as a compliment. But she had wanted to know, had wanted so badly to know what all the fuss was about.

He moved against her and tingling, driving sensation awakened in her pelvis again. She relaxed a little. The slow, almost provocative thrusts became enticing and she relaxed completely, indeed began to arch up to greet him with an enthusiasm she had never expected to feel. His skilled acceleration delivered sensation like nothing she had ever experienced and her excitement soared to delirious heights that climbed and climbed until she reached a peak and soared effortlessly over it and then down and down into the cocoon of lethargy and satiation, exhaustion pulling at her every sense.

Cesare settled her back down on the pillows and smoothed her tangled hair off her damp brow. His hand trembled a little because he was struggling to do two opposing things: firstly treat Lizzie like the bride she was and, secondly, suppress the anger tearing at him. 'Why didn't you tell me I'd be your first lover?' he demanded in a roughened undertone.

His tone, his exasperation, cut through Lizzie in her sensitive state like the sudden painful slice of a knife and she sat up abruptly, clutching the sheet to her chest. 'I didn't see that it was anything to do with you.'

'In other words, you chose to deliberately conceal it,' he condemned, leaping out of bed in one lithe, powerful movement. 'How the hell could you still be a virgin when you were once engaged?'

'Don't you dare raise your voice to me, Cesare Sabatino!' Lizzie yelled back at him furiously, but she was trembling with an innate fear she could not have expressed at that moment. 'As for why I was still a virgin, that's private.'

'You're married to me now, *cara*. I don't think it's unreasonable of me to expect an answer to something so basic.'

'When you have the right to ask me private questions, I'll let you know,' Lizzie slung back flatly, snaking out of the far side of the bed to avoid him and yanking the sheet free of the mattress with a violent jerk to wrap it round her body. 'Now, I'm going for a bath.'

'*Lizzie...*' Cesare ground out in frustration to her rigid back as she reached for the door of the en suite.

'I'm not feeling nice, *wifely* or the slightest bit chatty right now, so please excuse me,' Lizzie breathed icily and stepped into the bathroom, shutting and locking the door behind her within seconds.

Lizzie filled the glorious antique bath to the brim, filled it with bubbles and lowered her body into the warm water. Angry, Cesare could be incredibly intimidating, towering over her, dark eyes glowing with hostility in his lean dark face. She couldn't help that her first reaction to an angry man was to run to the nearest place of safety. Her mother's violent second husband had taught her to get herself and Chrissie out of harm's way fast.

But Lizzie refused to *be* intimidated by Cesare, whom she sensed would never be violent. What did he have to be so angry about? Hadn't their lovemaking been good for him? It had certainly been good for her, apart from the hiccup as such in the middle when she had discovered that her first experience of intimacy could actually be painful. Ironically she was more hurt by Cesare's withdrawal and grim mood in the aftermath, which had made her feel—all over again—inadequate. Why couldn't he have simply let the subject go? Had he no sensitivity? Couldn't he see that she didn't want to talk about it?

Cesare paced the bedroom in fierce frustration. Why hadn't she warned him? Had she been embarrassed about being untouched? He recalled the blushing and gritted his teeth, acknowledging that he was totally unfit to deal with sexual innocence when he had failed to recognise it even though it was right there in front of him. He had screwed up, screwed up even worse when he sprang an immediate interrogation on her.

This was not how he had pictured their marriage kicking off. She was all emotional now, very probably weeping in the bath and regretting their new agreement while wishing she had never laid eyes on him. And yet the sex had been amazing…so amazing he couldn't wait to repeat it. Galvanised into motion by that shameless motivation, Cesare threw on a disreputable pair of jeans and padded downstairs, pondering possibilities to redeem himself in his offended bride's eyes. Before he even got that far he heard the distant howls of Archie marooned in an outside kennel and he grinned at the sound. He was a very clever man and he would turn the wedding-night breakdown back into a honeymoon regardless of what sacrifices it demanded of him!

Archie broke off his cries mid-howl and pranced towards him on three little legs. Archie was not particularly attached to Cesare but he recognised him as a potential lead to his mistress…

CHAPTER SEVEN

ARCHIE WHIMPERED OUTSIDE the bathroom door.

'You know you can do better than that,' Cesare told him, tossing him a fragment of chicken from one of the plates on the table by the bed.

For a three-legged dog, Archie could move fast and he caught the scrap in mid-air.

'Now…you have a mission,' Cesare reminded the scruffy little animal. 'You get her out of the bathroom.'

Archie hovered by the door, tried to push it but the balloon collar round his neck got in the way. Sitting back on his haunches, Archie loosed a sad howl that would not have shamed a banshee. Cesare threw him another piece of succulent chicken in reward. Archie gave a grand performance.

Lizzie woke up feeling cold, water sloshing noisily around her as she sat up wide-eyed. Archie was howling at the door…or had that just been a dream? Clambering hastily out of the bath, she snatched up a fleecy towel and wrapped herself in it, just as Archie howled again. Glancing at the watch on the vanity to see how long she had slept, she was taken aback to realise that a couple of hours had passed and that it was now almost one in the morning. Depressing the lock, she opened the door in haste.

'Oh, pet, I forgot about you! Have you been lonely?' Lizzie asked, squatting down to the little dog's level.

'Want some supper?' Cesare asked lazily from the bed on which he reclined.

Small bosom swelling at that insouciant tone, Lizzie was about to tell him in no short order what he could do with supper and then her tummy growled and she registered in surprise that she was actually very hungry. Of course, she hadn't eaten very much at dinner...

Straightening, she looped her damp hair back behind her ear and focused on Cesare's lean, darkly devastating face, clashing with the banked-down glitter of his stunning eyes. 'You still want answers, don't you?'

'I'd be a liar if I said otherwise,' he admitted, sprawling back with his hands linked behind his head, a position which only threw into prominence the muscular torso and flat ribbed stomach beneath his black T-shirt.

Lizzie breathed in slowly, belatedly registering the table of snacks by the bed and the candles that must have been relit while she slept. A surprising sense of calm after the storm enclosed her. The worst had already happened, hadn't it? What did she have to fear now? Not marriage, not sex, she decided, her chin coming up. Cesare had...*briefly*...scared her but that wasn't his fault. No, that fault could be laid at the door of her late mother's misjudgement of men and a stepfather who had given Lizzie nightmares long after he had passed out of her life.

'You know, when you got so angry, you scared me,' she told him baldly. 'My mother was married to a man who beat her up when he got angry.'

Cesare sprang off the bed, a frown pleating his ebony brows. 'I would never hurt you.'

'I think I know that already,' Lizzie said quietly. 'But running is still a reflex for me when men get angry. I can't help it. The two years Mum was married to that man were terrifying for Chrissie and me.'

'Did he hit you as well?' Cesare growled in disgust, appalled that he could have, however unwittingly, frightened her.

'He tried to a couple of times but he was drunk and clumsy and we were fast on our feet,' Lizzie confided. 'Let's not talk about it. It's in the past. But I should make one thing clear…' She hesitated. 'I'm only willing to talk about Andrew if you're willing to talk about Serafina.'

'And exactly who has been talking to you?' Cesare demanded, a muscle pulling taut at the corner of his stern, handsome mouth.

'Your grandmother mentioned her…and I'm curious too,' Lizzie confessed while she walked into the dressing room in search of a nightdress. Shedding the towel behind the door, she slipped it on, catching a glimpse of herself in a tall mirror. What remained of her fake glamour had evaporated in the long bath she had taken. The moist atmosphere had added frizz to her formerly smooth tresses and she suppressed a sigh. Cesare was getting the *real* Lizzie Whitaker on this particular night.

Emerging from the dressing room with Archie at her heels, she tried not to visibly shrink from Cesare's acute appraisal. The silk nightie was long and, to her, the very antithesis of sexy because it revealed neither leg nor cleavage. Her face coloured as she stilled for a split second, disturbingly aware of the intensity of that assessment from his smouldering dark golden eyes. A wave of heat shimmied over her, settling at the tips of her breasts and between her thighs in a tingling, throbbing awareness that mortified her. She knew he was thinking about sex. She also knew that he was making *her* think about sex. And she didn't know how he did it. Hormonal awareness was like an invisible electric current lacing the atmosphere.

Cesare watched the candlelight throw Lizzie's slender legs into view behind the thin silk and his mouth ran dry while the rest of him ran hot and heavy. Her pert breasts shimmying below the material in the most stimulating way, she curled up at the foot of the bed and reached for a plate of snacks. 'So, who goes first?'

'I will,' Cesare surprised himself by saying. Although he had initially been disconcerted by her demand he was now more amused that she should want to travel that far back into his past. It simply irritated him, though, that his grandmother was willing to credit that a youthful love affair gone wrong could still have any influence over him.

'Serafina…it's a beautiful name,' Lizzie remarked thoughtfully.

'She is very beautiful,' Cesare admitted, quietly contemplative as he sprawled back indolently against the headboard of the bed. 'We were students together. I was doing business, she was doing business law. It was first love, all very intense stuff.'

Lizzie watched him grimace at that admission. 'My first love was a poster of a boy-band member on the wall,' she confided in some embarrassment.

'A poster would've been a safer option for me. I fell hard and fast and I wanted to marry Serafina. She said we were too young and she was right,' he conceded wryly. 'She was always ambitious and I assumed that I'd have to start at the bottom of the business ladder. But then I made a stock-market killing and took over my first company and my prospects improved. Serafina started work at an upmarket legal practice with some very rich...and influential clients...'

'And at that point, you were still together?' Lizzie prompted when the silence dragged, his delivery becoming noticeably less smooth.

'Very much so. We were living together. Second week in her new job, Serafina met Matteo Ruffini and he invited her out to dinner with a view to offering her the opportunity to work on his substantial account.' His beautiful mouth took on a sardonic slant. 'Suddenly she became unavailable to me, working late in the evening, too busy to join me for lunch.'

His tension was unhidden. Lizzie registered that Serafina had hurt him and hurt him deep because he still couldn't talk about the woman with indifference. 'She was seeing Matteo?'

'Sì...and the moment *Prince* Matteo proposed, I was history. He had everything she had ever wanted. Social position, a title and immense wealth. The only flaw in his perfection was that she was twenty-five and he was seventy-five.'

'Good grief! That's a huge age gap!' Lizzie exclaimed. 'Did she tell you she'd fallen in love with him?'

'No. Possibly that would have been easier to accept, if not believe. No, she told me that he was just too good a catch to turn down and that if she contrived to give him a son and heir, she'd be rich and blessed for the rest of her life,' Cesare breathed with derision. 'I realised I'd never really known her. It crushed my faith in women.'

'Of course it did,' Lizzie agreed, the nails of one hand biting into her palm while odd disconnected emotions flailed her, particularly when she found herself thinking aggressive thoughts about the woman who had broken Cesare's heart. She had read him *so* wrong when they first met. He had been prepared to leap into the commitment and responsibility of marriage at a very young age. Clearly, he had genuinely loved Serafina and yet she had betrayed him in the worst possible way when she chose a life of rich privilege over love.

'Andrew?' Cesare pressed in turn.

'He was my best friend growing up. We had so much in common we should've been a perfect match and we stayed great friends although he never actually asked me out until I was in my twenties. I was already in love with him…at least I *thought* it was love,' she said ruefully. 'Everybody assumed we would be great together and when he asked me to marry him, Dad was ecstatic. I said yes but I wanted us to just date for a while.' Her face paling, she studied her tightly clasped hands. 'It was in private that Andrew and I didn't work out.'

'Obviously you didn't sleep with him,' Cesare murmured softly, watching the fragile bones of her face tighten, the vulnerable curve of her mouth tense, feeling his own chest tighten in response.

'No, I just didn't want to sleep with him,' she admitted in an awkward rush. 'I froze every time he got close and he said I was frigid but I didn't find him attractive that way. I thought I had a real problem with being touched. That's why I wouldn't date anyone after him and why I never blamed him for turning to Esther.'

'You don't have *any* kind of a problem,' Cesare asserted with quiet confidence. 'You were inexperienced; maybe he was as well—'

'No,' Lizzie broke in, running back through her memories while remembered feelings of inadequacy and regret engulfed her.

Yet even before she had fallen asleep in the bath she had realised that her enjoyment of Cesare's attentions had shed a comforting light on the past, which had always troubled her. Her only *real* problem with Andrew had been that he had always felt like the brother she had never had. She could see things as they had been now, not as she might have wished them to be: sadly, there had been zero sexual attraction on her side. She had sincerely cared for Andrew but he had always felt more like a good friend than a potential lover. When she compared how she had reacted from the first moment with Cesare, she could clearly see the difference and finally understand that what had happened with Andrew was not her fault.

'I liked and appreciated him but I never wanted him that way,' Lizzie admitted with regret. 'I still feel guilty about it because I was too inexperienced to realise that he was just the wrong man for me…and my rejections hurt him.'

'He seems happy enough now.' Cesare toyed with another piece of chicken.

Encouraged to think that further treats were in the pipeline, Archie got up on his haunches and begged.

'Oh, my goodness, look what he's doing!' Lizzie exclaimed, sitting forward with wide eyes to watch her pet. 'He can beg…I didn't even know he could *do* that.'

Cesare rewarded Archie with the chicken because he had made his mistress smile and laugh.

'Of course, I've never fed him like that. If he'd come to me for food when I was eating my father would have called that bad behaviour and he would have blamed Archie. I kept Archie outside most of the time.'

'I suspect Archie would've been clever enough to keep a low profile around your dad,' Cesare surmised.

'Did you ever have a pet?'

'I would have liked one when I was a kid,' Cesare confided. 'But I was constantly moving between my grandmother's home and Goffredo's apartment and a pet wasn't viable.'

'Did you organise all this food?' she asked, smothering a yawn.

'The staff are in bed. I don't expect service here late at night,' he told her quietly. 'I emptied the refrigerator.'

'And let Archie up to lure me out of the bathroom,' Lizzie guessed, settling their discarded plates on the low table and clambering in the far side of the bed to say apologetically, 'I'm tired.'

'Brides aren't supposed to get tired, particularly not when they've been lazing in the bath for hours,' Cesare informed her, amusement dancing in his dark golden eyes.

He could still steal her breath away at one glance, she acknowledged wearily as she closed her eyes. It was, as he had termed it, 'just sex' and she had to learn to see that side of their relationship in the same casual light. She wondered if that would be a challenge because she was already drifting dangerously close to liking him.

'Archie can sleep under the bed,' Cesare decreed. 'He's not sharing it with us.'

'We can't do anything, you know,' she muttered in a sudden embarrassed surge, her cheeks colouring. 'I'm…I'm sore…'

'It's not a problem.'

Relieved, she smiled and closed her eyes. As he stripped by the side of the bed Cesare studied her relaxed features and thought, *Mission accomplished, honeymoon back on track.* It was the same way he handled problems at work, mentally ticking off items on a to-do list while always seeking the most successful conclusion. But as he slid into bed beside Lizzie he reached for her and it wasn't a pre-programmed task. He reasoned that she was a very restless sleeper and if he left her free to move around she would annoy him.

Strangely enough, he acknowledged, in spite of the bathroom shenanigans, she hadn't annoyed him once. But then she wasn't the greedy, grasping type of woman he had deemed her to be. Why had he been so biased? After all, he had a stepmother, a grandmother and three sisters, none of whom were rich *or* avaricious. Had he deliberately sought out lovers who only cared about his wealth? And if he was guilty of that, had it been because he genuinely only needed carefree sex with a woman? Or because he preferred to avoid the possibility of anything more serious developing? Almost ten years had passed since Serafina had waltzed down the aisle to her prince. He refused to think that she had burned him so badly that he had declined to risk getting deeply involved with anyone else. Yet he hadn't even got an engagement or a live-in relationship under his belt during those ten long years.

In the darkness, Cesare's wide, sensual mouth framed a silent but vehemently felt swear word. He did not appreciate the oddity of having such thoughts about the sort of thing he had never ever felt the need to think about before. It was that ring on his wedding finger that was getting to him, he brooded impatiently. It was feeling married and possibly just a tiny bit trapped…with Archie snoring beside the bed and Lizzie nestled up against him like a second skin.

Just like him, she was in this marriage for the end game and the prize, he reminded himself squarely. It wasn't a normal marriage but, if they planned to conceive a child, the marriage had to work on a daily basis and why should physical intimacy always lead to a closer involvement than he wanted? The answer was that sex didn't need to lead to anything more complex, he reminded himself stubbornly, certainly nothing that would break his rules of never getting more closely involved with a woman. And it was no wonder that he was feeling unsettled when he was in such unfamiliar territory. He hadn't tried to please a woman since Serafina and he wasn't going to make a fool of himself trying to please Lizzie, was he?

Archie's snores filtered up in direct disagreement.

CHAPTER EIGHT

CESARE GLANCED AT his wife and then at the party of men watching her every move in a pantomime version of dropped jaws as she alighted from his Ferrari. She was a lissom figure in a turquoise sundress, her gorgeous silvery mane blowing back from her delicately flushed face in the breeze, her shapely legs tapering down to impossibly delicate ankles and high-heeled sandals. He pushed up his sunglasses and gave the men a warning look before closing his hand round Lizzie's in a display of all-Italian male possessiveness that he could not resist.

Lizzie sank down at the table in the *piazza* and the waiter was at their side within seconds, doubtless drawn by one glimpse of Cesare's sleek sophistication. He had an air of hauteur and command that got them fast service everywhere they went and it was so inbred in him to expect immediate attention that he rarely even noticed the fact, although she was very sure he would notice if he didn't receive it.

Now she feasted her attention on his lean bronzed face. She was magnetised by his stunning dark golden eyes as they rested on her and wondered what he was thinking. She was *always* wondering what he was thinking, had to bite her tongue not to ask, but it was hardly surprising that she was living in a state of constant befuddlement because their business-based marriage of convenience had become something else entirely…at least for *her*…

They had now been in Italy for a solid month. Cesare had made several business trips. He had flown his family *and* Chrissie in to visit for one weekend and the two days had passed in a whirlwind of chattering liveliness and warmth. Lizzie had never been so happy before and it scared her because she knew she was nourishing hopes that would ultimately lead to disappointment and the stark biting pain of rejection. *What? Only possibly?* jibed her more truthful self. Lizzie's emotions had got involved the very first night they'd slept together and she'd wakened in the morning to find herself secure in Cesare's arms.

For four whole weeks she had been living an idyllic life with an attentive husband, who was also a passionate lover, by her side. He had taken her out sightseeing, shopping, out to dinner in sun-baked *piazzas*, fashionable squares, and to wander through old churches lit by candles and the sunlight piercing the stained-glass windows. Today they had walked the seventeenth-century ramparts of Lucca. Her fingers toyed momentarily with the slender gold watch encircling her wrist, her most recent gift. If he went on a trip or even noticed that she lacked something he considered essential, he bought it for her. He was incredibly generous in bed and out of it. He was curious about her, knew everything there was to know about her childhood. His interest was intoxicating because she had never seen herself as being particularly interesting.

In fact, being the focus of attention of a very handsome, entertaining male had made her see herself in a kinder, warmer light.

In truth, when Cesare Sabatino was faking being a husband, he faked with the skill and panache of a professional, she conceded ruefully. He hadn't asked her to fall in love with him. It wouldn't occur to him that bringing an ordinary woman out to beautiful Tuscany and treating her like a much appreciated, highly desirable wife while keeping her in luxury might turn her head. But Lizzie knew her head had been thoroughly turned. She found him fascinating. He was a spellbinding mix of rapier-sharp intellect and disconcerting emotional depth and, of course, she had fallen head over heels for him. Archie now rejoiced in a collar with his name picked out in diamonds and a four-poster bed of his own. How could she *not* love the man who had given her adored pet those quite unnecessary, ridiculously expensive but deeply touching things?

And the result was that now she was terrified of falling pregnant, fearing that that announcement would ensure that their marriage cooled back down to a businesslike arrangement in which Cesare would expect her to be terribly civilised and behave as if she didn't give a damn about him. Within days of the wedding she had had the proof that she had not yet conceived and Cesare had just laughed and said that they had all the time in the world, as if it truly didn't matter to him if it took months to reach that goal.

'What if there's something wrong with one of us and it doesn't happen?' she had asked him anxiously.

He had shrugged and suggested that they give it a year before seeking medical advice. If for some reason having a child turned out not to be possible, they would deal with it when it happened, Cesare had told her fatalistically while urging her not to stress about getting pregnant.

'I hope you've got something special lined up to wear tonight,' Cesare mused over their wine. 'It's a real fashion parade.'

'I thought it was a charity do.'

'In Italy such events are always fashion parades.'

'I have at least four long dresses to choose from,' Lizzie reminded him. 'I won't let you down. Don't worry about it.'

'*Ma no*...certainly not,' Cesare cut in, stroking a long forefinger soothingly over her hand where it curled on the table top. 'You always look fantastic, *gioia mia*. Why would I be worried about you letting me down?'

'I'm not part of your world and I never will be. It's a challenge for me to put on fancy clothes and pretend I'm something I'm not,' Lizzie admitted in an undertone.

'You only need to be yourself. You have two, no, three...' he adjusted reflectively, amusement gleaming in his gilded gaze '...advantages.'

'Which are?'

'Beauty and class and my ring on your finger,' Cesare completed with cynical cool. 'I'm a powerful man. You will be treated with respect and courtesy.'

An involuntary grin lit up Lizzie's face and she laughed, biting back foolish words of love. What an embarrassment it would be if she were to lose control of her tongue around him now! After all, he was playing a very sophisticated game with her, utilising his charm and a whole host of other extraordinary gifts to make their marriage work as if it were a real marriage. If she were to suddenly confess how she felt about him, he would be embarrassed and appalled to learn that she didn't know how to play the same game.

'We should head back soon,' she commented unevenly.

'Would that leave us time for an hour or so in bed?' Cesare sprang upright, dropping a large-denomination note down on top of the bill, smouldering dark eyes flashing over her with a sexual intensity that never failed to thrill.

'*Again?*' There was a slight gasp in her low-pitched response because she had yet to adapt to Cesare's high-voltage libido. He seemed to want her all the time, no matter where she was, no matter what she was wearing or what she was doing. She thought he was possibly a little oversexed but she didn't complain because she always wanted him too and, in any case, the whole point of their marriage was for her to conceive a child.

A light hand resting in the shallow indentation of her spine, Cesare urged her back to the Ferrari. As she clambered in beside him he turned his head and closed a hard hand into the tumble of her hair to hold her fast while he kissed her. His mouth was hungry and hot and erotic on hers and every sense was on overdrive by the time he freed her again and started up the car.

The air conditioning cooled her overheated skin but the ache throbbing between her thighs was far less controllable. Cesare skimmed up her skirt to bare her thighs. 'I like looking at your legs, especially when I know I'm about to part them,' he husked soft and low, laughing when her cheeks flamed.

Early evening, Lizzie inspected her reflection in a black shimmering dress that delineated her slender figure with a spare elegance that appealed to her. She was learning what she liked and didn't like in her wardrobe and she didn't like fussy trims or frills or neon-bright colours that seemed to swallow her alive.

Warmth speckled her cheeks as she thought about the intimacy of the late-afternoon hours. She moved slowly in her heels, a touch of tenderness at the heart of her reminding her of Cesare's passionate energy between the sheets. In bed, sensual excitement ruled her entirely and she was enjoying every moment of exploring that brave new world.

Even so the image that lingered longest was of Cesare, lithe and bronzed and breathtakingly beautiful, relaxing back against the tumbled pillows and finally admitting how very relieved he was that Athene was now well on the road to recovery, having initially suffered a setback in the aftermath of her cardiac surgery. For days, he had tried to pretend he wasn't worried sick even though Lizzie had watched him freeze at every phone call, fearful of receiving bad news. That he had finally abandoned that macho pretence of unconcern to share his true feelings with Lizzie had meant a lot to her. She valued the little signs that revealed that Cesare was behaving more and more like one half of a couple rather than an independent, entirely separate entity. They had visited his grandmother in her convalescent clinic in Rome several times and Athene's sparkling personality even in a hospital bed and her strong affection for Cesare had touched Lizzie's heart.

In the morning they were flying out to Lionos and

one day after that Athene was coming out to join them. Cesare had married Lizzie purely to gain that right to bring his grandmother out for a stay on the island and Lizzie regularly reminded herself of that unflattering reality. But she was looking forward almost as much as Athene was to seeing Lionos, which the older woman had described in such charmed terms. She only hoped that the enhancements engineered by the imperturbable Primo lived up to Cesare's expectations.

A limousine ferried Cesare and Lizzie to the venue for the charity benefit in Florence. It was being held in a vast mansion with every window lit and crowds of paparazzi waiting on the pavement to take photographs of the guests arriving. Lizzie froze in surprise when they were targeted, belatedly appreciating that she was married to a male who, when in his homeland, received the attention worthy of a celebrity for his looks and spectacular business accomplishments.

'Did you enjoy having your photo taken?' Cesare asked.

'No, not at all. I didn't feel glossy enough for the occasion,' she confided.

'But you spent ages getting ready,' Cesare countered with all the incomprehension of a male who had merely showered and shaved before donning a dinner jacket.

Her hazel gaze roving swiftly over the level of extreme grooming clearly practised by the other female guests, Lizzie suppressed a rueful sigh. She didn't look perfect and she knew it, reckoned she should have foreseen that the attentions of a hairstylist and a make-up artist would be necessary. But then how important was her image to Cesare? Did he really care?

Or would he soon be comparing her, to her detriment, to the women who had preceded her in his bed? Lizzie had done her homework on the Internet and she was uneasily aware that in recent years Cesare had spent a lot of time in the company of fashion and beauty models, invariably the very image of feminine perfection. Possibly she needed to make more of an effort, she conceded, uncomfortable with the comparisons she was making.

As they were surrounded by the leading lights in the charity committee of which Cesare was a director, the crowd parted and an exquisite brunette, wearing a very fitted pink dress overlaid with a see-through chiffon layer that simply accentuated her stupendous curves, approached them. Cesare performed the introduction. 'Our hostess, Princess Serafina Ruffini... Serafina, my wife, Lizzie.'

'Welcome to my home, Lizzie.' Serafina air kissed her on both cheeks and gave her a wide, seemingly sincere smile.

Shock winged through Lizzie and she was furious that Cesare hadn't warned her that the benefit was being held at his former girlfriend's home. Impervious to her mood and the manner in which her hand clenched tensely on his arm, Cesare talked about cancer research to an older man who seemed to be a doctor while Lizzie made awkward conversation with his wife, who spoke very little English. Italian lessons were going to be a must in the near future, Lizzie promised herself. Her attention crept back to Serafina, holding court on the other side of the room with a lively group who frequently broke into laughter.

Cesare had described his ex as *very* beautiful and

he had not been kidding. Serafina had almond-shaped dark eyes, skin like clotted cream, a wealth of dark tumbling curls and one of those enviable cupid's-bow scarlet mouths that men always seemed to go mad for. And, more worryingly, Serafina appeared to move in the same social milieu as Cesare, possibly to the extent that Cesare had not even felt it necessary to mention that Lizzie would be meeting her that very evening. For goodness' sake, he broke up with her almost ten years ago, Lizzie reminded herself impatiently. How likely was it that he was still hankering after what he had lost?

In conversation with one of the organisers, who spoke great English, Lizzie learned how indebted the charity felt to Serafina, not only for her recent decision to become their patroness but also for allowing her magnificent home to be used for a fundraising benefit. La Principessa, she learned, was worth a small fortune to the charity in terms of the PR and publicity she would bring their cause, which was raising sufficient funds to open a new hospice for terminally ill children.

It was very warm in the crowded room and perspiration began to bead on Lizzie's brow. She glanced longingly across the room to where several sets of doors stood open onto an outside terrace. As she stood there, a glass of water clasped in one hand, a sick sensation composed of both dizziness and nausea washed over her, leaving her pale.

'Excuse me, I'm warm and I think I'll step outside for a few minutes,' she told her companion and turned away, wondering if she should be taking refuge in the cloakroom instead, but praying that the cooler night air would revive her.

The terrace was furnished with tables and chairs, and lights and candles held the darkness at bay. Lizzie took a seat, gratefully feeling the clamminess of her skin and the faint sickness recede again and breathing the fresh air in deep while she wondered if she was simply tired or if, indeed, she could be in the very earliest stage of a pregnancy. Wonder at that faint suspicion curved her mouth into a ready smile but delight at the prospect was swiftly tempered by fear of what such a development might mean to her relationship with Cesare. Would he back off from their current intimacy? Would he stop treating her like a real wife?

'I saw you come outside,' a female voice said lightly. 'I thought we should get acquainted. I've known Cesare for so many years,' Serafina Ruffini told her with apparent warmth. 'You haven't been married long, have you?'

'No, only for a month,' Lizzie admitted, struggling to maintain her relaxed attitude in the face of Serafina's shrewdly assessing gaze.

'My husband, Matteo, passed away last year. I'm fortunate to have my seven-year-old son to comfort me,' Serafina confided.

'I'm sorry for your loss,' Lizzie murmured, guiltily dismayed at the news that the brunette was a widow. 'It must be hard for you and your son.'

'We're getting used to being a twosome.' Serafina signalled a waiter hovering by the door with an imperious gesture wholly in keeping with her rather royal air of command. 'Champagne?'

'No, thanks.' Lizzie smoothed a fingertip round the

rim of her glass of water while smiling valiantly as the brunette continued to watch her closely.

The champagne was served with a flourish. Serafina leant back in her upholstered seat. 'Of course, you'll know about my history with Cesare...'

Lizzie stiffened. 'Yes.'

'How honest can I be with you?'

'As honest as you like but I don't think Cesare would like us talking about him behind his back,' Lizzie opined quietly.

'He's an Italian male with a healthy ego.' Serafina laughed. 'Being wanted and appreciated by women is the bread of life for him.'

'Is that why you didn't marry him?' Lizzie heard herself ask helplessly. 'You believed he would be a womaniser?'

'No, not at all. I married for security. I didn't grow up like Cesare in a comfortable middle-class home,' Serafina confided, startling Lizzie with her frankness. 'I came from a poor background and worked very hard for everything I got and I had a great fear of being poor again. Matteo was a proven success while Cesare was only starting out in the business world. I loved Cesare but I'm afraid that the security which Matteo offered me was irresistible.'

Thoroughly disconcerted by that unembarrassed explanation, Lizzie murmured without expression, 'You made the right decision for you.'

Serafina saluted her with her glass in gratitude. 'I believe that I did but once I saw how well Cesare was doing in business, I naturally wished I had had more faith in him.'

'I expect you did,' Lizzie conceded tautly. 'But you

had a husband and a child by then and everything had changed.'

'But I still never stopped loving Cesare and, I warn you now, I intend to get him back.'

'You expect me to listen to this?' Lizzie asked, beginning to rise from her seat, having heard enough of Serafina's self-absorbed excuses.

'No, don't go,' Serafina urged impatiently. 'I'm sorry if I shocked you but I want you to understand that, right now, Cesare is set on punishing me for what I did to him almost ten years ago.'

Involuntarily, Lizzie settled back in her seat. '*Punishing* you?'

'What else could he have been doing when he married you? He married you to *hurt* me. Here I am, finally free and available and he marries you. What sense does that make?'

'Has it occurred to you that maybe he's over you and doesn't want you back?' Lizzie asked helplessly, provoked by the brunette's conviction that she would always be Cesare's most desirable option and reminding herself that she was supposed to be Cesare's real wife and should be reacting accordingly to Serafina's little spiel. 'Your affair ended a long time ago.'

'You *never* forget your first love,' Serafina argued with ringing conviction. 'He's even living in the house we planned together.'

'What house?'

'The farmhouse. We first saw it as students. It was a wet night and we made love in the barn,' Serafina admitted, a rapt look in her bright eyes as Lizzie hastily dropped her lashes to conceal her expression.

Too much information, Lizzie was thinking anx-

iously, an odd pain clenching her down deep inside.
She could not bear to think of Cesare making love
with Serafina and could have happily tossed Serafina's champagne into her sensually abstracted face.
Serafina had married her older man for security and
wealth while still loving and wanting Cesare. Lizzie
did not think the brunette had any right to expect to
turn the clock back or indeed any excuse to risk upset-
ting Cesare's new wife with intimate and threatening
images from the past she had once shared with him.

'Even though I was already married to Matteo, Cesare still bought the farmhouse as soon as it came on
the market,' Serafina told her smugly. 'Look across
the valley in the evening from the pool terrace and
you will see the Ruffini *palazzo* blazing with lights
on the hillside. He wants me back, Lizzie, he's simply
too proud to admit it yet.'

'I don't think he would've married me if that was
his intention,' Lizzie commented in a deflated tone.

'Oh, I guessed that he married you to get that stupid
island back into the family,' Serafina retorted with a
wry little laugh and she shrugged. 'I don't care about
that. Your marriage is temporary and I'll be waiting
when he decides to forgive me.'

'Whatever,' Lizzie mumbled, thrusting her chair
back and rising. 'You can hardly expect me to wish
you luck with my husband and I really don't understand why you wanted to talk to me in the first place.'

'Because you can make things a lot easier for all
three of us by quietly stepping back the minute Cesare
admits that he wants his freedom back,' the princess
pointed out smoothly. 'If it's a question of money.'

'No, I don't *need* money and I can't be bribed!'

Lizzie parried grittily, her cheeks reddening. 'I wish I could say it was nice meeting you…but it would be a lie.'

'You're a farmer's daughter with no education. Surely you don't believe you have what it takes to hold a man like Cesare's interest?' Serafina fired back with a raised brow. 'Cesare and I belong together.'

CHAPTER NINE

LIZZIE COMPRESSED HER LIPS, said nothing and walked back indoors.

A pounding headache had developed at the base of her skull. How she got through what remained of the evening, she had no idea, but she smiled so much her mouth felt numb and she made polite conversation until she wanted to scream. She was angry with Cesare for ever loving a woman as selfish and grasping as Serafina. Serafina only wanted Cesare now because he had built up an empire worth billions. Nevertheless a few of her remarks stayed with Lizzie like a bruise that refused to heal.

'You never forget your first love. He married you to hurt me. Cesare and I belong together.'

And who was she to assume that that wasn't true? Cesare had never dreamt of regaining the island of Lionos in the way his father and grandmother had. Never having seen it, he had never learned to care for it and could probably well afford to buy his own island should that have been his wish. Was it possible that Cesare had been willing to go through with marrying Lizzie because he had a stronger motive? A desire to punish Serafina for her betrayal all those years ago? *Revenge?* Certainly that was how the princess had interpreted his behaviour of getting married just at the point when she was finally free again. Exasperated by the pointless thoughts going round and round in her sore head, Lizzie tried to blank them out by acknowledging that she knew no more about what Cesare felt for Serafina than she knew about what he felt for herself.

'You've scarcely spoken since we left the benefit,' Cesare commented as the limo drew up outside the farmhouse. He had noticed that she had seemed unusually animated throughout the evening. That had proved a surprise when he had assumed she might feel the need to cling to him in such exclusive and high-powered company. When she failed to demonstrate any desire to cling, instead of being relieved he had felt strangely irked and could not explain why. He had always felt stifled by women who clung to him. He had always valued independence and spirit in a woman more than feminine weakness and soft words of flattery.

Yet when the spirited and independent woman whom he had once loved had approached him at the benefit for a private word, he had been totally turned off by the experience, he acknowledged grimly.

'I'm very tired,' Lizzie said stiffly.

Cesare followed her into the bedroom, unzipping her dress without being asked. Lizzie let the dress glide down to her feet, stepped out of it and, regal as a queen in her underwear, walked into the bathroom without turning her head even to look at him.

He knew when he was getting the silent treatment. She was sulking and that was childish. He had never had any patience for sulks. He pulled a pair of jeans out of a drawer and stripped off his suit. Casually clad, he noted the beady little eyes watching him from below the canopy of the four-poster pet bed and surrendered. 'Come on, Archie…time for something to eat…'

Archie limped across the floor. The cast had been removed from his broken leg only the day before but Archie still thought he was a three-legged dog and had yet to trust the fourth leg to take his weight again. Cesare scooped the little dog up at the top of the stairs and carried him down to the kitchen where he maintained a one-way dialogue with Archie while feeding them both as he raided the fridge.

Teeth gritted, Lizzie emerged from the bathroom to a frustratingly empty bedroom. She had decided that it was beyond cowardly not to ask Cesare why he hadn't warned her that the benefit was being staged at his ex-girlfriend's home. She had not been prepared for that confrontation and was convinced she would have made a more serious effort to look her very best had she known she would be meeting the gorgeous brunette. The problem was that she was jealous, she acknowledged ruefully, green and raw and hurting with ferocious jealousy. She looked out of the landing window at the dark silhouette of the old stone barn and her heart clenched as if it had been squeezed dry. Cesare had made love to Serafina there, love, *not sex.* He had loved Serafina, cared about her, *wanted* to marry her. Yet Serafina had turned her back on his love in favour of wealth and social status. Having achieved those staples, she now wanted Cesare back.

Pulling a silky wrap on over a nightdress, Lizzie

headed downstairs. Cesare was sprawled on a sofa in the airy living room. In worn jeans and an unbuttoned blue shirt, he was a long sleek bronzed figure and heartbreakingly beautiful. Her heart hammered out a responsive and nervous tattoo as she paused in the doorway.

'Why didn't you tell me?' she asked abruptly.

Cesare always avoided dramatic scenes with women and walking out on the risk of one came as naturally as breathing to him. One glance at Lizzie's set, angry face and the eyes gleaming like green witch fire in her flushed face was sufficient to warn him of what was coming. Springing lithely upright, he strolled out past her and swiped the car keys off the cabinet in the hall. 'I'm going for a drive…don't wait up for me. I'll be late,' he spelled out flatly.

Taken aback, Lizzie moved fast to place herself in his path to the front door. 'Are you serious?'

'Perfectly. I don't want to argue with you, *cara*. I'm not in the mood. We're flying to Lionos tomorrow and Athene will be joining us. That is enough of a challenge for the present.'

It was a shock for Lizzie to register how cold the smooth, perfect planes of his lean dark face could look. His spectacular eyes were veiled by his thick lashes, his superb bone structure taut, his shapely mouth, defined by a dark shadow of stubble, a hard line of restraint. Alarm bells sounded in her head. 'You could've warned me that we were going to Serafina's house and that she would be our hostess.'

'I am not going to argue with you about Serafina,' Cesare asserted, his jawline clenching hard as granite.

'I'm *not* arguing with you,' Lizzie reasoned curtly. 'And why won't you discuss her with me?'

Velvet black lashes flew up on scorching golden eyes. 'She's none of your business, nothing to do with you.'

Lizzie flinched and leant back against the door to stay upright. She felt like someone trying to walk a tightrope in the dark and she was terrified of falling. 'She spent ten minutes talking to me outside on the terrace and made me feel very much as if she was my business.'

Feverish colour laced his incredible cheekbones. '*You*...discussed me with...*her*?' he framed wrathfully.

Lizzie found it interesting that, instead of being flattered as Serafina had suggested, Cesare was absolutely outraged by the idea. 'What do you think?' She hesitated, hovering between him and the door. 'I only wanted to know why you didn't mention that she would be entertaining us.'

Cesare ground his perfect white teeth together because he *had* thought of mentioning it, only to run aground on the recollection that theirs was not a normal marriage. They were not in a relationship where he was bound to make such personal explanations, were they? He focused on Lizzie's pale face on which colour stood out only on her cheeks. She looked hurt. He saw that hurt and instinctively recoiled from it, frustration rippling through him. He didn't want to share what had happened earlier that evening with Lizzie, not only because it would rouse her suspicions, but also because it was tacky and he *refused* to bring that tacky element into what had proved to be a glorious honeymoon.

'Serafina is very much part of the local scenery. Many of my friends are also hers. I have no reason to avoid her. Seeing her is no big deal,' he delineated stiffly, reluctantly, willing to throw that log on the fire if it satisfied her and closed the subject.

'I don't believe you,' Lizzie whispered unhappily. 'If it had been no big deal, you would've mentioned it.'

'You know me so well?' he derided.

Lizzie paled even more. 'I thought I did.'

Cesare closed his hands firmly to her ribcage and lifted her bodily away from the door.

'If you walk out, I'm not going to Lionos with you!' Lizzie flung the worst threat she could think to make in an effort to stop him in his tracks.

'In what fantasy world are you living that you think you can threaten me?' Cesare breathed, freezing with the door ajar so that cooler night air filtered in to cool her now clammy skin.

'I only wanted you to explain.'

'I have nothing to explain,' Cesare parried drily. 'But you will definitely be telling me at some point what Serafina said to you.'

'Honesty has to be a two-way thing to work. We've been living like a married couple.'

'Because we *are* married.'

'You know what I mean…' Lizzie hesitated, reluctant to probe deeper but driven by turbulent emotional forces she could not suppress. 'You've been treating me as though I'm really your wife.'

There it was—the truth Cesare had hoped to evade

because he didn't know *how* that had happened, didn't know what to say to her, didn't even know how he felt about that development. Why did women always have to drag unmentionable issues out into the open and do them to death at a time of their choosing? How the hell had he got himself into such an untenable situation? He had started out fine, he acknowledged broodingly, laying down the rules, seeing what made sense, knowing what he should not do lest it lead to exactly this situation. And somehow it had all gone to hell in a hand basket in spite of *all* that careful pre-planning, *all* that practical knowhow and knowledge of the female sex. And here he was trapped as he had never wanted to be trapped…

'I want to know what Serafina said to you.'

'That she wants you back, that you married me to punish her, that I wasn't educated enough to hold you… Oh, yes,' Lizzie recounted and then, with a ghastly attempt at an amused smile, added, 'and that this was your mutual dream house, planned by you both on the wet night you made love in the barn…'

Cesare's eyes flashed flaming gold, his outrage unconcealed. He closed a hard hand to the edge of the door as if to emphasise the fact that he was still leaving. '*Madonna diavolo!* She shouldn't have involved you in this.'

At those words, at that suggestion that there was an involvement that she was unaware of, Lizzie swore her heart cracked right down the middle. 'No,' she agreed woodenly, because it was true.

Cesare steeled himself. He knew he had to speak, could not comprehend why ESP was suddenly warning him to shut up and say nothing. 'We don't have a genuine marriage. We are not a couple in the true sense of the word. We both know that...'

He paused as if he was hoping she would leap in and say something but Lizzie couldn't have found her voice had her life depended on it. At that moment she felt as if her life's blood were draining away in a pool on the floor and that dramatic image made her feel dizzy.

'I'm going to bed,' she mumbled, knowing that she was lying, knowing that sleep had never been further from her mind, but it seemed so incredibly important in that silence to act as if she were still able to function normally even if it was a complete lie to try and save face.

'This is all my fault,' Cesare breathed in a roughened undertone. 'Don't think I'm not aware of that. I shouldn't have brought something as volatile as sex into the equation.'

'And you were still doing it...only a few hours ago,' she framed unevenly.

Unusually indecisive, Cesare hovered in the rushing silence. Archie was looking at him from across the hall as if he had two heads, which absolutely had to be his imagination playing tricks on him, he reasoned wildly. He felt sick, he felt bad, he felt... No, he was being dangerously emotional and he knew what emotion did to him: it made him irrational and reckless and he wasn't going to go there again...*ever*! He was taking the right approach in correcting a serious mistake before it did any more damage. Aside of that aspect, they were both consenting adults.

'So, it's back to the business arrangement,' Lizzie assumed in a tight little voice.

'I think that would be wiser, don't you?'

Not recognising that cold, detached intonation, Lizzie finally dared to look at him again. He was poised by the door, devastatingly handsome, a long slice of bare brown torso showing between the parted edges of his shirt, tight jeans defining long, powerful thighs and lean hips. Slowly she raised her gaze, determined to be brave, determined to hold on to her pride even though he had rejected her in the worst possible and most hurtfully humiliating way. He had made it clear where he stood and she supposed that brutal honesty was for the best.

'Goodnight,' Lizzie said quietly and she turned on her heel.

In a split second the front door closed and he was gone. The Ferrari engine growled to life and she literally ran out to the terrace above the pool, frantically determined to see if she could pick out the Ruffini *palazzo* on the hillside. And there it was, a big white classical building lit up like a fairground. She had noticed it before but had never thought to ask about it. Now she watched the lights of Cesare's car heading down into the valley and she stood and she stood, arms wrapped defensively round herself while she waited to see if her very worst suspicions were correct.

At such a distance, she could not have been a hundred per cent certain but she was convinced that it was the Ferrari that she saw heading up the long, winding, steep drive to the *palazzo*. Cesare was going straight to see Serafina. Lizzie was in shock. Perhaps he had been seeing the other woman all along; Lizzie hadn't been keeping tabs on him everywhere he went. It seemed pretty obvious to her that Cesare had a dark

side and more secrets than she had ever had cause
to suspect and she had been ignorant and irrespon-
sible and very naive not to smell a rat sooner…but it
wasn't much good or any comfort to feel wise *after*
the event, was it?

CHAPTER TEN

THE FOLLOWING MORNING, with her heart beating very fast, Lizzie studied a test wand, relieved that she had taken the opportunity to discreetly buy a pregnancy kit some weeks earlier.

And there it was straight away, the result she had both feared and craved: she was pregnant. It changed everything, she acknowledged in shock, and she walked out to the bedroom and unlocked the door she had locked the night before. Cesare would need access to his clothes but had she cared about that last night when her dream world had collapsed about her ears? No, she had not.

But now that she knew for sure that she was carrying Cesare's baby, she had to look to the future and beyond the business agreement they had originally made. She could not afford to be at odds with her child's father. That would only foster resentment between them and their child would suffer in that scenario. Unfortunately that meant that she had to be a bigger person than she felt like being just at that moment. She had to rise above what had happened, bury the personal aspect and stick to the rules from here on in.

He'd broken her heart. Well, she'd recovered from

Andrew; she would eventually recover from Cesare. Of course, she had never loved Andrew the way she loved Cesare; consequently getting over Cesare would be more of a challenge. Andrew had hurt her self-esteem and damaged her trust but Cesare had torn her heart out. To think of living even one day without Cesare somewhere nearby tore her apart, teaching her how weak and vulnerable her emotions had made her.

Yes, Lizzie acknowledged, tidying her hair, adding more concealer to hide the redness of her eyes, she had a long, long way to go in the recovery process. But now that she knew about the baby, it would have to start right now. She would have to put on the act of the century. She couldn't afford to show the smallest interest in what was going on between Serafina and him. He had made it clear that she had no right to ask such questions and she would have to respect that.

Had Cesare behaved badly? She thought he had. Scrapping the business-agreement-based marriage had been *his* idea, not hers. But honesty forced her to acknowledge that he had suggested at the time that they would have to see how well their marriage worked. In short, their marriage as such had been on a trial basis. And obviously, while it had worked incredibly well for Lizzie, it had not worked at all for Cesare. That hurt; that hurt her very much. It was a complete rejection of everything they had shared in and out of bed over the past month and it made her feel such an idiot for being so deliriously happy with him while failing utterly to notice that he did not feel the same way.

Lizzie went downstairs for breakfast, Archie at her heels. The instant the dog saw Cesare, who spoiled him shamelessly and taught him bad manners by feeding him titbits during meals, Archie hurried over to greet him. Cesare vaulted upright the minute she appeared. Unshaven, noticeably lacking his usual immaculate grooming, he still wore the same jeans and shirt. He raked a long-fingered brown hand through his tousled hair, looking effortlessly gorgeous but possibly less poised than he usually was.

'I won't lock the bedroom door again,' Lizzie promised, her heart-shaped face as still as a woodland pool. 'I'm sorry, I didn't think about what I was doing but the room's free now.'

'I'll get a shower before we leave for the airfield,' Cesare countered, his dark golden gaze scanning her expressionless face as if in search of something. 'Lizzie, we need to talk.'

Already having foreseen that he might feel that that was a necessity, Lizzie rushed to disabuse him of that dangerous notion. The very last thing she needed in her current shaky state of mind was a rehash of the breakdown of their relationship the night before. It wouldn't smooth over anything, wouldn't make her feel any better. How could it? Essentially he was dumping her and nothing he could say would ease that pain.

'That's the very last thing we need,' Lizzie told him briskly. 'All that needed to be said was said last night and we don't need to go over it again.'

'But—'

'What you said made sense to me when I thought it over,' Lizzie cut in, desperate to shut him up. 'This is business, nothing else. Let's stick to that from now on and I'll keep to my side of the bargain while your grandmother is staying with us on the island. I see no reason why we shouldn't bring this…er…project to a successful conclusion.'

Cesare blinked, disconcerted by the sound of such prosaic language falling from her lips. He was relieved that she was calm and grateful that she now intended to accompany him to Lionos for Athene's sake but he didn't agree with a single word she was saying. While, uniquely for him, he hesitated in a frantic inner search for the right approach to take with her, Lizzie took the wind out of his sails altogether.

'And that successful conclusion I mentioned?' Lizzie continued, a forced brightness of tone accompanying her wide fake smile. 'We're almost there because I'm pregnant.'

'Pregnant?' Cesare exclaimed in almost comical disbelief, springing back out of his seat again and yanking out the chair beside his own for her use. *'Madre di Dio*…sit down.'

Taken aback by his astonished reaction to her news, Lizzie sank down on the chair. 'It's not earth-shaking, Cesare. Women get pregnant every day.'

'You're my wife… It's a little more personal than that for me,' Cesare parried thickly, stepping behind her to rest his hands down on her slim, taut shoulders.

Alarmingly conscious of that physical contact, Lizzie froze in dismay. 'Could I ask you not to do that?'

'Do what?'

'Touch me,' she extended in an apologetic tone. 'I'll understand if you're forced to do it when your grandmother's around to make us look like a convincing couple but we're alone here and there's no need for it.'

Off-balanced by that blunt response, Cesare released her shoulders and backed away. He was thinking about the baby and he was fighting off an extraordinarily strong urge to touch her stomach, which he knew was weird, not to mention an urge destined to go unfulfilled.

'Forgive me,' he breathed abruptly. 'My immediate response was to touch you because I am full of joy about the baby.'

He had never looked *less* full of joy to Lizzie. In fact he looked a little pale and a lot tense, eyes shielded by his ridiculously long lashes, wide, sensual mouth compressed. She wanted to slap him so badly that her hands twitched on her lap. Like a magician pulling a white rabbit out of a hat, she had made her unexpected announcement, depending on it to wipe away the awkwardness lingering after their confrontation the night before. She had just let him know that he would never have a reason to touch her again *because* she had conceived. He should have been thrilled to be let off the hook when he didn't deserve it. Instead, however, a tense silence stretched like a rubber band threatening to snap.

'I didn't think it would happen so...*fast*,' Cesare admitted half under his breath.

'Well, it saves us a lot of hassle that it has,' Lizzie pronounced with as much positive emphasis as she could load into a single sentence. Hovering on the tip of her tongue was the highly inappropriate reminder that, after the amount of unprotected sex they had had, she thought it was more of a surprise that they hadn't hit the jackpot the first week.

'Hassle?'

'If we'd had to go for the artificial insemination, it

might have been a bit...*icky*,' she mumbled, momentarily losing her grip on her relentless falsely cheerful front.

Icky, Cesare repeated inwardly. It was a pretty good description of how he was feeling. *Icky.* He had suffered a Damascene moment of revelation while he was with Serafina the previous night. A blinding light that even he could not ignore or sensibly explain away had shone over the events and emotions of the past month and he had finally understood how everything had gone so very wrong. Unfortunately for him, since Lizzie had joined him for breakfast, he had realised that 'wrong' was an understatement. He had dug a great big hole for himself and she was showing every intention of being perfectly happy to bury him alive in it.

Cesare went upstairs, ostensibly for a shower but he wanted privacy to make a phone call. In all his life he had never ever turned to Goffredo for advice but his father was the only touchy-feely male relative he had, who could be trusted to keep a confidence. His sisters were too young and out of the question. Each would discuss it with the other and then they would approach Lizzie to tell all because she was one of the sisterhood now and closer to his siblings than he was. Goffredo had one word of advice and it was an unpalatable one. Heaving a sigh, he then suggested his son imagine his life without her and take it from there. That mental exercise only exacerbated Cesare's dark mood.

Lizzie wore a floaty white cotton sundress to travel out to the island and took great pains with her hair and make-up. She knew that in the greater scheme of things her appearance was unimportant but was convinced that no woman confronted by a beauty like Serafina could remain indifferent to the possibility of unkind comparisons.

Close to running late for their flight, Cesare strode down the steps, a cool and sophisticated figure in beige chinos and an ivory cotton sweater that truly enhanced his bronzed skin tone and stunning dark eyes. Climbing into the car, he barely glanced at Lizzie and she knew all her fussing had been a pathetic waste of time.

Archie sat right in the middle of the back seat, halfway between them like a dog trying to work out how he could split himself into two parts. To Lizzie's intense annoyance, her pet ended up nudged up against a hard masculine thigh because Cesare was absently massaging Archie's ear, which reduced her dog to a pushover.

By the time they reached the airfield and boarded the helicopter, Lizzie was becoming increasingly frustrated. Cesare's brooding silence was getting to her and she wanted to know what was behind it. How could he simply switch off everything they had seemed to have together? It hadn't ever just been sex between them. There had been laughter and lots of talking and an intense sense of rightness as well. At least on *her* side, she conceded wretchedly.

His long, powerful thigh stretched as he shifted position and a heated ache blossomed between her thighs. That surge of hormonal chemistry mortified her. She reminded herself that that side of their marriage was over, she reminded herself that she was pregnant and she *still* ended up glancing back at that masculine thigh. Suddenly she was remembering that only the day before she would have stretched out a hand and stroked that hard male flesh, taking the initiative in a way that always surprised and pleased him. How had they seemed to be so attuned to each other when they so patently could not have been? Had she deceived herself? Had she dreamt up a whole fairy tale and tried to live it by putting Cesare in a starring role? Was this mess all her own wretched fault?

With such ideas torturing her and with a companion, who was almost as silent, it was little wonder that Lizzie had been airborne for over an hour when she was jolted by Cesare simply and suddenly turning round from the front passenger seat of the helicopter and urging her to look down at what he called *'her'* island.

'And Chrissie's,' she said unheard above the engine noise, stretching to peer over his broad shoulder as the craft dipped. She saw a long teardrop-shaped piece of land covered with lush green trees. *'That's* Lionos?' She gasped in astonishment for it was much bigger than she had expected. In her head she had cherished a not very inviting image of a rocky piece of land stuck in the middle of nowhere, for her mother had not made it sound an attractive place. At the same time their inheritance had never seemed very real to either her or her sister when they could not afford even to visit it.

Within minutes the helicopter was descending steeply to land in a clearing in the trees and for the first time in twenty-four hours a feeling of excited anticipation gripped Lizzie. Ignoring Cesare's extended hand, she jumped down onto the ground and stared up at the white weatherboard house standing at the top of a slope. Like the island, it was bigger than she had expected.

'Athene told me that her father built it in the nineteen twenties and she had five siblings, so it had to be spacious,' Cesare supplied as he released Archie and the dog went scampering off to do what dogs did when they'd been confined for a long time. 'Primo says it really needs to be knocked down and rebuilt but he's done his best within the time frame he's had.'

'He's frighteningly efficient,' Lizzie remarked, mounting the slope, striving to ignore and avoid the supportive hand Cesare had planted to the base of her spine and a little breathless in her haste.

'Take it easy. It's hot and you're pregnant,' Cesare intoned.

'For goodness' sake!' Lizzie snapped. 'I'm only a tiny bit pregnant!'

In silence, Cesare rolled his eyes at that impossibility. He had all the consolation of knowing that he was reaping what he had sowed. Lizzie was not naturally either moody or short-tempered. In fact, in spite of her troubled childhood she had a remarkably cheerful nature, he conceded grimly. At least she had had a remarkably cheerful nature until he had contrived to destroy everything in what had to be an own goal of even more remarkable efficacy.

Primo greeted them at the front door and spread it wide. 'Workmen are still finishing off the utility area,' he admitted. 'But I believe the house is now presentable.'

Wide-eyed, Lizzie drifted through the tiled hall, which had been painted white, and moved on into a spacious reception room furnished with pieces that were an elegant mix of the traditional and the more contemporary. French windows draped with floral curtains opened out onto a terrace overlooking a secluded sandy cove. The view down the slope of a path through the trees to the beach was incredibly picturesque and unspoilt.

She walked through the house and as she peered into rooms some of her tension began to evaporate. In the wake of her mother's unappreciative descriptions, she was surprised to discover that it was actually a very attractive house and full of character. A room with a bathroom had been prepared for Athene's use on the ground floor. Lizzie mounted the stairs, which had wrought-iron ornamental balusters and a polished brass handrail. A bedroom had been sacrificed to provide en-suite bathrooms. Everywhere had been freshly decorated and kitted out, fabrics stirring softly in the breeze through open windows.

'What do you think?' Cesare asked from his stance on the landing.

'It's magical. I can understand why your grandmother never forgot this island. It must've been a wonderful house for kids,' she confided.

'Soon our child will follow that same tradition,' Cesare said gruffly.

'Well, possibly when he or she is visiting you. I won't be here as well,' Lizzie pointed out, quick to puncture that fantasy.

Cesare hovered in the strangest way, moving a step forward and then a step back, lashes suddenly lifting on strained dark golden eyes. 'And what if I wanted you to be here as well?'

'But you *wouldn't* want that,' Lizzie countered with

unwelcome practicality. 'You will either have remarried or you'll have a girlfriend in tow.'

'What if I don't want that? What if I want you?' Cesare shot at her without warning, unnerved by that veiled reference to the divorce that would be required for his remarriage.

Lizzie lost colour, wondering what he was playing at, wondering if this was some new game on his terms. 'But you *don't*…want me, that is. You made that quite clear last night.'

'I *do* want you. I want to stay married,' Cesare bit out almost aggressively. 'Last night, you took me by surprise and I was confused. I made a mistake.'

Lizzie shook her pale head slowly and studied him in angry wonderment, temper stirring from the depths of the emotional turmoil she had been enduring since he had blown all her hopes and dreams to dust. 'I can't believe I'm hearing this. First you ask me for a business-based marriage, *then* you ask me to give our marriage a try and then you tell me we don't have a *real* marriage. As I see it, that's pretty comprehensive and not open to any other interpretation!'

She swivelled on her heel and deliberately walked past him to enter the room on the other side of the landing.

'I'm trying to say I'm sorry and you're not even listening!' Cesare growled from behind her.

'You can't apologise for what you feel…neither of us can,' Lizzie parried curtly as she lodged by a window, hoping to look as though she were entranced by the view when in actuality all she could think about was escaping this agonising going-nowhere conversation with Cesare, who seemed not to have the first clue about how she might be feeling. 'I'm going to get changed and go off and explore.'

'Alone?' Cesare exclaimed.

'Yes. I like my own company. I had to—I worked alone for years,' she reminded him doggedly, walking past him on the landing, relieved when she saw the cases being carried upstairs into the master bedroom. 'I realise once Athene arrives tomorrow it'll be "game on" or whatever you want to call it...but could we... please not share a bedroom tonight?'

'Why are you not listening to anything I'm saying?' Cesare demanded in apparent disbelief. 'You won't even look at me!'

Lizzie had only felt free to look at him when he was *hers*. Now that he wasn't any more, she didn't want to fall victim to his essential gorgeousness all over again. Not looking was a form of self-defence, she reasoned wildly.

'Lizzie...' he breathed in a driven undertone.

Lizzie stiffened, tears prickling behind her wide eyes. 'I can't afford to listen to you. You upset me a lot last night and I really don't want to talk about that kind of stuff. It's pointless. I'm not really your wife. I may be living with you—'

'Expecting *my* child!' Cesare slotted in with greater force than seemed necessary.

'But you didn't choose to marry me because you cared about me, therefore it's not a proper marriage,' Lizzie replied as she reluctantly turned back to face him. 'And in your own immortal words everything else we've shared can be written off as "just sex".'

Cesare flinched at that reminder, his pallor below

his bronzed skin palpable. 'I care about you *now*. I want to *keep* you.'

'I'm not a pet, Cesare…' Lizzie stared at him and frowned. 'Are you feeling all right? You know, you're acting very oddly.'

Goffredo's one-word piece of advice returned to haunt Cesare. 'I'm fine,' he said brusquely, lying through his teeth.

All of a quiver after that pointless exchange, her nerves jangling, Lizzie vanished into the bedroom, closed the door and opened her case to extract a sun top and shorts. She needed to blow the cobwebs off with a good walk. Cesare was nowhere to be seen when she went downstairs again and she went into the kitchen where Primo reigned supreme and eventually emerged with Primo's luxury version of a picnic meal and a bottle of water. With a little luck she could stay out until dark, then dive into bed and wake up to a new day and the big show for his poor grandmother's benefit.

Cesare was furious when he discovered that Lizzie had left the house. He strode down to the beach but there was no sign of her and not even a footprint on the pristine strand to suggest that she had come that way.

Several hours later, sunburned, foot weary and very tired after her jaunt across Lionos, Lizzie returned to discover that Cesare had gone out. Thankful, she settled down to supper as only Primo could make it. Sliding into her comfortable bed, she slept like a log.

Athene arrived mid-afternoon the next day. Cesare decided to be grateful for that because it brought Lizzie out of hiding. It had not once crossed his mind that she could be so intractable that she wouldn't even give him a hearing and then he thought of all the years she had slaved for her unappreciative and critical father and realised that she would have needed a strong, stubborn backbone.

Relaxed and colourful in a red sundress, Lizzie ushered Athene into her former childhood home. Tears shone in the old lady's eyes as she stood in the hall, gazing down the slope at the beautiful view. 'I thought it would all be overgrown and unrecognisable.'

'You showed me a photo once. I had the trees cut back,' Cesare told his grandmother softly. 'Shall I show you around?'

'Yes, this is your home and Lizzie's now,' Athene said a little tearfully and fumbled for a tissue. 'I have so many memories of my brothers and sisters here and now that they're all gone…'

Lizzie watched Cesare mop up his grandmother's tears with a deft touch and the right words and, minutes later, Athene was laughing as she recounted a childhood adventure with her brothers. She accompanied them on the official tour and Primo served afternoon tea out on the terrace, apparently an old tradition that Athene loved.

'Primo is an absolute treasure,' Athene told Lizzie as Cesare murmured an apology and withdrew to answer his phone before walking back into the house.

'And even better he *cooks*, which I'm not very good at,' Lizzie admitted, topping up the older woman's tea.

'Have you and Cesare had a row?' her companion asked without warning. 'I'm not an interfering old woman but I can feel that something's wrong.'

Lizzie felt that even an award-winning actress would have been challenged to carry off a smile at that point. 'A hiccup,' she downplayed studiously, her cheeks burning tomato-red as if the lie might be emblazoned on her forehead.

'My grandson has a remarkable brain, which serves him well in business. He's not quite so good at relationships,' Athene remarked wryly, gentle amusement in her warm brown eyes. 'There's bound to be hiccups as you call them. He's set in his ways and you'll challenge him. That's good for him. After all, anyone with eyes can see how deeply attached you are to each other.'

Lizzie's opinion of Athene's shrewdness nose-dived at that pronouncement but the awkward moment passed over and she managed to relax again. The old lady eventually nodded off in the shade and Lizzie went back indoors.

'I need to warn you,' Lizzie almost whispered round the corner of the door of the room Cesare had set up as an office. 'Athene thinks we've had a row but that that's normal, so not really anything to worry about...but we'll need to make a real effort to impress.'

'Wouldn't it be easier simply to talk to me?' Cesare suggested, rising from behind his desk, all sleek Italian designer style in his tailored oatmeal-coloured casuals.

Lizzie continued to hover defensively in the doorway. 'I just don't think we have anything to talk about.'

'Do you know what time I went to bed last night?'

Lizzie blinked in confusion. 'How would I?'

'I was out tramping round the island looking for *you*. Primo couldn't raise a signal on my cell phone until midnight and I only found out then that you had returned to the house hours earlier!'

Lizzie dealt him an astonished look. 'But why were you looking for me in the first place? I wasn't lost.'

Cesare studied her as if she were irretrievably dim. 'There are all kinds of hazards out there. Fast currents in the sea, steep drops, dangerous rocks...'

Definitely behaving oddly, Lizzie labelled as she breathed in deep. 'Cesare, I'm not some little fluffy woman who can't look after herself. I'm an outdoors woman, used to working in all weathers and accustomed to constantly considering safety aspects on the farm.'

'But I was *worried* about you!' Cesare shot back at her in furious frustration.

Lizzie tossed her head, platinum-blonde hair shimmering across her slight shoulders in the sunlight, green eyes wide and wary. 'Well, you didn't need to be. I should've thought you would've been more worried about how Serafina is managing while we're together here when you belong with her.'

'I do not *belong* with Serafina!' Cesare raked at her so loudly, she jumped.

'No?'

'Do I strike you as being an idiot? I was a boy when I fell in love with her and full of romantic idealism but I'm all grown-up now,' he completed grimly.

'Well, you went rushing over to that *palazzo* fast enough the other night,' Lizzie argued in a less aggressive prompt. 'That *was* where you went, wasn't it?'

His stunning gaze widened to smouldering gold eyes of challenge. 'You think I went over there to *be* with her?'

'What else was I supposed to think?' Lizzie asked tightly. 'You left me in anger...'

'I wasn't angry with you, I was angry with *her*!' Cesare exclaimed in full-volume contradiction and Lizzie hastily backed to the door to close it firmly shut. 'How dare she have the insolence to approach my wife with the tacky details of an affair that happened a decade ago? I'd never heard such rubbish in my life and I was determined to finally have it out with her.'

Tacky details scarcely dovetailed with Serafina's suggestion that the barn episode had been a very precious memory for them both. Furthermore Lizzie was transfixed by the idea that he had rushed out of the house in a rage because Serafina had dared to approach his wife. Lizzie went pink over her misreading of the situation. 'And did you have it out with her?'

'*Sì*...I said a lot that she will not forget in a hurry. If she wasn't so vain, she would have accepted a long time ago that I would sooner chew off my own arm than have anything to do with her again. How could you think *that* of me?' Cesare raked at her in apparent wonderment. 'A woman who walked out on me because I wasn't rich enough? A disloyal, deceitful woman with the morals of a whore... She first offered herself back to me three years after she married Matteo and she did it again last night, which outraged me.'

Lizzie was so astonished by what she was finding out that she was rooted to the floor where she stood. Not only did he no longer care about Serafina, he evidently despised her and her eagerness to get him back. There was nothing fake about the driving derision he exuded. 'And of course you said no?'

'I never thought about her again after that first incident,' Cesare admitted flatly. 'By that stage I was grateful that, by marrying her, Matteo had saved me from making a serious mistake. No sane man would want a treacherous woman but, unfortunately for him, Matteo was besotted with her.'

Lizzie nodded slowly.

'Serafina won't be bothering either of us again, I assure you,' Cesare spelled out. 'She told me that she's bored with the countryside and will be moving back to her home in Florence.'

Lizzie was thinking about him having spent hours searching for her the night before because he was concerned that she might have met with an accident. Even though she was a seasoned outdoorswoman, she could not help but be touched by his naive assumption that she required his protection. She had made so many silly assumptions about Serafina and suddenly it was obvious that she had been listening to an extremely vain and spoilt woman spouting her belief that she was both irresistible and unforgettable. Cesare, on the other hand, had recovered from Serafina's betrayal by appreciating what a narrow escape he had had. That, she recognised, was absolutely in line with his character while rushing off to be with Serafina while he was married would not have been.

'I'm glad she's moving…I didn't like her,' Lizzie confided in a case of severe understatement. A light-headed sensation engulfed her and she gripped the back of a chair. 'Sorry, I get a bit dizzy now and again.'

'Is that like being only a tiny bit pregnant?' Cesare enquired, scooping her up as she swayed and planting her carefully down into the armchair. 'You need to be taking more rest and eating more food.'

'And what would you know about it?' Lizzie mumbled, momentarily giving way to the heaviness of her body and slumping into the depths of the chair like a sagging cushion.

'Possibly as much as you,' Cesare dared. 'I contacted an obstetrician for advice.'

Her lower lip dropped. 'You did…what?'

'It's my baby too,' he countered defensively. 'I had no idea how to look after you properly. It made sense to consult someone with the relevant knowledge.'

Her eyes stung again. Against all the odds, he was making such an effort to put across the point that, although he didn't want a real marriage with her, he did care about her welfare and their child's. Her throat convulsed. The tears she had been holding back were gaining on her, no matter how hard she tried to hold them back.

As Cesare stared across the barrier of his desk he saw two tears rolling down Lizzie's cheeks and his last defences fell to basement level. *He* had caused this fiasco. *He* had made her unhappy.

'I'm sorry…I'm *so* sorry,' Cesare told her gruffly.

Lizzie opened her wet eyes to find Cesare on his knees at her feet, stunning dark golden eyes stricken. 'Sorry? What about?'

'I'm sorry I hurt you. For years I had this set of rules with women,' he breathed raggedly, grabbing both her hands and crushing them between his. 'I never got involved. I never got involved with anyone after Serafina. And then I met you and I…I thought it would be the same with you and I tried to stick to the same rules but you were too much for me, only I didn't see it…'

'Slow down…' Lizzie begged, struggling to work

out what he was telling her in such a rush. 'What are you saying?'

'That I'm mad about you, that I love you and I never want to lose you,' Cesare told her, crushing the life out of her poor fingers, his physical intensity as great as the emotional intensity now clear in his eyes.

Her lashes fluttered in bemusement. 'But you *said*—'

'Forget what I said. I was still trying to stick to my rules but it was idiocy,' he told her with a fierce fervour that was in itself impressive. 'I drove to Serafina's in a rage because she'd dared to try and upset you and I was driving back, thinking about what a vicious witch she is and thinking about you too…and that's when I realised.'

'That you love me?' Lizzie probed numbly, unsure what to believe, her thoughts spinning.

'I think I was scared to deal with what I was feeling for you, so I avoided thinking about it altogether…' Cesare hesitated. 'You know, I'm not much like Goffredo. I don't spend much time thinking about feelings and stuff.'

Lizzie was pleasantly surprised to learn that he had spent *any* time thinking about feelings but she couldn't smile when she was in shock. For the first time ever outside the bedroom she was seeing Cesare without the cool front he wore to the world and he wasn't half as smooth with words in the emotional category as he was with other things. Yet there was something hugely endearing about that inept surge of sentiment and confession because every syllable of it rang with raw honesty.

'So, you think you love me?' she pressed a little

shakily, scared to hope, scared to dream, scared he didn't yet know his own heart.

'I *know* I love you. I only had to think of how warm and happy everything has seemed since we got married. I only have to think of being without you to know that what I feel for you is so much more than I ever felt for Serafina,' he confessed huskily.

A huge smile suddenly lit up Lizzie's face as she finally dared to really look at him again, scanning the superb bone structure, the straight nose and the perfect mouth. This time around, she revelled unashamedly in his essential gorgeousness because for the first time ever he felt like *hers*.

'I didn't want to fall for you either. Mum made so many mistakes and she was never really happy. I was afraid of falling for you,' Lizzie admitted, freeing a hand to brush his thick black hair off his brow in a gesture that came very close to an adoring caress. 'I really did think we were going to go the business route and then…my goodness, I couldn't stop thinking about you, couldn't take my eyes off you, couldn't keep my hands off you. You're sort of addictive but I didn't want to get hurt.'

'I hope I will never hurt you again.'

'Why are you still on your knees?' Lizzie whispered, genuinely bewildered.

'I rang my father for advice. I didn't give him *details*,' Cesare stressed when she looked at him in dismay. 'I just admitted that I'd said some very stupid things and he had only one word of advice…'

Lizzie viewed him expectantly.

Cesare bit the bullet and confided, *'Grovel.'*

'Seriously?' Lizzie giggled, tickled pink.

'I'm only going to do it once because I'm never ever likely to screw up as badly with you again, *amata mia*,' Cesare delivered, springing back upright without any loss of presence to open the door before striding back to scoop his wife up out of her chair. 'I've learned a lot from this experience.'

'Have you?' Lizzie asked curiously, resting back against his broad chest, sublimely happy just to be in his arms again, breathing in the delicious scent of him and free to think about all the wicked bedroom skills he was undoubtedly about to unleash on her.

'For a whole month I took you for granted. I'll never make that mistake again. I love you. My family loves you.'

'Even my father said that you were a sensible man,' Lizzie inputted with amusement.

'Very sensible. You're a wonderful woman, *cara mia.*' Cesare lowered her the whole formidable length of his lean, hard body to the landing floor and kissed her with hungry, driving passion.

Lizzie was more than ready to drown now in his potent fervour to reconnect with her. Excitement laced her happiness with a heady sense of joy and quiet security. She simply knew that she had a glorious life ahead of her with her husband and her child.

On the ground floor, Athene was in a self-congratulating mood.

'I do hope I've sorted them out. Cesare's stubborn but his wife is soft. As if I would simply fall asleep in the middle of a conversation!' Athene chuckled as she took over Primo's kitchen to make her grandson's favourite cake. 'I think we'll have a rather late dinner tonight, Primo…'

* * *

Three years later, Lizzie relaxed on the front veranda of the house on Lionos while she awaited Cesare's return from a business trip. Her children were with her. Max was two, a toddler with the unusual combination of his mother's pale hair and his father's dark eyes. He was industriously racing toy cars on the boards beneath her feet and making very noisy vroom-vroom sounds. In a travel cot in the shade a dark-haired six-month-old baby girl slumbered, sucking her thumb, while Archie dozed on the front doormat.

Gianna had not been planned, Lizzie reflected, her eyes tender as she bent down to try and extract her daughter's thumb from her rosebud mouth. She managed it but even in sleep within minutes the thumb crept back. She gave up when she heard the distant beat of the helicopter's approach, sliding upright to get a better view over the bay.

Max abandoned his cars and joined her. 'Papa… Papa!' he exclaimed, well aware of what that sound presaged in his secure little world.

Lizzie stroked her son's silky head and smiled dreamily. She always enjoyed the sunshine and the peace on Lionos but it would soon be disrupted by Cesare's forceful, exciting presence and she couldn't wait; she really couldn't wait. Three years had not dimmed the chemistry between them.

Athene spent spring to summer on the island, preferring her Rome apartment and its greater convenience in the winter. Lizzie had grown to love her husband's grandmother as much as she loved the rest of his family. He had been so blessed by all that love and warmth and to give him his due becoming a parent had made Cesare more sensitive towards his own relatives. He was much more relaxed with his large and convivial family than he had once been and his father and his sisters were frequent visitors to their homes in London, Tuscany and Lionos. Lizzie often teased her husband that she had stayed married to him because she couldn't bear the thought of losing his family.

Sadly, since her marriage she had seen much less of her own father and sister. Brian Whitaker came on occasional visits but he didn't like flying or foreign food or even people talking their own language in his vicinity. Lizzie had purchased a compact home for the older man in the village where he had grown up and he seemed as happy there as he would be anywhere. She had taken him to see a consultant for his Parkinson's disease and he was on a new drug regimen and showing considerable improvement.

Disconcertingly, although Chrissie regularly hitched a flight home with Cesare when he was in London on business, she had become fiercely independent and now had secrets she was reluctant to share. Lizzie had watched anxiously from the sidelines of her sister's life as things went badly wrong for the sibling she adored and troubled times rolled in. Cesare had advised her to let Chrissie stand on her own feet and not to interfere when Lizzie would more happily have rushed in and tried to wave a magic wand over Chrissie's difficulties to make them vanish. She had had to accept that Chrissie was an adult with the right to make her own decisions...and her own mistakes. That said, however, she was still very close to her sister and very protective of her.

The helicopter finally appeared in the bright blue

cloudless sky and descended out of sight behind the trees. Max was jumping up and down by that stage and clapping his hands. In a flash he was gone and running down the slope to greet his father with Archie chasing at his heels, shaggy ears flying, tongue hanging out.

'Go ahead,' a voice said softly from behind Lizzie. 'I'll sit with Gianna.'

Lizzie flashed a grateful smile at Athene and raced down the slope after her son like a teenager. Cesare took one look at his wife, pale hair flying, cheeks flushed below brilliant green eyes full of warmth and welcome, and set Max down again to open his arms.

'I really missed you!' Lizzie complained into his shoulder. 'You're far too missable.'

'I'll work on it,' Cesare promised, smoothing her hair back from her brow, wondering whether or not he should admit that he had worked night and day to get back to her within a week. He missed his family more every time he left them behind and planned complex travel schedules that minimised his absences.

'I shouldn't be whingeing,' Lizzie muttered guiltily, drinking in the familiar musky scent of his skin, her body quickening with the piercingly sweet pleasure-pain of desire that made her slim body quiver against his long, lean length.

'It's not whingeing. You missed me…I missed you, *amata mia*,' Cesare said huskily. 'We are so lucky to have found each other.'

They walked slowly back up the slope, Max swiftly overtaking them, Archie lagging behind. Cesare stilled to turn Lizzie round and curve loving hands to her cheeks to gaze down at the face he never tired of studying. 'I'm crazy about you, Signora Sabatino.'

'And me…about you.' Beaming in the sunshine, Lizzie linked her arms round his neck and tilted her head back invitingly.

She slid into that kiss like melting ice cream, honeyed languor assailing her in the safe circle of his arms. Cesare was home and a rainbow burst of happiness made her feel positively buoyant.

* * * * *

THE WEDDING
NIGHT DEBT

CATHY WILLIAMS

To my three wonderful and inspiring daughters

CHAPTER ONE

DIVORCE. IT WAS something that happened to other people: people who didn't take care of their marriages; who didn't understand that they were to be nurtured, looked after, handled as delicately as you would handle a piece of priceless porcelain.

At any rate, that had always been Lucy's way of thinking, and she wondered how it was that she was standing here now, in one of the grandest houses in London, waiting for her husband to return home so that she could broach the subject of divorcing him.

She looked at her diamond-encrusted watch and her stomach knotted in anxiety. Dio was due back in half an hour. She couldn't remember where he had spent the past week and a half. New York? Paris? They had places in both. Or maybe he had been in their Mustique villa. Maybe he had gone there with another woman. Who knew? She certainly didn't.

Self-pity threatened to engulf her and she stemmed the tide with ease of practice born of habit.

She'd been married for nearly a year and a half, plenty of time to get accustomed to the way her youthful dreams had crumbled to ashes.

When she glanced up, she could see herself reflected in the huge, hand-made contemporary mirror which dominated the ultra-modern drawing room. Five foot ten, slender as a reed, long blonde hair that dropped to her shoulders, vanilla-blonde and poker-straight. When she was sixteen, she had been spotted by an agency and her father had tried to shove her into a career in modelling, because why waste a pretty face? After all, women weren't cut out for anything more challenging, not really… But she had resisted—not that it had done her any good at all, in the end, because what good had been her degree when she had ended up…here? In this vast house, wandering in and out of rooms like a wraith, playing the perfect hostess? As if perfect hostessing was any kind of career for someone who had a degree in maths.

She barely recognised the woman she had turned out to be. On a warm evening in the middle of July, she was languishing in silk culottes with a matching silk vest top, just a few discreet bits of fairly priceless jewellery and high heels. She had turned into a Stepford Wife, except without the adoring husband rolling in at five-thirty every evening and asking what was for dinner. That might have been a distinct improvement on what she actually had, which was…nothing.

Or, *had* been nothing. She allowed herself a little smile because things weren't quite as sterile as they had been. Her situation had changed in the past two months and she hugged that secret pleasure to herself.

It made up for all the time she had spent dressed up like an expensive doll, administering their various properties, smiling politely when she needed to smile politely and hosting dinner parties for the great and the good. Or, at any rate, the very, very rich.

And now…a divorce would set her free.

Provided Dio didn't kick up a fuss. Although she told herself that there was no reason for him to, she could still feel a prickle of nervous perspiration break out over her body.

When it came to the concrete jungle, Dio Ruiz was the pack leader. He was an alpha male who played by his own rules. He was the sexiest man on earth and also the most intimidating.

But he wasn't going to intimidate *her*. She had spent the past few days telling herself that, ever since she had decided which turning she would take at the crossroads—the turning that would put as much distance between herself and her husband as possible.

The only slight fly in the ointment was the fact that this would be the last thing he would be expecting and Dio didn't do well when it came to flies in the ointment, not to mention the unexpected.

She heard the slam of the front door and her stomach lurched sickeningly but she only turned around when she sensed him at the door, his powerful, restless personality permeating the room even before she looked at him.

Even now, after everything, hating him as much as she hated him, his physical beauty still managed to take her breath away.

At twenty-two, when she had first laid eyes on him, he had been the most sinfully stunning guy she had ever seen and nothing had changed on that front. He was still the most sinfully stunning guy she had ever seen. Raven-black hair framed arrogantly perfect features. His pale, silver-grey eyes, so unusual against his bronzed skin, were dramatically fringed with thick, dark lashes. His mouth was firm and sensuous. Every little bit of him relayed the message that he was not a guy to be messed with.

'What are you doing here? I thought you were in Paris…' Lounging in the doorway, Dio began tugging at his tie, strolling into the room at the same time.

Surprise, surprise. It wasn't often he found himself anywhere with his wife that hadn't been meticulously planned
in advance. Their meetings were formal, staged, never,
ever spontaneous. When they were both in London, their
lives were hectic, a whirlwind of social events. They each
had their separate quarters, readied themselves in their
own private cocoons and met in the vast hall, both dressed
to the nines and ready to present the united image that
couldn't have been further from the truth.

Occasionally, she might accompany him to Paris, New
York or Hong Kong, always the perfect accessory.

Smart, well-bred…and most of all stunningly beautiful.

Tie off, he tossed it onto the white leather sofa and
circled her, frowning, before coming to rest directly in
front of her, where he began undoing the top two buttons
of his shirt.

'So…' he drawled. 'To what do I owe this unexpected
pleasure?'

Her nostrils flared as she breathed him in. He had a
scent that was peculiarly unique to him. Clean, woody
and intensely masculine.

'Am I interrupting your plans for the evening?' She
averted her eyes from the sliver of tanned chest just visible where he had unbuttoned the shirt.

'My plans involved reading through some fairly dull
legal due diligence on a company I'm taking over. What
plans did you think you might be interrupting?'

'No idea.' She shrugged her narrow shoulders. 'I don't
know what you get up to in my absence, do I?'

'Would you like me to fill you in?'

'I don't care one way or another, although it might
have been a little embarrassing if you'd come home with
a woman on your arm.' She gave a brittle laugh, hating
herself for how she sounded—hard, cold, dismissive.

It hadn't started out like this. In fact, she had actually been stupid enough, at the very beginning, to think that he was actually interested in her, actually attracted to her.

They had gone out on a few dates. She had made him laugh, telling him about some of her university friends and their escapades. She had listened, enthralled, about the places he had seen. The fact that her father had actually approved of the relationship had been a green light because her father had made a career out of disapproving of every single boy she had ever brought home, all three of them. In fact, he had made a career out of being critical and disapproving of everything she had ever done, and every choice she had ever made, so the fact that he had been accepting, *encouraging*, even, of Dio had been a refreshing change.

If she hadn't been so wet behind the ears, she might have asked herself why that was, but instead, heady with the joy of falling in love, she had chosen to overlook his sudden benevolence.

When Dio had proposed after a whirlwind romance she had been over the moon. The intense but chaste courtship had thrilled her, as had the fact that he hadn't wanted to wait. No long engagement for him! He had been eager to slip the ring on her finger and his eagerness had made her feel loved, wanted, desired.

Sometimes, she wondered whether she would have stupidly continued feeling loved, wanted and desired if she hadn't overheard that conversation on their wedding night. She'd been floating on a cloud, barely able to contain her excitement at the thought of their honeymoon in the Maldives and their wedding night, the big night when she would lose her virginity, because until then he had been the perfect gentleman.

He'd been nowhere to be seen and she had eventually

floated away from the marquee in her father's garden, from
the music and the people dancing and getting drunk, and
had drifted off towards the kitchen and past her father's
office, where she had immediately recognised the deep
timbre of his voice.

A marriage of convenience…a company takeover…
He had got her father's company, which had been losing
money by the bucket load, and she had been an accessory
thrown in for good measure. Or maybe, when she had
bitterly thought about it later, her father had insisted on
the marriage because if she was married to Dio he would
remain duty-bound to the family company. No doing the
dirty once the signatures had been written on the dotted
line! No dumping her father in the proverbial because he
was no longer an asset!

She would be her father's safety net and Dio—as her father had spitefully told her when she had later confronted
him with what she had overheard—would get the sort of
class that his vast sums of money would never have been
able to afford him.

Lucy, in the space of a couple of hours, had grown up.
She was a married woman and her marriage was over before she had even embarked on it.

Except, she couldn't get out of it, her father had told her,
not that easily. Did she want to see the family company go
under? There'd been some uncomfortable stuff with some
of the company profits…a little borrowed here and there…
he might go to prison if it all came out. Did she want that,
to see her father behind bars? It would hit the news. Did
she want that? Fingers pointed? People smirking?

She had acquiesced to her sham of a marriage although,
frankly, her father might have escaped a prison sentence
but only by handing the prison sentence over to her.

The one thing she had resolved, however, was to be

married in name only. No sex. No cosy time together. If Dio thought that he had bought her body and soul, she had been determined to prove him wrong. When she thought of the way she had fallen for his charm, had thought he'd actually been interested in inexperienced little *her*, she had burned with shame.

So she had quietly put her dreams into a box, shut the lid and thrown away the key...and here she was now.

'Is there a problem with the Paris apartment?' Dio asked politely. 'Can I get you a drink? Something to celebrate the one-off occasion of us being in the same room alone without prior arrangement? I can't think of the last time that happened, can you?' But, at a push, he would have said before they'd got married, when she had been studiously courting him, even though at the time he had thought it to be the other way around.

He had set his sights on Robert Bishop and his company a long, long time ago. He had covertly kept tabs on it, had seen the way it had slid further and further into a morass of debt and, like any predator worth his salt, he had bided his time.

Revenge was always a dish best eaten cold.

He just hadn't banked on the daughter. One glimpse of Lucy and her innocent, ethereal beauty and he had altered his plans on the spot. He had wanted her. She had touched something in him with her innocence and, cynic that he was, he had fallen hook, line and sinker.

He hadn't banked on that complication, had thought that she would hop into bed with him, allowing him to get her out of his system before he concluded business with her father. But, after a few weeks of playing a courting game that wasn't his thing at all, he had concluded that he wanted more than just a slice of her.

Only thing was...nearly a year and a half later and their

marriage was as dry as dust. He still hadn't touched that glorious body, leaving him with the certainty that, whilst he had thought he had the upper hand, she and her conniving father had actually played him for a fool. Instead of swinging the wrecking ball to the company and setting the police on Robert Bishop—who had been embezzling for years—he had ended up saving the company because he had wanted Lucy. He had wanted her at his side and in his bed and, if saving the company came as part of the deal, then so be it. Course, he had saved it and made money from it, ensuring that Robert Bishop was firmly locked out with just enough pocket money to teach him the joys of frugality, but still...

He had been unwittingly charmed by her open, shy, disingenuous personality. When she had looked at him with those big, grave brown eyes, her face propped in the palm of her hand, her expression enraptured, he had felt as though he had found the secret of eternal life and it had gone to his head like a drug.

She'd led him on. God knew if her slime of a father had kick-started the idea but that didn't matter.

What mattered was that they had got what they wanted while he had certainly missed out on what *he* had banked on getting.

She was shaking her head at the offer of a drink and he ignored her, fetching himself a glass of whisky and a glass of wine for her.

'Relax,' he said, pressing the glass on her and then retreating to the bay window where he sipped his drink and watched her in absolute silence. She had made it crystal clear on their wedding night that theirs was not a real marriage. No sex, no chit-chat, no getting to know one another. So he'd taken over her father's company but that didn't mean that she came as part of the package deal and, if he thought he'd been short-changed, then that was too bad.

He hadn't asked how she knew, what her father had said or what she had been told. He'd been duped and that was the end of the story.

The thought of having any kind of soul-searching conversation about the quality of their marriage had never crossed Dio's mind. He had made no effort to talk things through. And no one could ever accuse her of not being the 'perfect wife'. She certainly looked the part. Willowy, blonde, with a devastating *prettiness* that conveyed an air of peculiar innocence underneath the polished exterior. It was a quality that no model or socialite could replicate. She looked like someone waiting for life to *happen* and people fell for it. She was the greatest business asset a man could have. The woman, Dio had often thought, had missed her career as an Oscar-winning actress.

'So, if you're not in Paris, it's because something's wrong with the apartment. You should know by now that I don't get involved with the nitty-gritty details of my houses. That's *your* job.'

Lucy stiffened. *Her* job. That said it all. Just what every young girl dreamed of…a marriage completely lacking in romance which could be described as a *job*.

'There's nothing wrong with the Paris apartment. I just decided that…' she took a deep breath and gulped down some wine '… I decided that we needed to have a talk…'

'Really? What about? Don't tell me that you're angling for a pay rise, Lucy? Your bank account is more than healthy. Or have you seen something you'd really like? House in Italy? Apartment in Florence? Buy it.' He shrugged and finished the remainder of his whisky. 'As long as it's somewhere that can be used for business purposes, then I don't have a problem.'

'Why would I want to buy a house, Dio?'

'What, then? Jewellery? A painting? What?'

His air of bored indifference set her teeth on edge. This was worse than normal. Usually, they could manage to be polite for the five minutes they were forced to spend in one another's company—cooped up in a taxi, maybe, or else waiting for his driver to take them to some opening or other; or else back in one of their grand houses, removing coats and jackets before disappearing to opposite ends of the house.

'I don't want to buy *anything*.' Restively she began walking, stopping to look absently at some of the expensive artefacts in the room. As with all their houses, this one was the last word in what money could buy. The paintings were breath-taking, the furniture was all hand-made, the rugs were priceless silk.

No expense was ever spared and it was her *job* to ensure that all these high-end properties with their priceless furnishings ran like clockwork. Some were used by him, if he happened to be in the country at the time; occasionally they both found themselves in one at the same time. Often he arranged for clients to have use of them and then she had to oversee all the arrangements to make sure that his client left satisfied, having experienced the last word in luxury.

'In that case,' Dio drawled, 'why don't you get to the point and say what you have to say? I'm having a night in because I need to get through some work.'

'And of course, if you'd known that I would be waiting here like a spare part,' Lucy retorted, 'you would have made sure you didn't bother returning.'

Dio shrugged, allowing her to draw her own conclusions.

'I feel...' Lucy breathed in deeply '...that circumstances

between us have changed since...since dad died six months ago...'

He stilled and dropped his empty glass on the side table next to him, although his silver-grey eyes remained on her face. As far as he was concerned, the world was a more pleasant place without Robert Bishop in it. Certainly a more honest one. Whether his wife would agree with him, he didn't know. She had been composed at the funeral, her eyes hidden behind over-sized sunglasses and, since then, life had carried on as normal.

'Explain.'

'I don't want to be shackled to you any more, and there's no longer any need.' She did her best to get her thoughts in order but the cool intensity of his gaze was off-putting.

'You also happen to be shackled to a lifestyle that most women would find enviable.'

'Then you should let me go and you should find one of those women,' she retorted, her cheeks burning. 'You'd be happier. I'm sure you would because you must know that I'm...not happy, Dio. Or maybe,' she added in a lowered voice, 'you do know and you just don't care.' She sat and crossed her legs but she couldn't meet his eyes. He still did things to her, could still make her feel squirmy inside, even though she had done her best over time to kill that weak feeling. It was inappropriate to be attracted to a man who had used you, who had married you because you happened to be a social asset. That didn't make sense. Yes, when he had pretended to be interested in her, she could understand how she had been hot for him, so hot that she had spent her nights dreaming about him and her days fantasising about him. But not when she had found out the truth, and certainly not now, after all this time of cold war.

'Are you telling me that you want out?'

'Can you blame me?' She answered a question with a

question and finally met those cool, pale grey eyes. 'We don't have a marriage, Dio. Not a real one. I don't even understand why you married me in the first place, why you took an interest in me at all.' Except, of course, she did. Robert Bishop had been happy enough to tell her. Dio had wanted more than just his company; he had wanted social elevation, although why he should care she had no idea.

It was something she had never asked her husband. It was humiliating to think that someone had married you because you could open a few doors for them. She had been a bonus to the main deal because she had looked right and had had the right accent.

'You could have bought my father out without marrying me,' she continued, braving the iciness of his eyes. 'I know my father tried to shove me down your throat because he thought that, if you married me, he wouldn't end up in prison like a common criminal. But you could have had your pick of women who would have flung themselves in your path to be your wife.'

'How would you have felt if your dear daddy had ended up in jail?'

'No one wants to see any relative of theirs in prison.'

It was an odd choice of words but Dio let it go. He was shocked at the way this evening was turning out but he was hiding it well.

Had she really thought that she could play games with him, reel him in, get the ring on her, only to turn her back on his bed on their wedding night? And then, as soon as her father died, turn her back on him a second time?

'No, a relative in prison tends to blight family gatherings, doesn't it?' He rose to pour himself another drink because, frankly, he needed one. 'Tell me something, Lucy, what did you think of your father's…how shall I put it?… *creative use* of the company's pension pot?'

'He never told me in detail…what he had done,' she mumbled uncomfortably. Indeed, she had known nothing of her father's financial straits until that overheard conversation, after which he had been more than willing to fill her in.

Lucy thought that Dio might have been better off asking her what she had thought of her father. Robert Bishop had been a man who had had no trouble belittling her, a man who had wanted a son but had been stuck with a daughter, a chauvinist who had never accepted that women could be equal in all walks of life. Her poor, pretty, fragile mother had had a miserable existence before she had died at the tender age of thirty-eight. Robert Bishop had been a swaggering bully who had done his own thing and expected his wife to stay put and suck it up. He had womanised openly, had drunk far too much and, behind closed doors, had had fun jeering at Agatha Bishop, who had put up with it with quiet stoicism because divorce was not something her family did. Cancer had taken her before she'd been able to put that right.

Lucy had spent her life avoiding her father—which had been easy enough, because she had been farmed out to a boarding school at the age of thirteen—but she had never stopped hating him for what he put her mother through.

Which wasn't to say that she would have wanted to see him in prison and, more than that, she knew her mother would have been mortified. There was no way she would have sullied her mother's reputation, not if she could have helped it. She would rather have died than to have seen her mother's friends sniggering behind their backs that Agatha Bishop had ended up with a crook.

Looking at her, Dio wondered what was going through that beautiful head of hers. There was a remoteness there that had always managed to feed into his curiosity. No woman had ever been able to do that and it got on his nerves.

'Well, I'll fill in the gaps, shall I?' he said roughly. 'Your father spent years stealing from the pension fund until there was nothing left to steal. I assume he had a drinking problem?'

Lucy nodded. At boarding school and then university she had not had much time to observe just how much of a drinking problem he had had but it had been enough, she knew, to have sent his car spinning off the motorway at three in the morning.

'The man was an alcoholic. A functioning alcoholic, bearing in mind he was crafty enough to get his greedy hands on other people's money, but the fact of the matter was that he nicked what didn't belong to him to the point that his entire company was destined to sink in the quicksand if I hadn't come along and rescued it.'

'Why did you?' she asked curiously. She assumed that he must have come from a working class background, if what her father had implied was true, but certainly, by the time he had crash-landed into her life, he was a self-made millionaire several times over. So why bother with her father's company?

Dio flushed darkly. Such a long and involved story and one he had no intention of telling her.

'It had potential,' he drawled, his beautiful mouth curving into a smile that could still make her heart beat a little faster. 'It had tentacles in all the right areas, and my intuition paid off. It's made me more money than I know what to do with. And then,' he continued softly, 'how many failing companies come with the added bonus of...*you?* Have you looked in the mirror recently, my darling wife? What red-blooded male could have resisted you? And your father was all too happy to close the deal and throw you in for good measure...'

He saw the way her face reddened and the way her eyes suddenly looked as though they were tearing up. For a split second, he almost regretted saying what he had said. *Almost.*

'Except,' he carried on in that same unhurried voice, 'I didn't get you, did I? You went out with me; you smiled shyly as you hung onto my every word; you let me get so close, close enough for me to need a cold shower every time I returned to my house, because you had turned re-treating with a girlish blush into an art form... And then, on our wedding night, you informed me that you weren't going to be part of any deal that I had arranged. You led me on...'

'I...I...never meant to do that...' But she could see very clearly how the situation must have looked to a man like Dio.

'Now, I wonder why I find that so hard to believe?' he murmured, noticing with some surprise that he had fin-ished his second drink. Regretfully, he decided against a third. 'You and your father concocted a little plan to make sure I was hooked into playing ball.'

'That's not true!' Bright patches of colour appeared on her cheeks.

'And then, once I had played ball, you were free to drop the act. So now you're talking about divorce. Your father's no longer in danger of the long arm of justice and you want out.' He tilted his head to one side as another thought crept in. For the first time, he wondered what she got up to in his many absences.

He could have put a tail on her but he had chosen not to. He had simply not been able to imagine his frozen ice-maiden doing anything behind his back. Except she hadn't always been that ice maiden, had she? There was more to her than that cool detachment. He had seen that for himself before she had said 'I do'... So *had* she been getting up to anything behind his back?

Was it a simple case of her wanting to divorce him, having given a sufficiently adequate period of mourning for her dear old daddy? Or was there some other reason lurking in the background...?

And, just like that, rage slammed into him with the force of a sledgehammer.

Had she been seeing some man behind his back? He couldn't credit it but, once the nasty thought took hold, he found he couldn't jettison it.

'I want out because we both deserve something better than what we have.'

'How considerate of you to take my feelings into account.' Dio raised his eyebrows in a phoney show of gravity that made her grit her teeth. 'I never realised you had such a thoughtful, pious streak in you.'

First thing in the morning, he would have her followed, see for himself where this was all coming from. He certainly had no intention of asking her whether there was some guy in the background. In this sort of situation, nothing could beat the element of surprise.

'There's no need to be sarcastic, Dio.'

'Who's being sarcastic? Here's what I'm thinking, though...' He allowed a few seconds, during which time he pretended to give what was coming next some careful thought. 'You want out—but you do realise that you will leave with nothing?'

'What are you talking about?'

'I had a very watertight pre-nup made up before we married, which you duly signed, although I'm not entirely sure whether you read it thoroughly or not. My guess is that you were so eager to get me on board that signing anything would have just been a formality. Am I right?'

Lucy vaguely remembered signing something extremely long and complicated and very boring. She decided that she wouldn't take issue with his accusation that she'd been eager to get him on board; with his accusation that she had been in cahoots with her father to lure him into buying the company with her in the starring role of sacrificial lamb. She wasn't going to get involved in any sort of argument with him because he would emerge the winner. He had the sharpest brain of any person she had ever known in her life.

She would get out, never see him again. For a fleeting second, something wrenching and painful tugged inside her and she shoved the feeling away.

'As a rich man,' he said, 'I thought it best to protect myself. Here's what you signed up to. I got the company. Lock, stock and smoking barrel. Just recompense for rescuing it from imminent collapse and saving your father's frankly unworthy skin. I'm not sure if you know just how much he skimmed off the pension funds, how much I had to inject back in so that your employees didn't find themselves of pensionable age with nothing but a begging bowl for company? Enough for me to tell you that it was millions.' He breathed an exaggerated sigh and looked at her from under sinfully thick lashes. It had always amazed him that such a stupendously pretty face, so stunningly guileless, could house someone so cunning. It took all sorts to make the world.

Lucy hung her head because shame was never far away when her father's name was mentioned. She looked at her perfectly manicured nails and thought how wonderful it would feel never to wear nail polish ever again. She might have a burning-of-the-nail-polish ceremony.

She distractedly half-smiled and Dio, looking at her, frowned. So…what was the joke? he wondered.

More to the point, what was the little secret? Because that had been a secretive smile.

'As long as you are my wife,' he informed her, banking down the simmering rage bubbling up inside him, 'you get whatever you want. There are no limits placed on the amount of money you can spend.'

'You mean provided you approve of the purchases?'

'Have you ever heard me disapprove of anything you've ever bought?'

'All I buy are clothes, jewellery and accessories,' Lucy returned. 'And only because I need them to…play the part I have to play.'

'Your choice.' He shrugged. 'You could have bought a fleet of cars as far as I was concerned.'

She made a face and his frown deepened. He considered the possibility of giving her a divorce and dismissed the idea, although the reasons for that instant dismissal were a bit vague. Was he that possessive a man that he would hold on to a woman who wanted to escape? He had wanted revenge. And it might have come in a different shape from the one he had planned, but it had still come. He had still ended up with Robert Bishop's company, hadn't he? So what was the point of hanging on to Lucy and an empty marriage?

But then, she wasn't just any woman, was she? She just happened to be his wife. The wife who had promised a lot more than she had ended up delivering. What man liked being short-changed?

'You leave me,' he told her in a hard voice, 'and you leave with the clothes on your back.'

Lucy blanched. She loathed the trappings of wealth but wasn't it a fact that that was all she had ever known? How would she live? What sort of job had years of being pampered prepared her for? She had never had the opportunity to do the teacher training course she had wanted to do. She had, instead, jumped into a marriage that had turned her into a clone of someone she didn't like very much.

'I don't care,' she said in a low voice and Dio raised his eyebrows in a question.

'Of course you do,' he told her. 'You wouldn't know where to begin when it came to finding a job.'

'You can't say that.'

'Of course I can. You've grown up in the lap of luxury and, when most other girls would have branched out into the big, bad world, you married me and continued your life of luxury. Tell me, what has prepared you for that ugly, grim thing called reality?'

He would turf her out without a penny. She could see that in his eyes. He had never cared a jot about her and he didn't care about her now. He had wanted the company and she had been a useful tool to acquire along with the bricks and mortar.

She just recently might have dipped her toe in that grim thing he was talking about called reality, but he was right. A life of creature comforts hadn't prepared her for striking out with nothing. It would take ages for her to find her feet in the world of work, and how would she survive in the meantime? When he told her that she would leave with nothing but the clothes on her back, she was inclined to believe him. The clothes on her back wouldn't include the expensive jewellery in the various safes and vaults.

'I can see that you know where I'm coming from...' He leaned forward, arms resting loosely on his thighs. 'If you want out, then you have two options. You go with nothing, or...'

Lucy looked at him warily. 'Or...what?'

CHAPTER TWO

DIO SMILED SLOWLY and relaxed back.

Sooner or later, this weird impasse between them would have had to find a resolution; he had known that. Always one to dominate the situations around him, he had allowed it to continue for far longer than acceptable.

Why?

Had he thought that she would have thawed slowly? She'd certainly shown no signs of doing anything of the sort as the months had progressed. In fact, they had achieved the unthinkable—a functioning, working relationship devoid of sex, a business arrangement that was hugely successful. She complemented him in ways he could never have imagined. She had been the perfect foil for his hard-nosed, aggressive, seize-and-conquer approach to business and, frankly, life in general. He hadn't been born with a silver spoon in his mouth, he had had to haul himself up by his boot straps, and the challenges of the journey to success had made him brutally tough.

He was the king of the concrete jungle and he was sharp enough to know that pretenders to the throne were never far behind. He was feared and respected in equal measure and his wife's ingrained elegance counterbalanced his more high-voltage, thrusting personality beautifully.

Together they worked.

Maybe that was why he had not broached the subject of all those underlying problems between them. He was a practical man and maybe he had chosen not to rock the boat because they had a successful partnership.

Or maybe he had just been downright lazy. Or—and this was a less welcome thought—vain enough to imagine that the woman he still stupidly fancied would end up coming to him of her own accord.

The one thing he hadn't expected was talk of a divorce.

He poured himself another drink and returned to the chair, in no great hurry to break the silence stretching between them.

'When we got married,' Dio said slowly, 'it didn't occur to me that I would end up with a wife who slept in a separate wing of the house when we happened to be under the same roof. It has to be said that that's not every man's dream of a happy marriage.'

'I didn't think you had dreams of happy marriages, Dio. I never got the impression that you were the sort of guy who had fantasies of coming home to the wife and the two-point-two kids and the dog and the big back garden.'

'Why would you say that?'

Lucy shrugged. 'Just an impression I got.' But that hadn't stopped her from falling for him. She had got lost in those amazing eyes, had been seduced by that deep, dark drawl and had been willing to ignore what her head had been telling her because her heart had been talking a lot louder.

'I may not have spent my life gearing up for a walk down the aisle but that doesn't mean that I wanted to end up with a woman who didn't share my bed.'

Lucy reddened. 'Well, both of us has ended up disappointed with what we got,' she said calmly.

Dio waved his hand dismissively. 'There's no point trying to analyse our marriage,' he said. 'That's a pointless exercise. I was going to talk to you about options…' He sipped his drink and looked at her thoughtfully. 'And I'm going to give you a very good one. You want a divorce? Fine. I can't stop you heading for the nearest lawyer and getting divorce papers drawn up. Course, like I said, that would involve you leaving with nothing. A daunting prospect for someone who has spent the last year and a half never having to think about money.'

'Money isn't the be all and end all of everything.'

'Do you know what? It's been my experience that the people who are fond of saying things like that are the people who have money at their disposal. People who have no money are usually inclined to take a more pragmatic approach.' Having grown up with nothing, Dio knew very well that money actually was the be all and end all of everything. It gave you freedom like nothing else could. Freedom to do exactly what you wanted to do and to be accountable to no one.

'I'm saying that it doesn't always bring happiness.' She thought of her own unhappy, lavish childhood. From the outside, they had looked like a happy, privileged family. Behind closed doors, it had been just the opposite. No amount of money had been able to whitewash that.

'But a lack of it can bring, well, frustration? Misery? Despair? Imagine yourself leaving all of this so that you can take up residence in a one-bedroom flat where you'll live a life battling rising damp and mould on the walls.'

Lucy gave an exaggerated sigh. 'Aren't you being a bit dramatic, Dio?'

'London is an expensive place. Naturally, you would have some money at your disposal, but nothing like enough to find anywhere halfway decent to live.'

'Then I'd move out of London.'

'Into the countryside? You've lived in London all your life. You're accustomed to having the theatre and the opera and all those art exhibitions you enjoy going to on tap… But don't worry. You can still enjoy all of that but, sadly, there's no such thing as a free lunch. You want your divorce? You can have it. But only after you've given me what I expected to get when I married you.'

It took a few seconds for Lucy's brain to make the right connections and catch up with what he was telling her but, even so, she heard herself ask, falteringly, 'What are you talking about?'

Dio raised his eyebrows and smiled slowly. 'Don't tell me that someone with a maths degree can't figure out what two and two makes? I want my honeymoon, Lucy.'

'I…I don't know what you mean…' Lucy stammered, unable to tear her eyes away from the harsh lines of his beautiful face.

'Of course you do! I didn't think I was signing up for a sexless marriage when I slipped that wedding band on your finger. You want out now? Well, you can have out just as soon as we put an end to the unfinished business between us.'

'That's blackmail!' She sprang to her feet and began restively pacing the room. Her nerves were all over the place. She had looked forward to that wretched honeymoon night so much…and now here he was, offering it to her, but at a price.

'That's the offer on the table. We sleep together, be man and wife in more than just name only, and you get to leave with an allowance generous enough to ensure that you spend the rest of your life in comfort.'

'Why would you want that? You're not even attracted to me!'

'Come a little closer and I can easily prove you wrong on that point.'

Heart thudding, Lucy kept a healthy distance, but she was looking at him again, noting the dark intent in his eyes. The desire she had shoved away, out of sight, began to uncurl inside her.

She'd been foolish enough to think that he had been interested in her, attracted to her, and had discovered that it had all been a lie. He had strung her along because he had decided that she would be a useful addition to his life.

There was no way that she would sleep with him as some sort of devil's bargain. She had watched the car crash of her parents' marriage and had vowed that she would only give her body to a man who truly loved her, that she would only marry for the right reasons. Her parents had had a marriage of convenience, the natural joining of two wealthy families, and just look at where they had ended up. The minute she had realised that her marriage to Dio had not been what she had imagined was the minute she'd made her decision to withhold the better part of herself from him, to remain true to her principles.

She watched, horrified, as he slowly rose from his chair and strolled towards where she was standing by the window. With each step, her nerves shredded a little bit more.

'A matter of weeks…' he murmured, delicately tracing his finger along her cheek and feeling her quiver as he touched her.

She was the only woman in the world he had never been able to read.

There had been times during their marriage when he had surprised her looking at him, had seen something in her eyes that had made him wonder whether his dear wife was slightly less immune to him than she liked to portray, but he had never explored the possibility. There was such a thing as pride, especially to a man like him.

He was willing to explore the possibility now because he knew that, if she left and he never got to touch her, she would become unfinished business and that would be a less than satisfactory outcome.

'Weeks...?' Transfixed by the feel of his skin against hers, Lucy remained rooted to the spot. Her breasts ached and she could feel her nipples tightening, sensitive against her lacy bra. Liquid was pooling between her legs and, although she remained perfectly still, she wanted to squirm and rub her legs together to relieve herself of the ache between them.

'That's right.' Plenty long enough to get her out of his system. She was his and he intended to have her, all of her, before he allowed her her freedom.

At which point, he would close the door on a part of his past that had gnawed away at him for as long as he could remember.

His erection was hard enough to be painful and he stepped a bit closer, close enough for her to feel it against her belly. He knew that she had from the slight shudder that ran through her body. Her eyes were wide, her mouth parted.

An invitation. One that he wasn't going to resist. He hadn't been this physically close to his wife since he had tied the knot with her and he wasn't about to waste the opportunity.

Lucy knew he was going to kiss her. She placed her hand flat on his chest, a pathetic attempt to push him away before he could get too close, but she didn't push him away. Instead, as his mouth found hers, treacherous fingers curled into his shirt and she sighed, losing herself in the headiness of feeling his tongue probing into her mouth, his tongue moving, exploring, with hers, sparking a series of explosive reactions in her body.

Like a match set to tinder, she felt her whole body combusting. Their brief courtship had been so very chaste. This wasn't chaste. This was unrestrained hunger and his hunger matched her own.

She felt him slip his hand underneath the silk top to cup her breast and, when he began to rub her nipple through the lacy bra, she wanted to pass out.

Or else rip off his shirt so that she could spread trembling, eager fingers against his broad, hard chest.

He pulled back. It took her a couple of seconds to recognise his withdrawal and then horror at what she had allowed to happen filtered through her consciousness and washed over her like a bucket of freezing cold water.

'What the heck do you think you're doing?'

Dio smiled. 'Giving you proof positive that we could have a couple of weeks of very pleasant carnal adventures…' Keen eyes noted the hectic flush in her cheeks and the way she had now prudishly folded her arms across her chest, as if she could deny the very heated, very satisfactory, response she had just given him.

He hadn't been mistaken when it came to those little looks he had surprised her giving him after all.

'I have no intention of…of sleeping with you for money!'

Dio's lips thinned. 'Why not? You married me for money. At least sleeping with me would introduce the element of fun.'

'I did not marry you for money!'

'I have no intention of going down this road again. I've given you your options. You can decide which one to go for.' He spun round on his heels, heading for the door.

'Dio!'

He stilled and then took his time turning to face her.

'Why?'

'Why what?'

'Why does it matter whether you sleep with me or not? I mean surely there have been…women in your life over the past year or so more than willing to jump into bed with you… Why does it matter whether I do or not?'

Dio didn't answer immediately. He knew what she thought, that he spent his leisure time between the sheets with other women. There had been no need for her to vocalise it. He had seen it in her face on the few occasions when he had happened to be in conversation with another woman, an attractive woman. He had seen the flash of resentment and scorn which had been very quickly masked and he had seen no reason to put her straight.

He didn't think that there was any need to put her straight now. Not only had he not slept with any other woman since his marriage, but he had not been tempted. There wasn't a human being on earth who wasn't driven to want what was out of reach and his wife had been steadfastly out of reach for the past eighteen months. During that period, he had not found his eyes straying to any of the women who had covertly made passes at him over the months, happy to overlook the fact that there was a wedding ring on his finger.

'I just can't,' Lucy breathed into the silence. 'I…I'm happy to leave with a small loan, until I find my feet.'

'Find your feet doing what?' Dio asked curiously.

'I…I have one or two things up my sleeve…'

Dio's eyes narrowed as hers shifted away. He was picking up the whiff of a secret and he wondered, again, what was going on behind his back. What *had* been going on behind his back? Had the mouse been playing while the cat had been away?

'What things?'

'Oh, nothing,' she said evasively. 'It's just that…I think we'd both be happier if we brought this marriage to an end, and if I could borrow some money from you…'

'Lucy, you would need a great deal of money to begin to have any life at all in London.'

'Money which you are not at all prepared to lend me, even though you have my word that you would be repaid.'

'Unless you're planning a big job in the corporate world or have a rich backer,' he said dryly, 'then I can guarantee that any loan I make to you would not be paid back. At least, not while I have my own teeth and hair.'

'How do you think it would look if your wife was caught with a begging bowl, looking for scraps from strangers?'

'Now who's being dramatic?' When he had met her all those months ago, she had been blushing and shy but he had had glimpses of the humour and sharp intelligence behind the shyness. Over the past year and a half, as she had been called on to play the role of perfect wife and accomplished hostess, her self-confidence had grown in leaps and bounds.

He also knew that, whatever she felt for him, she wasn't intimidated by him. Maybe that, too, was down to the strange configuration of their lives together. How could you be intimidated by someone you weren't that interested in pleasing in the first place?

'You will, naturally, walk away with slightly more than the clothes on your back,' Dio admitted. 'However, you would still find it a challenge to have a lifestyle that in any way could be labelled comfortable. Unless, of course, there's a rich patron in the background. Is there?'

Asking the question was a sign of weakness but Dio couldn't help himself.

She shrugged. 'I'm not into rich men,' she told him.

'I've always known that and having been married to you has confirmed all my suspicions.'

'How's that?' Frankly, he had never heard anything so hypocritical in his life before, but he decided to let it pass.

'Like you said, there's no such thing as a free lunch. I know you say that it's the most important thing in life...'

'I can't remember saying that.'

'More or less. You said it *more or less*. And I know you think that I wouldn't be able to last a week unless I have more money than I can shake a stick at but—'

'But you're suddenly overcome with a desperate urge to prove me wrong...' His gaze dropped to her full mouth. Something about the arrangement of her features had always turned him on. She wasn't overtly sexy, just as she wasn't overtly beautiful, but there was a whisper of something other-worldly about her that kept tugging his eyes back to her time and time again.

She had screwed up his clear-cut plans to buy her father's company at a fire sale price before chucking him to his fate, which would undoubtedly have involved wolves tearing him to pieces. He had been charmed by that other-worldly *something*, had allowed it somehow to get to him, and he had tempered all his plans to accommodate the feeling.

She had, over time, become the itch he couldn't scratch. He might have had her signed up to a water-tight pre-nup but, even so, he would never have seen her hit the streets without any financial wherewithal.

In this instance, though, he was determined to have that itch scratched and, if it meant holding her to ransom, then he was pretty happy to go down that road.

Especially now that he knew that the attraction was returned in full.

'I'm just trying to tell you that there's no rich anyone

in the background.' Did he imagine that she fooled around the way he did? 'And there never will be anyone rich in my life again.'

'How virtuous. Is it because of those free lunches not coming for free? Do you honestly think that hitching your life to a pauper would be fertile ground for happily united bliss? If so then you really need to drag your head out of the clouds and get back down to Planet Earth.' He abandoned the decision to go back to work, not that he would have been able to concentrate. 'I don't know about you, but I'm hungry. If we're going to continue this conversation, then I need to eat.'

'You were about to leave,' Lucy reminded him.

'That was before I became intrigued with your radical new outlook on life.'

He began heading towards the kitchen and she followed helplessly in his wake.

This felt like a proper conversation and it was unsettling. There were no crowds of people around jostling for his attention. No important clients demanding polite small talk. And they weren't exchanging pleasantries before heading off in opposite directions in any one of their grand houses.

She knew the layout of the kitchen well. On those occasions when they had entertained at home, she had had to supervise caterers and familiarise them with the ins and outs of the vast kitchen. When he was out of the country, as he often was, this was where she had her meals on her own, with the little telly on, or else the radio.

However, it was a bit different to see him here, in it.

For a few seconds, he stared around him, a man at sea trying to get his bearings.

'Okay. Suggestions?' He finally turned to her.

'Suggestions about what?'

'Thoughts on what I can eat.'

'What were you planning to eat if you hadn't found me here?' Lucy asked jerkily, moving from doorway to kitchen table and then sitting awkwardly on one of the chairs while he continued to look at her in a way that made her blood sizzle, because she just had to see that mouth of his to recall his very passionate kiss. Her lips still felt stung and swollen.

'I have two top chefs on speed dial,' he drawled, amused when her mouth fell open. 'They're usually good at solving the "what to eat?" dilemma for me. Not that it's a dilemma that occurs very often. If I'm on my own, I eat out. Saves hassle.'

'Go ahead and order what you want from your two top chefs,' Lucy told him. 'Never mind me. I…er…'

'Ate already?'

'I'm not hungry.'

'And I don't believe you. Don't tell me,' he said, 'that you feel uncomfortable being in a kitchen with me and breaking bread? We're a married couple, after all.'

'I don't feel uncomfortable,' Lucy lied. 'Not in the slightest!'

'Then where are your suggestions?'

'Do you even know where to find anything in this kitchen?' she asked impatiently.

Dio appeared to give that question a bit of thought then he shook his head. 'I admit the contents of the cupboards are something of a mystery, although I do know that there's some very fine white wine in the fridge…'

'Are you asking me to cook something for you?'

'If you're offering, then who am I to refuse?' He made for a chair and sat down. 'It doesn't offend your feminist instincts to cook for me, does it? Because, if it does, then

I'm more than happy to try and hunt down one or two ingredients and put my cooking skills to the test.'

'You don't have cooking skills.' From some past remembered conversation, when she had still had faith in him, she recalled one of his throwaway remarks that had made her laugh.

'You're right. So I don't.'

This wasn't how Lucy had imagined the evening going. She had more figured on dealing with shock at her announcement followed by anger because she knew that, even if he heartily wanted to get rid of her, he would have been furious that she had pre-empted him. Then she had imagined disappearing off to bed, leaving him to mull over her decision, at which point she would have been directed to a lawyer who would take over the handling of the nitty-gritty.

Instead she felt trapped in the eye of a hurricane...

She knew where everything was and she was a reasonably good cook. It was something she quite enjoyed doing when she was on her own, freed from the pressure of having to entertain. She expertly found the things she needed for a simple pasta meal and it would have been relaxing if she hadn't been so acutely aware of his eyes following her every movement.

'Need a hand?' he asked as she clanged a saucepan onto the stove and she turned to him with a snappy, disbelieving frown.

'What can you do?'

'I feel I could be quite good at chopping things.' He rose smoothly to join her by the kitchen counter, invading her space and making her skin tingle with sexual awareness.

Stupid, she thought crossly. But he had thrown down that gauntlet, brought sex into the equation, and now it was on her mind. And she didn't want it to be. She had spent the past months telling herself that she hated him and hating him had made it easy for her to ignore the way he made her feel. It had been easy to ignore the slight tremble whenever he got too close, the tingling of her breasts and the squirmy feeling she got in the pit of her stomach.

He'd never been attracted to her, she had thought. He'd just seen her as part of a deal. He'd used her.

But now...

He wanted her; she had felt it in his kiss, had felt his erection pressing against her like a shaft of steel. Just thinking about it brought her out in a fine film of perspiration.

She shoved an onion and some tomatoes at him and told him where to find a chopping board and a knife.

'Most women would love the kind of lifestyle you have,' Dio murmured as he began doing something and nothing with the tomatoes.

'You mean flitting from grand house to grand house, making sure everything is ticking over, because Lord help us if an important client spots some dust on a skirting board?'

'Since when have you been so sarcastic?'

'I'm not being sarcastic.'

'Don't stop. I find it intriguing.'

'You told me that most women would envy what I have and I told you that they wouldn't.'

'You'd be surprised what women would put up with if the price was right.'

'I'm not one of those women.' She edged away, because he was just a little too close for comfort, and began busying herself by the stove, flinging things into the saucepan, all the ingredients for a tomato-and-aubergine dish, which was a stalwart in her repertoire because it was quick and easy.

Dio thought that maybe he should have tried to find out what sort of woman she was before remembering that he knew exactly what sort of woman she was. The sort who had conspired with her father to get him where they had both wanted him—married to her and thereby providing protection for her father from the due processes of law.

If she wanted to toss out hints that there were hidden depths there somewhere, though, then he was happy enough to go along for the ride. Why not? Right now he was actually enjoying himself, against all odds.

And the bottom line was that he wanted her body. He wanted that itch to be scratched and then he would be quite happy to dispose of her.

If holding her to ransom was going to prove a problem then what was the big deal in getting her into his bed using other methods?

'So, we're back to the money not being the be all and end all,' he murmured encouragingly. 'Smells good, whatever you're making.'

'I like cooking when I'm on my own,' she said with a flush of pleasure.

'You cook even though you know you could have anything you wanted to eat delivered to your doorstep?' Dio asked with astonishment and Lucy laughed.

He remembered that laugh from way back when. Soft and infectious, with a little catch that made it seem as though she felt guilty laughing at all. He had found that laugh strangely seductive, fool that he had been.

'So...' he drawled once they were sitting at the kitchen table with bowls of steaming hot pasta in front of them. 'Shall we raise our glasses to this rare event? I don't believe I've sat in this kitchen and had a meal with you since we got married.'

Lucy nervously sipped some of the wine. The situation

was slipping away from her. How many women had he sat and drank with in the time during which they had been supposedly happily married? She hadn't slept with him but that didn't mean that she wasn't aware that he had a healthy libido. One look at that dark, handsome face was enough to cement the impression.

She had never, not once, asked him about what he did behind her back on all those many trips when he was abroad, but she could feel the questions eating away at her, as though they had suddenly been released from a locked box. She hated it. And she hated the way that fleeting moment of being the object of his flirting attention had got to her, overriding all the reasons she had formulated in her head for breaking away from him. She didn't want to give house room to any squirmy feelings. He had turned on the charm when they had first met and she knew from experience that it didn't mean anything.

'That's because this isn't really a marriage, is it?' she said politely. 'So why would we sit in a kitchen and have a meal together? That's what real married couples do.'

Dio's mouth tightened. 'And of course you would know a lot about what real married couples do, considering you entered this contract with no intention of being half of a real married couple.'

'I don't think it's going to get either of us anywhere if we keep harping back to the past. I think we should both now look to the future.'

'The future being divorce.'

'I'm not going to get into bed with you for money, Dio,' Lucy told him flatly. For a whisper of a second, she had a vivid image of what it would be like to make love to him—but then, it wouldn't be love, would it? And what was the point of sex without love?

'So you're choosing the poverty option.' He pushed his

bowl to one side and relaxed back in the chair, angling his big body so that he could extend his legs to the side.

'If I have to. I can make do. I...'

'You...what?' His ears pricked up as he detected the hesitancy in her voice.

'I have plans,' Lucy said evasively. And she wasn't going to share them with him, wasn't going to let her fledgling ambitions be put to the test by him.

'What plans?'

'Nothing very big. Or important. I just obviously need to think about the direction my life is going in.' She stood up and briskly began clearing the table. She made sure not to catch his eye.

Dio watched her jerky movements as she busied herself around the kitchen, tidying, wiping the counters, doing everything she could to make sure the conversation was terminated.

So she wanted out and she had plans.

To Dio's way of thinking, that could only mean one thing. A man. Maybe not a rich one, but a man. Lurking in the background. Waiting to get her into bed if he hadn't already done so.

The fake marriage was going to be replaced by a relationship she had probably been cultivating behind his back for months. Maybe—and the red mist descended when he considered this option—she had been cultivating this relationship from way back when. Maybe it had been right there on the back burner, set to one side while she'd married him and had done what she had to do for the sake of her father.

It might have come as a shock that she would face walking away empty handed but clearly, whatever her so-called plans were, they were powerful enough to override common sense.

Faced with this, Dio understood that first and foremost he would find out what those plans were.

Simple.

He could either follow her himself or he could employ someone to do it. He preferred the former option. Why allow someone else to do something you were perfectly capable of handling yourself?

The past year or so of their sterile non-relationship faded under the impetus of an urgent need that obliterated everything else.

'I'm going to be in New York for the next few days,' Dio said abruptly, standing up and moving towards the kitchen door where he stood for a few seconds, hand on the door knob, his dark face cool and unreadable. 'While you're still wearing a wedding ring on your finger, I could insist that you accompany me, because I will be attending some high level social events. But, under these very *special* circumstances, you'll be pleased to hear that I won't.'

'New—New York?' Lucy faltered. 'I can't remember New York being in the diary until next month...'

'Change of plan.' Dio shrugged. He stared at her, working out what he planned to do the following day and how. 'You can stay here and spend the time thinking about the proposition I've put to you.'

'I've already thought about it. I don't need to do any more thinking.'

Over his dead body. 'Then,' he said smoothly, 'you can stay here and spend the time contemplating the consequences...'

CHAPTER THREE

LUCY HAD HAD better nights.

Spend her time contemplating the consequences? The cool, dismissive way he had said that, looking at her as if he had complete authority over her decisions, had set her teeth on edge.

Their sham of a marriage had worked well for him. She knew that. Her father had told her that Dio wanted someone classy to be by his side and she had fitted the bill. Whilst he had been alive, he had never ceased reminding her that it was her duty to play the part because, if she didn't, then it would be within her husband's power to reveal the extent of the misappropriated money—and if he went down, her father had told her, then so too would the memory of her mother. The dirty linen that would be washed in public would bring everyone down. That was how it worked.

That had been Lucy's Achilles' heel so she had played her part and she had played it to perfection.

The day after their wedding, Dio had taken himself off to the other side of the world on business and, during the week that he had been away, she had obeyed instructions and had overhauled her image with the aid of a top-notch personal shopper.

Like a puppet, she had allowed herself to be manoeuvred into being the sort of woman who entertained. He had returned and there and then the parameters of their personal life had been laid down.

He had said nothing about her physical withdrawal. The closeness that had been there before her father's revelation had disappeared, replaced by a cool remoteness that had only served to prove just how right she had been in reading the situation.

He had used her.

What he had wanted was what he had got. He had wanted someone to whom the social graces came as second nature. He mixed in the rarefied circles of the elite and she could more than hold her own in those circles because she had grown up in them.

As far as she knew, the sort of woman he was attracted to was probably completely the opposite to her.

He was probably attracted to dark-haired, voluptuous sirens who didn't hang around the house in silk culottes and matching silk vests. He probably liked them swearing, cursing and being able to drink him under the table, but none of *them* would have done as a society wife. So he had tacked her on as a useful appendage.

And now he wanted her.

With divorce on the horizon, he wanted to lay claim to her because, as far as he was concerned, she was his possession, someone he had bought along with the company that had come with her.

He'd even set a time line on whatever physical relationship he intended to conduct!

Did it get any more insulting?

He knew that he'd be bored with her within a month!

She burned with shame when she thought about that.

She hated him and yet her sleep was disturbed by a series of images of them together. She dreamt of him making love to her, touching her in places she had never been touched before and whispering things in her ear that had her squirming in a restless half-sleep.

She awoke the following morning to an empty house. Dio had disappeared off to New York.

She'd used these little snippets of freedom to her benefit and now, as she got dressed, she felt that she should be a little more excited than she was.

It irritated her to know that, thanks to Dio, the glorious day stretching ahead of her was already marred with images of his dark, commanding face and the careless arrogance of what he had told her the evening before.

She made a couple of calls and then she headed out.

Dio, in the middle of a conference call, was notified of her departure within seconds of her leaving the house.

His personal driver—who had zero experience in sleuthing but could handle a car like a pro and could be trusted with his life—phoned the message through and Dio immediately terminated his conference call.

'When she stops, call me,' he instructed. 'I'm not interested in whether she's leaving the house. I'm interested in where she ends up.'

Suddenly restless, he pushed himself away from his desk and walked towards the floor-to-ceiling glass panes that overlooked the busy hub of the city.

He'd had a night to think about what she had told him and he was no nearer to getting his head around it.

So, she wanted out.

She was the single one woman who had eluded him despite the ring on her finger. To take a protesting bride to his bed would have been unthinkable. There was no way he would ever have been driven to that, however bitter he might have been about the warped terms of their marriage.

And he could see now that pride had entered the equation, paralysing his natural instinct to charm her into the place he wanted her to be.

With the situation radically changed, it was time for him to be proactive.

And he was going to enjoy it. He was going to enjoy having her beg for him, which he fully intended she would do, despite all her protests to the contrary.

And, if he discovered that there was a man on the scene, that she had been seeing someone behind his back...

He shoved his hands in his pockets and clenched his jaw, refusing to give in to the swirl of fury that filled every pore and fibre of his being at the thought of her possible infidelity.

When he had embarked on Robert Bishop's company buyout, this was not at all what he had envisaged.

He had envisaged a clean, fatal cut delivered with the precision of a surgical knife, which was no less than the man deserved.

Never one to waste time brooding, Dio allowed his mind to play back the series of events that had finally led to the revenge he had planned so very carefully.

Some of what he had known, he had seen with his own eyes, growing up. His father fighting depression, stuck in a nowhere job where the pay was crap. His mother working long hours cleaning other people's houses so that there would be sufficient money for little treats for him.

The greater part of the story, however, had come from his mother's own lips, years after his father's life had been claimed by the ravages of cancer. Only then had he discovered the wrong that had been done to his father. A poor immigrant with a brilliant mind, he had met Robert Bishop as an undergraduate. Robert Bishop, from all accounts, had been wasting his time partying whilst pretending to do a business degree. Born into money, but with the family fortunes already showing signs of poor health, he had known that although he had an assured job with the family business he needed more if he was to sustain the lifestyle to which he had become accustomed.

Meeting Mario Ruiz had been a stroke of luck as far as Robert Bishop had been concerned. He had met the genius who would later invent something small but highly significant that would allow him to send his ailing family engineering concern into the stratosphere.

And as for Mario Ruiz?

Dio made no attempt to kill the toxic acid that always erupted in his veins when he thought of how his father had been conned.

Mario Ruiz had innocently signed up to a deal that had not been worth the paper it was written on. He had found his invention misappropriated and, when he had raised the issue, had found himself at the mercy of a man who'd wanted to get rid of him as fast as he could.

He had seen nothing of all the giddy financial rewards that should have been his due.

It had been such an incredible story that Dio might well have doubted the full extent of its authenticity had it not been for the reams of paperwork later uncovered after his mother had died, barely months after his father had been buried.

Ruining Robert Bishop had been there, driving him forward, for many years...except complete and total revenge had been marred by the fresh-faced, seductive prettiness of Lucy Bishop. He had wavered. Allowed concessions to be made. Only to find himself the revenge half-baked: he had got the company but not the man, and he had got the girl but not in the way he had imagined he would.

Well, he just couldn't wait to see how this particular story was going to play out. Not on her terms, he resolved.

He picked up the call from his driver practically before his mobile buzzed and listened with a slight frown of puzzlement as he was given his wife's location.

Striding out of his office, he said in passing to his secretary that he would be uncontactable for the next couple of hours.

He wasn't surprised to see the look of open-mouthed astonishment on his secretary's face because, when it came to work, he was *always* contactable.

'Make up whatever excuses you like for my cancelled meetings, be as inventive as the mood takes you.' He grinned, pausing by the door. 'You can look at it as your little window of living dangerously...'

'I live dangerously every time I walk through that office door,' his austere, highly efficient, middle-aged secretary tartly responded. 'You have no idea what you're like to work for!'

Dio knew the streets of London almost as comprehensively as his driver did but he still had to rely on his satnav to get him to the address he had been given.

Somewhere in East London. He had no idea how Jackson had managed to follow Lucy. Presumably, he had just taken whatever form of public transport she had taken and, because he was not their regular evening driver, she would not have recognised him.

It was a blessing that he had handed the grunt work over to his driver because he had just assumed that his wife would drive to wherever she wanted to go, or else take a taxi.

Anything but the tube and the bus.

He couldn't imagine that her father would ever have

allowed her to hop on the number twenty-seven. Robert Bishop had excelled in being a snob.

He wondered whether this was all part of her sudden dislike of all things money and then he wondered how long the novelty of pretending not to care about life's little luxuries would last.

It was all well and good to talk about pious self-denial from the luxury of your eight-bedroomed mansion in the best postcode in London.

His lips curled derisively as he edged along through the traffic. She had been the apple of her father's eye and that certainly didn't go hand in hand with pious self-denial.

He cleared the traffic in central London, but found that he was still having to crawl through the stop-start tedium of traffic lights and pedestrian crossings, and it was after eleven by the time he pulled up in front of a disreputable building nestled amongst a parade of shops.

There was a betting shop, an Indian takeaway, a laundrette, several other small shops and, tacked on towards the end of the row, a three-storeyed old building with a blue door. Dio was tempted to phone his driver and ask him whether he had texted the wrong address.

He didn't.

Instead, he got out of his car and spent a few moments looking at the house in front of him. The paint on the door was peeling. The windows were all shut, despite the fact that it was another warm, sunny day.

His mind was finding it hard to co-operate. For once, he was having difficulty trying to draw conclusions from what his eyes were seeing.

He could hear the buzzing of the doorbell reverberating inside the house as he kept his hand pressed on the buzzer and then the sound of footsteps. The door opened a crack, chain still on.

'Dio!' Lucy blinked and wondered briefly if she might be hallucinating. Her husband had been on her mind so much as she had headed off but the physical reactions of her body told her that the man standing imperiously in front of her was no hallucination.

From behind her, Mark called out in his sing-song Welsh accent, 'Who's there, Lucy?'

'No one!' They were the first words that sprang into her head but, as her eyes tangled with Dio's, she recognised that she had said the wrong thing.

'No one...?' Dio's voice was soft, silky and lethally cool. The chain was still on the door and he laid his hand flat on it, just in case she got the crazy idea of trying to shut the door in his face.

'What are you doing here? You said that you were going to New York.'

'Who's the man, Lucy?'

'Did you follow me?'

'Just answer the question because, if you don't, I'll break the door down and find out myself.'

'You shouldn't be here! I...I...' She felt Mark behind her, inquisitively trying to peer through the narrow sliver to see who was standing at the door, and with a sigh of resignation she slowly slid the chain back with trembling fingers.

Dio congratulated himself on an impressive show of self-control as he walked into the hallway of the house which, in contrast to the outside, was brightly painted in shades of yellow. He clenched his fists at his sides, eyes sliding from Lucy to the man standing next to her.

'Who,' he asked in a dangerously low voice, 'the hell are you, and what are you doing with my wife?'

The man in front of him was at least three inches shorter and slightly built. Dio thought that he would be able to flatten him with a tap of his finger, and that was exactly what he wanted to do, but he'd be damned if he was going to start a brawl in a house.

Growing up on the wrong side of the tracks, however, had trained him well when it came to holding his own with his fists.

'Lucy, shall I leave you two to talk?'

'Dio, this is Mark.' She recognised the glitter of menace in her husband's eyes and decided that, yes, the best thing Mark could do would be to evaporate. Shame he wouldn't be able to take her with him, but perhaps the time had come to lay her cards on the table and tell Dio what was going on. Before he started punching poor Mark, who was fidgeting and glancing at her worriedly.

She felt sick as she looked, with dizzy compulsion, at the tight, angry lines of her husband's face.

'I'd shake your hand,' Dio rasped, 'but I might find myself giving in to the urge to rip it off, so I suggest you take my wife's advice and clear off, and don't return unless I give you permission.'

'Dio, please…' she pleaded, putting herself between her husband and Mark. 'You've got the wrong end of the stick.'

'I could beat him to a pulp,' Dio remarked neutrally to her, 'without even bloodying my knuckles.'

'And you'd be proud of that, would you?'

'Maybe not proud, but eminently satisfied. So…' He pinned coldly furious silver eyes on the guy behind her. 'You clear off right now or climb out from your hiding place behind my wife and get what's coming to you!'

With a restraining hand on Dio's arm, Lucy turned to Mark and told him gently that she'd call him as soon as possible.

Dio fought the urge to deal with the situation in the most straightforward way known to mankind.

But what would be the point? He wasn't a thug, despite his background.

His head was cluttered with images of the fair-haired man, the fair-haired wimp who had hidden behind his wife, making love to Lucy.

The heat of the situation was such that it was only when the front door clicked shut behind the loser that Dio noticed what he should have noticed the very second he had looked at Lucy.

Gone were the expensive trappings: the jewellery, the watch he had given to her for her birthday present, the designer clothes...

He stared at her, utterly bemused. Her hair was scraped back into a ponytail and she was dressed in a white tee-shirt, a pair of faded jeans and trainers. She looked impossibly young and so damned sexy that his whole body jerked into instant response.

Lucy felt the shift in the atmosphere between them, although she couldn't work out at first where it was coming from. The tension was still there but threaded through that was a sizzling electrical charge that made her heart begin to beat faster.

'Are you going to listen to what I have to say?' She hugged her arms around her because she was certain that he would be able to see the hard tightening of her nipples against the tee-shirt.

'Are you going to spin me fairy stories?'

'I've never done that and I'm not going to start now.'

'I'll let that ride. Are you having an affair with that man?'

'No!'

Dio took a couple of steps towards her, sick to his stomach at the games going on in his head. 'You're my wife!'

Lucy's eyes shifted away from his. Her breathing was

laboured and shallow and she was horrified to realise that, despite the icy, forbidding threat in his eyes, she was still horribly turned on. It seemed that something had been unlocked inside her and now she couldn't ram it back into a safe place, out of harm's way.

Dio held up his hand, as though interrupting a flow of conversation, although she hadn't uttered a word.

'And don't feed me garbage about being my wife in name only, because I sure as hell won't be buying it! You're my wife and I had better not find out that you've been fooling around behind my back!'

'What difference would it make?' she flung at him, her eyes simmering with heated rebellion. 'You fool around behind mine!'

'In what world do you think I'd fool around behind your back?' Dio roared, little caring what he said and not bothering to filter his words.

The silence stretched between them for an eternity. Lucy had heard what he had said but had she heard correctly? Had he really not slept with anyone in all the time they had been married? A wave of pure, undiluted relief washed over her and she acknowledged that resentment at her situation, at least in part, had been fuelled by the thought that he had been playing around with other women, having the sex she had denied him.

She would have liked to question him a bit more, tried to ascertain whether he was, indeed, telling the truth; if he was, more than anything else she would have loved to have ask him *why*.

'Now…' His thunderous voice crashed through her thoughts, catapulting her right back to the reality of him standing in front of her, having discovered the secret she had held to herself for the past couple of months. 'Who the hell was that man?'

'If you'd just stop shouting, Dio, I'll tell you everything.' Lucy eyed him warily.

'I'm waiting—and you'd better tell me something I want to hear.'

'Or else what?'

'You really don't want to know.'

'Oh, just stop acting like a Neanderthal and follow me…'

'Neanderthal? You haven't see me at my best!'

They stared at one another. Hell, she looked so damned hot! He should have obeyed his primitive instincts and laid down laws of ownership from the get-go. He should have had a bodyguard walk three inches behind her at all times. If he'd done that, he wouldn't be standing here now with his brain spiralling into freefall!

'Just come with me.' Lucy turned on her heels and disappeared towards a room at the back, just beyond the staircase that led upwards, and he followed her.

'There!' She stepped aside and allowed him to brush past her, then looked at him as he, in turn, looked around him. Looked at the little desks, the low bookshelves crammed with books, the white board and the walls covered with posters.

'Not getting it,' Dio said, after he had turned full circle.

'It's a classroom!' Lucy controlled the desire to yell because he was just so pig-headed, just so consumed by the business of making money, that he couldn't think outside the box.

'Why are you seeing some man in a classroom?'

'I'm not *seeing some man in a classroom*!'

'Are you going to try and convince me that the loser I got rid of was a figment of my imagination?'

'Of course I'm not going to do that, Dio! Okay, so

maybe I've been meeting Mark here over the past couple of months…'

'This has been going on for months?' He raked his fingers through his hair, but his blood pressure was at least getting back to normal, because she wasn't having an affair. He didn't know why he knew that but he did.

Which didn't mean that he wasn't interested in finding out just what *had* been going on…

'Oh, please, just sit down.'

'I'm all ears to hear what my wife's been getting up to when I've been out of the country.'

He dwarfed the chair and, even though he was now safely sitting down, he still seemed to emanate enough power to make her feel a bit giddy and unsteady on her feet.

'Did you plan this?' Lucy suddenly asked, arms still folded. 'I mean, when you told me that you were going to New York, did you lie, knowing that you intended to follow me?'

'A man has to do what a man has to do.' Dio shrugged, not bothering to deny the accusation. 'Although, if we're going to be completely accurate, *I* didn't follow you. Jackson, my driver, did. When he alerted me to your location, I drove here to find out what was going on.'

'That's as good as following me yourself!'

'It's better because I gather you took the tube and the bus to get here. It might have been difficult getting onto the same bus as you without you recognising me.'

'But why? Why now?'

'Why do you think, Lucy?'

'You never seemed to care one way or another what I got up to in your absences.'

'I never expected my wife to be running around with some man when I wasn't looking. I didn't think that I had to have you watched twenty-four-seven.'

'You don't. Didn't.' She flushed, recognising the measure of trust he had placed in her. She had met many women, wives of similarly wealthy men, whose every movement was monitored by bodyguards, who had little or no freedom. She had once mentioned that to Dio and he had dismissed that as the behaviour of paranoid, arrogant men who were so pumped up with their own self-importance that they figured the rest of the world wanted what they had.

It cut her to the quick now that he might think that his trust had been misplaced.

She hated him, she told herself stoutly, but she wasn't the sort of girl who would ever have fooled around.

Suddenly it seemed very, very important for her to make him believe that.

'I would never have done anything behind your back, Dio,' she said evenly. 'And I haven't. Mark and I are work mates.'

'Come again?'

'I follow a local website,' she told him. 'All sorts of things get posted. Advertisements for used furniture, rooms to let, book clubs looking for members. Mark posted a request for anyone interested in teaching maths to some of the underprivileged kids around here. I answered the ad.'

Dio stared at her, astounded at what he was hearing.

'I remember telling you once that I wanted to go into teaching.'

'I wanted to be a fireman when I was eight. The phase didn't last.'

'It's not the same thing!'

'Strange that you wanted to teach yet ended up marrying me and putting paid to your career helping the underprivileged.'

'I didn't think I had a choice!' Lucy answered hotly.

'We all have choices.'

'When it comes to…to…family, sometimes our choices are limited.'

Dio wryly read the subtext to that. There had been no way that she was going to leave Daddy to pay the price for his own stupidity and greed. Better that she put her own dreams and ambitions on hold. And of course, saving Daddy *had*, after all, come with a hefty financial sweetener…

'And, now your choices are wide open, you decided that you'd follow your heart's dream…'

'There's no need to be cynical, Dio. Don't *you* have any dreams you've ever wanted to follow?'

'Right now my imagination is working full-time on getting the honeymoon you failed to deliver…' And that was precisely how he intended to harness his roaming mind. He had fallen hard for what he had thought was her disingenuous innocence. If she thought that he was mug enough to repeat his mistake, by buying into the concept of the poor little rich wife whose only dream was to help the poor and the needy, then she was in for a surprise.

'You're not even interested in hearing about this place, are you?' she asked in a disappointed voice. 'When I told you that I wanted a divorce, you weren't even interested in asking me why.'

'Would you like me to ask you now?' Dio looked at her with raised eyebrows and Lucy drew in a couple of steadying breaths because he could be just so unbearable when he put his mind to it. He believed the worst of her and there was no way that he was going to revise his opinions, whatever she told him.

It didn't matter that *he* had married *her* for all the wrong reasons! He played by his own rules.

'Is all of this going to pay enough to keep the wolf from the door?' He spread his arms wide to encompass the little room but he kept his eyes fixed on her face. She looked as though she wanted to cry.

'It doesn't pay anything at all. It's all purely voluntary work.'

'Ah… And what's your relationship with the man who scarpered when I threatened to beat him up?'

'He didn't scarper.'

'Not the answer I want.'

'You're so arrogant, Dio!'

'I'm interested in finding out whether my wife has a crush on some man she met on the Internet!'

His voice was calm and only mildly curious but Lucy could sense the undercurrent of steel running through it. She shivered because, just for the briefest of seconds, she wondered what it would be like for that possessiveness in his voice to indicate jealousy.

She wondered what it would feel like to have this sinfully good-looking, charismatic and utterly arrogant man… *jealous*.

She shakily dismissed that insane curiosity before it even had time to take root.

'I don't have a crush on Mark,' she told him quietly. 'Although, he's just the sort of guy I might have a crush on.'

'What do you mean by that?' Dio was outraged that they were sitting here having this conversation.

'I mean he's a really nice guy. He's kind, he's considerate, he's thoughtful and the kids adore him.'

'Sounds like a barrel of laughs.'

'He can be,' Lucy retorted sharply. 'He can actually be very funny. He makes me laugh,' she added wistfully and Dio took a deep, steadying breath.

'And I don't?'

'We haven't laughed together since…'

Suddenly restless, he stood up and began pacing the room and, this time, he actually took in what he was seeing, all the evidence of classes in progress. He flicked through one of the exercise books lying on a desk and recognised his wife's handwriting. Ticks, corrections, encouraging smiley faces…

'So, no crush on the hapless teacher,' Dio eventually drawled. 'And is that reciprocated?'

For a moment, Lucy considered throwing caution to the winds and telling him that *the hapless teacher* was crazy about her. Something dark inside her wanted to see if she could make him jealous, even though she already knew that answer to that one.

'Mark isn't interested in women,' she said baldly. 'Not in that way. He's very happy with his partner who works for a legal firm in Kent. We're just good friends.'

Dio felt a bolt of pure satisfaction and he allowed himself to relax. It had been inconceivable that she had been fooling around behind his back. It was also inconceivable that he would allow her to walk away from him without him first sampling the body that had preyed on his mind ever since he had first laid eyes on her.

Whether she knew it or not, she was his weakness, and he was determined finally to put paid to that. The momentary threat of another man had shown him what he had casually assumed. He had allowed his pride to call the shots, to subdue a more primal instinct to assert himself under a civilised, remote veneer that just wasn't his style. No more. She was his and he wanted her, never more so than now, when she was stripped of the make-up and the designer clothes, when her raw beauty was on show. Her teacher friend might be gay but it still bothered Dio that the man had even seen her like this, in all her natural glory.

Her talk about some mythical man who was kind and caring, waiting out there for her, had also got on his nerves.

His eyes slid lazily to her face and he watched her for a few seconds in silence until he could see the tide of pink creep into her cheeks. When she began to fidget, he allowed his eyes to drift a little lower, slowly taking in the jeans, the tee-shirt and the jut of her pert little breasts underneath.

'So...' he murmured, finding a slightly more comfortable position. 'At least my woman hasn't been screwing around behind my back...'

'Since when am I *your woman*?'

'I like you like this.'

'What are you talking about?'

'Unadorned. It's sexy.'

Lucy went redder. She felt tell-tale moisture seep through her panties, felt an ache down there that throbbed and spread under the unhurried intensity of his gaze.

'I told you, I'm not interested...' But she could hear a wobble in her voice and the shadow of a smile that tugged his lips was telling. She straightened and gave herself a stern mental talking to. 'I'm going to build a life for myself, Dio. A real life—no pretending, no having to talk to people I don't want to talk to, no dressing up in clothes I don't like wearing!'

'Laudable.' He cocked his head to one side. 'So your plan is to continue your voluntary work here?'

'Like I said, it isn't all about money!'

'But you never qualified as a teacher, did you?'

'I will as soon as I can and the work I do here will be invaluable experience.'

'The place is falling down,' Dio pointed out. 'You might want to devote your talent for teaching here but, frankly, I doubt this building will stay the course. You may not have noticed, but there's a bad case of rising damp going on and I'd bet that the plumbing goes back to the Dark Ages.'

'Mark is doing an excellent job of trying to raise funds.'

'Really?'

Lucy didn't say anything for a while and Dio nodded slowly, reading what she was reluctant to tell him.

In hard times, it was always difficult to get well-meaning individuals to part with their cash and certainly, if they were providing a service to the needy, then the parents of those needy children would just not have the cash to give anyway.

The building was collapsing around them and neither of them would be able to stall the inevitable.

'I never knew you were so...engaged in wanting to do good for the community,' he murmured truthfully. 'And I'm willing to lend a hand here.'

'What are you talking about?' Lucy dragged her mind away from a brief picture of how her father would have reacted to what she was doing. With horror. He had always been an inveterate snob of the very worst kind. Women were not cut out for careers and certainly not careers that involved them dealing with people lower down the pecking order! A nice job working for a posh auction house might have met with his approval but teaching maths to school kids from a deprived background? Never in a month of Sundays.

To think of the kids not having this facility was heart breaking. She hadn't been there long, but she knew that Mark had poured his life and soul into trying to make something of the place. And the kids, a trickle which was steadily growing, would be the ones who fared worst.

'You want to walk away from our marriage with nothing rather than face getting into bed with me.' Dio didn't bother to gift wrap what he had to say and he didn't bother to point out that that kiss they had shared was proof positive that she wasn't immune to what he had to offer. 'I can't help that—but you want this building bought…? Repaired…? Turned into a functioning high-spec space…? No expense spared…? How does that sound to you, Lucy? You see…' He relaxed, met her bemused gaze coolly and steadily. 'I want you and I'm not above using any trick in the book to get what I want…'

CHAPTER FOUR

LUCY WAS APPALLED.

'What kind of thing is that for you to say?' she demanded shakily. 'You'd stoop so low?'

Dio inclined his beautiful head to one side and shrugged elegantly. 'I don't look at it that way.'

'No? And what way *do* you look at it?'

'I look at it as a form of persuasion.'

'I can't believe I'm hearing this.'

'You're my wife,' he said in the sort of voice that implied he was stating the glaringly obvious and irrefutable. 'When you started concocting your little plan to walk out of my life, you must surely have known that I wouldn't lie down on the ground waving a white flag and wishing you every success. Since when did I turn into that kind of person?'

Lucy shifted uncomfortably and then began fiddling with a pile of exercise books on the desk at which she had sat. Teacher in the front with wayward pupil facing her. Except Dio was far too intimidating to be any old wayward pupil.

'Well?' he prodded coolly.

'I just think it's out of order for you to jeopardise the welfare of lots of deprived children who happen to be benefitting from what is on offer here!'

'I'm not jeopardising anyone's welfare. You are.' He

glanced at his watch. He had been optimistic about getting back to the office at some point during the day and had thus dressed in his suit but, the way things were going, the office felt out of reach at the moment and, strangely enough, that didn't bother him.

He was far too invigorated by what was taking place.

'Is this taking longer than you expected?' Lucy asked with saccharin sweetness that wouldn't have fooled an idiot and he grinned.

Her stomach seemed to swoop and swirl inside her, as though she had been suddenly dropped from a great height without the aid of a parachute. That grin; it transformed the harsh, forbidding contours of his lean face. It reminded her of her youthful folly in letting it get under her skin until she had been walking on clouds, hanging onto his every word, waiting for the next meeting with barely bated breath.

And just like that it dawned on her why the thought of making love to him was so terrifying.

Yes, she hated him for the way he had manipulated her into marrying him for all the wrong reasons. Yes, she hated the way he had showcased her, like a business asset to be produced at will and then dispatched when no longer needed.

But what really scared her was the fact that he could still do things to her, make her feel things that were only appropriate in the domain of a real, functioning marriage.

When she thought of having him touch her, make love to her, she knew that somehow she would end up being vulnerable. He still got to her and she was scared stiff that, the closer he approached, the more ensnared she would become.

Like it or not, she was not nearly as detached as she had presented herself over time.

And that lazy grin was enough to remind her of that unwelcome reality.

'For my dear wife, I would be willing to put business on hold indefinitely.'

Lucy shot him a glance of scathing disbelief and Dio laughed, a rich, sexy, velvety sound that shot right past her defences.

'Or at least for a couple of hours, while we try to work out our little differences. Show me around.' He stood up and flexed his muscles. 'I can't carry on sitting in this chair for much longer. It's far too small. My joints are beginning to seize up. I need to stretch my legs, so give me the guided tour. If I'm going to revive this dump, I might as well start assessing what needs to be done.'

Lucy's full mouth compressed. Was he deliberately trying to goad a response out of her? Or was he just supremely confident of getting his own way, whatever she said to the contrary?

'You're not going to *revive this dump* and you're not interested in what I do here, anyway!'

Dio looked at her long and hard, hands thrust into his trouser pockets.

'I'm going to disagree on both counts,' he told her softly.

Lucy's eyes fluttered and she looked away hurriedly. The dark, naked intent in his gaze was unsettling. She decided that showing him around the school, what little there was of it, was a better option than standing here and having to brave the full frontal force of his personality.

She gave a jerky shrug and directed him to the exercise books on her desk. This was the main classroom, where she and Mark did their best to accommodate the children, whose abilities varied wildly, as did their ages.

She warmed to her subject.

Dio saw what had been missing all these months. She

had presented a beautiful, well-educated, cultured mask to the outside world but the animation had gone. It was here now as she talked about all the wonderful things the school was capable of providing; how much the considerate, funny and thoughtful Mark had managed to do with minimum help and almost no funding. Her eyes glowed and her cheeks pinked. She gestured and he found himself riveted by the fluid grace of her hands as she spoke.

There were several rooms on the ground floor. The building was like the Tardis, much bigger inside than it appeared from the outside.

'Volunteer teachers come whenever they can,' she told him, leading the way into another small room. 'Mark has managed to get a rota going and several subjects are now covered by experts.' She looked at Dio and her voice softened. 'You wouldn't believe the conditions some of the kids who come to us live in,' she explained. 'The fact that they're brought to us in the first place shows a great deal of parental support but there are stories of almost no food, noise pollution from neighbours, overcrowding in small flats…the list goes on.'

Dio nodded and let his eyes drift over that full mouth, the slim column of her neck, her narrow shoulders. Vanilla-blonde strands of hair were escaping the confines of the ponytail and the way they wisped around her face made her look incredibly young, barely a teenager.

'How safe is it?' he asked suddenly.

'Huh?'

'What are the safety procedures around here? Is there just the pair of you working here? And have you been working at night?'

'Are you telling me that you're concerned for my welfare?' Lucy's voice was mocking.

'Always.'

She felt the steady thud of her heart banging against her rib cage. His face was so serious that she was momentarily deprived of the power of speech and, when she did rediscover her vocal cords, she could hear a thread of jumpiness in her voice as she explained that neither of them worked nights and the place was always busy with people coming and going during the handful of hours in which they did work.

'Be that as it may,' Dio continued, 'now that I know where you spend your time, and what you get up to when I'm not around, you're going to have two of my guards close at hand whenever you come here—and, Lucy, that's not negotiable.'

'You used to say that you didn't agree with men who felt that they had to surround their wives with bodyguards!'

'You wouldn't require a bodyguard if you spent your time doing your nails and shopping…which was what I thought you got up to in your spare time.'

'What sort of impression is that going to give?' Lucy cried, feeling the wings of her freedom being clipped and resenting it even as she warmed with forbidden pleasure at the thought of him wanting to protect her.

To protect his investment. She brought herself back down to earth with a sobering bump. An investment he was keen to look after now that he wanted to take full advantage of it before he consigned it to the rubbish bin.

'I've never cared about what other people think. So, how many classrooms are there in this place and what's upstairs…?'

'I can't have great big, bulky men lurking around. They'll scare off the kids.'

'I doubt that in this neighbourhood.'

'Stop being provocative, Dio!'

'If you think I'm being provocative, then how would

you describe yourself?' He strolled towards her and she found herself nailed to the spot, mesmerised by the casual grace of his movements.

'I'm just…just trying to tell you that I don't want to…to…stand out when I come here.' Perspiration beaded her upper lips as he curled a strand of wayward hair around his finger. 'What are you doing, Dio?'

'I'm talking to you. You can't object if your soon-to-be ex-husband takes a little interest in the safety and wellbeing of his wife, can you?'

'That's not what I meant.'

'No?' He looked perplexed. 'Then what did you mean?'

'You…I…' Her sluggish brain could not complete the remainder of her thoughts. Her body felt heavy and lethargic. Right now, she yearned for him to touch her in other places; she absolutely yearned for him to take her to all those places he frequently took her to in her dreams.

She had to exert every ounce of willpower to drag herself physically out of his mesmerising radius, stepping back and sucking in a lungful of restorative air.

'It won't work having great big guys standing on either side of me. Plus, when I come here, no one knows who I am.'

'You're not recognised?' Dio frowned and she allowed herself a little smile.

'Why would anyone recognise me? I dress like this, in jeans, tee-shirts and jumpers, and I scrape my hair back and I don't wear tons of make-up and expensive jewellery.'

He heard the derision in her voice and was struck, once again, at hidden depths swirling just out of sight.

It confused him and that was a sensation he was not accustomed to dealing with. Least of all in a woman whose motivations had left him in no doubt as to the sort of person she was. Not one with hidden depths, for starters.

He raked his fingers through his hair and shook his head impatiently, clearing it of the sudden fog of doubt that had descended.

Did she enjoy the novelty of pretending to do good undercover? Was that it?

'Now, you were asking about the other rooms downstairs.' She briskly took him on the tour he had requested. More rooms with more low bookshelves and a scattering of stationery. She could have equipped the entire school with computers had she so desired simply by flogging one of the items of jewellery locked away in the safe in her bedroom. But she had chosen not to and he presumed that that was because she wanted, as she had told him, to keep her identity under wraps. To keep the extent of her wealth under wraps.

And yet how did that make sense?

She had been a Bishop, through and through. Surely the last thing she should have wanted would be…*this*.

He looked around at the shabby walls which someone had optimistically painted a cheerful yellow, similar to the walls in the hallway. Nothing could conceal the wear and tear of the fabric of the building, however, and the fact that it was practically falling down.

'Mark should be back shortly.' She ended the downstairs tour in a room that was very similar to the others he had been shown. 'If you're really interested, you can ask him whatever questions you like.'

'Think I'll pass on that one.' He leaned against the wall and looked at his wife whose face had become smudged with pencil at some point during their tour. 'I wouldn't want to have to administer smelling salts because he has a fainting fit seeing me still here.'

'Very funny,' Lucy muttered, making sure to keep a healthy distance.

'I have some questions to ask *you*, though. Is there any-where around here we can go for lunch?'

'Lunch?' she parroted, because lunch, just the two of them, was not something they had done since getting married.

'Unless you've travelled with sandwiches and a flask of hot coffee…? In your anxious attempts not to stand out…?' He could have told her that she stood out just looking the way she did.

'There's a café just round the corner.'

'Café?'

'It's not much but they make nice enough sandwiches and serve very big mugs of tea.'

'I'll give that one a miss. Any other suggestions?'

Lucy eyed him coolly and folded her arms. 'You're in my territory now, Dio.'

'*Your* territory? Don't make me laugh.'

'I don't care what you think but I feel I belong here a lot more than I belong in any of those soulless big houses, where I've had to make sure the fridges are stocked with champagne and caviar and the curtains are cleaned on a regular basis just in case…'

Dio's lips thinned. 'If you're trying to annoy me, then congratulations, Lucy—you're going about it the right way.'

'I'm not trying to annoy you but I meant what I said. If you want to continue this conversation and ask whatever questions you want to ask, including questions about the divorce I've asked you for, then you can jolly well eat in the café Mark and I eat in whenever we're here! I can't believe you're such a snob.'

'I'm not a snob,' Dio heard himself reply in an even, well-measured voice. 'But maybe I've seen enough of those greasy spoon cafés to last a lifetime. Maybe I come from enough of a deprived background to know that getting out of it was the best thing I ever did. I certainly have no desire to pretend that it holds any charm for me now.'

Lucy's mouth fell open.

This was the first time Dio had ever mentioned his background. She had known, of course, that he had made his own way up in the world, thanks to her father's passing, derogatory remarks. But to hear him say anything, anything at all, was astounding.

Dio flushed darkly and turned away. 'I'll talk to you when you return home this evening.'

'No!' Seeing him begin walking towards the door galvanised Lucy into action and she placed a detaining hand on his arm.

Just like that, heat from his body seared through her, and she almost yanked her hand back as if it had been physically burnt.

'We…we should talk now,' she stammered, stepping back. 'I know you must have been shocked at what I've asked and I never thought that you would…well, that you would see what I've been up to here…but, now that you have, well, I don't mind having lunch with you somewhere a little smarter.'

Dio sighed and shook his head before fixing fabulous, silver eyes on her flushed face. 'Take me to the café. It's no big deal.'

She locked up behind her and they walked side by side to the café where she and Mark were regulars.

She was desperate to ask him about his past. Suddenly it was as though locked doors had been opened and curiosity was bursting out of her.

He'd grown up without money but had he been happy? As she knew only too well from personal experience, a moneyed background was no guarantee of happiness.

She sneaked a glance at his averted profile and concluded that he wasn't in the mood for a soul-searching chit chat on his childhood experiences.

And it surprised her that she was so keen to hear all about them.

'It's not much,' she reminded him as they pulled up in front of a café that was still relatively empty and smelled heavily of fried food.

'Understatement of the year.' Dio looked down at her and noticed the way the sun glinted off her blonde hair; noticed the thick lushness of her lashes and the earthy promise of her full lips. His breathing became a little shallower. 'But I won't forget the virtues of the brimming cups of tea and the big sandwiches...'

They knew her!

Dio was stunned. Two of the people working behind the counter had kids who had started drifting in to do maths lessons and there was a brief chat about progress.

'And this...' she turned to Dio and glanced away quickly '...is a friend. Someone thinking of investing in the building, really turning it into somewhere smarter and better equipped...' She felt him bristle next to her. She'd always removed her wedding ring before coming here; it was just too priceless to take chances. She sneaked a sideways glance and caught the look of annoyance in his eyes and she returned that look of simmering annoyance with a special look of her own, one that was earnest and serious. 'He's very interested in helping the kids in this area really reach their full potential at school.'

'Because...' Dio said instantly, with the sort of charming smile that would knock anyone off balance, which it seemed to be doing to Anita, whose mouth had dropped open the second she had clocked him. 'Because I happen to have grown up not a million miles from here,' he said smoothly. 'On an estate not unlike the one we passed and, take it from me, the only way to escape is through education.'

Anita was nodding vigorously. John was agreeing in a manly fashion. Lucy was feeling as though she had been cleverly outmanoeuvred.

'This lovely young woman and I…are in discussions at the moment. It could all hinge on her acceptance of my proposal: no more rising damp, all the rooms brought up to the highest specification. Naturally, I would buy the building outright, and the cherry on the cake would be the equipment I would install. I find that computers are part and parcel of life nowadays. How else can children access vital information? Like I said, though, Lucy and I are in talks at the moment…'

As soon as they were seated, with mugs of steaming tea and two extra-large doorstop sandwiches filled to bursting in front of them, Lucy leaned forward, glaring.

'Thanks for that, Dio!'

'Any time. What else are friends and potential investors for? Why didn't you introduce me as your husband?'

'Because there would have been loads of questions to field,' Lucy said defensively. 'They would want to know who I really was…'

'To have snagged me?'

'You have a ridiculous ego.' She sipped some tea and looked at him over the rim of the mug. 'Were you lying when you said what you said?'

Dio knew exactly what she was talking about. Why had he suddenly imparted information about his past? He had always kept the details of his background to himself. Growing up on a tough estate, where the laws of the jungle were very different from the jungle laws of the business world, he had learnt the wisdom of silence. It was a habit that was deeply ingrained.

'Be more specific,' he drawled. 'Nice sandwich, by the way.'

'Did you grow up near here?'

'We *are* breaking into new and unexplored territory, aren't we?' he murmured, his fabulous eyes roving over the stunning prettiness of her heart-shaped face. It amazed him that he had never seen that body. His success with women had started at a very young age and was legendary and yet, with her, *his wife*, he had yet to discover what lay underneath the tee-shirt and the jeans.

Bitterness refused to dampen the sudden thrust of his erection and it occurred to him that he had spent an awful lot of time fantasising about the untouchable ice-maiden who had conned him into marriage.

Not for much longer. That was a very satisfying thought.

'Unexpected announcements, revelations all round, time together without high society peering over our shoulders… Where does it end, I wonder? Oh, yes, I know. In bed.'

Lucy flushed. Those amazing pale eyes sent her nervous system into freefall and as soon as he mentioned the word 'bed' she couldn't stop the tide of graphic images that pelted into her head at breakneck speed.

The principles she had held so dear became gossamer-thin under the impact of those images.

But for her, sex and love were entwined. They were!

'You were out of order implying to John and Anita that you were willing to sink money in the place if I agreed to your demands.'

'Was I?' Dio shot her a perplexed frown. 'I thought that I was only being honest. Nice people, by the way. They seem to have bought into the usefulness of having the after-school tutoring scheme there, but then I guess they would, considering they both have children who attend. Must be tough.'

Lucy was beginning to feel as though she had been stuck in a washing machine with the speed turned to full.

'What must be tough?' She knew what was tough. Tough was the way her carefully laid plans had unravelled at the speed of light in the space of twenty-four short hours. She had suspected that talk of divorce wouldn't fall on completely fertile ground, because her husband was nothing if not proud, but she had not banked on the route he had taken which had now landed them both up here.

With talk of sex shimmering between them.

'Tough being a working parent, trying to make ends meet while still attempting to find the spare time to sit and do homework with kids. I guess that's the situation with your two…friends.'

'They're going to repeat what you told them to Mark.'

'Oh dear. And would that be a problem?'

'You always have to get your own way, don't you?' Lucy looked at him resentfully and then immediately diverted her eyes, because he was just too sexy and too good-looking to stare at for very long. Especially now that the dynamics between them had changed, subtly but dramatically.

'Always,' Dio confirmed readily. 'What do you think your caring, sharing friend will think when he discovers that you're the person standing between the success and failure of his little baby…? Because, from what you've told me, this has been more than just a flash in the pan, try-it-on-for-size experiment for him.'

Lucy bristled. 'Are you implying that that's what it's been for me?' she demanded, sinking her teeth into her sandwich and chewing angrily on it.

'I never noticed just how cute you are when you're

angry,' Dio murmured. 'But then, anger didn't score high on the list of required emotions in our marriage, did it?'

It surprised him just how much he was enjoying himself. Was it the bizarre novelty of the situation? He didn't know and he wasn't going to waste time with pointless questions. He was in very little doubt that as soon as he had had her, as soon as he had slept with her, he would regain healthy perspective on just the kind of woman she was, at which point he would bid farewell to his manipulative wife. But in the meantime...

Lucy lowered her eyes, reminded of just how hollow and empty their marriage had been, and then further reminded of all the high hopes and girlish dreams that had driven her to marry him in the first place.

'I find working with these kids fulfilling,' she told him, ignoring his barb. 'Much, much more fulfilling than making stupid small talk to people I don't like and barely know. Much more fulfilling than going to the opening of an art gallery or a society wedding.'

Privately, Dio couldn't have agreed more. One of the more odious things he had to do in his steady, inexorable rise to the very top of the pecking order was attend events he couldn't give a damn about. But it came with the job and he was too much of a realist to think otherwise.

Funnily enough, it had never occurred to him that his well-bred wife would ever have found that side of life a bore. In fact, he would have thought that that might have been one of the many things she enjoyed about the position into which she had cleverly manoeuvred herself.

Now he looked at her with a frown, trying to work out the little inconsistencies he was beginning to spot underneath the polished veneer he had always associated with her.

'It's going to be all round the neighbourhood that a big

shot investor has taken an interest in our little local after-school club.'

'Not just any old big shot investor, though.'

'What am I supposed to say?' she demanded, pushing her plate to one side, making sure to keep her voice low and calm because people were beginning to filter into the café now and curious looks were being directed at them.

'You could tell them that you didn't care for the terms your big shot investor demanded.'

'You should never have followed me!'

'You know you want me…'

'I beg your pardon!'

'Shocking, isn't it?' He leant back in the chair and was amused when she leaned forward, all the better to make sure that their conversation wasn't overheard. 'You don't want to face up to it, but let's cut to the chase. You're hot for me.'

'I am not!'

'Would you like to put that to the test?' He cast his eyes round the small café and the curious faces. 'Why doesn't the hot shot investor apply a little physical pressure…? Hmm…? How about I reach across this table and kiss you? Remember that kiss? How about we have a repeat performance right here? Right now? Then we could take a vote… find out how many people agree with me that you're attracted to me…'

'You took me by surprise when you kissed me!' Patches of red had appeared on her cheeks. She knew that she didn't look like the calm, composed teacher everyone around here expected her to be. She looked just like she felt. Hassled, overwhelmed, confused.

Excited…

'So this time you'll be prepared. We can both gauge just how much you can withstand what's simmering between us.'

'There's nothing simmering between us!' Desperation threaded her voice.

'Of course there is.' Dio dismissed her in a hard, inflexible voice. 'And it's been there all the way through our sexless marriage.'

'Shh!'

He ignored her frantic interruption. 'I've seen the way you've looked at me when you thought you weren't being observed. You may have connived your way into marriage, and then pulled back once you'd got me hooked, but you still can't quite help what you feel, can you?'

Lucy rested her head in her hand and wondered if she could just wish herself some place else.

'Tell me…did you find it offensive to think of me in terms of being your lover?'

She looked at him, horrified. 'How can you say that? What are you talking about?'

'We couldn't have come from more opposite sides of the tracks,' Dio said drily. 'Did you imagine you might catch a working class infection if you got too close to me?'

'I'm not like that! We didn't have a proper marriage and I wasn't going to…to…'

He waved aside her half-baked, stammering explanation with an air of sudden boredom. 'Not really interested in going down this road,' he drawled. 'The only thing I want is *you*, my beloved wife. I want to feel your naked body writhing under me. I want to hear you scream out my name and beg me to bring you to orgasm.'

'That'll never happen!'

'Oh, it will. You just need to give the whole thing a little bit of thought and stop pretending that it'll be any great hardship for you. It won't be.'

'And you know this because…?' She was aiming for snappy and sarcastic; she got reedy and plaintive.

'Because I know women. Trust me. It won't be a hardship. And just think of the rewards… Fat alimony allowance…your little school shiny and well-equipped…grateful parents and happy little children… Could there be a better start to your wonderful bid for freedom…?' He leaned forward so that they were both now resting their elbows on the table, their faces close together, locked in their own private world. 'In fact, I have a splendid idea. Let's take our honeymoon, Lucy. Two weeks. After that, I have to be in Hong Kong to close a deal on a company buyout. I'll head there and you can… Well, you can begin your life of independence. How does that sound…?'

CHAPTER FIVE

PREY TO WARRING EMOTIONS, Lucy was left to consider her options for three days while Dio disappeared to Paris for an emergency meeting with the directors of one of his companies over there.

By her calculation, that left eleven days of honeymoon time before he vanished across the Atlantic to Hong Kong.

She knew that she had been cleverly but subtly outmanoeuvred.

For a start, the story of the brand new school spread like a raging wild fire. He had played the 'hot shot investor' to perfection. Now, as far as everyone in the neighbourhood was concerned, ordering computers, stationery and getting the builders in was just a little formality because everything was signed, sealed and delivered bar the shouting.

If the whole pipe dream collapsed, Lucy knew that she would have to dig deep to find an excuse that would work. The blame would fall squarely on her shoulders.

The day after she and Dio had lunched in the café, Mark had arrived at work clutching brochures for computers and printers. He had made noises about getting the national press involved to cover a 'feel good' story because 'the world was a dark place and it was just so damn heart-warming to find that there were still one or two heroes left in it'…

Lucy had nearly died on the spot. In what world could Dio Ruiz be classed as a hero?

No one had actually asked what the mysterious conditions were that had been imposed on her, for which she was very grateful, because she had no idea what she would have said.

They had been dependent on various money-raising ventures and government help to cover the scant lease on the building; now two members of the local council descended, beaming, to tell her that there were plans afoot to buy the place outright. They delivered a rousing speech on how much it would benefit the community to have the place brought up to scratch and in permanent active use.

They dangled the carrot of helping to subsidise three full-time members of staff who could perhaps assist in teaching non-English-speaking students, of which there were countless in the borough.

And, twice daily, Dio had called her on her mobile, ostensibly to find out how she was—given their new relationship, which involved conversation—but really, she knew, to apply pressure.

Two weeks…

And then, after that, freedom was hers for the taking.

Was he right? Would sleeping with him be such a hardship? They were married and, when she had married him, she had been hot for him, had counted the hours, the minutes and the seconds till they could climb into bed together. Her virginity was something precious to be handed over to him and she hadn't been able to wait to do it.

She was still a virgin but she was now considerably more cynical than she had once been. And how precious was it, really? So once upon a time she had had a dream of only marrying for love and losing her virginity to a guy she wanted to spend her life with. She had woken up. Big deal.

And she was *still* hot for him. It pained her to admit it, especially since he had gloatingly pointed it out to her and, worse, had proved it by kissing her, feeling her melt under his hands.

What was the point in denying reality? She'd been damned good at facing reality so far; she had not once shied away from the fact that she was trapped in a marriage and forced to play the part of the socialite she probably should have but never had been.

On day three she picked up her mobile to hear his dark, velvety voice down the line and, as usual, she felt the slow, thick stir of her heightened senses.

Once more or less able to withstand the drugging effect of his personality, Lucy had now discovered that her defences had been penetrated on all fronts. Even when he was on the opposite side of the world, she just had to hear his voice and every nerve inside her body quivered in response.

Overnight it seemed as though all the walls she had painstakingly built between them had been knocked down in a single stroke.

'What are you up to?'

Lucy sat down. Was she really interested in launching into a conversation about the porridge she had just eaten?

'Marie has handed in her notice. I knew she was going to at some point. She's far too ambitious to be cleaning. She's got a placement at a college. So I'm afraid you're going to have to find someone else to do the cleaning in the Paris apartment.'

'*I'm* going to have to find someone else?'

'Well, I won't be around, will I?' Lucy pointed out bluntly. She projected to when she would shut the door of their grand, three-storey mansion in London for good and she felt her heart squeeze inside her.

Sitting in the first class lounge at JFK airport, Dio frowned. By the time he returned to London, he wanted an answer from her, and the only answer he was prepared to accept was the one he wanted to hear.

That was what he wanted to chat about now. He certainly didn't want to have a tedious conversation about their apartment in Paris and finding a cleaner to replace the one who had quit. He didn't want her to start the process of withdrawing from the marriage. No way. Nor had he contemplated the prospect of not getting what he wanted from her.

It occurred to him that there really was only one topic of conversation he was willing to hear.

'I'll cross the bridge of hiring a new cleaner when the time comes.'

'Well, it'll come in the space of two weeks, which is when Marie will be leaving.'

'What are you wearing? It's early over there…are you still in your pyjamas? Does it strike you as a little bizarre that we've never seen each other in the confines of a bedroom, wearing pyjamas?'

Lucy went bright red and cleared her throat. 'I don't know what my clothes have to do with anything…' She automatically pulled her dressing gown tighter around her slender body and was suddenly conscious of her bra-less breasts and the skimpiness of her underwear.

'I'm making small talk. If we're to spend the next two weeks together—'

'Eleven days,' Lucy interrupted.

Dio relaxed and half-smiled to himself. He had made sure to phone her regularly while he had been away. Over the marriage, they had managed to establish a relationship in which she had been allowed to retreat. That retreat was not going to continue.

And now, without her having to say it, he could hear the capitulation in her voice. It generated the kick of an intense, slow burn of excitement.

'If we're to spend the next eleven days together, then we need to be able to converse.'

'We know how to converse, Dio. We've done a great deal of that over the course of our marriage.'

'Superficial conversation,' Dio inserted smoothly. 'No longer appropriate, given the fact that our relationship has changed.'

'Our relationship hasn't changed.'

'No? I could swear you just told me how long we're going to be spending on our long-overdue honeymoon...'

Lucy licked her lips nervously. The dressing gown had slipped open and, looking down, she could see the smooth lines of her stomach and her pert, pointed breasts.

She had made her mind up about his ultimatum and she hadn't even really been aware of doing so.

Soon that flat stomach and those breasts would be laid bare for him to see and touch.

A little shiver raced through her. She slipped her finger beneath her lacy briefs and felt her own wetness. It shocked her. It was as if her body was already reacting to the knowledge that someone else would be touching it—that *Dio* would be touching it.

'Okay,' she said as loftily as she could manage. 'So, you win, Dio. I hope it makes you feel proud.'

'Right now, pride is the very least of the things I'm feeling.' His voice lowered, sending a ripple of forbidden excitement through her.

Out of all the reasons she had privately given herself for yielding to his demands, she now acknowledged the only reason that really truly counted for anything.

It had nothing to do with the school, duty towards her students or, least of all, money.

She had yielded because she fancied him and because she knew, as he did, that to walk away from a dry marriage would be to wonder for ever what it might have been like to sleep with him.

Her head might not want to get into bed with Dio but her body certainly did and this was her window.

The fact that there were a lot of up sides and bonuses attached to her decision was just an added incentive.

'I'd tell you what I'm feeling,' he said roughly, 'but I'm sitting in the lounge at JFK and I wouldn't want anyone to start noticing the hefty bulge in my trousers…'

'Dio! That's…that's…'

'I know. Unfortunate, considering I'm going to have to wait a few more hours before I can be satisfied.'

'That's not what I meant!'

'No?'

'No,' Lucy told him firmly. To add emphasis to her denial, she very firmly tightened the dressing gown so that she could cover up her treacherously over-heated, semi-naked body. 'I…I'm happy to discuss the details of…er… our arrangement.'

'Speak English,' Dio said drily.

'I'll do this honeymoon business with you but only because I don't have a choice.'

'That's not very enthusiastic,' Dio admonished, hanging onto his temper. If he could put his feelings to one side, if he could forget her duplicitous take on their marriage, then he was damned if he was going to let her get away with dragging her feet and somehow blaming him for the fact that she wanted to sleep with him.

'Everyone expects you to descend and start flinging money at the school.'

'I find it doesn't do to mould your life according to other people's expectations.'

'How do I know that once this so-called honeymoon of ours is over you'll do what you say…?'

'You don't.' Dio was affronted. He had always been a man of his word, which was saying something, in a world where very few men were. He might not have been born with a silver spoon in his mouth but he knew one thing for sure: in his business practices, and in fact in his whole approach to life, he was a damned sight more ethical than a lot of his counterparts whose climb up the ladder had been a great deal less precarious than his had been!

'You'll have to rely on that little thing called trust.'

Lucy didn't say anything and Dio felt the significance of her silence like a disapproving slap on the face.

Rich, coming from the ice-maiden who had strung him along.

'I'm not a man who breaks his word,' he said coolly. 'I know many who do.'

Lucy thought of her father, who had cheated so many people out of their pensions, and she flushed guiltily. Were Dio's thoughts running along the same lines? He might have married her for all the wrong reasons but then he had never claimed to love her, had he? Even when they had been dating, he had never talked about love.

And something deep inside her knew that, if he had given his word, then he wasn't going to break it.

'Shall I book somewhere?' she asked stiffly. 'I expect you want to use one of the houses…'

'I think you can climb out of "personal assistant" mode on this occasion,' Dio said softly. 'It somehow ruins the… sizzle.'

His husky voice was doing all sorts of peculiar things to her body and she squirmed on the chair, idly glancing round at all the top-notch, expensive equipment in the very expensive kitchen.

'I surely need to book flights for us?' Lucy intended to do her very best not to let either of them forget that their weird honeymoon was built on stuff that was very prosaic.

This wasn't going to be one of those romantic affairs where they would spend their time whispering sweet nothings and staring longingly at one another over candlelit dinners before racing to their room so that they could rip the clothes off one another.

This was more getting something elemental out of their systems.

'Don't give it a thought,' Dio said briskly. 'I'll get my secretary to do the necessary.'

'But where will we be going? And when, exactly?'

'I'm at JFK now. When I return to London, I'll have a quick turnaround. Be prepared to be out of the country this time tomorrow.'

'What? I can't just leave here at a moment's notice.'

'Of course you can. My secretary will take care of everything. You just need to get ready for me...'

'Get ready for you?'

Dio laughed at the outrage in her voice. He was so hard for her right now, he was finding it difficult to move.

Small, high breasts... He had glimpsed the shadow of her cleavage in some of the more daring dresses she had worn to social events over the course of the marriage. He wondered what colour her nipples were. She was a natural blonde and he imagined that they were rosy pink, kissable nipples. He wondered what she would taste like when he buried himself between her thighs.

He wondered who else she had shared her body with before she had met him.

It was a grimly unappealing thought and he ditched it before it had time to take root.

'Use your imagination,' he drawled. 'Get into the head set...'

'Yes, sir...' Lucy muttered under her breath and she heard his soft laughter down the end of the line. Sexy laughter. The laughter of a man who'd got exactly what he wanted. She fidgeted a little more and forced herself to focus. 'And what should I pack?'

'Don't. I'll make sure that there are clothes waiting for you at the other end.'

'I don't want to be dressed up like a Barbie doll,' she told him quickly. 'That's not part of this arrangement.'

'I shall see you very soon, Lucy...'

'But you still haven't told me where we'll be going!'

'I know. Isn't it exciting? I, for one, can't wait.'

And he disconnected. Lucy was left holding a dead phone and feeling panicked because now there was no going back.

She tried to think of life after the next ten days but she found her mind getting stuck with images of Dio in bed with her. After she had discovered the truth behind their sham of a marriage, she had told herself that that was why he had not tried to get her into bed before they had tied the knot.

She had thought that he was being a gentleman, respecting her wish to wait until they were married before having sex. She had been too embarrassed to tell him that she was still a virgin, and anyway the subject had not arisen.

Instead, he had been stringing her along. She had stopped day dreaming about him but the day dreams were rearing their heads once again and she couldn't stop them.

How was she supposed to travel to some unknown destination? They could be going to the Arctic, the Caribbean or a city somewhere. Had he even decided or was he going to let his assistant choose where they went?

And what was it going to be like when he returned to the house?

The knowledge that they would be cooped up together for the better part of a fortnight would lie between them like a lead weight…

Wouldn't it?

She was a bundle of nerves as evening drew round. For the first time in as long as she could remember, she didn't dress up for his arrival. Usually, she never dropped the role unless she was on her own. Usually he saw her formally attired, even when she was in casual clothing.

But things were different and she had defiantly chosen to wear a pair of jeans and a faded old tee-shirt from her university days. Nor was she plastered with make-up and she hadn't curled her hair. Instead, she was a make-up-free zone and her hair hung heavily just past her shoulders, neatly tucked behind her ears.

She was in the same place as she had been when she had confronted him with talk of divorce, standing in the drawing room. And she was just as jumpy.

And yet, staring through the window into the, for London, relatively large garden with its row of perfectly shaped and manicured shrubs, she didn't hear him until he spoke.

'I wondered if you would wait up for me.' Dio strolled into the drawing room, dumping his jacket, which he had hooked over his shoulder. It had been a tiresome flight, even in first class, but he felt bright eyed and bushy-tailed now as he flicked his eyes over her.

He'd half-expected her to go into a self-righteous melt-down between speaking to her on the phone and showing up at the house. She was very good at adopting the role of blameless victim. He guessed that the lure of money was irresistible, however. She might play at her volunteer work and make big plans to teach but teaching didn't pay nearly enough for her to afford the sort of lifestyle to which she had always been accustomed.

Cynicism curled his lips when he thought that.

'Drink?'

A feeling of déjà vu swept over Lucy as she helplessly followed him into the kitchen, although this time she had eaten, and she expected he would have as well, so there would be no pretend domesticity preparing a meal.

'I thought we could chat about plans for tomorrow,' she began valiantly. 'I need to know what time we will be leaving. I…I've packed a couple of things…' He looked drop-dead gorgeous and she could feel the electricity in the air between them, sparking like a live, exposed wire. It made the hairs on the back of her neck stand on end.

And the way he was looking at her, his pale eyes skewering her, brought her out in a nervous wash of perspiration.

She wanted crisply to remind him that their arrangement was for the honeymoon period, which technically would only start when they reached wherever they were heading, and so for tonight they would retreat to their separate quarters as per normal. However, her tongue seemed to have become glued to the roof of her mouth.

'Have you been thinking about me?' Dio asked lazily. 'Because I've been thinking about you.' And marvelling that it had taken them this long to get where they were now, but then again the whole question of the penniless divorce had driven the situation.

He walked slowly towards her and she gave a little nervous squeak. 'I thought we were going to…er…well, when we were away…'

'Why stand on ceremony? The honeymoon's been cut

a little short by my unexpected meeting in New York anyway, so fair's fair, wouldn't you say? I don't want to be
short-changed on time. If I'm to pay for two weeks, then
I want my two weeks, or as good as…'

The last thing Lucy was expecting was to be swept off
her feet. Literally. The breath whooshed out of her body
as she was carried out of the kitchen. She felt the thud as
he nudged the door open with his foot and then she was
bouncing against him, heart racing as he took her up the
stairs.

To his bedroom, which she had been into many times
before. It was a marvel of masculinity. The colours were
deep and rich, the furniture bold and dark with clean lines.
Even with her eyes squeezed tightly shut, she could visual-
ise it. Once, when he had gone away, leaving the house a lot
earlier to catch a transatlantic flight, she had gone into the
bedroom to air it before the cleaner came and had remained
frozen to the spot at the sight of the rumpled bed, still bearing the impression of where he had been lying. She could
remember tentatively touching it and then springing back
because it had still held the lingering warmth of his body.

It had shaken her more than she had thought possible.

He dumped her on the bed and then stood back, arms
folded, for once lost as to what his next move might be.

He had been fired up with confidence downstairs, when
he had hoisted her into his arms like a true caveman and
brought her to his bedroom. But now…

She looked unimaginably beautiful and unimaginably
fragile, her eyes wide and apprehensive, making him feel
like a great, hulking thief who had snatched her from her
bed and carried her off to his cave so that he could have
his wicked way.

Dio raked his fingers through his hair and moved to the
window where he stood for a few seconds, looking out-

side, before snapping the wooden shutters closed, blocking out the street light.

Lucy stared at him from under her lashes. Her heart was still pounding and the blood was still rushing through her veins, hot and fierce. She wanted him so badly right now that she felt like she might die of longing, yet he was just standing there, looking at her with brooding stillness.

Maybe he had come to his senses, she thought.

Maybe he had realised that you couldn't just bargain with someone's fate the way he had with hers. Maybe he had seen the light and come to the conclusion that to blackmail someone into sleeping with you just wasn't on.

And if that was the case then why wasn't she feeling happier? Why wasn't she sitting up and making a case for having her divorce without a bunch of stupid stipulations? Why wasn't she striking while the iron was hot, trying to locate Mr Decent who must surely be there hiding behind Mr Caveman?

She wasn't feeling happier because she wanted him, simple as that.

Maybe if he had never mentioned sleeping with her, had never looked at her with those amazing, lazy, sexy eyes, she would have walked away from their marriage with her head held high and all her principles burning a hole inside her.

But he had opened a door and she wanted that door to remain open. She wanted to enter the unexplored room and see what was there…

She stirred on the bed then pushed herself backwards so that she was propped against the pillows, which she arranged under her, her vibrant blonde hair tangled around her flushed face.

Dio was her husband yet she felt as tongue-tied as a teenager on her first date with the cutest boy in class.

'Why are you just standing there?' she challenged, dry mouthed. 'Isn't this what you wanted? To carry me up here so that you could get *what you paid for*?'

Dio flushed darkly and scowled. Was that how he had sounded? Like a thug?

'Nearly a year and a half with no sex, Lucy. Are you telling me that I got a fair deal when I married you?' His voice was harsher than he had intended and he saw her flinch.

'Maybe neither of us got much of a fair deal.'

Personally, Dio thought the deal she had ended up with had been a hell of a lot better than his.

'You haven't answered my question.'

'You brought me up to your room for sex and here I am. You're getting what you paid for!' Brave words, but the way she cleared her throat alerted Dio to the fact that she might be talking the talk, but that was where it probably ended.

It seemed just one more thing that wasn't fitting into the neat slot he had shoved her into for the past year and a half.

A cold, opportunistic woman would surely not have been able to replicate the nervous wariness he could see beneath the brave statement of intent?

Her fingers wouldn't be digging into her arms to stop them from trembling…

'I find that I'm not as much into self-sacrificing martyrs as I had imagined,' Dio said, pushing himself away from the window ledge against which he had been leaning.

'Even the ones you forked out good money to buy?'

'You were never that cynical, Lucy.' He had a vivid image of her laughing at him with genuine, girlish innocence, the sort of girlish innocence that had made him lose his mind. She might not have been quite as innocent as she had pretended but she certainly hadn't been as sharp-tongued as she was now.

'I grew up,' she said with painful honesty.

'You can run along,' he told her, reaching to the top button of his shirt. 'I've had a long flight. I'm tired. I'm going to have a shower and hit the sack.'

She didn't want him to.

She could play the passive victim and scuttle off but she wasn't going to do that. She felt as though she had spent the past year or so playing the passive victim—had spent practically *her whole life* playing the passive victim—and now would be her only window in which to take control of a situation.

'What if I decide that I don't want to run along?' she asked with considerable daring.

Dio stilled, hand still poised to remove his shirt. Her chin was mutinously jutting out and he smiled, reluctantly amused by the expression on her face: stubborn, holding her breath, eyes squeezed tightly shut..

'What are you saying?'

'You know what I'm saying.'

'I like things to be spelt out in black and white. No room for error then…'

'I've wondered, okay?'

'Wondered what?' He was standing right by the bed now, looking down at her with a smile of male satisfaction.

'What it would be like…you know…? With you…'

'Even though you've spent many months being an ice-queen?'

'I've been very friendly with all your clients.'

'Maybe I've been longing for a few of those smiles to be directed my way,' Dio murmured. He slowly began unbuttoning his shirt, watching her watching him as his brown chest was exposed inch by inch.

Lucy was riveted. How long had she wanted this? How had this insane desire been so successfully hidden under layers of resentment and simmering anger, with a large dose of self-pity thrown in for good measure?

She watched as he tugged the shirt out from the waistband of his trousers, drew in a deep breath and held it as he shrugged off the shirt altogether, tossing it casually on the ground.

'So, you're curious…' He felt as though he was suddenly walking on clouds. It was an extremely uplifting sensation. In fact, when it came to the feel-good factor, this was as good as it got. Her eyes were huge and, yes, curious. He was bulging in his trousers, thick and hard and desperate for a release, which he was going to take his time getting to.

Drugged by the sensational vision of him half-naked… her bronzed god of a soon-to-be ex-husband… Lucy was deprived of speech. She nodded and didn't even bother trying to tear her eyes away from his glorious body.

'I confess I'm curious too,' Dio admitted, basking in her undiluted fascination with his body. 'So it's time for you to return the favour…'

'Huh?' Lucy blinked.

'One good turn deserves another,' Dio said drily. 'Or, in this case, one semi-striptease deserves another.'

'You want me to…?'

'We're man and wife.' He gestured broadly. 'A little bit of nudity should be as nothing between us.'

'I hate it when you do that,' she complained. He grinned and that grin erased all the forbidding, harsh lines of his beautiful face; made him seem almost boyish.

'Do what?'

'Oh, don't play the innocent with me.' But she smiled shyly and sat up. Her fingers were shaking; her hands were shaking. He had no idea that she had never done anything like this in her life before. Okay, at university there had been some good-natured fumbling with the two boys she had dated for six months and three months respectively. But they'd been boys and he was...

Dio...

Nerves ripped into her with a vengeance, but she had committed to this path, *wanted* this path, and she wasn't going to give in to cold feet now.

But that didn't mean that she wasn't shaking like a leaf as she dragged the tee-shirt over her head and flung it to the ground where it joined his shirt.

He had folded his arms and was staring, just as though she really was performing a proper striptease for his benefit only.

Which, she supposed, she was, in a way.

She closed her eyes, reached behind, unclasped her bra and, still with her eyes shut, flung the bra onto the little growing heap of discarded clothes.

'You can open your eyes,' Dio drawled. He was surprised he could talk at all because the sight of her was enough to take his breath away.

He loved the way she was sprawled there on his bed, her head averted. He could see the tiny pulse beating in her neck and, God, he wanted to fall on her, take her, sate himself with her body.

She was beyond captivating.

Pale, slender, her small breasts pert and pointed, her nipples as pink as he had imagined, but bigger. Perfect, circular discs that sent his blood pressure soaring.

Lucy opened her eyes and slid a hesitating, self-conscious sideways glance at him. She had no idea where she had found the courage to do what she had done, but she had had to do it, and one look at the naked hunger and desire in his eyes was enough to restore every scrap of her wavering self-confidence. She glanced at his trousers, then back to his face, and he laughed.

'So my beautiful ice-maiden thaws...' He slowly unlooped his belt from his trousers and then pulled down his zipper. He was utterly confident when it came to his own nudity and he really liked the way she was still looking at him. He pulled down the trousers and his boxers in one easy movement, and her eyelids fluttered as she took in the impressive girth of his erection.

'Your turn now...and then you can touch...' He loosely held himself and noted her quick, sharp intake of breath. Just one more of those little hot reactions and he knew that he wouldn't be responsible for what happened next.

Their eyes held and she wriggled her jeans down until she was left only in her panties. She couldn't stop looking at his big hand holding himself.

'Let me feel you first,' Dio said raggedly. He reached down and slipped his hand to cup the moist mound between her legs, then he pushed his finger in before sliding it along the slippery slit until he felt the throbbing nub of her clitoris.

Lucy gave a long, low groan and parted her legs.

There was no room in her head to contemplate her absolute lack of experience.

He would find out soon enough...

CHAPTER SIX

DIO STRADDLED HER and for a few seconds he just looked down at her. His fingers were wet from where he had touched her and felt her excited arousal.

She still seemed unable to meet his eyes in the shadowy darkness of the room and he gently tilted her face so that she was forced to look at him. He wanted to take her fast and hard…he was so aroused that he could scarcely breathe…but he could sense her nerves and, with a sigh, he lay down alongside her then hitched himself up on one elbow.

'Tell me you're not in the grip of second-thought syndrome,' he murmured, stalling her attempts to cover herself with his duvet.

Lucy's burst of self-confidence was fading fast. Her husband was the most beautiful man she had ever laid eyes on and, having spent far too long fantasising about him, she was even more bowled over at his beauty in the flesh. No fantasy could do him justice. He was a man in the very peak of his prime. No part of his impressive body was untoned. His stomach was washboard-flat, his shoulders broad and muscled. His sheer perfection not only made her teeth chatter with nerves but also made her very, very much aware of her lack of experience.

He would have slept with countless women. You could

tell that just from the way he was so comfortable in his own skin. He was a man who didn't mind women feasting their eyes on him, who probably enjoyed it.

She didn't imagine that *his* teeth were chattering with nerves at the thought of hopping into the sack with her.

She had to fight off the urge to leap off the bed and make a sprint for her clothes on the ground.

'No, of course I'm not,' she said, dry-mouthed. If he'd been short-tempered or impatient at her sudden shyness, she might have found sufficient anger to rally her mental forces and shrug off her attack of nerves. But his voice was low and curiously gentle and it reached something deep inside her that she hadn't revealed in the long months of their marriage.

Something vulnerable and hesitant. Gone was the hard veneer she had manufactured to protect herself.

'Then why the sudden reticence?' He traced the circle of her breast, running his finger in a spiralling motion until he was outlining her luscious pink nipple. He watched it stiffen and lowered his head to flick his tongue over the toughened nub.

Lucy took a dragging breath and stifled a groan.

'I…I just never thought that we would find ourselves in this situation,' she confessed, expecting the barriers that had existed between them to shoot back into place but, when he replied, his voice was pensive.

'Nor did I, not that I didn't want it.'

'I'm afraid,' she laughed nervously. 'The package without clothes might not be exactly what you'd expected.'

'What makes you say that?'

'I'm not the most voluptuous woman on the planet,' she said lightly. 'Too flat-chested. When I was at school, and all the other girls were developing breasts and hips, I just developed height and everything else stayed the same. I barely need to wear a bra. Men like women with big boobs. I know that.'

'You know that, do you?' He teased her throbbing nipple with his tongue and felt her melt under his touch.

'Yes. I do. Why else do you think those men's mags have always been so popular?'

'I can't say I've ever given it a passing thought. I've never read those things. What's the point of looking at a picture of a woman when you could be lying in bed with one?' Dio told her truthfully. He hadn't actually banked on doing a whole lot of talking in this arrangement. He had wanted the body she had deprived him of. And since when had sex involved long, soul-searching conversations?

Certainly they never had with him.

In fact, before Lucy, women had been pleasant interludes in a hectic, stressful work life. He had never become emotionally attached—had never encouraged any woman to think that he was, had never given any of that a passing thought. Meaningful conversations had been thin on the ground.

Against all odds, considering she should have been the last woman on earth he would want to have any sort of relationship with, Lucy had been the one woman to lodge underneath his skin. He had never delved deep into asking himself why that was. He had assumed that it was because she was also the one woman who hadn't made bedding him a priority.

Which—and why wouldn't this have been a natural conclusion?—was why he wanted her; why he had been unable to treat the marriage as the sham it had turned out to be and carry on playing the field. It had irritated the hell out of him that she had not given a damn one way or another whether he fooled around or not during their marriage and that, in turn, had been a source of slow-burning anger and dissatisfaction.

Now that she was within reach and he could see that burr under his skin finally being dislodged, he thought that conversation was the least he could do.

If she wanted to talk, then why not?

He couldn't, however, understand the self-denigration. Where had *that* come from? She had led a pampered, privileged life, the only child of wealthy parents. True, her father had been no better than a common criminal, but that didn't nullify all the advantages she had had.

She was, literally, the golden girl. Seeing her in action over the past year or more had really shown him just how easy she found those social graces; just how at home she was moving in the circles which he had been denied, thanks to her father.

He couldn't care less because he had made it to the top but he couldn't seriously credit that the self-confidence she had always oozed was anything but bone-deep.

He wondered where she was going with this and reluctantly was curious to find out.

He kissed the corner of her mouth and she squirmed and manoeuvred her body so that they were facing one another.

'Have you any idea how tough this is for me?' Dio asked her roughly and Lucy blushed.

'What?'

'Feeling your sexy little body pressed up against me. No, I take that back. I think you have a very good idea of how tough this is for me because you can feel my desire against your skin. That says it all.'

'You're…you're very big,' Lucy whispered, and Dio grinned.

'I'll take that as a compliment.'

'I mean…have you ever found that a problem?'

Dio frowned. 'What are you talking about? Why would I have found that a problem? A woman's body is engineered to accommodate a man of my size.'

'There's something I feel you ought to know,' she whispered, heart beating fast. 'I'm not as experienced as you probably think I am.'

'I never thought you were the sort of woman to sleep around.'

'I'm not. In fact, actually, I haven't slept around at all,' she admitted awkwardly and Dio edged back from her.

'Are you telling me that you've never made love to a man before?'

'It's not that big a deal,' she returned defiantly.

Dio remained silent for so long that she wondered whether he was trying to concoct an excuse to withdraw from the situation which he had been so keen to engineer.

'How come?'

'I don't feel comfortable having this conversation. I just thought that…that it was something you should know before…well…' She laughed nervously. 'When you're disappointed, then you'll understand why.'

Dio sat up.

His wife was a virgin. Incomprehensible. How had she managed to withstand the advances from men, looking the way that she did? *Why* had she? He raked his fingers through his hair then swung his legs over the side of the bed.

Lucy took advantage of the moment to yank the duvet over her.

This was a nightmare. What on earth had possessed her? Dio was a man of experience, a guy who had married her as something convenient that came as part of the package deal. He wasn't into virgins and he certainly wouldn't be into holding her hand while she lost her virginity.

She must have been mad.

Mortification swept over her in a hot wave.

Typically, he hadn't bothered to get dressed. While she had felt an urgent need to cover herself, he was as comfortable having this hideous conversation in the buff as he would have been in one of his hand-made Italian suits. He had moved to sit in the chair by the mahogany desk by the bay window.

'How come?' he repeated. 'And please don't tell me again that you don't feel comfortable having this conversation.'

'It just never happened for me.' Bright patches of colour delineated her cheekbones.

There was no way she intended pouring her heart out with some little-girl story of how unhappy her childhood had been; how she had witnessed her mother's miserable stoicism in the face of her father's selfishness and philandering. She wasn't going to drone on in a self-pitying manner about her lofty determination only to have sex with the man she truly loved which, frankly, would have been a confession too far—especially considering the man she had thought she loved had turned out to be just the kind of man she should never have got mixed up with in the first place.

'No testosterone-filled boys creeping through the windows of your prim and proper boarding school to have their wicked way with the innocent virgins?'

His lightly teasing tone was so unlike him that she felt herself begin to relax.

'None of that. There was always the house mistress on red-hot alert, waiting with a rolling pin for any daring intruders.'

She lowered her eyes but could still feel him staring

thoughtfully at her and she didn't like that. It made her feel exposed.

'And I suppose daddy was just as protective with his little girl?' His voice was hard-edged.

Lucy shrugged. Yes, he'd seen off potential boyfriends all right, not that there had been many of them, but only because he had been such a crashing snob that no one had fitted the bill.

In retrospect, taking into account his dire financial situation, none of them had had the necessary bank balances to provide a rescue package anyway. Dio had certainly fitted the bill and he had not been on her father's ridiculous social-climbing radar.

Watching her, Dio saw a shadow cross her face, gone as quickly as it had come, and he was struck by a sudden intense curiosity to find out what lay behind that shadow.

'I would completely understand if you'd rather call it a day right now.' She laughed a little unsteadily. 'It was a stupid idea, anyway. You can't just *have a honeymoon* and pretend that all the stuff that's happened between us never took place.'

'You'd be surprised,' Dio murmured.

He stood up and strolled over to the bed. She was a virgin. The thought rocked him, brought out a fierce possessiveness which he never knew he had. All those nervous little looks and shy glances now made sense. He'd never have guessed, but then he hadn't been looking, had he? He had accepted the cover version of her, the cool, elegant woman born into wealth and comfortable with it.

He hadn't thought to look any deeper. She had deceived him, as far as he was concerned, that that was the end of the story. He had closed the door and it had been a lot easier to keep it closed.

'I'm surprised,' he murmured, 'to think that you have

never made love to a man before…shocked, even…but not turned off. I have no idea where you got that notion from, my dearest wife.'

His voice was low and husky, his grey eyes glittering with intent.

'But can I ask you one thing?' He returned to the bed, depressing the mattress with his weight, and very slowly pulled down the duvet which she had dragged up to her neck in a vain attempt at modesty. 'Why choose the husband you're keen to divorce? Seems an unusual option.'

Lucy felt that if he listened hard enough he would be able to hear the steady, nervous thump of her heart.

Now, wasn't *that* a question?

'I fancy you.'

'And fancying me is enough to paper over the fact that you don't like me?'

Lucy felt that she could say the same about him, but men were different from women, weren't they? Women looked for love and men sought sex. That was why Dio had never been tempted in the past to hitch his wagon to any of the many women he had slept with. There had been no broken engagements or heart-rending tales of thwarted love. When they had been dating, during that brief window when she had actually believed that he was interested in her for herself, he had laughed when she had asked him whether he had ever been in love.

Dio might have used her, and certainly did not feel anything for her, not even affection—but he would still have no problem getting into bed with her because, as far as he was concerned, that was part of the marriage contract which he had been denied and, besides, he didn't think she was half bad-looking.

It was slowly dawning on her that she might hate him for stringing her along—might hate that core of coldness inside him that had allowed him to be the kind of man who could do that—but there was still something deep in the very heart of her that wasn't quite as immune to him as she would have liked to be.

She would rather have chewed her own arm off than ever admit that to him.

'Why not?' she asked.

Dio frowned. Their marriage had been little more than a business transaction and he wasn't sure why he now found her attitude unsettling.

'I was young when I married you, Dio. I'm only twenty-four now. Before you came along, I was totally wrapped up doing my maths degree and it didn't leave a whole lot of time for men.'

'You mean I was the first guy you really ever fancied...'

'You're a good-looking man.'

To his ears, that sounded like agreement, which made him wonder why she had retreated to her ivory tower the second the ring was on her finger.

'Then why wait until now?'

'Because maybe I've discovered that I'm more like you than I wanted to admit, even to myself.' She breathed with the panicked sensation of someone treading on thin ice.

So much safer when she had been able to keep her distance and set aside all the uncomfortable thoughts now besieging her.

'Now that we're going to be getting a divorce—'

'That's a matter that's still up for debate...'

'I know the conditions and I accept them,' Lucy told him bluntly. And then she added for good measure, for just that little bit of protection, 'And you're right—I can't see a way forward if I leave this marriage with nothing. I've never known what it was like to be broke.'

'Because Daddy protected you even when he was going under and all but waving a white flag…'

'Whatever.' She took a deep breath and did her utmost to disconnect from the contempt she felt for a man who had betrayed her mother and herself for pretty much all of his life. 'Now we're going to part company for ever in a couple of weeks' time, why deny the fact that I find you an attractive man? It makes sense to sleep with you, Dio. Like you said to me, it won't be a hardship.'

Pretty much everything she said got on Dio's nerves even though there was not a single thing he didn't agree with, not a single thing that shouldn't have eased his conscience.

'And what if I told you that you could have the money you want without the sex?' he heard himself ask.

Lucy looked at him, surprised.

'You mean that?'

'What if I told you that I did?' For a man who didn't deal in hypotheses, he discovered that he was a dab hand at dishing them out. He had seen nothing wrong with going after what he wanted, *what he was owed*, and likewise he had seen nothing wrong in using whatever tools were at his disposal to get there. After all, he owed nothing to a woman who had been his wife in name only for reasons that had suited her at the time. Why should he care about a woman who had turned out to be no better than a gold-digger?

Annoyingly, it now irked him to think that she was only going to hop into bed with him because he had dangled that money carrot in front of her. So she fancied him. Big deal. From the age of thirteen he had known what it was like to be fancied by the opposite sex. But did she fancy him enough to sleep with him if she didn't think that it made financial sense?

He loathed the direction his thoughts were taking but seemed unable to stop the flow now that it had begun.

'Are you? Because, if you're just speculating, then I don't want to be having this conversation. You're free to walk away cash in hand, Lucy, and you don't have to sleep with me as part of the deal.' He flung himself onto his back and stared up at the ceiling. If this was what it felt like to be the good guy, then he could say in all honesty that he'd felt better.

'Really?'

'Feel free to show your true colours, my beloved wife,' Dio said acidly, still staring up at the ceiling but conscious of her naked, sexy body next to his with every treacherous pore of his being.

'I meant what I said when I told you that I want to sleep with you—money doesn't have anything to do with it.'

Dio inclined his head to look at her. He couldn't credit the soar of triumph that greeted her unsteady admission.

'Is that the sound of you telling me that you're using me…?' He shifted so that he was lying on his side and lost himself in a shameless observation of her beautiful body, even though it was costing him not to touch that beautiful body. Yet.

'And what would you say if I told you that I was?'

'I'll live with it,' he murmured. 'Now, lie back. I don't think I've ever had so much talk before sex in my life before.'

Lucy's eyelids fluttered and she obeyed, sprawling with feline satisfaction, arching slightly so that her small breasts were pushed up.

With an unsteady groan, Dio planted a trail of kisses along her neck, then lower across her collarbone. He found heaven when he finally took one nipple into his mouth. It was sweet and succulent and he suckled on it, feeling it tighten in his mouth and hearing her moan as he swirled his tongue across the sensitive surface before drawing it long and deep into his mouth once again.

Gently he cupped her other breast, massaging it, and then rolling his fingers over her nipple, a warm-up for his mouth.

It was pure agony taking his time but he refused to let himself forget that she was a virgin. His virgin. His virgin bride. The thought of that fired him up on all fronts and appealed to the very essence of his masculinity.

He took his time as he straddled her, pushing her legs wide open to accommodate him, and gently stilling her instinct to snap them shut.

He was so aroused that he could scarcely breathe. If he began telling her what he wanted to do with her, he knew that he would find it impossible not to come.

This was a first for her and in some ways it was a first for him as well. The slight tremble which he knew she was trying hard to contain gentled his natural raw instincts.

Her other nipple was waiting for him and he took it gently into his mouth and teased and licked and sucked until she was writhing underneath him, arching up, her fingers curled into his hair so that she could push him down against her breast.

Her nipple was taut and glistening as he finally drew away. Hands flat on either side of her, he continued to trace a path along her rib cage, over her stomach, pausing to circle her belly button and then lower still…

Lucy's eyes flew open as his mouth moved to caress her inner thigh.

'Dio…'

He looked up and smiled. 'Dio…what…?'

'I…I…'

'Relax. Trust me. You're going to enjoy me kissing you

down there.' The scent of her filled his nostrils. 'And don't close your eyes,' he commanded. 'I want to know that you're watching me when I begin licking you...'

Lucy moaned as her imagination took wonderful flight. She was so wet for him, wanted him so much. She marvelled that she had spent so many months primly keeping her distance, little knowing that he had the power to melt every bone in her body until she was as pliant as a rag doll.

She watched as he settled between her legs, hands against the soft flesh of her inner thigh preventing her from closing her legs, making sure that she was open for him.

Delicately he slid his tongue between the soft folds, finding the throbbing bud of her roused clitoris with ease and tickling it.

The pleasure was exquisite.

She wanted to keep her eyes open so that she could see his dark head moving with purpose between her legs but she couldn't. She tilted her head up and arched her back, an instinctive response to what he was doing.

When he plunged his finger into her, whilst keeping up the insistent pressure of his tongue on her clitoris, Lucy could no longer hold herself back.

The waves of pleasure were too much, far too much. She didn't want this...she wanted him in her... But with a long, shuddering groan she gave in to the ripples that increased into an unstoppable riptide of her orgasm.

She came against his mouth, rising up, crying out, moving wildly as his tongue continued its ruthless plunder.

Her own lack of experience stared her in the face as she gradually came back down to earth.

'I'm sorry.' She turned away as he moved up to tilt her chin gently so that they were looking at one another.

'Only tell me you're sorry if you didn't enjoy it.'

'You know I did,' she whispered. 'But I...I should have

been able to hold off. I shouldn't have come…not like that…not when I want you in me…'

'I wanted to bring you to an orgasm, Lucy. This is just the foreplay…'

'It's pretty mind-blowing,' Lucy returned shakily.

'You're so beautiful and wet that I'll be able to slide into you, and I'll be gentle. I don't want to hurt you.'

Lucy found it remarkable that this powerful, ruthless man, accustomed to getting his own way at all costs, could be so tender between the sheets.

Yet, wasn't that the hallmark of the expert lover? That was what she told herself because it was bad enough that he was climbing out of the box into which she had securely placed him. She just didn't need yet another side of him to hit her in the face and overturn yet more preconceptions.

He said that she should trust him and that he didn't want to hurt her but some little voice inside cautioned her that it was within his power to deliver a great deal of hurt.

He already had! Surely the proof of the pudding was in the eating? He had married her so that he could socially elevate himself. Her father had been cruelly clear on that count. He had turned her into the cynical woman she was now! It would be wise to remember those things. She knew that the most important thing in the world was self-preservation.

She wanted a divorce, wanted to rid herself of a marriage that was a joke, and tellingly he hadn't argued against that. He wanted her but, once he got that out of his system, he would be more than ready to ditch her and move on with his life, find himself some woman he actually had feelings for and wanted to settled down and have children with.

That woman would never be her.

But, Lord, it was hard to marshal her thoughts when her whole system was in crazy free fall!

She felt him nudge against her and, just like that, a slow burn began. She wrapped her arms around him, loving the hardness of his body.

'Tell me what to do,' she whispered. Those were words that Dio had never heard from any woman and they were curiously thrilling.

'Do nothing but what feels good for you, and lose yourself, Lucy. It's what making love is all about.'

That sounded like a pretty scary concept to her but she nodded obediently and then stopped thinking altogether as he began to kiss her, slowly, taking his time.

She could taste herself as their tongues meshed. She reached down to hold him; he was massive, a hard shaft of steel that sent her senses spinning.

But she wasn't scared. She knew that he was going to be gentle.

And she wasn't filled with regret either. So what if this didn't make sense? So what if he had offered her the way out she had asked for without the blackmail? He had told her that she could walk away and that she wouldn't walk away penniless and she believed him.

But walking away would have opened the door to, if not regret, then a life of wondering what this husband of hers would have been like in bed, what it might have been like to have touched him.

No. She was doing the right thing.

He cupped her breast and played with it, idly stroking her roused nipple while he remained kissing her until she felt like she was drowning.

Then slowly, oh, so slowly, his hand smoothed over her stomach to cup the mound between her legs. Only then did he caress her down there, but so lightly that she had all the time in the world for her body to crank back into full gear, until she was throbbing and aching for more.

She wanted to push his hand in deeper, but instead she twisted so that she could taste him.

She'd never done anything like this before. She took him into her mouth and heard his sharp intake of breath as she began to lavish attention on the rigid shaft. She ran her tongue exploratively along it, sucked it, filling her mouth; cupped him between his legs and felt him expand under her attentions.

This time, he was the one spiralling out of control, but he pulled back before she could do what he had done to her and bring him to an orgasm with her mouth only.

Their bodies were slick with perspiration.

'Don't be nervous,' he whispered as he settled between her legs.

'I'm not nervous.' She felt the thickness of his erection and shivered with a mixture of wild excitement and apprehension.

'No?'

Lucy heard the amused disbelief in his voice and some of her apprehension drained away. 'Okay. Maybe a little.' Though he was someone whose very being posed a threat—who could be daunting and intimidating; whose presence she had contrived to avoid as much as possible from the very instant she had overheard that conversation on her wedding night—she trusted him wholly and completely with her body.

'You're so wet,' he murmured unsteadily, barely able to control his shaking hands as he blindly reached for protection in the little drawer by the bed, fumbling like an amateur. He nudged into her, feeling her tightness expand to hold him and fighting against a natural urge to ram himself in her right up to the hilt. 'You're going to enjoy everything I do...'

'I already have,' Lucy confessed honestly. She sensed

him taking his time and knew that it must be difficult for him. She didn't think that her husband was at all accustomed to taking his time with anything if he wanted it badly enough. It just wasn't in his nature. But he was taking his time now, gently probing deeper, but making sure to ease out before continuing to penetrate her in little stages.

'I like that.' He whispered things in her ear, sexy things he wanted to do with her, that had her blushing to her hairline. With each nudge, her nerves dissipated until she was desperate to feel all of him in her, desperate for the surge of his formidable strength inside her.

With the intuition of experience, Dio felt the change in her and offered a prayer of thanks because holding back was sheer torture.

He thrust deeper and more firmly inside. Rearing up on both hands, unable to hold back any more as he gazed down at her small, perfectly formed breasts, Dio moved with assurance, building up a rhythm until each thrust took her closer and closer over the edge.

Lucy had never thought that sex could feel so good. He'd been right. He had fitted into her as perfectly as a hand fitted into a glove; had fitted into her as though their bodies had been crafted to slot together. And now...

Her fingers dug into the small of his back as he continued to thrust, deeper and deeper, until she felt as though they were fusing into one. It was indescribable.

She hurtled over the edge in a wave of pure ecstasy. There was no room in her head for thought or analysis. Pure sensation took over. Every part of her body was on fire, soaring high, swooping thrillingly, until at last the crashing waves of pleasure became ripples and finally subsided, leaving her limp and utterly sated.

She clung shamelessly to him as he withdrew. Her mind

was still in a whirl. She couldn't think straight; her body was tingling and burning and as weak as a kitten.

'Enjoyed?' Dio didn't immediately feel his usual compulsion to vacate the bed the second love-making had come to an end but, then again, he told himself that it wasn't every day he made love to a virgin who also happened to be his lawfully wedded wife.

'It was lovely.'

'Lovely?' He gave a low growl of laughter and swept her damp hair away from her forehead. 'I prefer sensational…' And she had come to him without any pressure at all. Triumph made him heady with renewed desire.

'So, I guess that now we've…made love…' She shifted to disentangle herself from his embrace and he tightened his grip.

It had been easy not to think when she had been caught up in the wonder of making love but now reality began to drip in.

This was her first time and, yes, sensational was definitely the word to describe the experience. But for him this was all routine stuff. He had already given her a time limit of a fortnight, after which he anticipated getting bored, but perhaps she should establish a bit of cool and restraint herself. She'd acted like a limpet and the last thing she wanted was for him to get the idea that this strange situation was one that was out of her control.

Out of control were her physical responses. But that was where it ended.

She wasn't the foolish romantic she'd once been. She'd toughened up.

'Yes?'

The low timbre of his voice was a drag on her senses. 'Would you say we've put this thing between us to rest?' She chuckled lightly.

'What do *you* think?' Dio murmured. He'd been prepared to do the decent thing and let her escape with the money she wanted but things had changed since that bout of decency. He curved his hand possessively between her thighs and felt the slick moisture between her legs.

'You had your chance to fly away, my dearest wife, and you decided not to. Well, fair's fair, wouldn't you say? Ten days of happily wedded bliss and then we part company. Like I've said to you, Lucy, it won't be a hardship for either of us...'

CHAPTER SEVEN

LUCY GAZED DOWN as the plane dipped below the clouds and a vision of glittering blue water dazzled brightly up at her.

Originally, Dio said, he had thought about taking her on safari but had decided that a week and half making love in the sun was a far better idea.

'Why let some lions and elephants interrupt our journey of discovery?' he had drawled, catching her eye and holding it. 'Activity holidays are all well and fine but the only activity I want to do with you involves a bed and not much else…'

Heady stuff, she had thought with a strange pang.

The journey of discovery had not been the one she had contemplated in those giddy days before they had tied the knot. This journey of discovery would be a physical journey, and the only thing they would be discovering would be each other's bodies, but she had been utterly unable to resist.

After that first session of making love, they had made love again and again. Ingrained habit had propelled her out of his bed in the early hours of the morning but he had pulled her back to him and told her that he wanted to wake up next to her in the morning.

She had stayed and they had made love again in the morning, taking their time.

She found it almost impossible to keep her hands off him but she had uneasily given herself permission.

This was an arrangement of sorts, just as their marriage had been.

He could disconnect and so could she. It might not be in her nature but the option of walking away felt as impossible as climbing Mount Everest barefoot.

So the honeymoon that had never happened was arranged without delay. Given that he would then disappear off to the other side of the world to return to his high-octane life of big deals and even bigger money, time was of the essence for him, she guessed.

He had his catching up to do before she was dispatched without a backward glance.

They would be going to his place in the Caribbean. It was one of the few houses which Lucy had not had to personally see to as it hadn't been used since they had married. It was not on the map when it came to entertaining clients. Townhouses and apartments in city centres always received a lot more use.

'Excited?' Dio snapped shut his computer and devoted his attention to his wife, now that the plane was about to land.

He had worked for the duration of the journey even though he had felt her next to him, her floral scent filling his nostrils and driving him to the insanity of joining the Mile High Club.

The sex was going to be explosive. In fact, he couldn't wait to get her into bed again. If he had his way, they wouldn't make it as far as the private beach that surrounded his villa.

That said, he had no intention of losing perspective on this little episode, and keeping a firm hand on the situation was imperative. Raw physical instincts were all well and good provided they obeyed the order he had always imposed on himself. Work first.

'I've never been to the Caribbean before,' Lucy admitted.

'Never?' Dio was astounded.

'In fact, we didn't do a great deal of travelling at all.' Because, she could have added, that would have been a little too much family time for her father to deal with. For them all to deal with, come to it.

'You surprise me,' Dio murmured. 'I would have thought that you and your family would have been fully signed-up members of the playground of the rich club…'

Lucy shrugged and said lightly. 'Life is full of surprises.'

'As I'm discovering,' Dio breathed.

'So…' She dragged the conversation back to its starting point. 'When you asked me whether I was excited… I am. To see the island and to experience island life.' She had twisted to look at him and as their eyes met she felt a sliver of intense excitement race through her body.

'Is that all that's exciting you?'

Lucy reddened. Her mind shot back to the intimacy of their caresses, the way he had made her body come alive, and she licked her lips nervously. He was probably accustomed to women praising him to the skies but, since she wasn't one of his doting fans, she refused to do that.

'Tell me about your house,' she said a little breathlessly.

'What would you like to know?' Dio drawled, breaking off eye contact. 'It was a celebration purchase when I made my first million in profit. Since then, I've collected a few more properties along the way, as you know only too well.'

Because I look after them like an employee, Lucy thought. It was a timely reminder of their respective roles and the game they were playing and she was thankful for it.

'And you're right.' She dropped her voice to a husky whisper. 'The island and your house aren't the only things I'm looking forward to…'

Dio laughed appreciatively under his breath. This was more like it. The language of desire was a language he understood.

He was barely aware of disembarking. His head was caught up in all sorts of pleasant images of what he intended doing with her the very second they reached his villa. He had made sure that the place was aired, cleaned and supplied with sufficient food and drink to keep them going for the duration if they decided not to venture out. He had a person out there fully employed, even though their only job was to make sure an empty villa was looked after and unused gardens were kept under restraint.

All in all, he looked forward to smooth sailing and satisfying those physical needs he had foolishly underestimated over the past months.

His remarkably non-existent libido in the company of other women, including women who had done their utmost to distract him, should have sounded a warning bell that he still fancied the hell out of his opportunistic wife.

Life, as she had so succinctly pointed out, was certainly full of surprises—and, though never a man to enjoy the unexpected, he intended to enjoy this particular surprise to the full.

And then…divorce.

It made sense.

He squashed the surge of frustration that greeted that thought. Divorce made sense. He had married her, yes— because he had fancied her; because he had come round to thinking that a wife would be a handy accessory; and, of course, he had taken the company, and to take Robert

Bishop's daughter as well had seemed fitting retribution for the wrong that had been done to his father.

But life could hardly be called satisfying for either of them. He had not ended up marrying the woman he wanted to bed. He had ended up marrying a woman who had had her eye to the main chance.

He would be well rid of her.

Once he had cleared her from his system, which was what this little sojourn in the tropics would be about.

The same, he assumed, applied to her.

Having travelled the world, he was blasé about a lot. But now, as they were transported to his villa through small streets lined with the waving fronds of coconut trees, with glimpses of turquoise ocean glittering through the spaces, he had to admit that he had chosen a peach of an island on which to buy his villa.

It was tiny. They could cover it end to end in a handful of hours.

And Lucy...

She was as eye-catching as the scenery, as was her enthusiasm. He had never seen her as excited as this at any of the grand houses which had been at her disposal. She peppered him with questions, face flushed, eyes wide, like a kid in a toy shop.

How the hell had the Caribbean managed to pass her by? Wasn't that one of the bonuses of leading a pampered life? The long haul, over-the-top holidays?

How had *family holidays* passed her by? Unless Daddy had been too busy drinking and dipping his hands in the coffers to spare the time?

After the gluey, uncomfortable heat of summer in a city, it was balmy here, with a breeze blowing lazily through the swaying fronds of the coconut trees, only just disturbing the exotic colours of the flora.

In the twenty minutes it took for them to reach his villa, they passed three cars and many more people on foot. The economy was exclusively tourism-based, and every so often glimpses of millionaires' holiday mansions flashed past, along with several boutique hotels. They drove through the town centre, which was colourful and without a single department store in sight.

As soon as he had decided where they would be heading, he had got his long-suffering secretary to sort out a wardrobe. It would be waiting for them in the bedroom when they arrived.

New experience, new clothes. Simple as that.

'Wow, Dio. This is…spectacular.' Lucy had never seen anything like it. The villa sprawled in gardens that led down to a private cove. Surrounding the entire house was a broad, wooden-planked verandah with pale, sun-bleached railings and, from the overhanging eaves, baskets of brightly coloured flowers spilled out in a welter of extraordinarily diverse colours. Coconut trees fringed the gardens at the back. She could just about make them out. In front, it was picture-perfect, from the blazing blue of the sky, to the ocean stretching out ahead of them seeming so impossibly close to the lush, tropical gardens leading down to the cove.

She gaped.

'I wish I'd been to this house,' she said a little wistfully. 'It would have made a change from the city apartments and houses.'

'You grew up in London. I took you for an urban girl.'

'My mother's family came from Yorkshire,' Lucy said abruptly. 'She was an only child but she remained close to her cousin after her parents died.'

Standing next to her, staring out at the open ocean, Dio frowned at the sudden edgy tension in her voice.

Was she having second thoughts? he wondered. She had certainly gone back to her formal dress, the suitable attire of a rich man's wife. Slim, silk, loose-fitting trousers, a silk top, discreet items of gold jewellery, make-up.

It irked him.

He didn't want to have a hot ten-day fling with the wife he had known for the past few months. He wanted to spend it with the girl he had confronted in that shabby building in East London.

Was he being greedy?

'So your family holidays were in Yorkshire...'

'Mum and I used to go there often.'

'And stay in the family home?'

'That was no longer available to us. We stayed with Aunt Sarah.'

'I see...' He wondered where her slimy father had been when these trips had been taking place. 'I don't recall you disappearing off to Yorkshire after we married.'

'Well,' Lucy said lightly. 'It's not as though we were around one another twenty-four-seven. A lot of the time you were abroad and, when we *were* sharing the same space, well...'

'Which makes it all the more special that we will be sharing the same space here...but in quite a different way...'

Lucy didn't imagine that long conversations were going to play much of a part in this 'special way' they would be sharing space. Considering she had always placed such a high value on the quality of the relationship that defined a marriage, considering she had sold herself short and made a horrendous mistake, she still couldn't shake the simmering excitement at what lay ahead for the next ten days.

Since when had she ever been interested in sex for the sake of sex?

It baffled her but she was helpless to do anything about it.

'Shall we go in?' She changed the conversation, wondering whether she should play the sexy kitten he expected. 'I'm dying to see what the villa looks like and I feel rather hot and tired.'

'I'll lead the way.'

Inside was as exquisite as the outside. Wooden floors, soft muslin blowing gently in the breeze through open windows, with pale shutters keeping out the blast of the hot sun, bamboo furniture and a short staircase leading to spacious bedrooms and bathrooms on the landing above the ground floor.

He had had someone come in and make sure the place was ready for immediate occupation, although he had done away with having staff on the grounds while they were here. There was a little Jeep, if they wanted to go into the town or to explore other beaches, and enough food and wine to see them through.

It was paradise for the extremely wealthy and she should have taken it in her stride, for she was well accustomed to the palatial splendour of his other properties, but she was still knocked for six as they did a quick tour of the villa.

There was nothing she didn't adore about it, from the furnishings and the feeling of space and light to the magnificent views and the distant sound of the sea.

They bypassed four huge bedrooms and finally she was standing in the room they would be sharing.

The smiling man who had brought them from the airport had deposited her and Dio's scant luggage on the king-sized four-poster bed and it suddenly hit her...

This was their honeymoon. The honeymoon that had never been. She was with her husband and, even though their union had been a cruel joke, she couldn't stop the piercing thrill that filled her when she turned to look at his darkly sexy face.

The windows in the bedroom were sprawled open and she strolled to stare out, breathing in the wonderful balmy air and enjoying the way the breeze lifted her hair from her face.

'Are you going to survive for ten whole days without staff waiting at your beck and call?' she asked, eyeing him, and then nearly subsiding into a frantic, nervous coughing fit as he began to unbutton his shirt, exposing a sliver of hard, brown chest.

'It's a sacrifice I'm prepared to make because I don't want to have anyone around while we're both here.' He slanted just the sort of wicked smile at her that sent her senses shooting off into la la land. 'Come.'

Lucy walked slowly towards him and fell into his arms. His scent filled her nostrils with the punch of a powerful aphrodisiac. She almost lost it and groaned.

It didn't matter how many times her head was telling her that this was a pretend honeymoon; right here and right now, it felt *real*.

She wanted this man as though there had been no muddy water under the bridge.

Dio tilted her chin and kissed her, a long, lingering kiss; their tongues meshed and explored each other's mouths.

Lucy clung.

'You must be baking hot in this get-up,' he murmured.

Lucy thought that she was damned hot now and it had nothing to do with the temperature. In fact, the outfit was pretty cool, even though her body was on fire.

'I think we need to bath you…'

'We're going to shower…together?'

Dio laughed with open delight and led her to an amazing wet room in different shades of sand and tan marble. 'Now,' he said briskly. 'Clothes off.'

There was furniture in the bathroom. He proceeded to

sit on a clean, lined wicker sofa, legs indolently crossed, half-naked and all rippling muscle and sinew.

This felt very different from the safety of a darkened room.

'I can't.'

'Why not?'

'Stage fright.'

Dio threw his head back and laughed, a full-bodied laugh rich with genuine amusement.

'My virgin bride,' he murmured, his silver-grey eyes roaming appreciatively over her fully clad body. 'How about if I break the ice for you?' In one easy movement, he stood up and undressed, and Lucy watched, fascinated by his utter lack of self-consciousness.

'You make me feel so gauche,' she said nervously as he walked towards her, all powerful, all aroused and all one hundred percent alpha male.

'Touch me.'

Lucy took his heavy shaft between her slender fingers and a ripple of anticipation almost knocked her sideways. Her breathing quickened and her pupils dilated darkly as she played with him, enjoying the power she felt as he moved in her hand.

He controlled his surging response.

He was realising that he couldn't get within a metre of her without his body going crazy. Maybe it was just the natural after effect of all those months of keeping his distance. He should have handled this situation a hell of a lot sooner, but why go down that road? The fact was that they were here now and he intended to waste no time in exploring every single way he could discover his wife's sexy body.

The fact that she was so innocent was an unbelievable turn on.

'If you're self-conscious about doing a striptease for your husband…' he said unsteadily, holding her hand firm, because any more of what she was doing and he would respond in the only way he knew how '…then allow me to perform the task myself…'

Lucy succumbed. With every touch, she shed a little more of her inhibitions. This was what she had dreamed of when she had enthusiastically accepted his marriage proposal. Nothing had turned out quite the way she had expected, but she was determined to enjoy the physical pleasure he was offering her. Neither of them was looking for more than what was on the table.

They showered under jets of water that felt like warm rainfall. Halfway through, he switched off the jets and explored every inch of her with his hand and his mouth while she stood with the water drying on her, back pressed against the cool tiles, eyes closed, savouring every sweet lick. When he brought his mouth against the damp mound of her femininity, she parted her legs and let his tongue drive her to such dizzy heights that she could no longer contain the scorching orgasm that just seemed to go on and on and on as he kept his mouth firmly pressed against her, tasting her as she came.

The promised wardrobe was waiting for her when they finally made it out of the bathroom. Her body was singing.

'So, I had some clothes brought here for you.' Dio threw open the wardrobe doors and Lucy tentatively peered inside.

One by one she went through the things before turning to him where he lay sprawled on the bed in nothing more than a pair of unbuttoned jeans. His hair was still damp from the shower.

'But these aren't what I'm normally accustomed to wearing.'

Dio raised his eyebrows at her confused expression. 'I didn't think designer labels would be appropriate.'

Lucy tentatively stuck on a pair of small, faded denim shorts and the cropped top which could have come straight out of a department store.

These were the clothes she felt comfortable wearing and always had done. Even when she had been surrounded by money, growing up, designer labels had always made her feel like someone who had to be on show, the perfect doll which her father could parade in front of his chums to give an impression of the perfect family that had been far from the truth.

On the many trips she had made back with her mother to Yorkshire, she had ditched the silk and cashmere and enjoyed the freedom of wearing what she wanted. She had escaped the cloying confines of a life she didn't like and this was what it felt like now. A brief escape before she embarked on a whole different life. She was his wife and yet this felt like stolen time.

She told herself that her husband was a guy who knew what he wanted just as he knew what made women tick.

He wanted her and he was shrewd enough to work out that, yes, sophisticated London glamour would not set the scene for the sort of rapid-fire seduction he had in mind.

But there was still a treacherous part of her that was willing to overlook the cynicism behind his choices.

Not that he would have scoured department stores for the clothes himself. He would have told one of his minions what he wanted and that would have been the sum total of his contribution.

It was good that her head was still working, she thought.

'Nice,' he commented approvingly. 'I liked what I saw when I surprised you at that little club of yours and I like what I'm seeing now.'

'I'm not a puppet and you're not my puppet master.' And wasn't this just another form of him dressing her up for his own purposes?

'Is that what you've thought of me during our marriage? That I've tried to control you?' Dio's pale eyes flicked over her flushed face.

'Haven't you?'

'Most women would slice off their own right arm to be controlled by a man who gives them limitless spending money.'

'Dio, I don't want to argue with you about this. We're not here to…to argue…' They had never spoken as much during their marriage as they had done over the past couple of days and there had been times when Lucy had almost felt…*seduced* into telling him why she had pulled back from him the second the final guest had left on their wedding night. Whatever he thought of her and her father, she had wanted him to see her side of the story. She had had to remind herself that he had used her and that was the bottom line.

He had wanted her father's company, had been in a position to grab it for a knockdown price, and, even though he had certainly put right the wrongs her father had done financially, he had got *her* in exchange—the perfect hostess who could move seamlessly amongst his important clients, who actually *knew* some of them from times past.

She suspected that, had they consummated their marriage, he would have tired of her sexually within weeks and would have set his sights on other women.

Once, just once, she had done an Internet search on him to find out about the women in his past. There had been nothing aside from one photo taken from years and years ago of a curvy brunette clinging and laughing up at him as they emerged from a limo somewhere in New York. He had just signed a record-breaking deal.

That single photo had been enough to tell her the sort of women he was drawn to. It gave credence to her father's malicious taunt that Dio was little more than a jumped-up barrow boy who had made a few bucks and needed a suitable little woman to show off to the world that he'd come good.

She had overheard enough on her wedding night to know, for herself, that he was no saint when it came to manipulating an advantage. She had heard the low, cold intent in his voice when he had told her father that he had his company, and he could personally ruin him, but instead he would have his daughter, so he could count his blessings…

She hadn't needed to hear any more.

'No, we're not,' he told her softly. 'So why don't you come and sit here by me and show me why we're here…?'

'Do you ever think of anything but sex?' But she relaxed a little, pleased to close the door on that uneasy conversation between them.

'I'm finding it hard to in this particular situation,' Dio drawled, watching with satisfaction as she strolled towards the bed, looked for a moment as though she intended to take a flying leap on to the mattress but then gracefully settled next to him, though sitting up with her legs crossed.

'And, by the way, I don't like you referring to my project in East London as some *little club* of mine…' Lucy wondered where that had come from, considering she didn't want contentious subjects to get in the way of this arrangement of theirs.

'Following on from that, I've set things in motion to take care of all the finances there.'

'I know and I should have thanked you.' *But she'd had too much on her mind: him.* It made her cringe. 'Mark phoned just before we left and told me. He was very excited and he's waiting until I return so that we can break the news to the community together.'

'Cosy.' Dio frowned. Did she have a crush on the man, whatever she chose to tell him? 'You didn't mention that he called you.'

'I forgot,' Lucy told him honestly. 'Besides...' She lay down at a distance next to him until he pulled her against him and curved her so that they were facing one another, bodies pressed together.

'Besides what...?'

'Besides, there's no law to prevent me from talking to Mark, especially as we work together.'

'You can have however many cosy chats you want to have with him, and with anyone else for that matter, once you're no longer my wife.' Dio knew that he was overreacting. The man was a limp-wristed tree-hugger.

Except that was probably just the sort of guy Lucy would be attracted to. In an ideal world.

The thought got on his nerves and he found that he couldn't let it go.

'Who else comprises this little community of do-gooders?' he asked and Lucy tugged herself free of him and lay back to stare at the ceiling.

'Why do you have to be so condescending?'

'I'm not being condescending. I'm expressing curiosity.'

'I would have thought that you, of all people, would have sympathised with *do-gooders* who actually want to do something to help those who aren't so lucky in life.'

'Let's not get into my background, Lucy.'

'Why not?' She looked at him, glaring. 'You always feel free to get into mine.' Not that he knew the first thing about what her background had really been about!

'You're avoiding my question. Who else works with you? How long have you known them? Did you approach these people or did they approach you, via some kind of mutual acquaintance?' Dio heard the rampant possessiveness in his voice with distaste.

Lucy was bewildered at the harshness of his voice. What, really and truly, did he care one way or another?

'I approached them,' she admitted. 'I wanted to do more with my life than just be a hostess looking after your properties and mixing with other women who were married to similarly wealthy men. I wanted to use my brain and I saw an ad online so I applied. And there are a few of us who volunteer on a part-time basis. Mark is the key guy but there are... Well, do you want me to name them all?'

'Like I said, I'm curious. Humour me.'

With a sigh—because she couldn't recall him ever being that curious about what she got up to when he wasn't around and she saw his sudden burst of curiosity as just another controlling aspect of his personality—she listed the five other members of their team: three women, all much older than her, and two guys.

'And, when the cat's away, you socialise with these people?'

'Off and on.'

'Whilst concealing who you really are: no wedding ring in sight...'

'I wanted to be taken seriously, Dio. If they knew... Well, if they knew that I was married to you, that I lived in the house I live in, chances are they would just write me off as some rich young girl playing at helping out. Why are we having this conversation?'

Dio wasn't entirely sure himself. He just knew that nothing she said was filling him with satisfaction. 'So none of those guys know that you're married.'

'Not unless they're physic.'

'And what are they like?' he asked with studied casualness.

Lucy thought about Simon and Terence. 'Really, really nice,' she admitted. 'They're both full-time teachers and yet they still manage to find the time to come in whenever they can. They do at least three after-school classes a week. Simon teaches maths alongside me. Terry covers English and history. I can't wait to break the news about what…what you're going to do about injecting some cash into the organisation. They'll be over the moon.'

'Indeed…' Dio ran his hand along her smooth thigh and felt her quiver in immediate response. 'And, when the delighted celebrations kick off, I think it's only fitting that I attend as the wealthy benefactor…wouldn't you agree?'

Lucy shrugged and tried to imagine her husband mixing with the teachers and parents. She had a mental image of a lion being dumped into a litter of kittens.

But of course he would want to see where his money was going. He wasn't a complete idiot. He might have used that as a way of getting her where he wanted her, but he was shrewd enough not to write off the cash as money that could be blown.

And yet, did she want him invading this very private part of her life? The part of her life that she had mentally linked to her bid for freedom?

A sudden thought occurred to her and it was unsettling. Would he actually want to do much more than just throw money at the project? Would he want to oversee things? Would he still be a presence in her life, a dark, powerful, disturbing presence, even after they were divorced?

'I don't think we should talk about this,' she murmured, reaching down to hold him, feeling a surge of power at being able to distract him simply by touching him. 'I think there are far better things to do than talk right now...'

Dio swept aside the uneasy feeling that, for once, he wasn't entirely sure that he could agree...

CHAPTER EIGHT

OVER THE NEXT few days Lucy successfully managed to suppress those niggling, uncomfortable thoughts that occasionally bobbed to the surface.

What was going to happen once they left this paradise bubble they were in? Would he expect her to leave the house by the time he returned to London after his Hong Kong trip? Would he choose to keep working abroad until the coast was clear? Naturally, they would have to talk about the nitty-gritty business of the divorce. It wasn't something that would happen at the click of his imperious fingers but she had no intention of contesting whatever financial settlement he agreed to give her.

Strangely, the seductive lure of gaining her freedom no longer shone like a beacon at the end of a dark tunnel.

She assumed that that was because she was having the time of her life.

It amazed her, this ability to divorce her emotions from a physical side of her she'd never known she possessed.

It was as though something so powerful had awakened in her that it overrode all her common sense.

Sex. Everywhere and anywhere.

At night, they shared the same bed and, far from that feeling weird and abnormal, it felt absolutely brilliant. She enjoyed that period of being half-awake, half-asleep, curling into the warmth of his naked body and feeling it stir into instant response.

Everything else took a back seat. Misgivings. Unanswered questions. Simmering resentments. None of it mattered when they were making love. He'd been right. This so-called honeymoon, a time when they could both exorcise whatever it was they had to exorcise, was no hardship at all.

Today, a boat trip had been planned. Lucy looked up at the ceiling, missing the presence of Dio's body next to her because he had awakened at the crack of dawn and was in some other part of the villa working.

A little smile curved her mouth. Before he had left the bed, he had touched her, slipped his finger into her half-slumbering body and brought her to a climax while she had been in a glorious state of semi-sleep. It had been exquisite.

In a second, she would get up, have a shower, change into her bikini, with a wrap over her, and the flip flops which he had also managed to think about including in the wardrobe he had had imported from who knew where.

Right now, though, a nagging headache was sapping her of her energy and she remained in the bed with the overhead fan whirring efficiently over her and an early morning breeze wafting through the open windows.

Under the light sheet and blanket, her body felt hot and achy and she stirred, trying to find a more restful position.

She had no idea that she had fallen asleep until she heard his voice reaching her from a great height. At least, it felt like a great height, booming down into the room, making her feel a little faint.

'You're shouting,' she muttered, not opening her eyes and turning onto her side.

'I couldn't talk any lower if I tried.' Time had run away and it was after nine. Irritated by a pressing physical urge to take the steps two at a time, back up to the bedroom so that they could make love before setting off, Dio had controlled the impulse but now...

He frowned, standing at the side of the bed.

'It's nearly nine-thirty, Lucy...'

'Oh, no.' With a cry of dismay, she sat up and instantly fell back onto the pillow.

'What's wrong?'

'I...nothing; nothing's wrong. Just give me a couple of minutes. I'll get dressed and be down in, er, a little while.'

Everything was wrong, she thought faintly. Just three more days to go of living like this, far away from reality, and what did her body have to go and do? Fall ill!

She was in the grip of an oncoming cold at the very least. At worst, she was going to get the flu with all its nasty, debilitating side effects.

Right now, her head was banging, her limbs felt like lead, her mouth was dry and she knew that she was running a fever. She could feel it in the aching of her joints.

Disappointment speared her.

And if she was disappointed then she shuddered to think how furious Dio was going to be.

This was the honeymoon he had demanded and he had ended up with half of it and—worse—a wife who wasn't well. When she half-opened her eyes it was to find that he was still standing by the bed with a frown.

He reached down and pressed the back of his hand against her forehead.

'Nothing wrong? You're running a fever, Lucy!'

'I'm sorry.' Her reply was half-audible and addressed to his departing back.

She didn't blame him. He was so pissed off about the situation that he had headed back down to do something useful with himself. Like carry on working. Having had to cancel the boat and unravel the picnic hamper which had been delivered especially to the house the evening before.

Misery overwhelmed her. When she thought about leaving the island without having the opportunity to touch him again, she felt sick.

She didn't hear him re-enter the room until she felt his arm under her, propping her up into a sitting position.

He had a thermometer in one hand and a glass of water in the other.

'Why didn't you tell me that you weren't feeling well?'

'Because I was fine last night. I just…woke up this morning with a bit of a headache. I thought it would go away but I fell back asleep and…I'm sorry, Dio.'

Dio impatiently clicked his tongue and sat down on the bed next to her.

Sorry? Did she perceive him as that much of a monster that she would feel the need to apologise for not being well? He considered the way he had held the sword over her head, using the threat of sending her packing penniless as a means to an end. An end which he told himself he more than richly deserved.

He thought of the way he had announced, for all to hear, that renovation of the building that meant so much to them rested on her shoulders, doubly strengthening the case for her to get into bed with him.

He had seen taking her as a right which he had been denied. He had justified everything because she fancied him as much as he fancied her. Two consenting adults, all said and told, so what was the problem with that?

For him, he had had unfinished business and, typically, he had got exactly what he had wanted by using all the tools at his disposal—and gentle persuasion had not been one of them.

He was assailed by a rare attack of guilt and he flushed darkly as he stared down at her.

'I've phoned the island doctor.'

'Why?'

'Let me take your temperature.'

'There's no need! I have a cold, Dio. There's nothing anyone can do about that.'

'Open your mouth. Once I've taken your temperature, I've brought you some tablets.'

'What about the boat trip?' Lucy all but wailed. *What about the rest of our stolen honeymoon?* She was ashamed to find herself thinking about whether she could have some kind of IOU note, promising her three more days of snatched love-making once she was better. She found herself wishing his Hong Kong deal might not require his presence after all.

She found herself being *clingy…*

Appalled, she tried to recapture some of the hard-headed common sense that had been her constant companion for all the long months she had been married to him.

How had she suddenly become *clingy*? Was it because she was ill and far removed from her comfort zone? That line of reasoning at least made her feel a little less panicky.

'The boat trip is the least of your worries right now,' Dio told her drily. 'Now shut up and let me take your temperature.'

He did and then frowned. 'Okay, drink as much water as you can and take these tablets. You're running a high fever, Lucy. It's a bloody good job I called a doctor. He should be here any minute.'

'I told you, it's just a cold…'

'Mosquitoes can carry diseases in the tropics,' Dio said patiently. 'Not malaria, fortunately, but other diseases that can be almost as severe. Now, water—drink.'

Lucy did as she was told then she lay back, perspiring, eyes closed.

'You don't have to stay here, Dio. I know you probably have better things to do than tend to a sick wife.' She smiled but kept her eyes closed. Her words were composed and controlled but her thoughts were all over the place and she still couldn't seem to harness them. As fast as she got one under control, a swarm of others broke their leash.

'Name a few.'

'Work. It's the great love of your life.' She yawned and adjusted her position on the bed.

'It's had to be,' Dio murmured absently. 'When you have to drag yourself up by the boot straps, getting out of the quicksand becomes a full-time occupation.'

'And it's hard to let go,' Lucy said drowsily.

'And it's hard to let go,' Dio echoed, surprising himself by that sliver of confidential information he had passed on to her. 'Right. Don't move. The doctor's here.'

'Move? Where am I going to go? My legs feel like jelly.'

Dio grinned. His wife might have played the part she had been briefed to play perfectly over the past year or more, might have shown up at important events always wearing the right thing and always saying the right things and making the right noises. But he had learned what he had maybe suspected all along—that there was a feisty, stubborn streak to her lurking just below the surface, the same streak that had prompted her to break out of the box into which she had been sealed and look elsewhere for fulfilment.

He couldn't stand the thought of her having to look anywhere else beyond him, yet not only could he understand the urge that had prompted her but he reluctantly admired it.

Most women would never have thought to do anything but enjoy a life of stupendous luxury.

Most women would have slept with him.

He was finding it difficult not to think that there was far more to her than the opportunist working in cahoots with her father.

The doctor was a small, brisk man who bustled up to the bedroom, throwing little facts over his shoulder about germs, bugs and the innumerable things that could happen even on an island as small as theirs.

No snakes, he informed Dio crisply, shaking his head, but who said that mosquitoes couldn't wreak similar havoc?

There was a certain little mosquito...

Dio found himself bombarded with a litany of Latin names as he pushed open the bedroom door and followed the doctor into the room where Lucy was tossing restlessly on the bed, her cheeks bright red, her eyes glazed.

The doctor barely needed to examine her, although he was meticulous, taking his time and shaking his head before pronouncing his diagnosis.

Yet another long Latin term and Dio impatiently asked for clarification.

'Something similar to Dengue fever,' he pronounced, standing up and collecting his bag from the floor. 'Not as serious but nasty enough to wipe your wife out for as long as a week. No antibiotics needed. Just a lot of fluid and a lot of rest. The usual painkillers will do their best to fight the fever and the aching joints but, on the bright side, once it clears her system she'll be immune to catching this particular bug again.'

Lucy was appalled at the diagnosis. Drifting in and out of sleep, she woke as night was drawing in to find that Dio had brought his computer up to the bedroom and was working, keeping an eye on her. He hadn't signed up to any of this. She looked at him miserably. Even furious with her, which he would be, he still managed to draw her eye and hold it and, to his immense credit, he didn't show the annoyance on his face when he caught her staring at him.

'You're about to apologise again,' he drawled. 'Save it. You've caught something unpleasant from a mosquito bite and apologising isn't to make it go away. How are you feeling? You need to drink some more water and have something to eat.'

He stood up, stretched and strolled over to sit on the bed next to her. 'At least you're not so hot that I could cook a meal on you.'

'You're being very nice about this.'

'What would you have me do?'

'You don't have to be, you know. Nice. You don't have to be nice.'

'Are you giving me permission to be the sort of person you expect me to be?' There was an edge to his voice, although his expression was mild.

'This is supposed to be our overdue honeymoon.' Bitterness crept into her voice. 'A honeymoon is no place for getting sick.'

'And, on that note, I shall go and get you something to eat. My instructions are to keep you rested, fed and watered.'

He headed out to the kitchen where he banged his fist on the granite worktop.

How low was her opinion of him? Could it get any lower? This was supposed to have been an uncomplicated few days for him, during which he would get her out of his system the only way he knew how. And yet here he was now, frustrated by her unspoken insinuation that she might find him sexy, but that was as far as the complimentary thoughts went. On every other front, he was the sort of person she would have avoided at all costs.

She had apologised for being ill; had told him that getting ill had not been part of the honeymoon deal.

Was she afraid, deep down, that he would still see it as his right to have sex with her because he had effectively *paid* for it? He was repulsed by the idea.

Fifteen minutes later, he was on his way back up to the bedroom with a tray of food and her eyes opened wide when she took in the plate of bread and eggs and the long glass of fruit juice.

'You cooked this *yourself*?'

'You sound a lot better,' he drawled, setting the tray down on the bed next to her and dragging the chair closer to the bed. 'That sharp tongue of yours was missing in action while you were tossing and turning with a high fever. Headache gone? And yes, in answer to your question, I cooked it myself. I'd give myself a pat on the back if the meal was more complicated than bread and two scrambled eggs. Are you going to thank me profusely and tell me that producing some bread and eggs for you was not part of the honeymoon deal?'

Funnily enough, that had been on her mind, and she blushed and tucked into the food, losing her appetite after a couple of mouthfuls.

She had taken painkillers a couple of hours previously and she could feel all the aches and pains and soaring fever waiting to stage a comeback.

In the meantime…

'Maybe…maybe we should talk about the divorce,' she ventured hesitantly.

When he was touching her, she lost all power to reason or even to string a sentence together coherently. But he wasn't touching her now, *couldn't* touch her now, and she thought that it might be better to talk about the awkward elephant in the room rather than wait until they were back in London, when the barriers would be up again. Strangely, she didn't want to remember her final time with him as a cold war during which their communication was translated via lawyers and would revolve around money. At least if they sorted things out between themselves here in this setting, far removed from reality, they would part company with less bitterness between them.

Dio stiffened. He wondered whether she was making sure to pin him down to the details before the sex was over. Did she imagine that he would walk off into the sunset, having got what he wanted, without completing his half of the bargain? Maybe she thought that being ill had left her vulnerable to him having a rethink about the terms and conditions of their brief affair.

Despite the doubts he was beginning to have about all the assumptions he had made about her, Dio lost no time in allowing his imagination to jump to all the worst possible conclusions.

It was safe territory.

'Feel up to that, do you?'

'I'm not as groggy as I was earlier. I've got an hour or so before the painkillers really begin to wear off.'

'And why not use the time constructively?' He removed the plate of half-finished food, dumped it on the dressing table, returned to his chair by the bed and folded his arms. 'I get where you're coming from.'

Lucy breathed a sigh of relief. Should she try and explain that it would be better to get this awkward situation dealt with and put it behind them, like a boil that had to be lanced so that they could enjoy whatever brief time remained to them?

Or would that confession make her seem foolish? A bit of a loser? Over-sentimental?

And why should she feel sentimental anyway? Was it

some lingering after effect of having grown up to be the sort of girl who had believed in the sanctity of marriage? Had there been some part of her that still viewed divorce, whatever the circumstances, as a personal failure?

Even though this particular divorce couldn't happen fast enough…

It just showed how easily led the body was. It could veer off in a wildly different direction from the one the mind was telling it to stick to.

She wondered whether she could get over this stupid bug in double-quick time if she just stayed in bed for the next twenty-four hours. Then they could at least have the last bit of their stay here together…

It would be self-indulgent and probably a very bad idea but why not? And at least if they sorted the whole divorce thing out they wouldn't have that hanging over their heads like the Sword of Damocles…

She could pretend that it didn't exist, just like she had been pretending that this honeymoon wasn't what it really was.

'If you like, I can bring some paper and a pen and put my signature somewhere so that you don't think that I'm going to renege on the deal…'

'I…I just want to know when you'd want me out of the house.'

'This conversation is sordid.'

'Why?'

'You're sick and, even if you weren't, we haven't come here to talk about the details of our divorce. Call me mad but I've always thought that there's nothing more guaranteed to ruin a honeymoon atmosphere than talking about divorce.'

'I just thought…'

'The fact that you've been bitten by a mosquito and

ended up in bed ill won't affect your financial package.'
Dio knew that that was a brutal way of saying what he
wanted to say but he didn't take it back.

Nothing about what they were doing was real but, hell,
he was still enjoying it and the last thing he needed was
a reminder of just what had propelled her into his bed in
the first place.

'I wasn't thinking about the money side of things,' Lucy
said faintly.

Dio looked away, mouth drawn into a thin line. 'If
there's one thing life taught me,' he said with lazy cool-
ness, 'it's that when someone tells you that the last thing
on their mind is money it's invariably the one thing they're
thinking about.'

'If you don't want to discuss this then forget it. I just
thought that while we're both here it might be better to
talk face to face than for us to return to London and have
lawyers do it on our behalf. I mean, divorce is a really
personal thing.'

'And most divorces usually go down a slightly different route.' He raked his hands through is hair, outraged
that she would stubbornly persist with this even though it
must be obvious to her that it was an inappropriate topic
of conversation. More to the point, it was a conversation
he didn't want to be having.

'Most people usually end up facing one another across
a desk with lawyers at their sides after they've spent years
rowing and arguing. By the time most people hit the divorce courts, they'd tired and fed up of the arguments and
they're ready to bow down to the inevitable. That's a personal divorce, one where emotions have been exhausted.
This isn't one of those instances.'

'It doesn't make it any less personal.' She thought of her
parents and their lousy marriage. There hadn't been years

of shouting and arguing, just a quiet destructive under-current with insults and criticism delivered in a moderate tone of voice. Unless, of course, her father had been rolling drunk but even then he had never been a crashing around the house kind of drunk. Theirs had been a silent, failing marriage and was nothing like what she and Dio had.

'You're right. It's not.' She stared off into the distance quietly. 'But not all marriages that break down end up that way, after years of shouting and throwing plates. Some marriages just end up broken and useless with no shouting at all. In fact, shouting can be a good thing in a marriage. Anyway, I don't know why we're talking about this...' She shook her head and looked at him, resting back against the pillows. 'I shouldn't have brought this up in the first place.'

She did that.

Opened a conversation in which he had no desire to participate and then got him to a point where his curiosity had been stirred, only to back away, leaving him with a bit between his teeth.

Did she do that on purpose or was it just some fantastic ingrained talent she had managed to hone over the years?

He just knew that he now wanted to find out what she was thinking, why her expression had suddenly become so pensive. He wanted to know what the heck was going through her head.

'What are you going on about?' He placed one finger under her chin and directed her head so that she had no choice but to look at him. 'One minute you're telling me that you want to discuss our divorce so that you can make sure you get your financial settlement—'

'That's not what I said!'

'And the next minute you're generalising about broken marriages where there's no arguing. Are you talking about any marriage in particular?' It was a stab in the dark and he could see, immediately, that he had hit the jackpot. Her eyelids flickered and her mouth parted on some unspoken denial, her fingers compulsively twisting the thin sheet covering her.

'Some friend of yours, Lucy? Aunt? Cousin?' She didn't reply. 'Your parents?' he asked softly, for want of any other name to pull out of the hat, and she gave a terse nod.

Dio was astounded. He drew in a sharp breath and looked at her narrowly to see whether she was having him on but her eyes were wide and unblinking.

'I've never told anyone before.' Her head was beginning to throb. She closed her eyes, part of her knowing that she should just shut up because the fever and the aching limbs were a potent mix, making her want to say things she knew she shouldn't.

'And there's no need to now,' he murmured, instinctively knowing that once certain doors were opened they could never again be closed, and suspecting that this might just be one of those doors.

Did he want his assumptions overthrown?

Did he want to hear about her parents and their occasional well-bred tiffs? Frankly, when you thought about it, any wife in her right mind wouldn't have been able to stand Robert Bishop for longer than five minutes, because the man was a disaster area.

But the picture he had always had of the Bishop family had been one of the perfect nuclear unit blessed with beauty and wealth all round...

'You probably think that I had a great childhood,' she murmured drowsily. 'Actually, lots of people think that. Well, except for very close family friends and some relatives. Not many.' She slid her eyes over at him and smiled. 'In our circles,' she said with a trace of irony in her voice, 'it doesn't do to wash your dirty linen in public.'

'You should get some sleep, Lucy.'

'Maybe you're right. I guess I should.' She sighed and Dio grudgingly pinned his silver grey eyes to her flushed, rosy face.

'Tell me,' he commanded gruffly.

'Nothing much to tell,' she yawned. 'It's just that…we're going to be getting a divorce and I don't want you to go away thinking that I'm a prim and proper, pampered little princess who was born with a silver spoon in her mouth.'

'Which bit of that statement is not true?'

'You've always thought the worst of me, Dio.'

'God, Lucy. I didn't come over here so that we could end up having long, meaningful conversations about where we went wrong.'

'Because we should just have been out here pretending that we could spend time in one another's company and get through it with sex alone.'

'I thought we were managing just fine on that front.'

With every bone aching, Lucy still felt a crazy quiver at the wolfishness of his smile and the sudden flare of heat in his lean, handsome face.

A mosquito-borne virus made her feel less wobbly than his lazy, brooding eyes.

'I tried hard to forget that you only married me because you figured I would make a suitable wife.'

About to remove the tray of half eaten food on the bed, Dio paused and looked at her narrowly.

Fever made a person semi-delirious and he could tell that her fever was back. However, she sounded calm and controlled, even though her eyes were over-bright and there was a sheen on her face.

'A suitable wife…'

'Right background. You know.'

'Do I?' He sat back down. 'I'm not so sure that I do. Enlighten me.'

Lucy twisted the sheet between her fingers. 'On our wedding night,' she said so quietly that he had to lean forward to catch what she was saying, 'I overheard you talking to my father. Well, more of a heated conversation, to be honest. I heard you telling him that he had got what he deserved and that you were going to make sure that you took what was owed to you. The company...and everything that went with it...'

Dio cursed fluently under his breath as pieces of a jigsaw puzzle slotted into shape. She had heard snatches of conversation; she might have cast her own interpretation on what she had heard, but...

Was he going to provide a fuller explanation? No. He'd wanted revenge. It was something that had eaten away at him since he had been a young adult. He'd got it. But now he felt strangely disconcerted as he questioned that driving passion that had propelled him forward for years.

Stupid.

The man had deserved everything he had got, and not only because of what he had done to his father, but for what he had done to the people who had held shares in the company, the people he had been happy to throw to the wolves by embezzling their money.

So he'd been diverted by Lucy, had married her for not entirely honourable reasons, but her life had been pretty damn good.

Except...

'He told me that you married me because I was the sort of person who could give you social credence, you know. He said that...'

'That *what*...?'

'That you came from a deprived background and what

you wanted was someone who could promote your chances to go through doors you wouldn't normally be allowed to go through. That you might have made a lot of money but…but you didn't have…have…what it took to gain entry into certain circles.'

For a few seconds, Dio actually thought that he had misheard her, but as the meaning of her words sank in rage engulfed him.

If Robert Bishop hadn't been safely six foot under, he might have been tempted to send him there.

'And you believed him?'

'Why wouldn't I?' Lucy asked, confused. The dark anger on his face, which he was struggling to control, made her wish that she'd never broached the topic. 'Anyway, I'm beginning to feel really tired. Plus my headache's coming back and the fever…'

Fetching painkillers gave Dio a few minutes during which he suppressed a violent urge to punch something very hard.

Then, just like that, his thoughts veered off in a different direction and he was moderately calmer when he sat back down and watched her swallow the tablets and then lie back with her eyes closed.

'You're not going to fall asleep on me now, are you, Luce?'

Lucy didn't say anything. He hadn't called her that for a very long time, not since they had first started going out; not since they had been on one of those few early dates…

She was aching all over but still alert, fired up by the fact that she had confided in her husband for the first time in many long months. It felt liberating because what did she have to lose?

'When you said that your childhood wasn't what everyone assumed,' Dio said thoughtfully, 'what you really meant was that your father wasn't the man the world thought him to be.'

Her eyelids flickered and she sneaked a glance at him to see if she could figure out what was going through his head but Dio only ever revealed what he wanted other people to see. She knew that and right now he wasn't revealing anything at all about what he was thinking.

'Was his abuse…physical?' Just voicing those thoughts out loud was sickening but he had to know and he felt a wave of relief when she shook her head in denial.

'He was brutal to me and Mum but it was only ever verbal. My mother was such a gentle creature…'

'So you overheard our conversation and your father convinced you that the only reason I married you was because I wanted to use you to gain social entry to…God only knows where. It never occurred to you that I couldn't give a damn about gaining social entry to anywhere? No…' He pensively provided his own answer to that question before she could confirm his suspicions. 'It wouldn't because he appealed to all your insecurities…' And yet a lifetime of good schools where an ability to mask emotion and project the right image had stood her in good stead when it came to maintaining an air of cool.

'You mean you didn't…use me?'

'I mean…' Guilt seared through him as he trod carefully around his words. 'If you think I married you because you had the right background, or because I thought you could open doors for me, then you're very much mistaken.' He stood up, unwilling to go down any further roads, because those roads were riddled with landmines. 'And now, get some sleep, Lucy. Doctor's orders…'

CHAPTER NINE

LUCY WAS VAGUELY aware of time passing by over the next couple of days. The fever came and went in phases, as did the pain in her joints, making her feel as weak as a kitten.

However, when she did surface from the virus, her recovery was swift. She awoke to a room awash with pale light sifting through the closed shutters and the muslin drapes and the soft, overhead whirring of the fan.

A quick glance at the clock by the bed told her that it was a little after eight in the morning. Dio wasn't in the room.

She took time out to mull over certain flashbacks that floated to the surface.

He'd been around all the time. She could remember waking to find him sitting in the room with his laptop at a little table he had brought from some other part of the house. She could remember him bringing her food, which had been largely left uneaten, and making her drink lots of fluids. He had bathed her and helped her with whatever she had needed.

He hadn't signed up to look after her. She was pretty sure that he had never had to do anything like that in his life before and who knew? Maybe if they hadn't been stuck on an island where normal life had been temporarily suspended he would have called in people to pick up the slack so that he could remove himself from the thick of it, but they were on this island and he hadn't had a choice.

But he had risen to the occasion. Admirably.

She remembered something else, stuff they had talked about, and she was sure it wasn't her mind playing tricks on her. She had finally opened up about what her home life had really been like. Not given to personal confidences of that kind, it had been an enormous relief to let it all out. Growing up, not even her friends had known how much she had hated her father's mood swings, the sneering way he had of putting her down and putting her mother down, the atmosphere of tension that had been part and parcel of growing up. Her mother had maintained the front and a stiff upper lip and so, in the end, had she.

The last person she would ever have imagined talking to was Dio, yet she had, and she hadn't regretted opening up because he had proved to be a good listener.

And she'd been wrong. He hadn't used her. He'd said so. Her father had lied, had told her that Dio was a trumped up nobody who had married her for her social connections and her ability to fit in to the world he wanted to occupy—a world, her father had said, that was denied to him because he didn't come from the right background and didn't have the right accent.

She could have kicked herself for not really questioning that assumption. She should have known that Dio was so confident in himself, so much a born leader of the pack, that he wouldn't have cared less about any social pecking order.

But he'd hit the nail on the head when he had told her that her father had known how to manipulate her own insecurities.

She'd been wrong about Dio.

Whatever his reasons for buying her father's company,

and whatever bits and pieces of that awful conversation she had heard, she had misconstrued.

She'd had a lot of champagne and she had added up two and two and arrived at the wrong number and, because of that, they had had a sterile marriage in which all lines of communication had been lost. Indeed, she had ensured that those lines of communication had never been opened and he was far too proud a man to have initiated the sort of touchy-feely conversation he loathed.

He was proud, he was stubborn and…she was madly in love with him.

Her heart skipped a beat and she licked her lips, glad that she was alone in the room, because she would have felt horribly naked and vulnerable if he had been sitting in the chair, looking at her. Those amazing eyes of his saw everything.

She had fallen for him from the very first second she had laid eyes on him and she had papered over that reality with bitterness and resentment once they were married. She had told herself that he was just the sort of man she should have avoided at all costs; had told herself that the man for her was gentle, kind, thoughtful and considerate and that Dio was spectacularly none of those things.

How could he be when he had ruthlessly used her and married her for all the wrong reasons?

Now she felt as though the scales had been ripped from her eyes.

Not only had he proven just how considerate he could be, just how thoughtful and caring, but he was no longer locked up in that box that she had turned her back on.

The divorce, which she had insisted on, was a mocking reminder of how stubbornly she had held on to her misconceptions and panic swept over her in a rush.

She'd hankered after a bright, shiny new life, free from

someone who didn't give a damn about her, who had used her and who didn't care about whether she was happy or not.

But Dio...

She frowned.

Did he really care about her? She loved him. She knew that now. She had always loved him, which was why she had never been able to be in the same room as him without all her antennae being on red alert. She had fumed and raged but had still been so aware of him that her breathing became ragged whenever he was close to her.

But he had always been guarded around her and even here, making love, in the throes of passion, he had never—not once—let slip that he felt anything for her beyond lust.

She knew that she should take something from that, yet hope began to send out alarming little shoots.

Would he have been so solicitous if he didn't feel something for her?

Putting damp cloths on her forehead and cooking food, even if the food was usually the same fare of scrambled eggs and toast, counted for something...didn't it?

Alive to all sorts of possibilities, and feeling as right as rain, Lucy took herself off to have a shower. Then she slipped on the silk dressing gown hanging on the back of the door, making sure to leave her bra behind, and also making sure to wear some sexy lacy underwear, one of the few items of clothing she had brought with her.

She found him in the kitchen, some papers in one hand whilst with the other he stirred something in a frying pan. His back was to her and she took her time standing by the door, just looking at him.

She was seeing him in a whole new light. She had given herself permission to have feelings for this guy and now she appreciated the strength and beauty of his body, the muscular length of his legs, the powerful yet graceful arch of his back and the way his dark hair curled at the nape of his neck.

'I think you might be on the way to burning those eggs…'

Dio started and it took him a few seconds to register that Lucy was in the kitchen and looking so… So damned fresh-faced and sexy that it took his breath away.

She was in a dressing gown, loosely belted at the waist, flip flops on her feet, and she had draped her hair over to one side so that it fell in blonde, tumbled disarray over her shoulder.

No make-up. All one hundred per cent, natural woman.

His body clocked into a response that was fast, furious and immediate.

Just as it was, now, utterly inappropriate.

'What are you doing downstairs?' He salvaged the eggs. 'I was about to bring you your breakfast.'

Lucy strolled to the kitchen table and sat down. Here, as everywhere else in the villa, large windows allowed maximum light in and French doors led out to the lush back garden. It was already a warm, blue-skied day. The French doors had been flung open and a gentle, tropical breeze wafted in. She could smell the salty tang of the ocean air.

He was truly magnificent, she thought, in a pair of faded jeans and a white tee-shirt that did wondrous things for his physique.

'I woke up this morning feeling as right as rain.' She smiled and propped her chin in the palm of her hand. 'So I thought I'd come downstairs to have breakfast.'

'You should go back to bed,' Dio urged, abandoning the eggs to lean against the counter, arms folded.

'I know the doctor said that,' Lucy told him wryly, 'but I'm sure what he meant was that I could actually get out of it once I started feeling better…'

Dio gave her a long, considering look. She looked better. In fact, she looked in rude health, but was it an act? She had spent so much time apologising for her ill health getting in the way of why they were here that he wondered whether a sense of guilt hadn't propelled her into this act of sunshine and smiles.

'No need, Lucy.'

'No need for what?'

'Do you want breakfast? Of course you do. You need to eat.' Did he really want to get involved in a long, complex conversation? He'd already been knocked sideways by the last one.

And the last couple of days had thrown him off course even more. As marriages went, theirs had not been one that had involved any of the usual things he assumed were normally taken for granted. He had cooked meals—a first—and sat by her bedside, keenly aware that, whatever some doctor said, who knew whether this whirlwind virus would just miraculously disappear? He had mopped her brow and frankly put his own life on hold.

He'd barely managed to get any work done and his Hong Kong deal had been rearranged.

His life had always revolved around work so, like cooking meals, shoving it to the back burner had also been a first.

And she had told him things he had stupidly never suspected. How was it that it had never occurred to him that Robert Bishop, the man who had cold-bloodedly swindled his father, not to mention the people who had entrusted their pensions to him, might not have been the upstanding, loving family man he had assumed? If it walks like a duck, quacks like a duck and looks like a duck, then it was a duck. Robert Bishop had been a thoroughly unpleasant criminal, *ergo* he had been a thoroughly unpleasant man, full stop.

And Lucy…

So she might have got hold of the wrong end of the stick in one small detail, but if she only knew the half of it…

Yet his body was still on fire at the sight of her sitting there on the kitchen chair, looking as young and as fresh-faced as a teenager. The sun had brought out a scattering of freckles.

'Maybe we could have something aside from scrambled eggs…'

Dio forced a smile, while his mind continued to roam through all sorts of unexplored avenues. 'Are you telling me that you find fault with the chef?'

'Not at all. In fact, the patient couldn't be more grateful to the chef, although it has to be said that the chef's repertoire is very limited.'

'As you know only too well, I haven't made it my life's career to get to grips with a kitchen.'

'I'll help. Maybe we could cook something together. It'll do me good to be up and moving.'

Dio shrugged and Lucy stifled a sudden feeling of hurt but she stood up anyway and headed to the fridge, where she pulled out some ham, then she rifled through the cupboards and managed to locate enough ingredients for French toast.

'You sit, Dio. You've spent the past few days cooking for me; the least I could do is repay the favour.'

'Like you said, scrambled eggs don't exactly qualify as cooking.'

'I'll bet it's more than you've ever done.' She glanced over her shoulder and felt her heart constrict.

Had she disturbed whatever reading he had been doing? He couldn't have got much done while she had been ill and she knew that his Hong Kong trip had been postponed. He'd had to play the good Samaritan and she could hardly blame him if his mood wasn't all that great.

'You can prepare breakfast if you really want to, Lucy, but that's it. I'll get Enid in to take over the cooking arrangements for the remainder of the time that we're here. The last thing I need is for you to have a relapse.' This was what he had to do. Dio hadn't banked on long confessionals, and he hadn't banked on discovering what had really happened on their wedding night, what had led to her physical withdrawal from him. He got the uneasy feeling that something in her had changed towards him.

She had looked at him…differently after that little chat.

Maybe it was simply the fact that she'd been ill, running a high fever. Maybe that look in her eyes had been virus induced. Had she revised her rock bottom opinion of him because he had truthfully told her that he hadn't married her for her connections?

Did he want her to have revised opinions?

He recalled the way she had looked at him when they had been going out on their handful of dates. He had been charmed at the unexpected find of Robert Bishop's daughter.

Who'd have guessed…?

She had looked at him as though she were a starving waif and he were her specially prepared banquet.

He'd liked that too. What man wouldn't? He hadn't known just when it had occurred to him that she might play a part in the revenge plan that had been his companion for more years than he could remember. He didn't know whether that had been a conscious decision or not.

He just knew that emotions had never played a part in it for him. Emotions had never played a part for him in anything. He had absorbed one very simple reality growing up and that was that emotions were a train wreck waiting to happen.

Emotions had propelled his volatile, brilliant father into trusting a guy he considered a friend. It hadn't occurred to him to get signatures on a dotted line, to get lawyers involved when it came to his invention. He'd paid dearly for that oversight and they had all paid as well. Not just his father, but his mother, who had had to live with a bitter and disappointed husband and a son who had not been spared the details of a wrecked life.

No, Dio had learned from early on that emotions were not to be trusted. Logic, common sense, the intellect—those were the things to be trusted. They never let you down.

And money… With money came power and with power came freedom.

The only emotion Dio had allowed into his life was a healthy thirst for revenge and he had made enough money to ensure that, whatever form that revenge took, he would be able to cover it. His money had bought him the freedom to do just as he pleased when it came to ensuring that Robert Bishop paid for past sins.

He'd married Lucy because he'd fancied the hell out of her, because at thirty-two he'd been ready for marriage and the undeniable advantages it brought and because she'd been Robert Bishop's daughter—and how better to twist the knife than to parade her in front of her father as his wife?

But it would appear that nothing had been quite as it seemed.

He hadn't married a daddy's girl; he'd married someone who had been desperate to escape. For her the escape hadn't gone quite according to plan but, because she had been wrong about one small detail, did she now imagine that he was, in fact, the knight in shining armour she had originally placed all her trust in?

Because Dio didn't want that. Not at all…

She'd lost her virginity to him.

In the cold light of day, he was all too aware of the significance of that and it scared the hell out of him.

'I'm not going to relapse.' Lucy laughed uncertainly as she began focusing on food preparation.

'I've already had to postpone my Hong Kong deal…as you no doubt know.'

'Yes.' Tears stung the back of her eyes because he wasn't being cruel, he was just being honest. 'And I believe I apologised to you about being the cause of that. Several times over. But I'm happy to tell you again that I'm sorry I screwed up all your precious plans.' Lucy said all of this in a rush without looking at him.

Dio raked his fingers through his hair and glared. He could tell from the slump of her shoulders that she was close to crying.

'I'm not asking for your apologies. I'm making sure that you don't overdo it and end back up in bed.'

'I know.' She clattered and began dipping the bread in the egg and frying. She could detect the grim impatience in his voice and it dawned on her that the honeymoon was well and truly over. 'Don't worry. I'll take extra care to make sure I'm bouncy and in top form and, if I do feel a little tired, I'll make sure I don't bore you by saying anything. These are done, although suddenly I'm not very hungry.' She was mortified at the foolish hope that had propelled her down the stairs in a dressing gown and not much else. Still not looking in his direction, she spun round with the frying pan in her hand to find that he had somehow, stealthily, managed to creep up on her.

He should have been at the kitchen table. Instead, he was an inch away from her and now he was gently removing the frying pan from her vice-like grip.

'I've never been a fan of crying women,' he murmured.

'And I've never been a fan of crying.' Lucy's voice wobbled. 'So you're in luck.'

Dio sifted his fingers through her hair and knew that he

really shouldn't. She wanted out of the marriage and she would be a lot better off out. He was no knight in shining armour. He was, in fact, a lot worse than she had taken him to be.

What she needed—and he could see that, now that she had revealed her true colours—was a guy who could give her all those things she was looking for. Friendship, security of an emotional kind, a shoulder on which she could lean...

She needed one of those do-gooder, social worker types she had hitched up with at her out-of-hours teaching establishment. Her turbulent background had conditioned her for a guy whose ideal night in would be cooking together before settling down in front of the telly with just the dog between them. He didn't fit the bill, didn't want to and never would.

In which case, the kindest thing he could do would be to distance himself from her, starting from right now...

But when her hot little body was pressing up against him the way it was now, it was difficult to keep a handle on noble thoughts.

And she wasn't making things easy, either. She had pressed her face into his shoulder and he felt her body quiver as he stroked her hair with an unsteady hand.

Dio made a half-hearted attempt to create a little space between them and he wondered whether he was imagining that she held on to him just a little bit tighter.

'So you think I was being cruel when I reminded you of my deal in Hong Kong and the fact that I've had to reschedule it? You think I'm somehow blaming you?'

'I don't.' Her voice was muffled as she spoke into his shoulder. 'The only thing you really care about is work, isn't it?'

'How well you know me...'

A fortnight ago, had he said that, she would have shrugged and told herself acidly that that just about summed up why she didn't like the guy and never would—forget about what he had done to her, forget about how he had used her.

Now that she knew that he hadn't used her, she was seeing him in a different light—seeing his humour, the depth of his intellect and the way he had looked after her when she had been ill.

There was a warmth there she'd never known existed. He might tell her that the only thing he cared about was work, but there was so much more to him than that, whether he accepted it or not.

She had sensed that all along, hadn't she? Which was why her heart had remained his even though her head had tried to persuade her otherwise.

If she let him, he would turn her away. She sensed that. Maybe she should fight for him. Would it be possible for her to seduce him into a place where he might find her presence indispensable to him?

They had slept together! Why shouldn't they carry on sleeping together? Why shouldn't this marriage become the real thing? She couldn't remember why she had been so passionate about getting a divorce.

They could stay as man and wife, but their lives would change in so many ways! She could carry on doing her maths classes at the centre…at the new and improved centre! Of course, she would have to come clean about who she was, but why should that be a problem?

She wriggled against him and the silky dressing gown dislodged just a tiny bit.

She made no attempt to belt it back into shape.

Dio groaned softly as her soft breasts squashed against his chest. When he looked down, he could see the shadow of her cleavage, the gentle swell of her naked breasts, nipples tantalisingly half-concealed by the dressing gown.

All he had to do was shift his hand, dip it under the silky fabric and he would be able to cup her breast, feel its weight in the palm of his hand…

'I want you to touch me,' she said huskily, shocking herself with her forwardness. She guided his hand under the dressing gown and felt his big body shudder. Heady satisfaction overwhelmed her. She was damp between her legs and she shifted, rubbing her thighs together and, more than anything else, wanting to feel his hand down there…

Even here, she'd shied away from making love in broad daylight, preferring to have the curtains drawn, which he had found very amusing.

Now, though…

She clasped his hand and stood back. 'This isn't the place.'

Dio knew that he could step in now and make clear his intention to put this honeymoon behind them…

Unfortunately, his body had other plans.

Maybe, if she'd said 'bedroom', he would have come to his senses. Maybe if she'd been predictable in her wants…

But she inclined her head to the kitchen window, tugged his hand and smiled shyly.

Dio followed the direction of her gaze and felt a charge of supersonic adrenaline flood through him.

'You like the curtains closed,' he said gruffly.

'Maybe I'm ready to branch out.'

'Luce…'

Lucy took a deep breath, untied the barely tied belt on the dressing gown and then shimmied out of it, leaving it to pool at her feet so that she was stark naked aside from her underwear.

She watched the flare of his nostrils, the way his eyes darkened, and noted the sharp intake of breath.

She'd never wanted him more desperately than she wanted him now. She'd spent months making sure to keep her heart under lock and key and, now that it had been released from captivity, she couldn't bear the thought of them walking away from one another.

She'd misjudged him and that put everything in a whole new light.

'I want to make love on the beach,' she said, brazening out her absolute terror of her body being exposed in the full, unforgiving glare of daylight. She was long and slim but her breasts had always been smaller than she'd wanted, her figure not voluptuous enough. She wondered whether he was making comparisons with all those other women he had slept with, now that he was actually seeing her like this, then she squashed that thought which did nothing for her self-esteem.

This is still honeymoon time… Dio thought, waving aside the introspection that had led him to resolve that he had to get out of a situation that had developed like a swift-moving hurricane. That the man he was definitely wasn't the one she thought she'd unearthed; that he had done what he had set out to do—he had acquired the company that should have rightly belonged to his father, had acquired Robert Bishop's daughter. Job done.

Now she was standing there, bare-breasted, her rosy-pink nipples pointing at him, her skin paler where it had been covered by her bikini top…her long slender legs going on for ever.

How was any red-blooded man to resist?

He walked slowly towards her and decided, in a sudden brainwave, that it would be downright callous to turn her away. She had a lot of issues. He'd never realised that before, but he knew now. She'd grown into adulthood with deep feelings of insecurity, unable to enjoy the looks she had been given.

If he rejected her now, all those insecurities would return tenfold.

Would he be happy being responsible for that? No. So...

In one easy movement, he pulled his tee-shirt over his head and smiled wolfishly as her eyes dipped compulsively to his washboard-hard stomach.

He never failed to get a kick at the way she looked at him, as if she was compelled to and yet, at the same time, was mortified to be caught doing it.

She was looking at him like that right now.

He linked his fingers through hers and gently brushed her hair away from her face.

'If you're sure...' Dio drawled.

'I am. Are you?'

At this moment in time, with an erection bulging against his trousers, Dio had never been more sure of anything in his life.

Outside the sun was already hot. The villa was set in its own very private grounds and the only sound they could hear was the sound of the sea lapping lazily on the shoreline.

A couple of days in bed had dimmed Lucy's recollection of just how stunning the tiny cove was: powder-white sand, sea so clear that you could see every polished stone you were treading on as you waded out, a distant horizon that was blue meeting blue.

The breeze felt wonderful on her naked breasts. She turned to him, laughing, holding her hand to her hair to keep it out of her face and, for just a few seconds, she was literally dazzled by his masculine beauty.

'Are you going to make me beg you to remove the rest

of your underwear?' Dio's hand rested on the button of his jeans and he slowly pulled down the zip.

Lucy was riveted at the sight of him removing his jeans. The sun glinted over his bronzed body, exposing the flex of his muscles as he tossed the jeans behind him onto a rock, followed by his boxers.

Then, eyes not wavering for a second from her flushed, excited face, he touched himself and grinned.

'Okay. Your turn.'

Lucy slid out of her underwear, attempted nonchalantly to toss it to join his boxers, and then watched in dismay as a sudden gust of wind blew it into the sea.

Dio laughed and shielded his eyes from the glare. 'So...' He pulled her into him and she yielded without hesitation. His hard erection pressed against her belly made her quiver. 'Why the sudden sense of daring, my darling wife?' He nibbled her ear and she sighed softly and squirmed against him. 'What's happened to the shy little creature who wouldn't contemplate sex unless the curtains were tightly pulled?'

'Maybe you've kick-started a sense of adventure in me,' Lucy murmured and an unpleasant thought flashed through Dio's head like a depth charge...

Another man would be the recipient of her new found, so-called sense of adventure. He almost longed for the hesitant timidity that had made him keep those curtains tightly drawn.

His unexpected possessiveness was disturbing but thankfully short lived as he cupped her naked breasts in his big hands, teasing and thumbing the ripe swell of her nipples.

'Sand can be a nuisance,' he murmured, flicking his tongue against her ear, knowing just where she liked to be teased. 'So keep standing...'

He worked his way down until he was kneeling in front of her.

Lucy knew what he was going to do and her whole body thrummed with heady anticipation.

She loved it when he licked her down there. It had felt outrageously intimate the first time he had done it, and he had had to gently but firmly prise her legs apart so that he could settle between them, but having him tease her clitoris with his tongue was a mind-blowing experience.

She curled her fingers into his dark hair, arched back and parted her legs.

The sand was warm between her toes. She wanted to look down at his dark head moving between her legs but, on a soft moan, she closed her eyes and tilted her face up to the sun, losing herself in the wondrous sensation of the slow, inexorable build to her climax.

She cried out as she came against his mouth. Before she had time to return to planet Earth, he had hoisted her up, lifting her as easily as if she weighed nothing, and she wrapped her legs around him, feeling the thrust as he came in her.

No protection. And he was normally so careful. The realisation vanished as he pulsed inside her, driving her higher and higher until she was clinging, shuddering and coming in waves of intense pleasure, knowing that he was doing the same, feeling his release with an explosion of pure ecstasy.

Afterwards, they swam. Lucy would love to have been able to bottle the moment and treasure it for ever.

Failing that, as they returned to the beach towels he had brought down with him and lay on the sand, she wondered how she could engineer the conversation towards this very real thing that existed now between them.

Surely he must realise that things had changed?

They hadn't spoken about the divorce for days. She wondered whether her being ill had been a blessing in disguise. It had certainly been an eye opener for her. Had it been the same for him? So, he wasn't the kind of guy who was into long conversations about emotions, but that didn't mean that the emotions weren't there, did it?

She reached out and linked her fingers through his.

They were both gazing up, squinting at the bright blue sky through the fronds of the palm trees.

'So...' She allowed that one syllable to drag out tantalisingly.

'I should apologise.' Dio was down from his high and acknowledging that he had failed to take protection. He had known exactly what would happen out here, on the beach, and yet he had still failed to carry protection with him.

'Sorry?'

Furious with himself for overlooking something so vital, he stood up abruptly and strode towards the discarded clothing, slipping on his sandy boxers and jeans, which he brushed down.

Lucy immediately followed suit.

'I risked an unwanted pregnancy,' he said bluntly. 'I didn't use protection.'

Hearing him say those words, hearing the tone of his voice, was like a slap in the face and she almost stumbled back.

'I'm sorry if I sound harsh.' He raked his fingers through his hair and cursed himself for not having had the will power to resist her when he'd known he should have. Instead, he had fabricated a bunch of non-excuses for enjoying himself one last time. Maybe if he hadn't discovered just how innocent she really was, maybe if she had been the hard-nosed opportunist he had always assumed her to be, he might have felt better about himself.

No, he *would* have felt better about himself. He would have taken what he had seen as his right and he would have walked away. As things stood, by exposing her own vulnerability, by revealing a softness he had never, ever expected, she had likewise exposed him for what he was: cold, ruthless, a man who had played the long game to get what he wanted.

They were poles apart. He was a shark to her minnow and he wondered whether he would have been quite so keen to secure her in his bid for revenge had he known. Probably not.

'I'm sure,' he began, heading back towards the villa, 'that, like me, the last thing you would want is to discover that you're pregnant. Especially…' he turned to face her fully '…when you consider that we're going to be getting a divorce.'

'It's okay,' she whispered. 'We were caught up in the passion of the moment. I'm sure it will be fine.'

Pain assaulted her on all fronts. She was giddy with it. How could he look at her like that, as though they hadn't just shared the most amazing experience ever? And it wasn't just about making love. It was so much more that they had shared. At least, that was how it was for her…

How could he be so…*callous*?

Desperation ploughed into her with the force of a sledgehammer and she hated it.

'How can you be like this, Dio?' The pleading whisper made her wince.

'Be like what?'

'We've just…made love…'

Dio could feel the unexplained horror of something breaking inside him and, far, far worse, the knowledge that it was inevitable that he was now walking down this road. 'It's what we came here to do. To make love. To have our honeymoon…'

'I know that!' Stripped of words, she stared at him, heart pounding so hard that it hurt.

'Then…what?' This was where revenge had finally taken him, to this impasse, to the only place he had ever reached before where he was powerless. He had thought his heart to have been wrapped in ice, immune to pain. He was discovering that it wasn't.

'What we had… Do you feel *nothing*?' Lucy longed to be cool, to just let it go, because she knew that she was trying to fight a battle that she was destined to lose, but the black void opening up at her feet seemed to galvanise her into a terrifying urge to cling.

Dio banked down the wave of unfamiliar emotion surging through him.

Her hands were balled into fists, her body rigid with accusation, and he recognised the searing hurt that lay behind that accusation; knew that from that angry hurt would eventually come the return of the cold dislike she had nurtured towards him.

And he knew that it was deserved. Hell, he knew that with as much certainty as he knew that night followed day.

'I feel we've had our honeymoon.' The words felt like shards of glass in his mouth but, deprived of any choice, he ploughed on, every muscle in his body braced for the job at hand—because that was what it was. 'And now we have to have our divorce…'

CHAPTER TEN

Lucy stood and looked around the brand-new apartment which would now be her new home.

She knew that she should be feeling as pleased as punch. When she had finally garnered her courage all those weeks ago to bring up the matter of a divorce with Dio, this was exactly the sort of outcome she had had in mind.

No. This was a whole lot better than the outcome she had had in mind.

She had spent two weeks at the London house, during which time he had made sure to be abroad. He had fulfilled every single one of his promises, even though she knew, from what her lawyer had told her, that there had been no need because she had indeed signed up to a watertight pre-nup without even having realised it, idiot that she had been.

He had been generous beyond words. He had immediately arranged the purchase of the breath-taking apartment in which she now stood. It was in a prime location and there wasn't a stick of furniture she didn't like. Just as he had glimpsed the part of her that was the girl with the pony tail, the girl she really was, he had made sure that some member of staff chose items of furniture that were homely, comfortable and cosy.

She wasn't amazed that he had managed to acquire the perfect apartment so effortlessly.

Having spent a year and a half married to him, she knew that the one single thing money got when it came to purchase power was speed. What Dio wanted, Dio got. And what Dio had wanted had been this spectacular apartment.

What he had wanted was her out of his life, having got the honeymoon he had demanded when she had asked him for a divorce.

She sat on one of the boxes cluttering the living room and stared miserably out of the window. Her view, from here, was of the sky, a grey, leaden sky that seemed to reflect her mood.

She should be counting her blessings.

She was financially sorted for the rest of her life. The run-down building which had been her lifeline was in the process of a startling renovation which would make it the most desirable place in that part of London to which deprived children could go to further their education after school hours. She had no doubt that dozens would find their springboard to a better life. She had signed up to a teacher training course, something she had always wanted to do until marriage and Dio had swept her off her feet, and she would be able to do it without worrying about money. There were so many things for which she should be grateful.

And yet…

With a little sigh of pure misery, she strolled over to the window and stared down at the street below.

For a little window in time, out there in paradise, she had actually dared to hope. She had opened up to him, thankfully only stopping short of telling him how she felt about him—not that she was in any doubt that he didn't know—and she had dared to hope that destiny might veer off in a different direction.

She'd been such an idiot.

He might not have used her in the way she had been led to assume, but he hadn't cared about her either. Why had he married her? Probably because he had fancied her and had decided that she could be an asset to him. It had been a lazy decision and he hadn't banked on having a sexless marriage. Once sex had been put on the menu, he had been happy to grant her the divorce she wanted.

She knew that at least he had parted company caring enough about her to ensure her physical wellbeing, except what was the good of that when her emotional wellbeing was in pieces?

He had been ultra-courteous to her before they had parted company in London.

The sad truth was that she didn't want his bland concern. She wanted...

Frustrated with herself, she began unpacking. It was not yet ten in the morning and there was so much to do that she hardly knew where to begin. She had left most of her designer clothes behind but Dio had insisted she take the jewellery.

'It's worth a fortune, Dio,' she had protested half-heartedly and he had shrugged as they had boarded the plane.

'What do you suggest I do with it all?'

She had been tempted to tell him that he could always donate the lot to her replacement. *She* certainly had no intention of showing up to teach dripping in diamonds.

Now, she opened the first box of jewellery. It all belonged in a safe but instead she shut the lid and began placing the boxes at the back of the wardrobe, knowing that in due course she would have to do something more secure with them. Stick it all in a vault somewhere. Or maybe flog it all and donate the proceeds to charity. That seemed like a good idea.

She was so absorbed in her task, her thoughts so given

over to silly, pointless rehashing over how her life had changed for ever, that she was barely aware of her entry phone ringing, at which point she wondered who it could be.

Maybe she half-expected it to be Dio but she was still shocked when she saw his grainy image on the little screen. He was glancing impatiently around him and then he stared up and she felt a quiver of nervous excitement invade her body.

'Are you going to let me in?' he asked tersely.

Lucy gathered her scattered senses to reply in a composed voice. 'What are you doing here?'

'I've come to...' *To what?* 'Just let me in, Luce. I need to talk to you.'

'Is it about the divorce? Because I thought it was all pretty straightforward.'

'I'm not enjoying this conversation on your entry phone.'

Lucy didn't think that she would enjoy a conversation face to face but she buzzed him in, knowing that he had probably come to check and make sure everything was okay with the apartment. He would be polite and concerned and she would want to scream with frustration.

'When did you get back?' she asked, as soon as she had opened the door to him. Her voice hitched in her throat. Never had he seemed so gloriously good-looking, his dark hair swept back, his lean, sexy face reminding her all too painfully of the intimate moments they had shared before his passion had given way to cool indifference.

'An hour and a half ago.' And he had had a struggle not coming sooner; had had to endure the slow, dawning realisation that he had made a terrible mistake.

He'd let her go. He'd allowed her to walk away and had then had to live with his uneasy conscience which would not let *him* go.

'And you came straight here?'

'I don't like putting things off.'

'Putting what off?' She had to tear her eyes away from his handsome face and was dismayed to find that she was perspiring, that her hands were shaking so that she stuck them behind her back before launching into a grateful speech about the apartment—about how wonderful it was, nervously laughing at the boxes still to be unpacked, offering him something to drink.

Dio glanced around him but he was driven to look at her. She looked scruffy. Her hair was tied back and she was in a pair of faded jeans, a baggy tee-shirt and some old, stained trainers. She couldn't have looked less like the polished beauty who had entertained clients as though she had been born to it.

But then, hadn't he already realised that that polished beauty was not her at all?

She also looked nervous as hell which, he thought wryly, could only be a patch on how nervous *he* was feeling. It was a sensation that was utterly alien to him. He knew that there was only one person in the world who could inspire that in him and that person was looking at him anxiously, as though half-waiting for some hidden hangman's noose to fall.

'Have you…had a period?'

'I beg your pardon?'

Dio raked his fingers through his hair and glowered. 'We made love without protection. Remember?'

'You've stepped off a plane and rushed over here to make sure I wasn't pregnant?'

Dio shrugged and frowned at her. He was hovering in the middle of the cluttered living room but now he sought out one of the chairs and sat down.

'I told you that it would be fine and it is,' Lucy said

tersely, arms folded, as the reason for him descending on her became clear.

He hadn't come to make sure she had settled in all right. He had come to make sure there was to be no inconvenient situation to be dealt with. Woe betide her if he had dealt with one inconvenient situation only to find that another had come along! One that might be a little trickier to deal with!

'So you didn't have to dash over here in a flat-out panic thinking that there would be some other mess for you to try and clear up!'

'Why would I have panicked at the thought of you being pregnant?'

Lucy refused to give houseroom to anything stupid like hope. She'd been down that particular road already and look where it had got her. Nowhere.

His challenging remark was greeted with stony silence.

'Why don't you sit down?' Dio urged.

Likewise that was greeted with stony silence until Lucy replied with simmering resentment, 'What for? You've told me why you came here and I've answered you. What more is there to talk about?'

'A lot, as it happens.' He hunkered forward, arms resting loosely on his thighs.

Lucy watched, bemused, as he slumped into silence. He was hesitant. Had she *ever* seen Dio hesitant? Even when she had asked him for a divorce, he had immediately and confidently responded with his demand for his denied honeymoon. He was the most self-assured person she had ever encountered in her entire life, yet right now...

'A lot...like what?' she asked, bewildered.

'I didn't marry you because of your background, Lucy.'

'I...I know that. I didn't at the time, but I know now. And you know I know.'

'But because I didn't marry you because of your background, doesn't mean that my intentions were entirely... honourable.'

'Dio, I have no idea what you're talking about.'

'It's a long story.' He sighed heavily and glanced at her with that same uncertainty in his pale eyes that filled her with apprehension. 'Your father wasn't entirely unknown to me when I decided to take over his company. In fact, I've known about your father for a very long time.'

'But how?'

'It goes back decades, Lucy. Before you were born. Our fathers knew one another.'

'I don't understand.'

'Skeletons in cupboards,' Dio said wearily. 'All families have them.'

'They do,' Lucy accepted, thinking of her own skeletons, no longer a secret from this man sitting across from her.

'Sometimes those skeletons have bones that rattle so much, they create all sorts of problems down the line. A long time ago, my father invented something pretty big and at the time he was friends with your father. They were at university together. My father was a boffin, yours was... what can I say? The life and soul of the party. I have no doubt that my father was somewhat in awe of your father's rich, playboy lifestyle. He was studious, poor, everything your father wasn't. When your father decided that he was worth investing in, my dad believed him. Unfortunately, his trust was somewhat misplaced.'

Comprehension was beginning to drip in and Lucy's eyes widened. 'My father...'

'Took everything. He took his family business and built it into something huge on the back of my father's hard work. I grew up with that and it... Let's put it this way, for a very long time I've been hell-bent on revenge. I waited my time, Lucy. I went to university and I made sure that I was better than good at everything I did. Fortunately, I seemed to have a knack for making money. I traded but quit that pretty quickly, just as soon as I had enough capital, along with a bank loan, to begin the business of acquisition. I made more money than I knew what to do with but there was only one thing I wanted to do with my millions and that was to wait until the time was right. I knew it would come because I knew what kind of man Robert Bishop was.'

'He was drinking himself into a hole…stealing from pensions.'

'He was and I knew just when to strike. The conversation you semi-overheard that night was when I told him exactly who I was.'

'He must have known before—he would have recognised your name.'

'Of course he did but the man was so arrogant, so sure that he was top dog, that it never occurred to him that he had become involved in a game in which there could only be one winner and that winner would be me.'

'So you went out with me…'

'I hadn't planned to. In fact, whilst I knew to the very last detail the progress of your father's company, I never had the slightest interest in the progress of his personal life. I didn't know you existed until I met you on that very first visit when I came to enquire about buying the company.'

'And my father encouraged us to go out…'

'I needed no encouragement, trust me on that, Luce. He knew who I was but he still stupidly thought that he could somehow con me into paying full whack for his company whilst keeping him on, honour intact. Maybe he thought he could use you as a bargaining tool to get an even better deal out of me. He'd swindled my father and he thought that we were cut from the same cloth. I have to admit that I didn't immediately disillusion him. I got involved with you and I was having…a good time.'

'You were having a good time…' Lucy said slowly, driven to search for an answer she knew she wouldn't want to hear. 'But did you plan on actually asking me to marry you?'

Dio looked at her steadily. He'd brokered hundreds of edge-of-cliff deals but never had he felt more nervous about the outcome of any situation…or more desperate to secure the outcome he wanted.

'No.'

'You planned on having some fun with me and then getting down to the main business of ruining my father as payback.'

'That's about the sum of it.'

'Why did you change your mind? Why did you decide to ask me to marry you?' Her puzzled, questioning eyes tangled with his steady, cool ones and it dawned on her that a man hell bent on revenge might find that revenge in all sorts of ways contrary to what he might have planned originally. 'I get it,' she said in a small, appalled voice. 'You figured that not only would you get the company but you would take me with it, and that way you would have wiped my father out on all fronts…'

Dio said nothing. He found it impossible to understand the whole business of revenge that had motivated him for such a long time, but then something so much bigger had come along and knocked him to the ground.

'How could you?' She sprang to her feet and paced the room, dodging the packing crates, her mind in turmoil, her stomach churning with his revelations.

With a flick of his hand he caught her as she jerkily paced past him and pulled her so that she toppled onto him, only to push herself back immediately, shaking with mortification and anger.

'I thought I'd misjudged you,' she flung at him bitterly. She clenched her fist because she wanted to slap his beautiful face so much that it was a physical pain.

'I know you did,' Dio told her gently. 'Just like I knew that finding out the truth would…hurt you. Why do you think I decided that the best outcome would be for me to walk away? Spare you the details?'

'Oh, how generous of you,' Lucy jeered with biting sarcasm. She could feel the heat from his body against hers and the steady beat of his heart under her arm, which was pinned into position. He was only holding her lightly but she still couldn't move an inch. Tears stung the back of her eyes.

'Generous and, as it turns out, impossible,' Dio murmured. He could sense the effort she was making not to cry. He felt powerless to ease the pain and enraged that he was responsible for causing it, even though when all this began he had no idea that this was the route it would end up going down.

'Not impossible,' Lucy whispered. 'You could have just left me believing what I did.'

'You deserved to know the truth, Lucy, especially as…' He sighed, shook his head and released her abruptly.

Freed from his clasp, Lucy was dismayed to find that her body didn't immediately behave the way it should have. It took her a few seconds to leap away from him and sprint to one of the packing crates, where she sat, glaring at him.

'Especially as…*what*?' She wondered how many more revelations he had tucked up his sleeve.

'This isn't quite the end of what I have to say…'

'What more can there be, Dio? What more can you *possibly* have to say to me?'

'I thought I married you as a fitting way of making sure the wheel turned full circle. I took you for a daddy's girl and, yes, I thought that I could deprive him of more than just his company in one fell swoop. It never occurred to me that what I felt for you went far beyond anything to do with getting even with your father.'

'Oh, please…'

'I knew I fancied the hell out of you; I just didn't realise that I felt much more than that, which was why I was just so damned furious with myself when you decided that sleeping with me wasn't going to be on the table. I figured you'd strung me along to get me to sign on the dotted line, thinking, like your father, that I would be a sucker for your pretty face.'

Lucy flushed because, although that had been a horrible misunderstanding, she didn't emerge as flawless. They had both had issues with one another.

'I made sure I got what was mine, though… But I spared your father the humiliation of a prison sentence because of you.'

'Surely that would have been the ultimate revenge?'

'I found I couldn't do it.'

'Even when I refused to sleep with you?'

'Even then. Maybe…' he smiled wryly '… I wasn't quite as hard-nosed as I thought I was, or maybe I just fell in love with you and couldn't bring myself to take that ultimate step.'

'Fell in love with me?'

'It's why I lost interest in all other women the minute you came on the scene. The only woman I went to bed dreaming of was you. I thought that it was because I had never had the chance to take you to my bed. I thought it was a simple case of wanting what had been denied me…'

'Which was why you wanted the honeymoon, so that

you could get me out of your system.' *He'd fallen in love
with her?*

'I came here to tell you everything, Luce. I…I let you
go, and I never should have done that, but I didn't know
how to stop you, not when I knew that there was so much
muddy water under the bridge.' He looked at her, wondered what was going on behind that beautiful, expressive
face. If he lost her…

The thought filled his head like a blackness.

'When you say you *fell in love with me*…?'

'By that I mean I want you next to me for the rest of my
life. I don't want a divorce, Lucy, although if you insist on
one then I'll walk away. Unless,' he mused, 'I choose the
other option of pursuing you relentlessly until you can't
stand it any more and you just give in. I should warn you
that I can go to great lengths to get what I want.'

Lucy threw him a wobbly smile. 'I can hardly believe
what I'm hearing, Dio,' she confessed unsteadily. She
sighed heavily. 'I fell in love with you the second you
stepped into my life.' Her eyes flickered and got the response they wanted, the steady, tender gaze that warmed
her to her very depths. 'It was like I was waking up for the
first time in my life. I never thought…it never occurred to
me that what was happening between us might not be real.
I was so…inexperienced; when I overheard that conversation and then had it all confirmed by my father… You
have no idea. It was like something inside me shrivelled
up. I'd been bought, like something from a shop.'

'I was blind, Lucy. I hadn't been looking for love and
I was arrogant enough to assume that it wouldn't find me
unless I had been.'

'I was married to a guy I was crazy about but I was
forced to tell myself otherwise. I knew that if I just confronted that truth I would break apart.'

'You played a part and I was responsible for that, my darling. You'd spent your life playing a part and then you were forced to continue…' And that hurt him. 'Little wonder that you were searching for an exit.'

'And I thought I'd found it. I could get back to what I had always dreamed of doing. I thought I'd be free, like a bird released from a cage, but then we went on our honeymoon and all the truths I'd shoved away out of sight began creeping out of their hiding places—and this time round I couldn't hide any of it from myself. I was still crazy about you. I'd never stopped…' Never had she felt more naked but that look on his face was still there, still warming her, taking her heart to heights she had never known existed.

'My darling…'

'I love you so much, Dio.'

'Revenge might not be an honourable emotion.' Dio stood up and walked across to her, dragging another packing crate so that their knees were touching. 'But I wouldn't have changed a second of those dishonourable emotions because they brought me to you, Lucy, and being with you is coming home. So…' He went down on one knee and looked at her with such tenderness that her heart melted. 'My darling almost-ex-wife, can I ask you not to divorce me?'

'I never thought I'd have a marriage proposal as weird as that!' Lucy's heart took flight and she reached forward and ran her fingers through his hair. 'So how can I say no? The past is behind us, all of it, and now…now we just have the future.' She laughed, leant to kiss him and lingered a bit more as their mouths met. 'My dearest husband for ever…'

* * * * *

MILLS & BOON

THE HEART OF ROMANCE

A ROMANCE FOR EVERY READER

MODERN

Prepare to be swept off your feet by sophisticated, sexy and seductive heroes, in some of the world's most glamourous and romantic locations, where power and passion collide.

HISTORICAL

Escape with historical heroes from time gone by. Whether your passion is for wicked Regency Rakes, muscled Vikings or rugged Highlanders, awaken the romance of the past.

MEDICAL

Set your pulse racing with dedicated, delectable doctors in the high-pressure world of medicine, where emotions run high and passion, comfort and love are the best medicine.

True Love

Celebrate true love with tender stories of heartfelt romance, from the rush of falling in love to the joy a new baby can bring, and a focus on the emotional heart of a relationship.

Desire

Indulge in secrets and scandal, intense drama and plenty of sizzling hot action with powerful and passionate heroes who have it all: wealth, status, good looks…everything but the right woman.

HEROES

Experience all the excitement of a gripping thriller, with an intense romance at its heart. Resourceful, true-to-life women and strong, fearless men face danger and desire - a killer combination!

To see which titles are coming soon, please visit

millsandboon.co.uk/nextmonth

JOIN US ON SOCIAL MEDIA!

Stay up to date with our latest releases, author news and gossip, special offers and discounts, and all the behind-the-scenes action from Mills & Boon...

 @millsandboon

 @millsandboonuk

 facebook.com/millsandboon

@millsandboonuk

It might just be true love...

GET YOUR ROMANCE FIX!

Get the latest romance news,
exclusive author interviews, story
extracts and much more!

MILLS & BOON

MODERN

Power and Passion

Prepare to be swept off your feet by sophisticated, sexy and seductive heroes, in some of the world's most glamourous and romantic locations, where power and passion collide.

Julia James
Heiress's
PREGNANCY SCANDAL
MILLS & BOON
MODERN

Jennie Lucas
Chosen as the
SHEIKH'S ROYAL BRIDE
MILLS & BOON
MODERN

Kim Lawrence
A WEDDING at the ITALIAN'S DEMAND
MILLS & BOON

Sharon Kendrick
The
SHEIKH'S SECRET BABY
MILLS & BOON
MODERN

Eight Modern stories published every month, find them all at.

millsandboon.co.uk/Modern

MILLS & BOON
True Love
Romance from the Heart

Celebrate true love with tender stories of heartfelt romance, from the rush of falling in love to the joy a new baby can bring, and a focus on the emotional heart of a relationship.

MILLS & BOON

Desire

Indulge in secrets and scandal, intense drama and plenty of sizzling hot action with powerful and passionate heroes who have it all: wealth, status, good looks…everything but the right woman.